NEVER FORGET YOU

First published in Great Britain in 2022 by Farshore

An imprint of HarperCollins*Publishers*
1 London Bridge Street, London SE1 9GF

farshore.co.uk

HarperCollins*Publishers*
1st Floor, Watermarque Building, Ringsend Road, Dublin 4, Ireland

Extracts taken from:
A New Heaven by Wilfred Owen (1916)
Children's Wartime Diaries, edited by Laurel Holliday, Piatkus (1995)
Silent Words: A Selection of Poetry and Prose, Hermes Publishers (2004) in
collaboration with the International Centre for Dialogue among Civilisations
The Song of the Stormy Petrel by Maxim Gorky (1901)
High Flight by John Gillespie Magee Jnr (1941)

ISBN 978 0 7555 0334 6
Printed and bound in the UK using 100% renewable electricity
at CPI Group (UK) Ltd
1

Stay safe online. Any website addresses listed in this book are correct at the
time of going to print. However, Farshore cannot take responsibility for any
third party content or advertising. Please be aware that online content can
be subject to change and websites can contain content that is unsuitable for
children. We advise that all children are supervised when using the internet.

MIX
Paper from
responsible sources
FSC™ C007454

This book is produced from independently certified FSC™ paper
to ensure responsible forest management.

For more information visit: www.harpercollins.co.uk/green

NEVER
FORGET
YOU

AWARD-WINNING AUTHOR OF *CORAM BOY*

JAMILA GAVIN

Farshore

I dedicate this book in honour and in memory of Miriam Hodgson, who had hoped that, one day, I would write about this period.

A la claire fontaine
M'en allant promener
J'ai trouvé l'eau si belle
Que je m'y suis baigné
Il y a longtemps que je t'aime
Jamais je ne t'oublierai
Il y a longtemps que je t'aime
Jamais je ne t'oublierai

Part 1

WAR OR PEACE?

PROLOGUE
Flight

RUSSIA 1918

There were demonstrations and riots in the town the day they left. The gates of the city were closed by a barricade. An angry crowd surged round the strange foreigners: a pale woman who clutched a baby to her breast, and a very tall, very dark-skinned man who held her close. As the crowd threatened to overwhelm them, the man tenderly extracted the baby from its mother's arms, stripped it from its swaddling, and held its naked body above his head for all to see: a gently writhing, gleaming baby. Its cry rang out like a lost bird. The crowd gave a hushed moan. Every eye travelled from the pale mother to the dark-skinned man, so tall that it was as if he levitated above their heads, and so shining it was as if he were a living icon in his golden priest-like robe.

Suddenly silent, the crowd fell away respectfully, and the little family was allowed to leave.

ENGLAND 1937

You would have had to tip your head skywards to see the buzzard. It was so high, circling slowly over a golden, summer countryside with unblinking eye, scouring the woods and hedgerows, looking for a kill.

Its prey, those little voles, field mice, and rabbits, wouldn't have seen the killer – not until it dropped lower, its devouring shadow sliding silently over the land. Who knows what terror drummed in their tiny bodies as they made a run for it?

The buzzard was not interested in the limousine which, from that height, may have looked like a dark, burrowing creature, winding its way along the narrow country lanes. After a while, it swung away to scour another field. The passengers inside the car never saw the predator above, nor the life-or-death panic of the little creatures. They gazed silently at the unbelievably green hills and fields of wheat and barley, burnished by the July sunlight as if touched by Midas.

It was an English countryside.

But the family in the car were not English.

CHAPTER 1
The Princess

I will never forget the day my class was introduced to Noor. We had been told a new girl was joining us, and that she was an Indian princess. The excitement was palpable; none of the girls had only seen ever seen a real, live princess before – apart from photographs of the princesses Elizabeth and Margaret, or fairy-tale princesses in books. Most of them had never seen any kind of real Indian girl, except for a few who, like me, had been born abroad because their fathers were running the empire in various parts of the world. The words they liked to use were 'far-flung corners', which somehow always made me think of some vast tablecloth which someone had thrown out over half the world, as if it were their own great dinner table.

Chairs screeched back from desks as the class rose respectfully on the entry of the headmistress, Miss Heywood, accompanied by two distinctly Indian visitors. I felt my heart lurch with homesickness to see them. I had been born in India and lived there until they sent me and my

3

older brother, Eric, home, *home to England*, to go to school. For Eric, it was a boys' boarding school in Hertfordshire and for me, Barrowfield, a boarding school for girls in darkest Sussex, but I felt I was being sent *away* from home. India was my home, and my parents seemed so far away.

"Girls," proclaimed Miss Heywood, "I want you to meet His Highness the Sultan of Karanji and his daughter, Noor. Noor will be joining us next term, so they have come to Barrowfield today to finalise arrangements. We thought it was a good opportunity for you to meet your new classmate."

A polite greeting murmured round the classroom. They probably thought the girl was a disappointment. This was no glittering Indian princess, not like the ones they had read about in their colourful silken saris and sparkling adornments. She was small and bendy like a reed, as if she would blow about in a wind; she seemed shy and inscrutable, standing there with a bowed head from which hung two shining black plaits right down to her waist. She was wearing very unprincess-like clothes: a long tweed skirt, woollen stockings, sensible brown lace-up shoes, a dark blue hip-length cardigan beneath which was glimpsed a white blouse, lace-embroidered, and clipped at the throat with a silver brooch. Even our school uniform of light grey trimmed with red was far better. She stood there, leaning into her father as if she might hide behind him and, with a blank expression on her face, she seemed not at all as exotic as a princess ought to be.

But it was her father that we couldn't take our eyes off, and who caused everyone to gasp and stare most rudely. He was wearing a long peat-coloured woollen coat, mixed with raw linen and spun with gold silk. And at that moment, standing in a pool of sunlight which poured in through the windows, he gleamed. It felt as if everything in that dreary classroom had turned to gold.

He was tall, looming, gaunt, and very dark-skinned, like the trunk of an ancient tree, bringing a kind of wild nature among us. He had a long black beard which reached down to his chest, his cheekbones stuck out like rocky crags, and his nose curved like the beak of an eagle, between narrowed, searching eyes; eyes which hovered over us as if surveying us from a great height. Although it was late September, it had become suddenly cold outside, yet his feet were bare in open leather sandals.

But there was something about his face which was not just bird-like or king-like, but god-like. It was ethereal, spiritual; as if he was only partly of this earth, and that another part of him inhabited some outer, extra-terrestrial regions. Perhaps he had come from another time altogether: his golden coat made me think of medieval bishops, Byzantine icons, or the pharaohs of ancient Egypt.

"Our girls have been inculcated with the highest standards of duty, service and kindness, so I'm sure they will give Noor every consideration, and will ensure that she settles in quickly and smoothly," Miss Heywood said with a slightly obsequious flutter in her voice.

The Sultan spoke in reply, and we were spellbound by the depths of his rich bass voice: "My daughter and I thank you from the bottom of our hearts, don't we Noor?"

Noor looked up at him as if she looked up at the sun. She smiled, her face suddenly shining with such love and affection that she seemed transfigured from being boring and shy to beautiful and confident. "Yes, Papa," she replied, in a peculiarly accented voice, which rang out like a temple bell. "I'm sure I'll be very happy."

Then they were gone. The chairs scraped once more as we all sat down. There was an explosion of voices.

"Fancy having a real live princess in our class," hissed my friend, Dorothy – who we all called Dodo. "Do we have to call her 'Your Highness'?"

"That's enough girls!" exclaimed the History teacher, restoring order. "Let's carry on."

"She seems all right," Dodo whispered and I agreed, quite looking forward to next term when Noor would join us.

The buzzard was still circling when the limousine returned along the lanes buried among hedgerows. The relentlessly sinking sun heralded evening, creating dark reflections of cows which stood as if spellbound, their heads turned into the rays. The shadows of trees strode like giants across the landscape and, by the time they could see the lights of the city ahead, daylight had almost gone.

Flights of starlings soared and swooped in miraculous, ever-changing formations over the rich golden fields before settling for the night with babbling shrieks. Then silence.

"Our daughter will be in a place of safety," the Sufi prince reassured his wife when they finally reached their lodgings in London.

The newspaper boy was shouting at the top of his lungs: "Germany re-arms!"

CHAPTER 2

Friends and Fairies

Seeing we never spied frail Fairyland,
Though small we crouched by bluebells, moon by moon
WILFRED OWEN

I was pleased when, at the beginning of the Autumn term, it was me who was asked to befriend the Indian princess. And no, we didn't have to address her as 'Your Highness'; just 'Noor'.

"I want you to show her the ropes, Gwendoline!" said Miss Heywood. "You know India, and I'm sure you and Noor will have lots to talk about. She is in your house, 'Mary Slessor', and in your dormitory, so please be responsible for her until she has settled in. I'm sure you'll both get along well enough."

I saw Noor scrutinising me, probably realising what a contrast we made: me with my tight curly blonde hair, my bluest of blue eyes, and my strawberries-and-cream complexion. If you were being kind, you would say I had the makings of an English rose, whereas she could already be described as beautiful with her earth-coloured skin, luminous dark eyes, and long, thick black waist-length plaits. Where she was shorter than I and as slender as a willow, I was taller, chunkier and plump in a jolly hockey sticks kind of way, always liable to be picked for the sports teams. Did she think we'd get along? I wondered.

"Take Noor up to the dormitory," murmured Miss Heywood in a kindly voice. "Matron should be there to show you your bed and locker. Then when you've unpacked, Noor, Gwendoline can accompany you to the dining hall." My headmistress stared at me with her sharp, cat-like grey eyes as if to say, 'Don't let me down'.

Yes, Miss Heywood," I replied reassuringly and, giving Noor an encouraging smile, I led her out.

"Thank you, Gwendoline," said Noor in her tinkly voice. "It is so very kind of you to sacrifice yourself for me in this way. I hope I will not be a burden. I promise to learn to look after myself as quickly as possible." She looked up at me with stricken eyes, and I realised that she was desperately homesick.

"Oh, don't call me Gwendoline!" I replied, warmly. "Everyone calls me Gwen, except Miss Heywood. But we can't exactly shorten your name," I teased, "unless we call you N!"

Noor burst out in a cascade of laughter, which was catching. That was a good start.

"Come on," I said. "Let's dump your stuff in the dorm, and then I'll take you to the canteen. I hope you're going to be able to bear the ghastly boiled cabbage and mutton which passes for food in this institution."

Noor was pleased that her bed was near the window, which overlooked the vegetable garden at the back of the school. Being on the first floor, she could see over a redbrick wall and beyond to another garden – a somewhat neglected flower garden. To most eyes, it looked unkempt and overgrown, but Noor gave a gasp of delight.

"Oh, look at the flowers. Aren't they beautiful; so wild!" she exclaimed. "I love the way they grow among the weeds. And those long spiky grasses! They are like pointed spears, there to protect the fairies."

Fairies? Was she joking?

But Noor was staring at the garden, entranced, her face glowing with a kind of mysterious excitement. "Fairies find a garden like this so much more thrilling than those well-tended ones. Oh, I wish I could see you all from here," she breathed softly. "That is a stream over there, just behind that beech hedge, isn't it, Gwen?" Noor pointed.

"Yes," I said haltingly. "I believe it is."

"That's where they'll be, then. Fairies love making boats out of bits of bark or nut shells."

"You mean . . . you *see* them?" I asked, not knowing whether to laugh; but I didn't, as she seemed so intensely serious.

"Of course!" she exclaimed. "Don't you?"

"Er . . . no, actually." I stifled a giggle, not wishing to be unkind.

"Oh," she said with such disappointment, I felt I'd let her down. It didn't seem to dawn on her that not everyone believed in fairies, and that I might be surprised at an almost grown-up girl of nearly sixteen doing so. She suddenly seemed so fragile, and child-like, I couldn't bring myself to jeer.

"Come on," I said, gently pulling her away. "We've got to get you unpacked before the lunch bell."

After lunch, Noor vanished. One minute she was at my side – I had stopped to talk to Dodo – and the next minute she'd gone.

"She's probably gone to the lav," and Dodo.

We went to look. She hadn't, so we went back up to the dorm in case she'd wanted something. It was empty. Then I glanced out of the window, over the brick wall into the neglected garden – and there she was, crouched on the overgrown path, staring intently into a cluster of flowers.

"What's she doing?" cried Dodo.

"Looking for fairies," I replied seriously.

Dodo guffawed. "Really, Gwenny Penny! Not like you to be sarcastic!"

"No, truly. Let's go down and find her – but listen, Dodo," I said, holding her arm earnestly. "Don't tease her. I know it's nuts – but she really does seem to believe in fairies. You must be respectful."

"Do they have fairies in India?" asked Dodo, prancing about and flapping her arms.

"Of course!" I exclaimed. "Along with spirits, demons,

11

gods and goddesses. But don't tell the others. And for heaven's sake, don't tell Pamela. She'll tear her apart. Just be kind and go along with it. After all – it's her first day."

Noor was exactly as we had seen her from the dormitory window when we reached her, staring into the mass of weeds and flowers. We came up quietly and crouched beside her.

"Can you see anything, Noor?"

"Ssssh! There." She pointed into the depths of a yellow evening primrose. "Don't wake her."

Dodo gave me a silent look of utter astonishment.

"They'll have to find shelter in the hollows of trees when winter comes," Noor remarked seriously. She straightened up and stared at us with shining eyes. "I'm so glad there are fairies in the school garden."

As we got to know her, I decided that Noor was like a fairy herself – sometimes not quite visible; not quite present. I could easily believe that she was floating airily along or, being so still, had slipped into another layer of Time. But for a mortal, she was incredibly forgetful. It was maddening when she couldn't remember where she'd left her hat just at the point of going out, or her school bag, or her purse. Arrangements would be made and not kept. A Latin test would be forgotten, and she would fly into a panic of revising. Ordinary everyday things barely interested her. But we could never be cross with her for long – her laughter and self-deprecation cast its own spell, and we forgave her. We always forgave her.

CHAPTER 3
Outsiders

Fairies or no, we saw how hard it was for Noor to settle in. She had never been separated from her family before and, like mine, they were now thousands of miles away across the ocean in India.

Just as Miss Heywood predicted, we felt an instant bond. We could talk to each other about our beloved India, even though, as I teased her, I had lived there for longer than she had. Noor had been born in India, but had only lived a very short time there before they moved to Europe. "It's more my country than yours," I teased.

"Ah!" She wagged her finger at me. "But we're going to kick you out of India one of these days. We shall leave the British Empire!"

"Hmmm," I pondered, impossible as it seemed. "And how are you going to do that?"

"My father believes in Reason and the Goodness of people," answered Noor with gravity. "That's how you British will be defeated. We don't need bombs and bullets, just Goodness. My family doesn't believe in violence – and we'll still be friends."

Her father was not just a Sufi prince, but a philosopher too – like Noor's grandfather. They were Muslim, but also followers of Sufism. Her grandfather had been so famous that the Czar of Russia had summoned him to live in the Kremlin, and teach him about philosophy and Sufism. "My father brought us up in the same way," Noor explained. "He says we have to be beyond worldly things; to go deep into the Self to find purity, love, generosity and sacrifice. That's what Grandfather taught them in Russia. He was deeply upset when the whole of the Russian royal family was shot after the revolution."

"Shot?"

A group of us from our dorm were all sitting in a circle in the common room like courtiers, with Noor holding court.

"Yes," said Noor and, as if she had known the Russian princesses personally, solemnly chanted their names: Grand Duchesses Olga, Anastasia, Maria, and Tatiana and their little brother, the crown prince Alexei. "My grandparents had to flee for their lives with my father, who was only eight, and my uncle, who was a baby. They barely made it through a murderous mob. My grandfather told us he was sure that the rest of Europe would save the Czar and his family. But no one did – not even his cousin, the King of England. So, all five princesses and their young brother were shot with their parents, Czar Nicholas and Czarina Alexandra."

There was silence.

"My grandparents also had to flee from Russia to Poland with their family at that time, because of the pogroms," said a hesitant, rather peculiar voice. "My mother was just a baby."

Everyone turned and looked at Vera Bell, sitting on the carpet nearby, with her knees drawn under her chin. Vera had come to the school a year earlier. She was different from us; an outsider, who made no attempt to fit in, and had no real friends. She usually hovered on the edge of things and, at times, we could forget she was there. I'm afraid none of us had made any effort to get to know her.

"What's a pogrom?" whispered Dodo.

"Not sure," I hissed back. "Something bad."

"After the Revolution, there were bands of thugs who went on the rampage," said Vera. "My grandparents were attacked, so they fled to Poland. That's where I was born. My father is Polish; my mother, Russian." Vera faltered, as if she had said too much. "Then later, we . . . I mean, I came to Paris."

Noor gasped. "Do you know Paris, Vera?"

Vera nodded, replying in French with a broad smile. "I've lived there since I was six years old."

For a while, Noor and Vera chattered on in French.

"How amazing," exclaimed Noor. "We might have passed each other in the street and not known it. I went to school in Paris, and I sometimes feel more French than Indian. I even dream in French."

I think I heard Vera laugh for the first time since coming

16

to school. Briefly, the frowns which usually creased her brow vanished, as her expression changed from sad to happy in an instant.

"Excuse me!" joked Dodo, wagging a finger theatrically. "This is England, in case you hadn't noticed."

"And, we are English, and speak English here," I added with a flourish.

"Don't know about that, Gwen," said Pamela Dale with a mocking sneer. "You were born in India. What does that make you?"

"One of us!" said Noor sweetly.

There are some people who look for every opportunity to put others down. Pamela was one of those. Even though she herself was hardly nobility, she looked down on colonialists, and anyone remotely 'foreign'. To her, we were jumped-up, ladder-climbing opportunists, trying to wriggle out of the cesspit of the English working classes.

"What did you say your father did?" she once asked me when I was still new and raw with homesickness.

"He's a District Officer in charge of the Nagina region," I had replied innocently.

"Is that a sort of clerk?" she exclaimed with a peal of derisory laughter.

If anyone had ever brought me close to a violent act, it was Pamela and, at that moment, I had felt my face burn, my heart beat, and my fists clench.

"Don't rise to it, Gwenny Penny," Dodo had murmured, gripping my elbow and pulling me away.

Dearest Dodo had become my closest and most valued friend, and had helped me to settle in when I had arrived at school three years earlier. She was a hardened veteran, having been in boarding school since she was three years old. I don't know how I would have survived those first gut-wrenching weeks without her.

"And your name: *Vera Bell*?" she continued, unabashed. "Not exactly Russian or Polish, is it? It's not French, and you certainly don't sound English. What kind of accent is it?"

Vera looked oddly terrified, and I flew to her defence. "Who the hell do you think you are, Pamela, interrogating people; prying into their private lives? Leave her alone."

Pamela shrugged disdainfully and, seeing our hostile faces, walked off saying, "It was only friendly curiosity."

With her usual cruel precision, Pamela was right: it was odd that her name wasn't Polish, Russian or French. So why did she have an English-sounding name, *Vera Bell*? It wasn't clear who she was. And it's true, she did speak with an indeterminate accent, but this only added to the mystery. She found it difficult to meet your eye, as if afraid of giving away secrets, and she always spoke with her head lowered. I thought that it was because her eyes were so often filled with tears.

More disturbing was that if she occasionally flicked her hair back, I glimpsed lines scoured across her brow, as if she had aged before her time. It was hard to make her out: she was aloof, impenetrable, and no one really wanted to be her friend. Perhaps there was some tragedy in her life about which we knew nothing. But her reserve made us feel helpless.

I sometimes woke in the night to find her standing at the dorm window, weeping quietly, but did nothing. I'm afraid, in a boarding school like ours, you had to stick up for yourself. We could be callous as a group. The group hated weakness. Vera needed to make alliances, or else face exclusion, but she didn't have the knack – whatever that was – and we were not as sympathetic as we should have been. We had our own problems: difficult home lives, separation anxieties, insecurity, petty bullying, and downright homesickness. When Vera first came, the girl Miss Heywood chose to show her the ropes dropped her as soon as she possibly could, and, to that day, Vera had never acquired what you would call a 'best friend' – until Noor arrived. It was Noor who drew her out and could make her smile. It was Noor who drew her out, and made us like her.

Now, somehow quickly, we became a group: Noor, Vera, Dodo, and me. Maybe because all our parents were abroad: mine and Noor's in India, Vera's in Paris – though she never talked about them – and Dodo's parents everywhere.

Poor Dodo. Her parents didn't seem interested in her; they lived the high life cruising round the Mediterranean, skiing in the Alps, or taking the Orient Express to Istanbul. She sometimes went for a whole year, as I did, without seeing her parents at all. But whereas I had a letter nearly every fortnight from India, full of news and love and 'missing you', she might get an occasional postcard from somewhere exotic like Vienna, Paris, or Budapest.

But Dodo masked her sadness by being the clown of the class. She could be very funny, sometimes cruel: mimicking the teachers, pulling faces and telling wicked jokes. It was only because I slept in the next bed to her and heard her moaning in her sleep that I knew she, too, contained a well of misery.

When Dodo did get a proper letter, she would read it out in the dorm after lights out by torchlight to amuse us all. Because it had usually come from some exotic part of the world, she would mimic her mother and father, or foreign voices, which had us all rolling with laughter.

"Listen to this from Mummy in Monte Carlo!" She stood up on her bed.

"*Daddy and I went to supper with the Virgets. Madame Virget reminds me of a rat. She's very thin and has a long face ending in a pointed chin, with the hint of a few whiskers above her upper lip, like a moustache. I wager she spends hours in front of the mirror trying to pull them out with tweezers. Get it wrong and it leaves you with very sore red patches, which gives it away. Worst of all, she calls me Valerrrrie –*" Dodo exaggerated the French accent. "*You can tell I don't like her, and I don't like the way she flirts with your father, even though she's old enough to be his mother. But he seems impervious to my observations. By the way, that nice young man Lucien came too. He asked after you.*"

"Who's Lucien, Dodo?" asked a girl meaningfully.

"Oh Lucien!" Dodo jumped out of bed with her torch flashing and, like Juliet looking for her Romeo, cried, "Lucien, Lucien, *où es-tu, mon charmeur? Je t'aime, je t'aime.* Eeeet's me. *Moi.* Dodo. You re-mem-berrrr, zat Eeenglish girl whose virrrrrginity you wanted to take . . . naughty boy . . ."

We all giggled so loudly that the matron came storming in with threats of detentions, and we all made a dash for our beds, sliding under our sheets to muffle our laughter.

About a month later, unusually soon, there was a further letter from Dodo's mother. That night, in the darkness, with Dodo's torch flickering back and forth, I got an inkling of not just other places in the world, but something else; something disturbing, and exciting. Certainly, her mother seemed enthused.

"*Darling!*" droned Dodo. "*We're in Adolf Hitler's Munich! Such a beautiful city; you can see the mountains from here. Germany is so lucky to have a tough, straight-talking man like Hitler. I hope you're not so cut off in your expensive school that you are completely unaware of him. He's the Chancellor of Germany – and what a man. Everyone adores him. He gets things done; and he's so inspiring. We could do with a man like that in charge, in England. Chamberlain is so boring. Your father and I were invited to a country house up in the mountains for a hunting weekend, and guess who was there? Herr Hitler himself! We felt so honoured. Mind you, he didn't go hunting. He's a vegetarian and loves animals; such a kind man. You've got to come in the holidays.*"

Vera's querulous, accented voice drifted across the

darkened room. "Does she say anything about how they're *treating* people?"

I sensed Dodo frowning. She wagged her torch like a shaking head. "What do you mean?"

Vera's voice sounded hesitant. "My uncle had a business in Berlin. It got smashed up by the Brownshirts."

"Who on earth are the Brownshirts?" hooted Dodo. "Boy scouts?"

I joined in the laughter; then wished I hadn't.

"They murdered my uncle a few years ago," Vera said quietly.

We all fell quiet, then drifted into sleep. But I knew we hadn't heard the whole truth.

I noticed that, for the rest of the term, Vera didn't always join us – especially if Dodo was there. Dodo noticed too.

"What on earth have I done?" she complained. "She can't blame me for her uncle being murdered by the Brownshirts, whoever they are."

CHAPTER 4

Where to Go?

For boarders like us, school holidays were always a problem. Some had parents around Europe, so they were able to get on trains and go – even as far as Moscow, Istanbul, Rome or Paris. India was too far for me. It took at least three weeks on a ship out there, and another three back. My mother had only once managed to come over to see me and my older brother, Eric, and that was to bring my younger brother Archie to school. But at least we had our beloved Aunt Madge and Uncle Harold – not forgetting their sheepdog, Disraeli, who we all called Dizzy. Archie and I spent all our holidays with them on their farm, St Petroc's in Wales.

Poor Archie. He was still raw during that first year of being away from our parents and India. I'd hear him sobbing in his sleep, so I'd creep into bed with him and hold him tight, which made me feel better too. Eric sometimes came for a week or so to help on the farm, but otherwise, he was away with the air cadets. He was mad about flying.

Noor usually spent her holidays in London with an elderly English couple, the Baileys, who were devotees of her father. They had an apartment in Holland Park where they ran the Society for Sufi Philosophy.

Dodo was usually shunted off to friends or relatives she barely knew.

Vera went back to Paris. I often wondered why she had been sent to school in England in the first place, and what had produced the lines and sadness etched in her face. Was it her uncle's death? She had started to mention her mother, then stopped. I was curious, but hesitated to ask.

That summer of 1937 was the first time I properly wondered about Adolf Hitler and the Nazis. Even though the wireless was always on, I'd never really listened before, not like Aunt Madge, who was an avid listener, always arguing with it: frowning, puzzling, and debating. "The Germans are re-arming? Not again. The last war was supposed to be the war to end all wars!"

Then I heard the word 'Brownshirts' again.

"Who are they?" I asked.

Aunty Madge burst out angrily: "Thugs and bullies, that's who! Supporting Hitler in the early days, rampaging about, singing patriotic songs and beating up anyone who didn't agree with their politics – and especially terrifying Jews. They used to strut in bunches down the pavements, forcing other pedestrians to give way. If someone took a stand, they got beaten up, and the police did nothing."

"There were probably lots of ordinary, decent Germans who would have protested, and did," Uncle Harold pointed out, "but most seem to be utterly intimidated by these monsters – or worse, agreed with them."

"You should hear what your Uncle Reggie has to say," huffed Aunt Madge. Uncle Reggie was a diplomat in the British consulate in Munich.

"They're now called 'storm troopers', these Brownshirts – as if it makes it legal to be thuggish," said Uncle Harold, "and they've certainly got it in for the Jews, harassing and persecuting them. Hitler passed a law, can you believe, turning Jews into second-class citizens and closing their businesses! They can barely call themselves German at all."

"And no one lifts a finger," snorted Aunt Madge.

"Dodo's mother thinks Hitler's a jolly good sort," I said defensively. "She thinks we need a Hitler here in England. She's met him, too!'

Aunt Madge's face went puce. "We'd never stand for his sort in England!"

"Don't forget, we had that wretched Oswald Mosley and his Blackshirts," said Uncle Harold wryly, looking up from his newspaper. "He's no better than Hitler; caused enough trouble in London, goose-stepping around the East End, bringing war to the streets. He wanted us to go the same way as Germany. Thank God, most people have had the good sense to ignore him. So far."

"Playing silly boys' games! That's all it would be if they weren't doing so much damage," exploded Aunty Madge.

"Yes, they're dangerous," Uncle agreed. "Mosley's lot have been stirring up hate – especially against Jews. We'd better watch out or we'll get our own Nazis."

"Why do they hate Jews, these Blackshirts and Brownshirts?" I asked.

"Because –"

"Not now, Harold," Aunty Madge sighed, as if reluctant for me to hear any more. "Go on Gwendoline – shoo! I need to get on."

Poor Aunt Madge was only trying to protect me from knowing too much about what the world was like, and I barely had an inkling of how much worse it was likely to get.

"Hey Gwenny, ducky! Before you go," Uncle Harold stabbed at a page of his newspaper, "what's another word for *exasperation*? You're good at crosswords. Five letters. *Cross* doesn't work, and *peeved* is too long. Any idea?"

"*Pique*?" I suggested, and laughed when Uncle heaved a sigh of annoyance with himself as he put it in.

It was that summer Archie and I saw our first aeroplane. We were lying side by side on top of a newly constructed haystack, smelling the freshly mown hay, chewing the seeds from the husks, and watching the skylarks soaring upwards, when we heard a droning, like a distant bumble bee. Archie sat up quick as a jack-in-the-box, then got to his knees.

"It's an Avro," he shouted.

"How do you know?" I asked, jumping up excitedly.

"Saw it at the pictures. I remember the sound. Look! See? I was right!"

And there it was: a wobbly little yellow thing with four wings, looking like a wasp, getting bigger and bigger as it headed towards us in a dead straight line.

"It's going to hit us!" I shrieked, dropping flat into the hay.

"No it ain't," shouted Archie above the buzz, which had turned to a roar. He waved his hands madly above his head. "Hello! Hello!"

The plane dipped his wings, and the tiny speck of a pilot waved back.

"Did you see that?" cried Archie with awe. "He waved at us. When I grow up, I'm going to be a pilot."

"Me too," I vowed, with sudden passion.

"Don't be daft," said Archie scornfully. "Girls can't be pilots."

"They can too," I retorted defiantly, kneeling up covered in straw. "Just you see. Bet I'll be a pilot before you."

But it was our older brother Eric who got there first, and achieved that goal. It was early September, a few days before Archie and I each went back to our respective schools, when Eric turned up at the farm. He was wearing a spanking new uniform: neither blue nor grey, with braided epaulettes, and a badge with golden wings, and a smart peaked cap. He suddenly looked like a man, not a boy. We were silent with admiration. Yet I felt a sudden, plunging sense of loss: our brother, with whom we had shared memories of early childhood in India: rough-and-tumbling, or singing in the church choir, or accompanying our father on horseback round the villages, or squatting with the cook while he rolled chapattis, or watching our mother singing Gilbert and Sullivan with the church amateur dramatics – our brother Eric had suddenly grown up.

What had felt like the present rolled away into a distant past; lost to us forever. Eric stood before us, an airman, in the uniform of His Majesty's Service – the Royal Air Force – and there was talk of war.

The summer ended, and it was back to school, swotting for our exams, and enjoying what we could of school life. For Dodo, it was looking forward to the annual Shakespeare play. This year it was to be 'As You Like It'.

"I'm going to audition for Rosalind – they must see I'm the perfect Rosalind, and they owe it to me," raged Dodo, as if in anticipation of being turned down. "I should have been Juliet last year and they gave it to Maud just because she's an 'Honourable' and her parents were going to attend. It was embarrassing; she forgot her lines and, anyway, didn't look remotely like a Juliet."

Poor Dodo, how she craved to be an actress. She was passionate about the theatre, and ruthless with it, whether it was doing everything she could to get a part in the school play year after year, or skipping school to go to the theatre in London. She had a secret stash of clothes – suspenders, stockings, hat, gloves, the lot – and, with a dash of lipstick and powder, would cycle out of school unnoticed to the train station. When 'Me and My Girl' was on with Lupino Lane, she cried, "I'd rather be expelled than miss that!" How she got back without anyone finding out was a miracle.

The auditions for 'As You Like It,' arrived. Though Dodo had worked so hard to learn the speeches, she didn't get the part of Rosalind. "Why?" she wailed despairingly. "Is it my face? Is my nose too big? My eyes too close together?"

I studied her affectionately, with her pale white face, shining brown straight hair, and nut-brown eyes. "Dodo – you're YOU!" I cried.

And she was. The layout of her features did not conform to the ideal of perfect feminine beauty, it was true: her nose was a little too narrow, and a little bit long, and her brow quite high, her cheeks angular. But her intelligence, wit, the sparkle in her eye, and the mobility of her face when she was mimicking someone or pulling faces, were a million times more interesting than some dizzy chocolate-box pin-up girl. She was heartbroken when she wasn't chosen for Rosalind; then less so when she found they'd given her the part of Celia.

"I know it's my nose," she declared. "I shall get myself a new nose as soon as I'm able."

"You're an idiot," I retorted.

CHAPTER 5

The Post

Noor settled in to our English boarding school without any fuss.

She must have been homesick, though never referred to it, and never came seeking distraction or comfort. The only clue was when I once found her sitting totally still: not looking out of the window, not reading, just totally absorbed in her own thoughts. I had burst in on her unexpectedly while she was in this state of meditation, and it was as if I'd thrown a bucket of cold water over her. After that, I learned to make a slight noise before I entered the room.

And how Noor loved writing her letters! Every day she had a letter on the go; usually a long one, and mostly to her father who, she said, read them out to the rest of the family. How envious we were of the frequency of the letters she received, often three in a week. Her father's letters were easily identifiable: fat chunky envelopes with coiled handwriting in black spidery ink.

One day, the postman delivered an extraordinarily

large, strangely shaped object almost as big as himself, but addressed to Noor in that same spidery hand. It was wrapped in brown paper with stickers all over it in red letters: FRAGILE. It was more than wrapped; it was positively entombed in padding to withstand the roughest of handling.

"What is it? What is it?" A bevy of girls and even staff gathered round.

"It's a body!" declared Dodo, dramatically. "Murder most foul!" And everyone laughed.

"It's come at last!" exclaimed Noor, joyfully. "I told Papa how much I missed playing it – and look what he's done!"

It took her five minutes to unwrap all that padding – but how we gasped at what emerged.

Noor held in her arms the most beautiful object most of us had ever seen. It was made out of highly polished, honey-coloured wood, beautifully carved, and inlaid with mother-of-pearl. It ballooned out like a gourd at the bottom, and went up a long neck with five metal strings. A silver-fretted finger board stretched to a dragon's head at the top. Beneath was another small gourd hanging from the neck.

"What is it?" voices called out in hushed whispers as though in the presence of something magical.

"A veena."

The musical instrument immediately transported me back to India, remembering an evening when we had a gathering in our bungalow for my mother's birthday.

An Indian musician came to play the veena for us with his tabla player – a boy barely ten years old. They seated themselves on the carpet and began to play. It was monsoon, and the rain was hurtling down like thousands of drumming fingers.

I knew Noor played the piano; she and Vera loved playing duets together. But this beautiful exotic instrument was quite another thing.

"Play it, Noor!" I begged.

Noor pressed the veena to her face, and stroked the shivering strings; then, as if possessed, carried it away like a beloved child, saying, "I must tune it first."

In India, the Hindu goddess Sarasvati plays the veena, sitting on a lotus flower, floating on the waters of Creation. It is said that those who play the veena commune with the gods. Somehow, it seemed the perfect instrument for Noor.

That night in our dorm after lights out, Noor sat on the floor in a pool of moonlight, holding the veena across her body. She began to play, her face lifted upwards as if her soul soared with the magical sounds coming from beneath her fingers. Her belief in fairies now made sense; she was a fairy herself, or a goddess on her lotus flower, looking as if she might float away into the blackness of that night. It was more than just a moment of beauty. Some people use the word bliss; it was bliss.

A slight quivering next to me made me turn in the darkness. It was Vera, quietly weeping.

Vera had become more relaxed with us, especially now that she and Noor could speak in French to each other, and they often went off to the practice rooms to play piano duets. She even laughed at Dodo's jokes, and we really did feel like a band of friends – though, unexpectedly, Vera could suddenly withdraw back into herself.

Noor would shrug helplessly, muttering, "I don't know what's wrong with her."

But it was the year which would end in mock exams before our Leaving Certificates – so we all studied assiduously, and there was little time to be introspective.

The grand ending of the year was the school play itself.

Even, though Dodo played Celia rather than Rosalind, it was obvious what a talented actor she was. I clapped like hell and joined in the cheers when she took her bow, feeling sad and furious that neither of her parents had thought to put space in their diaries to come and see her.

The following summer of 1938, Vera invited Noor to spend the holidays with her family in Paris. Noor was stunned and came to consult me.

"It's one thing to be a school friend of Vera's, but another to go and spend the whole of the summer holidays with her and her family. She's so moody. What if we fall out?"

"You won't! You couldn't fall out with a scorpion – dear Noor," I reassured her. "And, after all, Paris was your home. You've got friends there, haven't you? Anyway, it's only for five weeks."

"Six," she corrected.

"Paris. Gay Paree! You lucky thing!" I exaggerated my envy. "Think of me haymaking while you're making hay."

"I'll have to get permission from my guardians," murmured Noor. I could tell her mind was already coming round to the idea. "Vera's parents will have to write to them and invite me."

"Will they mind?" I asked.

"I don't think so. They won't have to keep finding things for me to do."

"You'll be able to play duets for hours, won't you," I cried, "though I suppose you'll miss your veena. You can't possibly carry it around with you?"

"Ah!" Noor clapped her hands. "We had friends in Paris who played the veena – the Bonnards – Pascal and Marianne. I can go and track them down! Oh, what a thought – I'll see them again." At a stroke, Noor turned from anxious and tentative to madly enthusiastic.

"Noor," I asked mischievously, "do the French have fairies too?"

"Oh yes!" she breathed. "My very first fairies were French: *les fées*."

"That's settled then," I declared. "Accept. Whatever happens, you'll have your friends and your *fées*."

"You think I'm childish," muttered Noor, looking suddenly deeply sad – as if to lose her world of fairies would be to lose her own reality. "Have you really never seen one, Gwen?"

"No, I haven't, though I used to believe passionately in fairies when I was little. I'm afraid I'm not like Peter Pan," I added thoughtlessly. "I grew up."

I saw Noor's face nearly crumple with humiliation at my cruel retort.

"Darling Noor!" I cried remorsefully. "How I wish I could see fairies. But it doesn't matter. Never grow up – otherwise you won't be you. *You* see them – lucky you."

Strangely, as soon as it was cleared for Noor to spend the summer holidays with Vera in Paris, Vera became withdrawn again. She seemed to disappear behind her fringe, and kept to herself. Odd, since she had been so thrilled that Noor was going to spend the holidays with her.

Noor whispered anxiously to me, "I wish you were coming to Paris as well. She's become all moody again."

"I almost wish I was too!" I sighed. "It'll be fine, Noor. You'll have a wonderful time."

We had been talking earnestly as we wandered through the school gardens. We saw Dodo and Vera sprawled on the grass a little way ahead.

"I just wish we could all stay together," murmured Noor quietly. "I *do* like Vera; but . . . am I just being her friend out of duty? My father always said, we should attend to the weakest and help them." She laughed wryly. "So I know he would approve. But can you imagine how humiliated Vera would feel if she thought that was true?"

"Darling Noor!" I took her arm. "I know you. Your principles aren't something separate from who you are. They are in your nature. Look how you stand up for Vera when Pamela gets going! You're like a tiger. You always leap to her defence if anyone makes an ugly remark. I know you hate violence – but you're still a warrior; a kind of peaceful warrior."

"But Gwen – six weeks!" groaned Noor. "And what if her parents are awful?"

Before we could continue our conversation, Dodo spotted us and waved madly. "Trust you two to turn up just when I've opened up some chocolate," she quipped. "Come and have some – if you must!" She glanced over at Vera and raised her eyebrows with a minuscule shrug as if to say, 'I don't know what's up with her.'

Vera wasn't smiling, but was staring at the grass as if she were counting every blade. We flopped down next to them, and Dodo, a little too brightly, handed round some chocolate squares with great flourishes. We sat in awkward silence as we allowed the sweetness to fill our mouths.

Suddenly Vera got to her knees, as if she had been preparing for this moment for a long time. "I've got something to tell you," she said. "I can't go on pretending."

We looked at each other, bewildered.

"What do you mean?" asked Dodo.

"You all need to know . . . especially you, Noor," said Vera. "You can't spend the next six weeks with me in Paris, and not know that – well – I'm Jewish."

Vera looked at us as if expecting some explosive effect. But we were baffled, and didn't know what to say or how to react.

"You can change your mind if you want to," said Vera.

"Good grief!" exclaimed Dodo. "I thought you were going to tell us you were pregnant or something!"

I kicked her. "Shut up, Dodo!"

Noor put a reassuring arm round Vera. "Don't be silly. Why would it matter to me what religion you are? I'm a Muslim. Does that matter to you?"

"Being Jewish matters to an awful lot of people," murmured Vera. "You know I'm different. "

"Only a little," teased Dodo. "You've got rather pointy ears."

We sniggered light-heartedly, but Vera didn't laugh.

"I've been living a lie," whispered Vera, as if ashamed. "I've lied to you all at school, and if the girls ever get to know, they'll hate me even more than they do now. Even in England, Jews are not popular, and here at school, they suspect there's something odd about me – especially Pamela. I'm sure she's guessed."

"And if she has, it can't possibly matter!" Dodo cried. "What's wrong with being Jewish? Jesus was Jewish. Don't take any notice of Pamela, she's nasty to everyone."

"What about your parents?" Noor asked. "What do they say?"

"That's a lie too." Vera's voice was almost a whisper. "They're not my parents. They are my aunt and uncle, Monsieur and Madame Moskowski. Aunty Minnie is my mother's younger sister, and Uncle Victor is her husband. They told me I should explain all this to you to avoid misunderstandings."

There was total silence. I knew there had to be something more serious than being Jewish. "Where are your parents, Vera?"

Vera twisted her fingers then, in the smallest voice said, "I don't know," and refused to look any of us in the eye. "I was born in Poland, like I told you, into a small village near Kielce."

Poland. For Vera, the word had faded, but never gone away. The land of her birth lurked in her bloodstream. Generations of memories became her memory. The poverty-stricken shtetl *she had lived in where everyone eked out a living as best they could. The make-do ethos. The 'waste not want not' of everyday life: of making things, growing crops, stitching and patching. The hand-me-down clothes, the buying and selling; the not enough to eat, too many mouths to feed; the poverty that could make you count every penny. The land where trust was fragile, and suspicion hung like a cloud with the hate that surrounded the Jews.*

"Where we lived, everyone was poor," whispered Vera. "Though there was always some anti-Jewish feeling, it was a mixed village, and we all got along. Every now and then thugs would attack Jewish houses, but they were usually drunk.

"My uncle had left years earlier and set up a successful business in Berlin. He used to send us money. All was going well till Hitler came in, and Uncle began to suffer attacks on his business.

"His letters became increasingly worried. He said attacks against Jews in Germany were becoming more and more common. 'I warn you,' he wrote to us, underlining his words, 'Hitler has ambitions to change the world and purge it of "undesirables" and those who contaminate the Aryan blood. He has his eyes on Poland. Believe me, you should think of leaving.'

"Aunt Minnie had always wanted to leave. She was young and adventurous. Her dream was to go to Paris; to see the world. But my parents couldn't just leave and, anyway, they still felt safe enough in Poland. 'Our family's known worse,' they said. But Aunt Minnie said she wasn't going to spend her days rotting in poverty and, one night, she ran away. We would get an odd message from time to time; she had been working her way through Germany, to Luxembourg and Belgium. Then suddenly – she was in Paris! Her dream city. Within a few months, she wrote to say she was married! She had met a businessman and gallery owner, Victor Moskowski. Her dream had come true. She was set to live happily ever after."

No one said a word. Vera continued.

"Back here in our village, more attacks began to happen.

No sooner had my father replaced the broken glass in his windows, then another brick would come through. The attacks became more frequent and more vicious. They wanted to drive Jewish families out of Poland as they were doing in Germany. We often had terrified people coming to our house for refuge. Finally, there was another anti-Jewish pogrom in our own village. Two families were beaten up and had their houses burned to the ground."

Pogrom. Dodo and Gwen looked at each other. Now they knew what it meant.

"Then we heard that uncle himself had been murdered defending his business," Vera went on quietly. "My father shouted and slammed his fist on the table. 'That's it! We're leaving!' he said. 'We have to give our children a better future than this. We'll go to your Aunt Minnie in Paris, until we can get on our own feet.'

"My mother wrote to her sister, to ask if we could all come and stay with her and Uncle Victor. It was hard for her to write a begging letter; my mother and her sister had never really got on. But we were running out of time. A reply finally came. Aunt Minnie had agreed.

"I remember that day: the fearful excitement, the rush to pack – taking only our most treasured possessions. Oh, the things I left behind!"

The others were listening now in intense silence.

"We took a bus to the railway station at Kielce: me, my mother and father, and my baby brother, Ethan."

Vera was speaking quickly, as if she couldn't bear to

articulate the truth of her own words. "My father put me on the train first. He was heaving our suitcases on board when there was an attack. A band of local bully-boys came running down the platform, chanting and lashing out at people – anyone – just to scare them. Then they saw us. My father always wore his cap – his yarmulke – with pride, so they knew we were Jewish. They struck my father to the ground, and when my mother rushed to help, they beat her up too, even though she had my baby brother Ethan in her arms.

People stared, as if turned to stone; nobody helped. The guard was blowing his whistle frantically. The train started moving. I was leaning out of an open door, screaming for my mother and father, and trying to jump off, but someone dragged me back and slammed the door. A voice hissed in my ear. 'Shush!' and a hand was put over my mouth. I was held tightly until I had stopped struggling, while the train gathered speed.

"I left them behind."

Vera looked at the others, stricken, full of guilt and remorse.

Noor threw her arms round her. "Oh Vera! How have you lived with this? You poor thing! What happened to them?"

"What happened to them?" All Vera knew was the pain she lived with; the fear and the nightmares – and the sorrow; the sorrow she went to bed with each night, and the sorrow she knew would be there when she awoke the next morning.

"I don't know," she replied in a flat voice. She had

tried to answer the question to herself a million times. "We never heard from them again. Perhaps they're dead.

"The man who had grabbed me and calmed me down was an Englishman." Vera was tired now. "He spoke to me in Russian. He held me till I stopped screaming, then got me to sit in his carriage. He was kind. He gave me a piece of chocolate. He told me not to worry; that I would be all right; that my parents would come later and find me. He looked at my suitcase, which had come on board with me, and the label with my Jewish name, as well as the address in Paris. He ripped off the label, tore it into bits and threw them out of the window. He told me not to worry. He said he was going to Paris and would take me to that address. 'You're with me now,' he said. 'I'll say I'm your guardian.'"

"And what about your name? Vera Bell?" asked Noor.

"Another lie," Vera wailed. "My real name is Bielawski. It's Polish because my father is Polish. My Uncle Victor changed it to Bell when they sent me to England. They thought it was better to have a more English name. You see, Jews can have a hard time anywhere. In France too. It's the same all over Europe."

"Do your aunt and uncle feel safe in Paris?" asked Dodo.

"Uncle Victor does," replied Vera. "Although he's Jewish, he was born French from generations back, so he doesn't see himself as an immigrant. He owns an art gallery and is well-known and respected. My aunt is more nervous. That's why I troubled her. My father is a rabbi, and we lived a very traditional life in our *shtetl* – our village – but Aunt Minnie found me a nuisance, always remembering the Jewish festivals, asking to light menorah candles every Friday, and demanding to go to the synagogue. My aunt and uncle aren't at all religious. They are proud to be secular and never go to the synagogue, except for bar mitzvahs or other ceremonies of their friends. Paris is full of people from everywhere; no one used to care. But recently, people are openly turning against Jews again."

The school bell rang. The others enveloped Vera reassuringly and, arm in arm, went in for tea.

CHAPTER 6

Dilemmas

It was early evening, Noor's favourite time of day during the summer, when the sun was lower in the sky, the shadows longer, the air softer, warmer, and perfumed. Now all the colours of the flowers seemed so vibrant: the pinks, blues, lavenders, whites; the roses of orange, and red, and cream, and yellow. She went looking for her fairies – and yes – there was one: deep among the sky-blue Canterbury bells, inside the heart of the flower.

She halted, enchanted; enraptured. The fairy lifted its head, smiled, and waved. Noor waved back and felt deep happiness. How she wished she could have shared this magic with someone. Noor had never met anyone else who saw fairies. Not even Papa. When she told him, he just smiled tenderly and said, "Darling daughter, you and I will always see things others can't – but we are blessed because we see Beauty and Goodness, and that's the most important thing."

Noor felt she could think more clearly when she talked to her fairies. "Should I go to Paris with Vera?" she asked the fairy. Noor was still unsure.

"Noor, what is it you like about Vera?" asked the fairy.

"She lives in France and like me, speaks French, and she loves music as I do."

"What else?"

"She's an outsider as I am."

"And?"

"And I feel a duty to protect her. But I'm not sure if we're real friends yet. Should I go to Paris?"

"Be friends. Go to Paris. It will be good," the fairy murmured.

"Yes." Noor sighed with acceptance. "Thank you. I will go."

I too got an invitation.

Dodo's parents were still in Germany and had summoned her to Munich for the summer holidays. *"Why not bring Gwen? You'll both get invited to lots of dances, and maybe hunting weekends. We think you should see something of German life. Having Gwen would be good for you, and useful for us to know you'll be entertained, as we'll be terribly busy."*

"Please Gwen, please come to Munich with me," begged Dodo. "We'll have such fun."

I was sceptical. "I don't think for a single minute my aunt and uncle will let me go. They think Germany's descending into hell, as far as I can make out. And there's Archie. But look," I added, when I saw Dodo's disappointment. "I'll mention it to them and see what they think."

CHAPTER 7

Will There Be a War?

"Do you think there's going to be a war?" Vera's voice quavered through the darkness of their first night in Paris.

Noor was so tired she was tempted to pretend that she was asleep. It had been a long journey, travelling all day from school by train to Victoria, then the boat train to Dover, and the cross-channel ferry to Calais – where, even though it wasn't that rough, she had spent most of the time being sick over the side. But it was exciting to see the coastline of France emerging out of the sea mist, and she sang under her breath: *"The farther off from England, the nearer is to France,"* as the whiting sang to the snail in *Alice in Wonderland*.

Swarms of blue-coated French porters had swept up their suitcases when they docked, and deposited them on the train to Paris. Two hours later they arrived at the Gare du Nord to be met by Vera's aunt and uncle.

They were not what Noor expected. She felt suddenly unsettled, and not sure that she had made the right decision to come after all.

Aunt Minnie was vivacious: very young and bright, very Parisienne, glamorously made up with lipstick and rouge and a carefully placed black beauty spot on her cheek. She was fashionably dressed in a sweeping black coat fitted into a tiny waist, a fox-fur stole tossed round her shoulders, and a neatly fitted amber velvet hat with a coil of shining yellow and black feathers perched on her head, allowing a few locks of her close bobbed, rich brown hair to frame her moon-white brow. Loops of pearls clustered round her throat and matching drop earrings added to her glamour; high-heeled shoes showed off shapely legs glistening in silk stockings; and she had a way of moving that made everything swish and swirl. Black velvet gloves covered her hands. She was beautiful. Noor couldn't see anything of Vera about her at all; no clue that she, with her shy, hiding personality, could be related to this fashionable woman. Aunt Minnie was chin-up confident, with wide dark eyes which swept critically over Noor before she smiled. Noor wondered whether she disapproved of her. Perhaps she was not the kind of person she hoped would be Vera's friend.

Uncle Victor was quite short and bulky, with a sharply intelligent face and narrow, twinkly blue eyes beneath gingery eyebrows. He was wearing a very expensive tweed coat, a fedora hat, highly polished shoes and fawn calf-skinned gloves in which he kept pressing his fingers impatiently, as if they were late for the opera. Vera didn't run to either of them, but let each of them approach her.

"Vera!" boomed Uncle Victor with loud affection, and

he kissed her, right cheek, left cheek, right cheek and left cheek again.

"*Chérie!*" exclaimed Aunt Minnie in a high tinkling voice.

Noor was shocked and puzzled to find that Vera addressed them as *vous* in the formal way rather than *tu* and that there was barely any difference between the way they greeted their niece and the way they greeted her. Noor, too, got the intimate peck, peck, peck, peck.

But it was Paris! They walked out of the noisy, steam-hissing, soot-grimy station, following their red-jacketed porter into the blinding blue of a Parisian summer. There was an aroma of sugared almonds, and flower sellers thrust perfumed bunches into their faces. Busy streets clattered with horses, the shrill ringing of bicycle bells, and the beep-beep of taxis. Noor felt a rush of joy. She was back!

The porter hailed a taxi and, after Vera's uncle had placed a wodge of notes in his hand, they were off – driving across Paris. Noor was thrilled to see gleaming, horse chestnut tree-lined boulevards, the familiar buildings and parks and landmarks again. Memories flooded through her: the language, the food, and cafés, the sound of music, cars, buses, trams and voices – singing, laughing, loving, arguing.

When they arrived at the Moskowskis' apartment in the Rue d'Assas, overlooking the Jardin du Luxembourg, it was not unlike the apartment Noor had lived in a few years earlier. She felt she had come home.

They entered through a high, broad wooden door off the street, into the sharp-shadowed square of a cobbled courtyard, on to which four storeys of windows gazed down. From one of the windows the Moskowskis' maid, Jeanne, had been watching and waiting. It was almost as though she had to restrain herself from flying out of the third-floor window. She vanished and quickly reappeared: a plump, rosy, round-faced young woman, who looked as if she were more of a country girl from a farm than a Parisian maid. She rushed over cooing and squeaking with affection, to help with the luggage.

"Jeanne!" Vera gave her first cry of joy as she flung her arms round the maid, and addressed her as *tu*, and Jeanne responded warmly calling her *"ma petite!"*

They trooped passed a window where, in the dim yellow light, Madame Boucher, a grim-faced concierge, invigilated, and combined skilful knitting with darting eyes which checked every person who came and went through the street door. The family acknowledged her, but Noor felt there was contempt in her barely nodded, unsmiling response, her focus having already returned to her clickety-clackety needles. They climbed three flights of a broad dim stairway, up, up, up, the dark, yellowing walls lit only by low, spluttering gaslight, and arrived outside the imposing, polished oak door of the apartment.

Vera's aunt was helped off with her coat. As she removed her gloves, Noor was startled at the sight of her hands: although her fingernails were manicured, long, and painted red, her wrists, the breadth of her hands, and her knuckles were curiously large, as though they had been used to extreme hard work, as on a farm or outside in the

52

fields. It was a mild observation, swiftly passing and gone while she took in the apartment.

It was like stepping into another world of rich carpets and glowing wall lamps, with as many pictures hanging on the walls as in an art gallery; and spindly, polished tables with vases and figurines; and gold-gilt mirrors which reflected crystal chandeliers. A grand piano gleamed walnut brown, in the French windows, with a balcony beyond.

"What a lovely piano!" exclaimed Noor. "Can't wait to play duets on it."

"I'm sorry we don't have a veena," mourned Vera.

"Oh, but I have friends here in Paris who do," cried Noor. "Perhaps we can go and see them soon?"

"Yes, we must," agreed Vera without enthusiasm. She suddenly looked vague and disconnected. But just when Noor began to feel uneasy at what she perceived was the strangely formal and unloving atmosphere she had come into, there was an unexpected, whooping scream of delight. A small boy of about five came bursting in like a wild thing, and flung himself into Vera's arms. "Veroshka! *Tu es venue!* You've come," he cried, kissing her passionately.

"My nickname," laughed Vera, swinging him round and round, full of joy.

"*Viens, viens!*" He struggled from her arms. "I want to show you my new room."

"Manners!" Vera reminded him. "Louis meet Noor; Noor meet Louis."

"*Bonjour mademoiselle,*" Louis whispered.

"*Bonjour* Louis," answered Noor, formally shaking his thin, small hand.

"Noor comes from India," explained Vera, as Louis stared at Noor's brown skin, and dangling black plaits.

"Have you seen tigers?" he asked.

"No, Louis, I haven't seen tigers. Maybe one day."

"Come and see my room, Veroshka," he yelled, and dragged Vera away.

Noor was relieved that no one expected them to eat a hearty supper.

"So sorry, my dears!" Aunt Minnie exclaimed with effusive apologies. "I have such an important meeting. Forgive me for rushing off. But your Uncle Victor will guard you. You don't mind, do you sweetie?" She bent her face into the back of Vera's head with an extravagant kiss. "We're going to see lots of each other this summer."

Vera stared stonily ahead. Then Aunt Minnie was gone.

Supper was a bowl of onion soup and crusty bread which they ate amid much amiable banter from Uncle Victor. Later, when they said goodnight, he hugged his niece warmly.

"It's wonderful to have you home again, Vera; and you too, *mademoiselle*." He turned to Noor. "We're so pleased to welcome one of Vera's friends here." He took her hand and, with courteous formality, kissed her fingers, and she felt he meant it.

They were sharing a room with a bed on each side of shuttered French windows leading to an wrought-iron balcony, festooned with flowering potted plants.

Before getting into bed, Noor peered out into the darkness, wondering if fairies were listening among the flowers. "*Salut, mes amis!*" she whispered. She reached out to close the shutters, but Vera called, "Noor, would you mind if we left them open?"

Noor didn't mind. She felt nothing could have kept her awake, even the sounds of Paris by night, and she tumbled into bed. But after a few minutes, Vera's next question brought her wide awake.

"Do you think there's going to be a war?"

Noor heard the fear in Vera's voice. She pretended to be asleep. She had no idea how to answer.

"Goodnight, Noor. I'm so glad you're here," Vera murmured.

As there was still no reply, she said nothing more. Noor lay awake for a long while, before falling into troubled dreams.

Grandpa, who had seen many wars, said, "War not only kills people, it kills people's souls."

JANINE PHILLIPS, AUGUST 1939
Children's Wartime Diaries

CHAPTER 8

Daniel

They walked into the Jardin du Luxembourg, smelling roasting chestnuts and sugared almonds; a distant busker played the accordion. But there was a peculiar, unsettling energy in the air. Clusters of people argued volubly. The Nazis had marched into Austria; where next? Is that why Vera had asked that question last night?

Crossing the park, they arrived at the dappled tree-lined Boulevard Saint-Michel, passing cafés where people leaned towards each other in intense conversation, debating and gesticulating. A small group of people waved banners. Vera said they were communists proclaiming "Bread, Peace, and Liberty!" or *"Non au Fascisme!"* to a mixture of boos and cheers. Later another march chanted, *"Non au Communisme!"* equally passionately.

Vera walked on – a little faster, no longer lingering before shop windows. Noor hurried to keep up with her. Vera finally stopped outside a café with tables on the pavement. She looked troubled.

"I'd love a lemonade, would you?" she said.

A waiter bustled out quickly and took their order. They sipped quietly, then Vera asked again, "Do you think there's going to be a war?"

"Oh, dearest Vera!" exclaimed Noor. "Surely not!"

"I think there will be a war," Vera said, staring at the lemony light fragmenting in the fizz of her glass. "Didn't you hear the news, see the headlines? They've already gone into Austria. They're giving the Jews a hard time: beating them up, and burning their businesses and synagogues. It makes me scared."

What do your aunt and uncle think?" asked Noor.

"They're not scared," Vera exclaimed harshly. "They don't think anything like that could happen here. I mean, they're well off: middle class, not refugees or foreign workers. My mother always said Aunt Minnie had done well for herself; that she despised the rest of us for not getting out of our village like she had, and for accepting our lot. She said Aunt Minnie always expected to hear we had been killed in some pogrom or other, and she dreaded us turning up to scrounge off her.

"Then I appear. So, you can imagine what she felt when I arrived at their door: a scruffy little girl who spoke mainly Polish and Yiddish. An embarrassment; but, of course, they took me in."

"Your Uncle Victor seems very kind," suggested Noor.

"He is, he is," agreed Vera. "But Aunt Minnie is very touchy. Hates people knowing where she came from. She wants me to assimilate, and discouraged me from going to the synagogue. Uncle Victor wasn't so bothered, but my aunt argued with him, telling him that I should forget Poland and that damned rat-infested *shtetl*. 'If she stays with us, then she must be French like us,' Aunt Minnie had said. 'With things being so troubled at the moment, it's better if she keeps her head down, learns French, and just fits in.'

"Uncle Victor winked at me. 'Better do as your aunt says.'

"At first, I was too young to disobey. But one day, when I was older, I was walking with Jeanne and we passed a big red brick building. It was hot. A window was open. I could hear a cantor singing. It was a synagogue. I ran up to the door, and burst into tears, as memories came back of my father taking a service, and me sitting with my mother in the gallery.

"Jeanne was so kind. 'Listen, *ma petite*,' she whispered. 'If you want to go inside, you go. I won't tell anyone.'

"So, I did. Listening to the Hebrew prayers, and the music, and the calls of the cantor, brought an almost unbearable happiness and sadness all mixed up – but also a sense of belonging again, for the first time since I had arrived in Paris. After that, Jeanne often dropped me off at the synagogue on a Saturday morning, and collected me again afterwards. Dearest Jeanne, she is my best friend, you know!"

"I can tell that," Noor said with a smile.

My aunt and uncle didn't find out about the synagogue

for quite a while. They were always busy, and Jeanne had a boyfriend, so she was only too pleased if I looked after myself. But I knew if they ever discovered I had disobeyed them, my aunt especially, would be furious.

"But they found out soon enough."

"Oh no! How?" asked Noor.

"Someone told them; probably the concierge – Madame Boucher. She's the sort that would have knitted under the guillotine during the French Revolution, and smiled as people's heads were chopped off," cried Vera bitterly. "They were furious. My aunt sacked Jeanne on the spot. It was only because I screamed that I would die if they sent her away that Uncle persuaded Aunt Minnie to keep her on. So, she gave in, but warned Jeanne that if she ever colluded with me again against their wishes, she would be instantly dismissed.

"It was as if I had betrayed my aunt. But it was she who had betrayed me and my mother – her own sister. I argued with them. I had a right to go to the synagogue. I called them cowards and traitors to their faith; didn't they care what had happened to my parents and my baby brother? And didn't it mean anything that my great uncle in Berlin, my aunt's own uncle, had been murdered for being a Jew?"

Vera's eyes were blazing with anger.

"My aunt called me an ungrateful good-for-nothing. How she ranted at me. Didn't I know how difficult it was to be Jewish? Uncle Victor tried to soothe things over, but he just liked to keep the peace.

"Then she had this idea: to send me away. 'Why don't we send her to school in England. It would be better for all of us,' she insisted. 'We have to be careful these days with so much prejudice around. All these refugees pouring in – thousands of them – they're ruining it for us.'

"Uncle Victor told her to stop worrying. 'We're assimilated French citizens; we've lived here for hundreds of years. There's no reason why we should feel insecure.'

"'Vera is not a French citizen,' my aunt pointed out. 'She has no papers, nothing. It will take a long time to regularise her.'

"So, they sent me to England for my safety! Huh!" Vera snorted scornfully. But suddenly, with great affection, she leaned over to Noor and held her arm. "But if they hadn't, I wouldn't have met you, dear Noor. Thank you for spending the summer with me."

A voice called out from across the road. "Hey Vera! It *is* you!" A young man darted towards them.

"Daniel!" Vera adjusted her hat, looking uncertain and embarrassed, but pleased too; so pleased that a change swept over her face. She jumped to her feet and they greeted each other with formal kisses on both cheeks. But with a sudden impulse, he gave her a quick hug and clasped her hand.

"How great to see you, Veroshka. When did you get back? We've missed you."

Vera introduced Noor. "This is my friend from England. She's spending the holidays with me."

"*Pardon, pardon!*" cried Daniel. He held out his hand. "Daniel Alkan."

"Noor Khan," replied Noor, taking his hand and greeting him in her best French. "*Je suis enchantée.*"

He broke into a surprised grin and spread his arms. "Oh ho! You speak such good French! *Merveilleux!*"

"Noor used to live in Paris," explained Vera. "I met Daniel at the synagogue," she told Noor, and soon the three of them were chatting away in French together and catching up on news.

Daniel was nice, Noor decided. He was a little older than they were – about eighteen or so – long and gangly, with tight curly black hair and steel-rimmed glasses behind which dark eyes sparkled mischievously. She knew he was studying her as he sipped his coffee, but Noor also quickly got the impression he was holding something back. He looked secretive, wary; the same expressions she had grown used to seeing with Vera.

As Daniel walked them home, he took Vera's arm. Pulling her closely to him, he talked urgently. "Things are getting bad, Veroshka. The Nazis –" he called them *les boches* – "they want to overrun the whole of Europe. And do you know what they're doing in Spain? They're helping Franco and his fascists to win. Who can stop them? If they aren't stopped in Spain . . ." His voice trailed away helplessly. "But they must be stopped. I think it's our only hope. Listen! Can you come to a meeting tomorrow night? Seven p.m. at the Café Rigaud? We have a Republican who escaped from Catalonia living here in exile. He's going to speak to us. Try and come."

It began to rain. Daniel and Vera walked on, out of Noor's hearing, but she could see the intensity with which he clutched her arm, and spoke into her ear. Then he kissed her fiercely on both cheeks in farewell.

The rain was falling more heavily now. Daniel turned to Noor and clasped her hand. *"Mademoiselle,* I hope to see you tomorrow with Vera."

Back in the apartment, Vera sat at the piano and began playing Chopin very quietly. Noor resorted to their bedroom and started a letter to her father:

Darling Papa,

You always told us war was wrong.

Above all, you said we must never be violent and hurt another person, even if they were our most dire enemy. But if the enemy perpetrates violence on innocent others, shouldn't we ever intervene?

CHAPTER 9

Letter From Munich

The first letter that came, however, was to both of them from Gwen in Munich. Her usually neat handwriting was a scrawl, as if she had written fast and furious. Noor read it out loud.

Dearest Noor and Vera,
I hope you get this letter. I had to write. I saw them – those Brownshirts that you, Vera, were so scared of. They call them stormtroopers now. It was terrible; revolting. Dodo and I had joined her parents to stay with their friends the von Garstadts. After a few days in Munich, the von Garstadts drove us all into the mountains for a change. We saw a commotion on the pavement as we passed through one of the suburbs on the way out of the city. "What's that?" I cried. "What are they doing to that man?" A gang of youths were hurling stones and bricks through a shop window. The shopkeeper rushed out to confront them, and they jumped on him. He was obviously Jewish, and they were trying to grab the yarmulke from his head. He stumbled and fell face down, and they set about kicking him. A couple of stormtroopers just stood

by and watched. I begged the von Garstadts to stop the car. "You've got to help him," I cried. But they just drove on. I begged Dodo to ask them to stop. But Herr von Garstadt understood English, and he just said, "Best to stay out of these things. There are a lot of disturbances these days. Jews are usually at the bottom of it."

"I don't know how it can be kind to beat up an old man," I protested.

I know Dodo was upset too, and looked as if she wanted to disappear.

"You don't understand," said Herr v.G. "We have many problems here in Germany, and sorting them out can seem a little brutal. We must be cruel to be kind – is that not what you say in England?"

"Absolutely," agreed Dodo's mother.

I couldn't believe my ears – let alone my eyes. "Can't we stop and help?"

Dodo's parents just stared ahead and didn't say a word.

Dodo poked me with her elbow. "Oh please shut up, Gwen," she begged me in a whisper. "Be polite."

I wanted to jump from the car. I wanted to go home. Now I knew why Aunt Madge was so upset with what she was hearing on the radio.

It's true, Vera – all those stories you told us about the Nazis are true. And do you know, everywhere – everywhere are banners and flags with swastikas. (Gwen had drawn a picture of a swastika.) And whenever people greet each other it's "Heil Hitler" this and "Heil Hitler" that, with a clenched fist salute into the air.

Now I'm writing to you from the prettiest wooden chalet – like the musical clocks they have in Switzerland, with window boxes full of geraniums, and painted shutters at the windows with hearts carved into them – and we have a view of the mountains. It's so beautiful, like paradise; so I could hardly believe the ugly scene we had witnessed on the way up. I think Dodo's cross with me. I embarrassed her. She's lying on her bed reading. I hope we're still friends.

LATER

Dodo asked if we could go for a walk. She was very pale and quiet – not like our dear Dodo. She's terrified by the way her parents and the von Garstadts seem besotted by the Nazis. They even give the Nazi salute – can you believe it?

2 DAYS LATER

Surprise, surprise! Charles Brandon has come. He drove up in a glamorous Alvis. Hooray! That will cheer things up. He bounds about like a puppy, laughing a lot, and he's very good looking. Dodo thinks he looks like Laurence Olivier – and you know how potty she is about him. Charles has got the same magnetic, glowering eyes that challenge you to resist him. Aunt Madge would definitely warn me to beware of a man who looks at you like that! What's more, he's got this wavy, dark brown hair and a shadow of a moustache which makes him look incredibly dashing. Just like a film star! He was very polite, though he didn't click his heels and kiss our hands, as German men do. I think Dodo's rather keen on him. It bucked her up no end, especially when he took us for a whirl *in his amazing car. He cracked loads of jokes, and fooled about pretending to be Hitler. Good job no one else was watching. We got back in time to change for supper. Dodo was quite excitable and giggly. We both put on our evening gowns, and felt very grown up adding some lipstick and powder to our faces which Dodo pinched from her mother's make-up case. I thought she looked radiant, and that Charles was sure to fall in love with her.*

Then something awful happened after supper. We were in the drawing room, and Herr von Garstadt began to play songs and dances at the piano. Everyone began singing and knee-slapping. Even the staff joined in. Then Dodo's mama ordered Dodo to recite a poem. She really didn't want to, but they wouldn't take no for an answer, so she stood up and read that Shakespeare sonnet about the Darling Buds of May. When she had finished and everyone clapped, that horrible Frau von Garstadt quipped to Dodo's parents, "What a darling pretty daughter you have. Pity about her nose – a little too Jewish." It was supposed to be a joke – ha ha – and everyone laughed uproariously, and Dodo's mother said, "Our dear Dodo has always wanted a new nose," and they laughed even louder.

You can imagine her humiliation. Charles immediately took to the piano and began to sing that song by Noël Coward, 'Don't Put Your Daughter on the Stage, Mrs Worthington,' winking at Dodo, and fooling about with the words, making her laugh. I liked him for that. Everyone was so impressed, and afterwards he paid Dodo attention for the rest of the evening. But later that night when we went to bed, Dodo had a good cry and said she hated her mother, and felt ashamed for ever having wanted to change her nose. I told her to forget it. Look how gallant Charles was! She said he was just being kind and would never look at her again without seeing her nose. She still felt utterly humiliated. Poor Dodo.

I do hope you two are having a terrific time and love being back in Paris. Write, write, write . . . At least you're not seeing those beastly stormtroopers.

If you write immediately, your letter should reach us before we leave. I can't wait to see you.

Heaps and heaps and heaps of love,

Gwen

P.S. I didn't tell you, but Dodo and I went to some balls in Munich before we came up into the mountains. Three in a row! The von Garstadts arranged for two young English-speaking men from the local military academy to be our escorts. Oh goodness – we nearly swooned when we saw them. Frightfully handsome they were, with wavy blond hair and blue eyes just like Wagnerian gods – and one of them was actually called Siegfried! The other was Kurt. Dodo and I argued over who we wanted as our partner! I felt quite excited about going with them. Dodo did too. We wore those gowns we bought in Harvey Nichols in Kensington – do you remember? We looked gorgeous – even if I say so myself. These balls are very grand – just like the debutante balls in England. Everyone is so formal and civilised: the young men click their heels and bow, and kiss your hands, and are so incredibly polite. The girls curtsey to their elders. Yet outside in the streets shopkeepers are being kicked to death for being Jewish.

"Shall we try and play a duet?" asked Vera quietly. She went to a cupboard and took out some music. "I love Schubert. Top or bottom?"

"You do top," said Noor, pulling up a chair at the bottom end of the keyboard. "I'll do bottom and hope you don't notice my mistakes."

She had two bars on her own of lilting chords, like a child's cradle gently rocking, until Vera entered with a lullaby tune of such aching beauty, it was impossible to think of the evil that lurked outside.

The sufi said:
Listen to music
And find the secrets therein.

CHAPTER 10

A Cause Worth Dying For?

Vera's aunt and uncle now turned a blind eye when every Saturday, Vera went to the synagogue. On one such Saturday morning, Noor borrowed Vera's bicycle and cycled off to the house of Marianne and Pascal Bonnard, her family's old friends. She had sent a postcard asking if she could visit them, and an enthusiastic YES! had come by return.

She cycled through familiar streets. The bustle of the boulevards quietened as she entered the side streets of houses and gardens strewn with bougainvillea and clematis; streets of acacia and geraniums, of wrought-iron gates and balconies shaded by magnolia. She cycled faster, remembering her old friends' hospitality; their affection for her mother, their playfulness with Noor and her younger siblings, and their passionate interest in her father's philosophy. They loved all things Indian, even though they had never been there. "One day we shall go to India," they would say with enthusiastic certainty.

She remembered their house was full of Indian carpets,

and hangings and ornamental carved wooden tables, and beautiful Indian miniatures, and carvings – many of which had been given to them by Noor's family; and most of all the veena, which her father and mother had given Marianne on her fortieth birthday. Noor remembered an evening of birthday celebrations when the two families and friends gathered in their drawing room, sitting on carpets and cushions and bolsters, to listen to Noor's mother playing the veena and singing, and Noor's father reciting Sufi poetry.

Noor propped her bicycle at the bottom of the steps, and leaped up to a large, dark blue front door. She rang the bell. It jangled just as she remembered; its metallic clangs sounded all the way through the house.

The length of time it took for the door to open was longer than she expected – or was it just her impatience? She remembered how Léonie, the Bonnards' maid, always seemed so swift to open the door to them, beaming and welcoming, taking their coats and ushering them through; and Pascal, more like a young boy than the master of the house, leaping down the main staircase, shouting, *"Les hindous sont arrivés"* – the Indians have arrived. The French commonly called Indians "hindou" – even though Noor and her family were Muslims, they had never minded. Marianne would appear from somewhere, her tumble-down auburn hair falling into her eyes, racing to embrace them all; and other doors would open at the top of the house, out of which their young children, Marcel and Constance, would come clattering down to greet them. They adored her father, the Indian philosopher, mesmerised by his sweeping golden coat, his long black beard, and deep black eyes. But as if suddenly overcome by shyness, they would pause and flop halfway down the stairs and stare, till he would open wide his arms for them to leap into and be whirled around with shrieks of laughter.

She waited for the door to be opened. Where was Léonie? Had she left them? That was the trouble with memories: they could freeze in the mind; remain unchanged by Time.

At last, the knob turned. The door opened a crack; a blue eye stared through the narrow gap. It opened further, and there was Marianne's face, curiously anxious, thinner, older. At the sight of Noor, she flung open the door and her face creased with smiles.

"Darling Noor!" She kissed her joyfully, and pulled her into the house. "I can't believe what a beautiful woman you have become!" she exclaimed. "Of course, you were always a beautiful child, so why should I have expected anything different? Ah, come! Come, into the drawing room. Let me get you a coffee or lemonade – what would you like? And tell me how you come to be in Paris, and who you are staying with, and what it is like to be at school in England! Yes – your parents wrote to me and told me . . ."

She chattered on and on, leaving no room for answers, like a chain smoker, barely pausing for breath – and though Marianne had always smoked, Noor wondered if she had indeed become a chain smoker as she smelled the heavy fog of tobacco, and noted ashtrays piled high with stubs.

Marianne clutched Noor's hand, stroked her face, and played with her long plaits. Finally, she excused herself to fetch the lemonade which Noor had managed to convey she would like. At last, with a brief moment alone, Noor took a deep breath to reconfigure her memories into the reality of what she was seeing.

Where was Léonie? Where was Pascal? Where were their children, Marcel and Constance? The place looked empty, devoid of family; dusty, fading – even cold for a summer's day. At the far end of the room was the piano she remembered, but looking unplayed, draped in a heavy fringed maroon chenille with an array of dusty family photographs displayed on top.

In a corner nearby was the veena – the beautiful, ornate, lacquered veena. The sight of it brought tears to Noor's eyes as more memories – happy, happy memories – rushed back. She stroked the strings. They were untuned, but sound reverberated round the room like the wave of a magic wand, and it seemed to her that ghostly figures of the Bonnard family and Noor's family thronged into the drawing room, laughing and filling it up with friendship.

Marianne reappeared, and set down a tray of lemonade on a table. "Ah! You've found the veena!"

In the past Noor and her family had always called these friends by their first names and used the informal *tu*. Yet now, Noor felt suddenly awkward, and formal. She hung her head shyly. "Are you still playing it, *madame*?"

"I am still your old friend, *Marianne*," said Marianne gently. "We have been like family, yet better than family:

all equal – adults and children. Please, we are still *tu* – with each other. Remember how your father called us anarchist! How we laughed then – yet he knew – he knew us – and he was right. We are anarchist; we are all equals. How silly labels are!" She laughed.

"What's happened here?" Noor blurted out. Something had changed; something profound. "Where is Pascal? Where are Marcel and Constance?"

Marianne extricated a cigarette from the packet lying on the side table. She lit it, inhaled deeply, and slowly exhaled, watching the blue smoke coil into the room. She laughed again; a nervous, brittle laugh. "Have you forgotten how Paris empties in the summer? Everyone has gone on holiday – to the Côte d'Azur or some holiday destination. Constance and Marcel have gone to Roussillon to stay with their grandparents for the holidays."

"And Pascal?"

Marianne took a couple more draws on the cigarette as if trying to think what to say. "Noor, I don't know how much you know of what is going on in the world. You are so young, and you've been living in a girls' boarding school far away in England. But here, we feel as though it is we who live on an island. A great cloud sweeps towards us from Europe and envelops us in anxiety. We are in danger. We are afraid of the rise of fascism: in Hitler's Germany, and Italy's Mussolini, and in Spain with Franco. There is a war raging right now in Spain – a civil war – between fascists and socialists. It's bitter; it's going to be a war to the death. What happens there may influence what happens to the rest of us. Even here in France, we have splits between left and right. That is why . . ." Her voice trailed away. "We've become more cruel."

Daniel had said the same thing. "But Pascal?" Noor repeated urgently. "What has that got to do with him?"

"Thousands of French people have gone to Spain to fight for the Republicans – the anti-fascists."

"Pascal has gone to Spain?" whispered Noor.

"Pascal says he must fight. We too believe in non-violence, but . . . Hitler's goal is to conquer Europe. I begged him not to go. I'm so afraid. It's a real war with guns and bombs and horrible cruelty; thousands of people are getting killed and wounded and losing their homes and jobs. Did you hear what the boche did to Guernica? They razed the whole village to the ground, killing everyone: women and children too."

Noor remembered Vera's fearful question: *Do you think there's going to be a war?*

"I haven't heard from Pascal for over a month. I don't know if he's alive or dead. Pascal's last letter was very gloomy. The fascists, especially Hitler, want to make the whole of Europe fascist, and are helping Franco."

Marianne had aged; grey threaded through her once rich hair, making it look dull. The woman – whom Noor remembered as always being immaculate, like most Parisian women from shop girl to duchess – was now plain, pale, wearing no lipstick and powder, or eye make-up, or that subtle dusting of rouge which could bring a glow to her skin. Her appearance, which had always been chic with smart tailored clothes, looked shabby and almost unkempt, and she was devoid of all adornment: those earrings, bracelets, and necklaces which in the past had been 'a must'.

Suddenly, Marianne stubbed out her cigarette and leaped to her feet. "Forgive me, dearest Noor! How could I greet you with such gloom? You poor child – what must you think of me? Why don't you go into the garden while I make lunch? you always loved flowers more than the others.".

It was just a small courtyard garden, and had once been Marianne's pride and joy, but now, the flowerpots looked neglected and overgrown. Long tall weeds overwhelmed the once neat herbaceous beds; the shrubs had become unwieldly and in need of cutting. A swing, the same one Noor remembered, still hung from the horse chestnut tree. More ghosts appeared as little Marcel and Constance grabbed the ropes, pushing each other, leaping on two at a time, twirling the ropes round to spin like tops, their laughter and protests: "My turn now!"

Noor sat on the cracked and faded wooden seat, gently rotating in her memories.

As she swung to and fro, Noor heard a tinkling and rustling behind her. What joy! It was a sound she knew: the sound of the fairies singing, like birdsong, like crystals, like trickling water. Noor's feet hit the ground, bringing her to an abrupt stop. She crept into the undergrowth, the part that was in deep shade, hoping . . . hoping . . . that the fairies would be waiting for her. She parted the weeds, searching from flower to flower till suddenly – there was one, peeping at her through the leaves and petals; and another, and another.

"Hello, Noor! You're back!"

I missed you," cried Noor, overjoyed to see her fairies.

"We've missed you too." But their welcome seemed muted and guarded – just as Marianne's had been.

"Things at the house have changed," Noor said. "Have you noticed?"

"Oh yes. Things have changed," agreed the fairies, their voices rippling like small eddies across a dark surface of water. "The trolls are around, watching and waiting."

"The trolls? What trolls?" asked Noor, knowing only the trolls of myth and legend and fairy tale.

The fairies shivered. "They threaten us. We try to drive them away but they just go underground to wait and plan. We've glimpsed them under stones, beneath the bridges and archways of Paris; in ditches and wastelands; hiding in stagnant waters and dark places; just biding their time; watching, waiting. You have your trolls too: in elegant drawing rooms, in seats of office, smiling at cocktail parties, going to the opera, parading down the boulevards. Watch out for them, Noor. We are afraid; the Bonnard family is afraid. Sometimes Marianne comes into the garden, sits on the swing and weeps."

"I wish she could see you, and that you could cheer her up," murmured Noor.

"We've ruffled her hair, blown gently into her ears, and flicked our wings in her eyes. Sometimes we sing; surely, she would hear us? But she takes us for the wind or birds or fluttering leaves, and now it's too late for cheering her up. Play for us, Noor! Go and play the veena. Open the windows so we can hear you. It will cheer up Marianne too, perhaps."

Noor returned to the drawing room. She opened a window wide and picked up the veena. String by string, she tuned it, then sat down on the carpet and began to play. Somehow, the strains of the plucked strings made the house feel even more empty and desolate. She halted, filled with apprehension.

Marianne appeared, wiping her hands on an apron. "Don't stop, please don't stop! I wondered when I would ever hear it played again properly." So, Noor continued playing, accompanying herself as she sang a soft Indian song. Marianne insisted on eating in the dining room. The long shining oak table was set, her silver cutlery laid out formally with two crisp white napkins, two crystal glasses which stood like gleaming sentinels to the side, and in the middle of the table, flanked by silver candlesticks, stood a bottle of champagne.

"Oh Marianne!" Noor was overwhelmed. "How lovely – and all this for me?"

"For you, for me, for us, our families, our love and friendship; for those who are not here; for those who must come back." Marianne was weeping and smiling at the same time. "Pascal must come back." She lifted a bottle of champagne, eased back the golden wires, then, pressing its head into a white napkin, eased off the cork with a *pop*. Tears coursed down her cheeks as she poured the champagne into each glass, bubbles dancing with rainbows.

"*Santé!*" Marianne exclaimed in a broken voice. "Health to us all; health to our nations and our peoples; health to our loved ones, our husbands, and children, friends and lovers. Go on, drink. Our wishes won't count till we drink!"

Noor drank. Marianne brought in dishes of fish casserole, and potatoes and vegetables, and insisted on serving her guest, sniffing and wiping her cheeks with her sleeve as she did so. At last, she sat down to eat.

Noor thanked her and ate a mouthful. "You must be so lonely, Marianne. I do hope you will go to Roussillon and join your parents and your children. Why are you still here?"

"Someone needs to keep the house going!" Marianne laughed without happiness. "And besides . . ." She stopped abruptly, then continued. "Pascal wants me to stay. He says we must use the house; it must always be open for anyone who needs it." She paused again. "It is a place . . . a refuge . . . It's . . . our refuge."

Noor was sure there was something Marianne had almost told her, but had stopped herself, and swiftly turned the conversation to Noor's family, asking in detail how they were. Noor told Marianne about where she was staying, about Vera and how brave she was, and how difficult it seemed to be Jewish – that she had to lie about it, even at their boarding school.

"Ah yes! Poor child. I fear things are going to get worse. All over Europe, the Jews are suffering."

"Do you think there's going to be a war?" Noor asked, echoing Vera.

"Impossible that we should repeat our mistakes so soon – isn't it?" Marianne shook her head hopelessly. She looked Noor directly in the eye as if she – her distinguished philosopher-father's daughter – might have the answers. "Do you remember that poem your father taught me by Rumi, *One Light?*" And Marianne began to recite it with a voice faltering with emotion:

One Light
What are 'I' and 'You'?
Just lattices
In the niches of a lamp
Through which the One Light radiates.
"I" and "You" are the veil
Between heaven and earth;
Lift this veil and you will see
How all sects and religions are one.
Lift this veil and you will ask –
When "I" and "You" do not exist
What is mosque?
What is synagogue?
What is fire temple?

"We are facing the question again: what is worth fighting for, worth dying for? What do you think your father, the pacifist, would say now, Noor?" Marianne's voice was edgy with irony; bitterness, even. The question hung there, unanswered. She lit another cigarette.

But Noor knew what her father would say, and so did Marianne. Violence was never the answer.

When it was time to go, and Noor stepped out into the late afternoon sun, Marianne said, "I hope when you write to your father and tell him about Pascal, he will remember us kindly. I hope he won't hate us."

"Marianne," Noor murmured, as they embraced, "my father may be saddened when I tell him that Pascal has gone to fight in Spain, but he will always love him and think of him with the utmost kindness."

As she cycled back to Vera's, she was already composing her letter to her father:

If you see your family – even children – beaten up, innocent people killed, towns and villages bombed and razed to the ground, really evil people taking more and more power, is there never a time when it's right to fight back? How does Good stand up to Evil?

CHAPTER 11

The Catalan

She got back to the sound of little Louis singing in the bath as Jeanne scrubbed his back. How sweetly his voice rang through the apartment:

"*Il y a longtemps que je t'aime, Jamais je ne t'oublierai, Il y a longtemps que je t'aime, Jamais je ne t'oublierai . . .*" Never shall I ever forget you.

"Ah! I'm so glad you're back, Noor!" cried Vera from the bathroom. "Remember the meeting Daniel mentioned tonight at the Café Rigaud? We must go!"

"Don't go!" begged Louis. "Stay and read me a story!"

"I've read you a story every night since I came," laughed Vera, flipping water on to his back, as shining as a dolphin's. "Jeanne can read to you tonight."

"I want a story from Noor!"

Noor had been making up stories for Louis, and they had become enthusiastic friends.

"Let Noor go out tonight, darling," said!" said Jeanne. "We'll read *Babar the Elephant*. You love *Babar*, don't you?"

"I love Babar!" exclaimed Louis, splashing the water.

"Noor, have you ever been on an elephant? I have. We went to the zoo and I rode on one. It was marvellous."

"I've ridden on one too," laughed Noor boastfully. "I love elephants. We have two or three of our own at home."

"*What!*" exclaimed Louis. "Elephants! You have real live living elephants?"

"Yes! In India they work in the fields for us. We paint and decorate them on special occasions."

"Tell me more! Please Noor, tell me about your elephants."

"Tomorrow, I promise, I'll tell you all about elephants and tigers, and my pet squirrel – and all about the monkeys who swing around in the trees and jump on our roof," said Noor.

"And we'll go somewhere fantastic," said Vera. "Perhaps take a picnic to the Bois de Bologne." Vera splashed Louis' glistening skin and blew bubbly kisses into his neck, making him shriek with giggles.

"Goodnight, little Louis. Sleep well!"

"*Bonne nuit!* Good night!" Louis trilled as Jeanne took over.

"So? Will you come tonight?" Vera asked Noor again as they left the bathroom.

"Of course!" Noor had never heard a soldier speak before; someone who had fought in battles. What were they like, these people who could kill? Her father called his pacifism '*action*'. But how did you take action if you believed in non-violence? She wanted to feel active rather than sink into a stupor of passive fear, bewilderment and ignorance – ignorance above all. How could she explain to her father why Pascal had gone to fight?

Café Rigaud was alive with gossip and music and people, eating, drinking and smoking – some in cosy candle-lit corners, others at tables of six, arguing and debating, and pouring more and more carafes of wine – so that the pitch of noise rose higher and higher. The proprietor, Georgie, wove in and out of the tables like a dancer, serving drinks and chatting cheerily with his customers. Noor was glad when Daniel arrived with friends Antoine, Simone, Levi, Tibor, and Yvette. He introduced them all and they shook hands, then trooped through to the back of the café, leaving behind a muffled sound of laughter and clinking glasses as they climbed the narrow stairs to a room above.

The atmosphere was sombre and intense, blue with the haze of tobacco. People hunched together patiently in rows of wooden benches: men and women, young and old; some who would have fought in the Great War. Vera, Noor, Daniel and their other friends took up the best part of one row, their eyes fixed on the empty low platform before them.

A man and woman entered and stood side by side at the front facing their audience. The chatter ceased.

"*Bon soir*," the man greeted them. "For those of you who don't know me, I am Paul Barrault. This is my wife, Yvonne. We run the local Communist group round here. We've observed the events round Europe with horror – and especially the Civil War in Spain over the last two years. We've been raising money for the Republican side, and supporting the wounded and their families. Many of our comrades have gone out there to fight alongside other comrades of the Left from all over Europe and even America. Tonight, I want you to meet Antoni Cardona. He is from Catalonia. He will remind you what is at stake here and why the whole world is looking." He thrust a clenched fist up into the air and cried, "*Vive Communisme! Vive la Révolution! Vive la France!*"

There was wild applause. Antoni Cardona came on to stage. The crowd fell silent. He looked exhausted and despairing, shrunken, pared down to his frame, yet his eyes burned with fierce pride

"I am a Spaniard; I am a Catalan, I am a Republican, I am a Communist, I am a worker, I am a peasant," he began. "Above all, I am a human being. I believe in the value of all of us, not just the rich. I believe in Spain, in Catalonia. I believe in freedom. We wanted to show the world what we could do. But the world laughed. 'What can filthy, ignorant, illiterate peasants do?' They couldn't even arm us properly. When they did, it was with weapons that were broken or so outdated they were more dangerous to the friend than the enemy. All the while, Germany was arming Franco, giving him aeroplanes, guns and bombs. Comrades, we are being annihilated. Only Russia comes to our aid."

The audience broke out into angry comments, arguing among themselves.

"Do you think we're just fighting for ourselves?" Antoni Cardona cried. "No, we're fighting for all of you – especially for the poorest, the smallest, weakest, the least educated, the sickest. We want to do away with hierarchy. The prince and pauper must be equal; the colonel and foot soldier too, and the priest and bishop. Why should kings and generals tell us what to do?"

"Russia is dictating to the communists!" someone cried. "Do you really believe Russia is interested in the Spanish people?"

"Huh!" yelled another. "Taking over the whole world is all they're interested in. Communists are no better than fascists. I am an anarchist. That is the only way."

Some jeered and some cheered.

Antoni Cardona's face seemed to shrink into a death skull. "I warn you, my friends, this war is no longer about Spain or Catalonia. It is about you. Believe me, if Spain falls and becomes fascist, you will know about it – every single one of you."

"Rubbish!" called a voice. "France is strong. They can't get into France."

The Catalan wagged his finger. "The boche have already gone into Austria. This is your war too; it is the world's war. Believe me! Don't look to the British to help. They sit on their colonial verandas drinking tea while the world goes to the dogs. France needs another glorious revolution. And you can have it with Russia on your side."

The room exploded: anarchist against communist, communists against the left alliance, both against conservative clerics and the church. Suddenly the Catalan looked spent. Perhaps he had said all he wanted to say. He staggered a little, and Yvonne Barrault was immediately at his side.

"Enough," she said. "I think we need a drink."

Noor got up and lifted her coat from the chair. It was only then that she noticed Marianne standing at the back. She must have come in late; too late for a seat. If she had seen Noor, she didn't show it.

"Marianne's here," Noor whispered to Vera. "I want you to meet her."

But before Noor could even make eye contact or call out, Marianne turned and left. Noor elbowed through the crowd, but by the time she reached the top of the stairs, there was no sign of her.

Daniel found a table outside. He was still at fever pitch. "What a man!" he exclaimed. It was a warm night, which enabled them to sit easily with legs outstretched. They all pitched in as Georgie came and took their orders: carafes of house wine, coffee or grog, whatever students could afford. Cigarettes were lit, glasses filled as they argued volubly for this position or that; was it better to be communist or anarchist or socialist, religious or atheist; each friend taking up sides, their voices rising.

Noor noticed a figure shuffling down the boulevard: a slight youth of about seventeen years old, with a shabby coat swinging free over worn trousers, and boots.

"Oh Lord!" sighed Yvette. "It's Herschel Grynszpan on the scrounge again."

"*Salut, salut!*" the boy mumbled, pulling up a chair at their table.

"What'll you drink, Herschel?" asked Daniel, waving for the waiter.

"How kind, kind!" mumbled the young man. "Red house wine would be great!" He spoke French with an accent like Vera's.

"And a basket of bread too, please," Daniel added,

"You shouldn't encourage him Daniel," hissed Simone. "He's always on the take."

Noor watched the young man with curiosity. His face was a pallid white, framed by lank black hair hanging over his ears, glowering black eyebrows which almost met across his brow, and full lips which he kept chewing nervously.

"What news, Herschel?" asked Levi. "Got a job yet?"

"I'm trying, I'm trying," muttered the youth, not looking him in the eye.

"He's an illegal," Antoine whispered to Noor. "They would deport him if they found him trying to get a job."

Georgie brought a further carafe of wine and a basket of bread. They watched – some with sympathy, some with scorn – as Herschel gulped his wine and tore chunks from the bread rolls.

"As Jews, we should side with the communists," declared Levi, continuing the conversation. "They are the only ones who are truly secular and egalitarian."

"But what makes you think they'll be fair to the Jews? Is Stalin to be trusted? There are rumours he's already cosying up to Hitler," argued Antoine.

"Filthy boche," muttered Herschel vehemently. "Do you know how they treat us in Germany just because we're Jewish? Even though my parents have lived there for over twenty years, and I was born in Germany, that doesn't matter any more; oh no! I've heard they've been stuffing Jews into trucks and taking them away to some holding camp. That's why I came here." Herschel sniffed. His tears flowed, and he wiped his streaming nose across his sleeve.

"It's all he ever talks about," grunted Daniel. Noor looked on with a mixture of abhorrence and pity, as Herschel wept and snuffled into his wine, gobbling the bread like a starving man.

Vera's mind was full of imagining how her family had also suffered like this. She felt herself shaking. She glanced at the faces of Daniel and his friends. They didn't like Herschel. It was as if he reminded them too much of their own fears.

"Have you been listening to that Catalan? Huh!" sneered Herschel. "They're just throwing their lives away in Spain. Franco and the Nationalists are far stronger. The boche have given them planes and bombs and guns, and the Republicans barely have pitchforks."

"You talk the talk of failure, Herschel." Daniel's words were quiet but sharp and intense. "I've made a decision; I'm going to Spain. For every man and woman who dies or falls wounded and can't fight any more, there must be another to take his place. I will go."

"Daniel?" Simone leaned forward fearfully to touch his hand. But Daniel reached for his wine, and Simone moved her fingers away.

"You criticise the rest of us, but what is your contribution, eh, Herschel?" challenged Daniel.

"Yeah!" agreed Yvette. "You should go too, instead of slinking down the boulevards like a stray cat looking for a handout."

"Fat lot of good that will do. Just another pointless sacrifice," Herschel said. "I'll fight, all right. Just you see. But I won't waste my energies fighting a losing battle in a Spanish war. When I fight, I'll fight the boche – not shadows."

"It isn't just a Spanish war. It's a war for the freedom of Europe and for justice," Yvette responded earnestly.

"It's all right for you, Yvette. You're not Jewish," retorted Herschel. "Do you think any of them care about us? They will all be united against Jews! They'll just leave us to sink or swim. Sink more likely. We Jews are going to have to fight our own battles."

"That's why I'm going to Spain," said Daniel. "Action is needed!"

"Don't leave us, Daniel," said Levi quietly. Levi was Daniel's best friend; they were like brothers. But Levi had been born with a disability which meant he walked with a limp and could never be accepted into any army. "We can't afford to lose you."

"I can't just go to University studying law, when we may be overrun by the boche!" said Daniel angrily.

"I'll go with you," yelled Tibor.

"Me too," exclaimed Vera. "Why not! What's to stop me?"

"Vera, this is not a battle you can take part in," said Daniel intensely. "You will fight, but yours must be a different battle. Not because you're a woman – many women have gone to Spain and given their lives. But you will do more good by staying back. Return to England. Bide your time; see what happens. Don't come back to Paris till you know what you're coming back to." He gripped her arms across the table. "Do you understand?" He turned to Noor. "Make sure Vera returns to England. She will know what to do when the time comes."

"When what time comes, Daniel?" Noor asked quietly.

"Vera knows what I'm talking about. It's already happening in Germany and Poland. It's what happened to her uncle in Berlin; it's what may have happened to her mother, father, and brother and uncle."

"And mine," said Herschel.

"And so many thousands of others," continued Daniel. "She knows the truth of what I'm saying, don't you Veroshka? Your duty is to survive."

Noor realised that Simone was staring hard at Vera.

Daniel accompanied Vera and Noor home. He walked between them, his arm linked through each of theirs. At the door, he suddenly turned to Vera and hugged her as if he would never let her go, then briefly kissed her lips.

"One day, this will all be over," he said. "Believe it."

As Vera looked up into Daniel's face, with the rain dripping from the rim of her hat, Noor saw, if briefly, that all those lines on her face had disappeared. Vera looked her age: sixteen, almost a woman, and suddenly beautiful.

Daniel released her and turned to Noor. He kissed her on each cheek. "Look after Vera. Promise me?"

Noor nodded. "I promise." And she meant it.

Then he departed into the rain, his head and beret tucked down under his collar. Vera lingered, watching his receding figure, and Noor watched Vera, and saw the light die in her face.

Back in the apartment, Jeanne's boyfriend had gone. Aunt Minnie and Uncle Victor were not yet back, and Jeanne was asleep in Louis's room, lying spread-eagled on the spare bed, snoring gently. Vera closed the bedroom door and went into the living room. She sat at the piano and played softly, as if only music could make sense of what they had heard that evening. While she played, Noor wrote her father the letter she had been composing in her head ever since she left Marianne that afternoon.

Two days later, Daniel left for Spain. Then they heard that Simone had gone too.

CHAPTER 12

Waiting For News

"She's in love with him," said Vera, as if to herself.

"Who?" asked Noor.

Vera hesitated.

Noor filled in for her gently. "Simone?"

Vera looked unsettled. "I've always known Simone likes him. But when she went to Spain with him, I knew for sure – she more than *likes* him, she loves him."

"But that doesn't mean it's reciprocated," replied Noor.

"But he didn't try to stop her as he did me," Vera said, her voice suddenly a plaintive wail.

"That's because he cares deeply about you. It's obvious." Noor held Vera's arm. "He doesn't want you to sacrifice yourself unnecessarily. He wants you to be here, helping at the synagogue, staying alive so that you can help him when he gets back. Daniel has this sense of the future; of what can happen. He's seeing beyond Spain. Simone made her own decision to follow him."

The summer went by, filled with cycling trips with Vera's friends from the synagogue, spending all day in the countryside, eating bread and cheese, and discussing the state of the world. When Daniel or Simone's names came up, Vera went quiet. Noor was relieved that they weren't the only ones who hadn't received news. No one had.

There were times when Noor could get Vera laughing; even being girlish and giggly, especially when they played hide and seek with Louis round the apartment.

"Louis! Come out, you rascal. You've won. We can't find you. So please come out!" cried Vera one time, after they had hunted and hunted for Louis until they were alarmed.

He appeared, grinning all over his face.

"Where did you hide?" asked Vera, scooping him up for a hug.

"Ah!" cried Louis. "It's my secret hiding place." And nothing would make him tell.

Two weeks to go before the end of the holidays, and there was still no news from Spain. Vera and Noor were cycling near the 4th arrondissement.

"We're not far from Daniel's home," murmured Vera.

"Let's go then!" said Noor. "Why didn't you say?"

"I don't know," said Vera doubtfully. "His parents hate Daniel's activities, and they disapprove of me and his friends. They think people should keep their heads down. 'Don't rock the boat.' Just like my aunt and uncle."

"Let's try," Noor said persuasively. "What's the worst they can do? Eat you?"

They pedalled across the Seine into a maze of narrow streets and alleyways, where scraggy, bare-footed children played ball and swung each other around.

Daniel's father owned a small bookshop off the Rue des Rosiers. Through stripes of dust-speckled light pouring through the shutters, Noor saw it was packed from ceiling to floor and wall to wall with books. Somewhere in the darker rear of the shop, a man hovered over some ledgers. He looked up and, for a moment, his face was caught in a dingy yellow light bulb from an angled lamp. Noor was startled. She thought it was Daniel, with the same steel-rimmed glasses, the same gaunt intense face and the tight curly hair; except the curls were streaked with grey, and his face was lined with signs of worry.

He saw Vera, and looked embarrassed, but greeted her with civility. "*Bonjour, mademoiselle.*"

"*Bonjour* Monsieur Alkan," replied Vera. She introduced Noor. "This is my friend from England. She's met Daniel."

Daniel's father shook Noor's hand, and lowered his eyes, sighing deeply.

"Have you heard from him, *monsieur*?" Vera blurted out. "I'm so worried."

"*You're* worried?" Monsieur Alkan exclaimed with heavy sarcasm in his voice. "You young people, with your high and mighty ideals! You think life and death aren't anything to do with you. You think you are immortal and go off to war as if you wear a cloak of invisibility, with winged sandals and the shield of Hermes; you think you are gods. Nothing matters but your cause. Not your parents or siblings or anybody. I won't say friends – because you're all in it together." His voice broke.

"I'm sorry, *monsieur*," said Vera, "but you are wrong. If people like Daniel do nothing, *then* you have something to fear. Of all of us, he has understood the full picture. He knows what the future can be if people like us don't take action. I know we live in dangerous times. I have already lost my parents and baby brother, trying to escape violence in Poland."

Daniel's father jerked with surprise. There was a long pause. Then he said quietly, "I regret that deeply, *mademoiselle*. He didn't tell me."

"Have you heard anything recently?" Vera's voice shook. "He's been gone for weeks."

"If you hadn't come to me, I would have eventually swallowed my pride and come looking for you," murmured Monsieur Alkan. "No, he hasn't written. We too are desperate for news." He indicated his wife, a lingering shadow in the corner.

"*Bonjour, madame*," Vera and Noor both murmured respectfully.

"Will you have some coffee or a lemonade?" she asked with formal kindness.

"No, no, thank you," said Vera. "We really don't want to disturb you. We just came in case you had news. I promise, if we hear anything, we will tell you immediately – and you also . . . will you . . .?"

"Leave us your address, *mademoiselle*," Monsieur Alkan said. "If I hear any news, you will be the first to know."

He pushed over a piece of paper and pencil and Vera wrote her address.

"How useless all this will be," Monsieur Alkan suddenly burst out, "if the English and French governments make a peace deal with the boche – and our Daniel gets himself killed in Spain."

His wife put an arm round him. Vera and Noor quietly left.

By the time the holiday ended, Vera hadn't heard from Daniel, and Noor had not received a reply from her father.

CHAPTER 13

Aufwiedersehen Deutschland

The holidays ended. I can't say I was sorry to leave Munich and the platoons of parading Nazi soldiers, tramping down the street behind banners with the Swastika insignia. How the people of Munich loved it; how quickly crowds formed to cheer marching soldiers, their faces glowing with fervour, women tossing bunches of flowers and lifting their children to see. Almost daily, there was a parade, or demonstration of strength: the cavalry, the motorbike platoons, jeeps and armoured vehicles, and the roar of fighter planes overhead. But it was the *left right left right* of a hundred jackbooted feet, like an ominous drumbeat hammering on cobbled streets, that entered the blood-stream of a warlike heart. Sometimes, it seemed as though the whole city was an army of marching soldiers. And when they chanted – *Sieg Heil, Sieg Heil* – on and on and on . . . it became a continuous roaring. If someone noticed you weren't shouting too, or raising your arm in the Nazi salute, they stared at you, frowning, then threatening, so that you either did it too, or slipped away.

In cafés and restaurants – where one might have expected to find calm, and more of a daily rhythm of eating and drinking and chatting and laughing – even there, someone would break out into a patriotic song, and everyone would join in with knee-slapping and beer glasses clinking, toasting *Heil Hitler*!

It was almost as though in every public place someone had been planted to start up a cheer group for Herr Hitler, linking arms and swaying to and fro, loudly singing national songs like the Horst-Wessel-Lied:

> *Clear the streets for the brown battalions,*
> *Clear the streets for the storm division!*
> *Millions are looking upon the swastika full of hope,*
> *The day of freedom and of bread dawns.*

We went for supper to a lakeside restaurant where the von Garstadts and Dodo's parents joined us. We had just ordered when there was a sudden outburst of national fervour. A group of young people began singing loudly, clinking their wine glasses and slopping their beer tankards. "*Toast auf Herr Hitler*!" Other tables cheered too, raising their glasses.

An elderly German couple in a far corner refused steadfastly to join in. A young man noticed and called, "Hey you! Grandpa! Why aren't you joining in? Aren't you true patriots of the Fatherland? Do you not honour our Chancellor, Herr Hitler, as your true leader? Join in join in, like good German citizens!"

The couple, stony-faced, carried on eating with lowered eyes.

"Excuse me?" persisted the young man, getting to his feet. "Have you no answer? Are you true patriots of Germany and the Third Reich?"

The old man looked up with patient eyes. "Do I know you, sir?"

The whole restaurant had gone quiet now, all eyes on the blazing young man, as the elderly couple steadfastly tried to continue their meal.

The young man strode over and slammed his fist on the table, making their wine slop and the cutlery rattle. "All you need to know of me is that I am a patriot," he sneered. "All of us here are patriots, are we not?"

"Yes!" cheered the majority.

"Daddy!" Dodo gripped her father's arm. "What a bully that man is. What's he going to do?"

"I don't know, darling. We're English visitors in Germany. It's not for us to say anything," he replied uncomfortably.

I caught Frau von Garstadt's eye. She twisted her napkin looking embarrassed. Good.

"Do we want such spineless people here in our midst? Hey – Herr Grigo!" The bully called for the proprietor. A tall pleading man appeared from a back room, his pale hands outstretched, silently beseeching them not to create a disturbance in his restaurant.

"Do we want such people in your restaurant, who are

not prepared to openly support and praise our Third Reich and our Führer?" demanded the young man. "What are they? Communists? Perhaps Jews – are you Jews?" He leaned over the couple menacingly.

"No, no!" whispered Herr Grigo urgently. "He is a distinguished writer, sir – an academic – and his wife. They are loyal Germans, I assure you."

The young man scoffed. "Ah! *Loyal* Germans! Well, why didn't you say so?"

At this, the old man laid down his cutlery, and wiped his mouth with his napkin. His wife did the same. He waved to a waiter for their bill and coats and then, with the restaurant in total silence, he linked his wife's arm in his, and walked slowly and steadily towards the exit.

Herr Grigo leaped ahead to open the door for them, and bowed respectfully as they left, with soft words that no one else , He then returned to his office at the back of the restaurant, leaving the young man still standing. The young man, who at first had looked so puffed up and sure of himself, realised all the eyes were on him.

"It is our duty to demonstrate loyalty at all times. *Heil Hitler*!" he blustered, thrusting out his right arm. No one else joined him in the salute, and he returned to his table.

The holidays ended, and it was time for us to leave. It was with relief that we piled ourselves on to the night train at Munich and headed through the flickering darkness towards home. Dodo was quiet: no jokes, no chatter. We lay silently on our bunks listening to the intermittent shriek of the train whistle, smelling the steam and soot from the engine streaking past our window. I awoke at some point in the night with a sense of dread at the sound of clumping feet and, still half dreaming, thought they were the Nazi boots of a soldier coming to arrest us.

Voices outside were blaring in my sleep – *"Sieg Heil! Sieg Heil!"* – but as I properly awoke, it was "Karlsruhe! Karlsruhe!": the name of the station.

There was a sharp rap on our door. We both sat bolt upright. "Passports!" demanded a voice.

"We're at the French border," murmured Dodo.

A light came on and, bleary eyed and embarrassingly dishevelled, we fumbled in our bags and produced our documents.

The customs boarder guard stamped each page to prove we were leaving Germany and, with a polite *"Danke schön"*, slid shut our compartment door.

As the wheels churned and the train finally ground its way into France, Dodo muttered, *"Auf wiedersehen, Deutschland."*

CHAPTER 14

Changes

Had we been blind when we left England? Had there been preparations for war going on which I simply hadn't seen? Back on English soil as our train pounded through Kent heading for London, it seemed everywhere was preparing for war: piles of sandbags in doorways, trenches dug in gardens, Red Cross lorries on the streets, and groups of servicemen in the uniforms of the army, navy and air force. Suddenly, I thought of my brother, Eric, and felt a wave of terror sweep over me.

Victoria Station was seething with servicemen carrying duffle bags and rifles. We struggled through the mêlée, and there was Dodo's nanny, Griggy, at the barrier, waving and smiling. Dodo made a rush for her. I saw Aunty Madge, and –

"Eric!" I screamed with joy to see my brother. He wasn't in uniform, and for a moment I forgot that if war broke out, he would go off to fight. I rushed into his arms. Then we were hugging each other, drawing Dodo and Griggy into our embrace.

Aunt Madge said she had booked us all into a little hotel round the corner so we could have some proper time together before returning to school the next day. She had missed us, and worried about us – and wished we hadn't gone to Germany. But now we were back. Safe? Well – for the moment. But Aunty Madge said there was so much turmoil and uncertainty, and she had been getting more and more worried with so much talk of war. She held me at arm's length. Yes – I had caught the Alpine sun and looked as though I'd had a holiday. She chatted sweetly to Dodo, asking after her parents and thanking her for taking me to Munich.

Dumping our stuff at the hotel, we caught a taxi and all of us went off to Claridges for tea. "After all," exclaimed Aunt Madge, clasping Eric's arm, "who knows when we'll next be able to do this? We must live for the moment."

It had been a sweet ending to our holiday, trailing up Regent Street looking at the shops, and Dodo gasping at the theatre billboards advertising John Gielgud; perhaps she preferred him to Laurence Olivier. She was thrilled when Eric suggested we pick up a theatre matinée – he thought there was a Noël Coward playing somewhere.

Before we parted, the next morning, I clung to Eric, questioning him fiercely. I told him what we'd seen in Munich, and how the whole city was like a war machine: how the German young men were all ready to march off and fight for the Führer. They hadn't looked as if they would pop off to see a theatre matinée. I laughed, and then asked bleakly, "Are you going back to your barracks?"

"Yes, back to the mountains of Norfolk!" Eric joked, and saluted mockingly. "Just remember, Gwen," he said with sudden seriousness, "war is war, and if it breaks out, I'll do my duty. But war or no war, I love flying. It's what I want to be doing. Do you understand?"

His eyes were shining. I did understand, though I burst into tears.

The next morning, Dodo and I were put on the train for Barrowfield, with Aunt Madge, Eric, and Griggy chorusing goodbye. "See you at half term!" they cried.

"Give my love to Archie, and Uncle Harold, and –" My words were swallowed up by the shriek of the train whistle; great clouds of steam enveloped them as the train ground slowly out of the station. I stood for a long time, leaning out from the open window until my tears had dried.

As the train plunged into the Sussex countryside, the fields were golden, as they were every late summer, with sunlight streaming through the trees. No sign of war. The familiar buzzard circled: tipping and soaring, describing predatory circles in the blue air.

Our taxi had barely turned into the drive leading to Barrowfield when any illusion we might have had about war being somewhere else was shattered. Teams of men milled about the grounds with shovels and tarpaulin. Long lines of trenches zigzagged across the usually immaculately mown lawns.

"What's going on?" we exclaimed with alarm.

"Preparing air raid shelters, miss," said our driver. "Got to be ready in case, eh?"

"It's not going to happen," declared Dodo. "Chamberlain will make a deal with Hitler."

"Let's hope you're right. Don't want another blinking war like last time."

The school building came into sight. We gasped at the sight of vast piles of sandbags all up the main steps, almost blockading the front door, and more surrounding the entire ground floor.

Our housemistress, Miss Conway looked harassed as we climbed out of the taxi. "We're preparing for war, girls," she said, "though it probably won't happen. They're just going to the brink. Now get your stuff to your dormitories, and wait for instructions."

We peeped into the gym. It was lined with mattresses on the floor, each holding two sheets, one pillow and two blankets. People I hadn't seen before stood around, chatting.

"We've been asked to take children evacuated from London," Miss Conway said as she passed us in the hall. "Including at least thirty unaccompanied refugees from all over Europe. The volunteers are here to help them settle in. The children will be with us until they can be placed in families elsewhere."

All through the late afternoon there was a procession of cars and coaches winding their way down the drive. Most were bringing back Barrowfield girls, but one of the coaches held a gaggle of refugee children: a mixture of girls and boys, from goodness knows where, of all ages and backgrounds. Some were neatly dressed and cared for; others grubby, bedraggled, in hand-me-downs that didn't fit. All had placards round their necks labelled with their name, age, and nationality. Their faces were blank with shock. Big ones looked after little ones; siblings and friends clutched each other's hands as if they would never allow themselves to be parted. They carried battered suitcases, and cloth bundles with their belongings rolled up and tied into bows like bundles of laundry. They were taken into the gym, where volunteers marched up and down allocating mattresses with high-pitched voices, on to which the children piled their stuff, then sat staring bleakly at nothing in particular.

Noor and Vera were almost the last to arrive. When their taxi drove up, piled high with their suitcases, we raced out to meet them. How we hugged each other – we group of friends. We helped them up to the dorm with their baggage, and flung ourselves down on our beds as they unpacked, talking ten to the dozen. What was Paris like? What was Munich was like? Did Lucien turn up? How about Charles? Did you meet any other boys?

But we had all changed. After the first excitement of seeing each other, we giggled a little less, and paused longer before expressing a thought. We could see it in each other's eyes; hear it in our sombre voices: things would never be the same again. We were on the brink of womanhood – and war would accelerate it.

We were summoned to the gym to lend a hand.

"Vera Bell! Could you come here please?" called Miss Sargeant. "You speak Polish. Help me out and translate for me."

Vera knelt down next to a small, miserable child who clutched the large hanky pinned to her front and dabbed her dribbling nose. After a few words from Vera, a small smile crept across her face, and she wound her arms round Vera's neck in desperate need of a hug.

"Not many *English* girls can do that," remarked Pamela tartly.

As Vera hugged the child, it sounded like she was asking questions. Had the girl met anyone from Poland with the name Bielawski? Ruth and Eli Bielawski? They had a baby with them called Ethan? But she was met with a bewildered face.

At the back of the hall were trestle tables covered in dozens of half-opened cardboard boxes with tubes dangling from them. Gas masks for everyone. How they stank, these gasmasks; a horrible rubbery cloying smell which made us retch. I really thought I'd suffocate. There were all sorts of warnings about when and how to use them – and terrifying stories of people who'd died when they tested their gas masks by putting their heads into the gas oven.

Every day, we had gas mask practice. The horrible things had to be carried at all times in case the alarm went off. The alarm was a beastly wooden rattle with cogs and ratchets, which was whirled around fiercely, making an ear-splitting clackety-clacking sound. But the sound that sent terrifying shudders through everyone was the air-raid siren: a heart-stopping wail which made some girls burst into tears.

"When you hear this," shouted a teacher through a megaphone, "drop whatever you are doing and grab your gas masks. There are blankets and pillows on every landing. Take one each and go immediately to the front lawn."

The disruption seemed unbearable at first, and it was hard to settle back to work. "We'll never get our Certificates," I moaned. But we adapted, and soon were working away, doing our homework, our revision, our classes, and carrying on as though war was just another part of our school routine.

The evacuees were eventually collected in buses and cars and taken to homes all over the country. There were pitiful cries as friends and sometimes siblings were parted from each other. I couldn't bear hearing it, and rushed off to have a weep. But the school was ours once more, and we tried to recover some normality – still wondering if war really would break out.

I received more letters than usual from India. My parents were worried. They seemed unsure whether to bring us back to India, but after reassurances from Uncle Harold and Aunty Madge, they felt we should stay put and, if necessary, go to the farm.

Dodo's parents were full of optimism. *Chamberlain will see sense and make a deal with Hitler. The Führer is a good friend of the British. Prefers them to the French! Of course, he doesn't want war.*

As usual, there were always plenty of letters for Noor: from her mother, sister, brothers, aunts, uncles, grannies – the whole of India seemed to write to Noor. But today, even though she clutched a bundle to herself, she looked as sad as if no one had written to her at all.

There was one letter from a friend in Paris called Marianne, which Noor read out.

"There was a crisis with Pascal. I had to rush to the French border. Pascal was wounded, and I was terrified he would have difficulty getting out of Spain.

"They're so brave, my friends, Marianne and Pascal," Noor murmured. "And Vera's friends too, Daniel and Simone. They believe in something, and they are fighting for it. What do I believe in? What would I be prepared to die for?"

I shrugged. "Has your father written yet?"

"Not once all summer," Noor said quietly. "I know something's wrong."

Never had I seen her so disturbed, her usual poise and serenity so unsettled. "What does your mother say?" I asked.

"She says my father is very preoccupied; he doesn't seem himself. I mustn't worry. But Gwen! I wrote three letters from Paris, asking the same question. He must know how important it was to me. I need an answer."

She didn't tell me what her question was, and suddenly I felt unable to ask her.

The sufi said: You who wrote a hundred letters and did not receive a reply; this too is an answer.

At last, one morning Noor got a letter. It was among three others. She snatched them up, then paused, looking almost terrified.

We were interrupted by Dodo rushing up, clutching a letter. "Gwenny!" she cried. "Guess what?"

Noor stuffed her unopened letters into her satchel.

"Noor?" I said.

But she headed off, calling, "See you later!"

"Gone to talk to her fairies?" teased Dodo. "Gwen, Laurence Olivier's playing Iago in Othello at the Old Vic! I'm damn well going. You will cover for me, won't you? Oh! It's the best news! You've got to help me. I'll die if I don't go."

"When?" I asked anxiously.

"The eleventh of November. That's only a couple of weeks away. Charles has bought the tickets already."

"That's very irresponsible of him!" I exclaimed. "He could get you expelled!"

"Darling, I've been doing this for ages – you know I have," said Dodo. "Charles or no Charles, I would still have gone. Griggy's niece would have got the ticket for me. Now just be a sport and leave the garden door open for me so I can get back in afterwards, won't you?"

I hated it when Dodo took risks like this, sneaking out of school to go to London. I couldn't bear to think of her getting caught.

"Gwen?" She peered at me fiercely.

"I'll see to the garden door," I sighed. "Noor was just telling me something. I must find her. See you later!"

"Enjoy the fairies!" chortled Dodo.

I found Noor in the garden, sitting on the bank staring blankly into the stream. "Have you heard from your father at last?" I asked, flopping down next to her.

She nodded.

"Was it a good letter?" I asked gently, seeing her sad face.

"He hasn't answered my question! I mean, he has, but it doesn't help." She spoke with an extraordinary vehemence, which I had never heard before.

"What was your question?"

Noor fished out her notebook from her satchel, where she had drafted the letter to her father.

Darling Papa,

You have brought us up to believe in non-violence. Under no circumstances should we take up arms against an enemy. But that's all very well when they are words in a book about philosophy, or when you sit at the feet of a guru in some mountain cave removed from the world.

But if you see mothers and fathers being beaten up, old men shot and innocent people killed, what should you do? If towns and villages are being bombed and razed to the ground, and really evil people are taking more and more power, is there never a time when it's right to fight back?

How does Good stand up to Evil? I need to know.

"That's what I asked him," she cried furiously. "And look at his useless reply!"

She handed me her father's letter.

My darling Daughter,
Please remember: existence is suffering, and suffering finds its origin in desire, which can never be satisfied. Do not hurt another in a way that would hurt you. Have only one passion: the happiness of others. All those who are unhappy are so because they have been looking for their own happiness. All those who are happy are so because they looked for other people's happiness.

Nothing is more courageous than non-violence. This is true action. This is your weapon to overcome evil.

Your ever-loving father

"It's beautiful," I said thoughtfully.

"Yes – that's the trouble with words. They can make the most terrible things sound beautiful," said Noor bitterly. "But if you see a baby being kicked by a thug? Can you find beautiful words to describe that?" She shook her head in bewilderment. "Is it right to stand and do nothing? Why doesn't he answer me? My own father has toured America, Russia, Europe, saying beautiful things about how the answer to evil is non-violence. People revere him, worship him; yet my own father can't tell me how I should react. What would he have done if he had had to watch me, and my mother and my brothers and sister get beaten up, or go before a firing squad? Would he have just stood by?"

I linked a comforting arm into Noor's. She venerated her father like a god; always believed he had the answer to everything. But just when she most needed him, his answer didn't help.

"You know what, Noor," I said, "there are moments when you're on your own. *We* are on our own. We have to make our own minds up, and come to our own decisions. We can have the wisest teachers or parents, but in the end, we have to be the judge of our own actions."

She stared at me, tears suddenly rolling down her cheeks. I had never seen Noor cry.

CHAPTER 15
Kristallnacht:
The Night of Broken Glass

9-10 NOVEMBER 1938

The night before Dodo played truant to go and see her beloved Laurence Olivier in London, she put her hair in rollers. We all watched with amusement.

"It's hell sleeping in these," she moaned, "but one has to suffer for art and beauty."

We all giggled, familiar with the prickly rollers that some of us endured through a night to look like a Hollywood film star the next day. Of course, we had all been pledged to absolute secrecy, but we were used to Dodo sneaking out of school, and we were all in the conspiracy to cover for her.

We usually played hockey on a Friday afternoon. It wasn't hard for Dodo to plead being unwell. Her plan was to catch the 4.15 train, see the play, and catch the 10.30 back. It would be midnight before she returned, and my job was to make sure the garden gate was open, and the boiler-room door unlocked.

"How do I look?" asked Dodo. She backed away from the mirror, before which she had spent several silent minutes intently making up her face. I had popped up to see her before going to hockey, and to reassure her that I had left my bicycle for her in the hedge by the garden door. It was a half-hour cycle ride to the station.

"You look amazing," I sighed.

Dodo's theatrical instincts had enabled her expertly to outline her eyebrows and eyes, with a touch of mascara on her lashes, a brush of face powder, a hint of blusher, and exactly the right shade of lipstick. From her secret cache, she had produced silk stockings, suspender belt, silk petticoat, cherry red silk blouse, a grey twinset, and a loop of pearls. She would add layers of school uniform over the top – skirt, school shoes, coat, and hat – so that she could cycle inconspicuously out of school; then, within the shelter of a nearby copse, she would remove all her school clothes, tuck them in a suitcase and hide them in the bushes. Slipping on patent leather court shoes, and a pretty net and feather fascinator over her shining curls, who would know she wasn't twenty-one?

I watched her with admiration and a little bit of envy. "Send my best to Charles," I said.

"I'll try to remember," she said coyly.

I wagged my finger at her. "And if you can't be good, be careful!"

"Yes, aunty!" she mocked.

I was restless that night. I didn't usually wait up for

116

her: the garden door was open, and I'd unbolted the boiler room last thing before bed. I had dozed off, but woken to hear it raining outside. Checking my watch, I saw it was after midnight, but Dodo's bed was still empty.

"Oh Lord," I muttered to myself. "Where is she? She'll be drenched."

Pulling on my dressing gown, I crept downstairs, down, down, through the boiler room and out. It was raining steadily. I tucked my head into my dressing gown and squelched across the garden. The door wasn't open. Double drat! Someone must have come after me and locked it.

I drew back the bolt, hissing, "Dodo! Are you there?"

"Is that you, Gwenny Penny?" I heard a desperate voice breaking with relief. "I always knew you were an angel personified. Open the bloody door!"

"Language!" I scolded as I pulled the bolt across, letting in a bedraggled girl clutching a suitcase, looking for all the world like one of those refugees.

"Gwen!" Dodo flung her arms round my neck, and I smelled alcohol. She giggled and hiccoughed. "I missed my train. Charles had to drive me all the way back!"

"You're a bad girl, Dorothy Bridges-Smith," I chided.

"You're just jealous!" she retorted and then hiccoughed again. "Whoops! Sorry. Charles had a bottle of fizz in the car so I'm a little tiddly!"

"But he didn't stop long enough to make sure you got back into school, the irresponsible clot!" I cried. "What if I hadn't come down to check?"

"Well, you did, darling! So, don't go all aunty on me."

And with Dodo clinging to my arm, we staggered back across the garden, through the boiler room and up to the dorm. She giggled and clattered and hiccoughed all the way, and I was terrified we'd be caught.

Of course, she woke everyone up in our dorm.

"How was Larry?" drawled Pamela.

"Divine! Not sure who I prefer – him or Charles. But Charles can't quite say *"Oh beware my Lord of jealousy.*

"It is the Green-eyed monster which doth mock

"The meat it feeds on."

Giggling, Dodo knocked over a box which clattered to the floor, sprinkling pencils and pens everywhere. "Oh dear! Sorry! I'm bringing the Night of Broken Glass into the dorm," she exclaimed.

"What?" we asked.

"You should have seen the headlines," babbled Dodo. "The newspaper boys in London were all yelling about the Night of Broken Glass. Some idiot in Paris went and shot the German attaché a few days ago, thinking he was the ambassador. When it became known the assassin was Jewish, they went bonkers all over Germany, smashing up the place. It's in all the papers. Charles says that's done it. It'll be like the assassination of Franz Ferdinand and could lead to war."

"Why? Who did it?" asked Noor.

"Some Polish chap – a Jewish student! Even though they caught him, the Nazis and anti-Semites still went round beating up any Jew they could lay their hands on. Even killing them, would you believe it? They've been trashing all the Jewish shops, burning synagogues and throwing bricks through shop windows – the sound of breaking glass was everywhere," tittered Dodo stupidly. "Oh God!" Suddenly her voice broke. "Sorry. It's awful and I'm giggling because I'm drunk. Sorry, Vera. Must be horrible for you. I mean, the Jewish thing."

"Did they name the assassin?" asked Vera, now tense and bolt upright in bed.

"Hursh, Hersch, Herschle . . ." giggled Dodo with a sob. "Hershy Marzipan – something like that. They caught him red-handed." She scrummaged in her suitcase and brought out a soggy newspaper.

"Not Herschel Grynszpan?" said Noor sharply. "Vera! Could it be that boy we met in Paris?"

"That's his name: Herschel . . . Look there's a photo of him." Dodo held out the newspaper under the torchlight. "Apparently his parents and sister in Germany had been thrown into trucks and taken away, and he wanted revenge."

Vera stared at the pale haunted face of a young man with flattened black hair and desperate dark eyes staring out at us. "That's him," she exclaimed. "We met him. Noor and I, we met him."

"You *met* him?" I said.

Now everyone was awake. We read the newspaper account again. It said he had been arrested on the spot and thrown into prison.

"You actually met him?" I cried.

"The foolish idiot!" Vera's moan was heartfelt. "How stupid! How brave! Perhaps it should have been me who fired the gun. How can I learn to fight?"

"No, no! You must believe me, Vera, violence is not the answer." Noor's words were emphatic. "Doesn't this prove, after all, that violence begets violence? Look at the terrible suffering his revenge has caused." It was as though she was trying to convince herself. "How can Herschel live with the consequences?"

Noor was right. Herschel Grynszpan's act triggered a terrible revenge. Here, the papers called it the Night of Shattered Glass; in Germany, they called it Kristallnacht.

The weather got colder. They predicted a white Christmas. Before we all separated, the school took us to see a pantomime at Drury Lane. It was 'Babes in the Wood', and how we loved it. But the weather forecast was for heavy snow, so a week later, trickles of girls were being collected early and taken home. No one wanted to be snowed in at school.

We had our last midnight feast of the term in our dorm. We tuned the radio, keeping the volume down in case our matron heard it, and scanned through the stations till we found Fred Astaire singing 'Dancing Cheek to Cheek' from the film 'Top Hat'. We danced too, whirling each other around the dormitory. How we yearned to see it. That night we lit candles, and roasted marshmallows over the flame, and Dodo performed an extract from 'A Christmas Carol' which, a few days earlier, she had managed to sneak out and see in the theatre with Charles. She hammed it up, playing all the parts, and had us rolling around with muffled laughter. *"I am the ghost of Christmas past . . ."* she intoned, while Noor twanged along on her veena, adding to the sound effects.

I would look back on that night, and realise it was the last time we would all be together as silly schoolgirls, roasting marshmallows over a flickering candle.

CHAPTER 16

Pain and Joy

CHRISTMAS 1938

Letters, letters, letters! How dependent we were on them; how they punctuated our lives, enabling us to look forward – but how their absence left a void. Term drew to a close; there were no further letters from Noor's father, but one from her mother. I saw Noor's stricken face as she read and reread her letter.

Her father had suffered a spiritual crisis. He had left home; walked out without telling anyone, leaving a note to say he would stay away until he had resolved a problem. He took no clothes or money. The night watchman thought he saw a holy man wearing just a dhoti and shawl, carrying a bundle, a metal bowl, and a long stick, walking down the road just before dawn, heading north. The figure was unusual because he was tall, straight, and walked with a purpose.

"The only other time my father took to the road on a pilgrimage was when his father died, and he went to the

Himalayas," whispered Noor. "Why couldn't he have told me?"

I thought of Noor's father – so commanding, gleaming, god-like in his shining gold coat. I couldn't imagine him having a spiritual crisis, or what could have caused it.

Perhaps Noor couldn't either. Her whole body crumpled as she told me. During the following weeks she became more tense and introspective, and I was so saddened to see it: our Noor – so scatty, so ready to laugh and be mischievous; who could shift from friendship, fun and hard reality to otherworldliness, with her music and her fairies. She was a mysterious blend of what my Aunt Madge would have called 'an old soul', yet also an innocent, and as naïve as a young child. Now she looked as wounded as though her spirit had been damaged.

Ever since her holiday in Paris with Vera, Noor had seemed bewildered, drifting, not knowing where she was going. Her father had abandoned her – at least that's how she saw it. She spent more time alone, as if an invisible shield had gone up, and none of us could reach her.

We all separated for the Christmas holidays with affectionate calls. "Have fun! See you next term! Next year!"

Vera went back to Paris, hoping for news of her friend Daniel, who had gone to fight in Spain. Noor, who had heard nothing further from her mother or father, could have gone with her – I think Vera would have liked that – or with me to Aunt Madge, but decided instead to spend the holidays in Holland Park in London with the Baileys at the Centre for Sufi Philosophy. Perhaps she felt closer to her father there, and more likely to get news of him.

Dodo thought she had been going to join her parents in Vienna. She read out her mother's letter: *"Darling, we know how you find our friends boring, all those parties utterly tedious, so we've been in touch with Gwen's aunt and uncle, and they've agreed you can go to them for Christmas. I'm sure you'll have lots more fun."*

Dodo's expression was that of an abandoned child as she crumpled up the letter and chucked it away. But it was fleeting, and replaced quickly as she quipped, "Well, Gwenny Penny! Looks like you're landed with me, old chum."

"Oh dearest Dodo! I'm thrilled. We'll have a whale of a time – just you see," I replied, throwing my arms round her.

"Better make sure your Christmas isn't boring, that's all I can say! Of course, I could go and look for Charles. You wouldn't tell, would you?" Dodo looked at me, her tear-filled eyes flashing with rebellion. "I wonder what he's doing? Skiing, I expect."

"Dodo, NO!" I cried, gripping her arm. "You damn well won't."

"Course not, silly! I was only joking. But if I didn't like you so much, I might have considered it."

Dodo came with me to Wales, and we only just made it before the snow arrived. The next day, you could barely see your hand in front of you for the thick, noiseless, descent of huge white flakes falling, falling, falling, as though the sky was one vast quilt of goose feathers being shaken out. All night long they must have fallen, for when we woke the next morning, it was to a stifling silence: no sound of birds or winds or rattling barn doors, not even Dizzy barking as usual. An eerie white glow filled the bedroom we were sharing. I tiptoed to the window and gasped to see snow drifts as high as the downstairs window ledges. The roads and ditches became as one, and suffocated fields lay pristine, as white and as unmarked as Antarctica.

We couldn't open the doors until Uncle Harold managed to get out and shovel away the snow, creating great mounds on either side of the path. But we loved being snowed in. It was as though we had been cocooned from all the troubles of the world. When I look back now at that Christmas, I realise that, maybe for the last time, we were children; just children, living in the present with Time on hold.

Archie had come with his friend, Edward, and we knew that Eric was hoping to get leave and be with us for Christmas Day – and that was the only concern we had: that with the snow disrupting the roads and trains Eric might not make it. When it stopped snowing, the temperature dropped and it was unbelievably cold, but how we played! We joined the village children having snowball fights or sledging down the hills, and skating on the iced-up dew ponds – and we all built the most gigantic snowman ever. We got so frozen that, when we finally rushed to the fire to warm up, we screamed with pain. Uncle Harold had to drag us away from the heat, saying it was because we were thawing out too fast.

Perhaps this would be the last time I would accept Christmas, and everything it meant, with a childish joy. Perhaps because Aunt Madge, of all of us, had intimations of a dangerous world, she made it an especially traditional Christmas, bringing all the elements together as creatively as a theatre director: the carol-singing, the decorations, the Christmas tree dug from the woods, roots and all, the same one as last year, and the year before, and the year before . . . so it was taller and taller, and this year so tall that we would need a ladder to put the silver star on the top.

Dodo was at her funniest – especially when we played charades in the evening, and she imitated first Laurence Olivier as Hamlet, then John Gielgud as Iago. And she sang all the songs from 'Babes in the Wood', with Uncle Harold rollicking away at the piano, and the boys mocking us like clowns.

Smells of cooking and baking permeated the house for days on end, and there was no shortage of mulled wine, pies and cakes as we hosted the tenants from the cottages, and friends from the neighbouring farms, or those who could plod their way across the fields up to their knees in snow, or ride on the hay wains pulled by their farm horses.

And if any carol singers braved the freezing cold and the perilous drifts, they were welcomed in and plied with hot cocoa and minced pies.

Christmas cards lined the mantelpieces and window ledges: from India, Kenya, and even Vienna from Dodo's parents – but we heard nothing from Vera or Noor and briefly, thoughts of them clouded my mind. I wondered what was happening with Vera in Paris, and how Noor was doing in London – so unlike Noor not to write – and I wondered whether she'd heard further news of her father.

We opened our letters, their stamps carefully steamed off by Archie and fiercely competed for with his friend, Edward, before being inserted into stamp albums.

Oh, my darling children, our mother sighed far away across the ocean in India. *If only we could all be together. I sometimes think my heart will break I miss you so much.* And we swore that the slight inky smudges on the paper were her tears, and I went off to the lav – even though it was the chilliest room in the house – and wept buckets.

Would Eric make it? There was no message – what with the phone lines being down, and the wireless reporting snow blocking the tracks. We had feasted on our Christmas Eve high tea, playing ludo and cards in front of the fire, when suddenly Dizzy began barking his head off and leaping at the door.

"If they're carol singers, they're rather late," frowned Aunt Madge. But we were already anticipating who it might be and sprang to open the door.

A deep male voice sang, "God rest you merry gentlemen, let nothing you dismay!"

"Eric! It's Eric!" we screamed joyfully and, with Dizzy barking and jumping, Uncle Harold unbolted the front door and pulled it open. A white figure stumbled in – as though our snowman had come to life and wanted to enter and sit by the fire. But it was Eric, his thick, grey overcoat and cap utterly snow-encrusted. We threw ourselves into his arms. He had managed to get a train, stopping and starting, and crawling along so slowly, but getting as far Swansea, eight miles away. With no buses or cars or any kind of transport, he had walked.

It was as complete a gathering as we could have hoped for. Only our parents would have made it better. That night when we had finally got to bed, Dodo whispered, "Gwenny – thank you. Thank you for the most magical Christmas I've ever had."

It was January 1939 when we all convened back at school – all of us, except Vera. News came that she was not returning.

Noor was stunned. "She never told me!"

CHAPTER 17

I Can't Go Back!

PARIS 1939

"I can't go back!"

She hadn't planned it; had barely thought about it. It just came to her in a moment. But once lodged in her brain, it was utterly clear to Vera that she could not return to England.

There had been a terrible row. "Don't be so ridiculous!" her aunt had exclaimed. "Of course you must go back."

"Aren't you happy there?" asked Uncle Victor more gently. "We liked your friend, Noor. Won't she be disappointed?"

"I want to be here in Paris," said Vera, not sure how to express her anxieties. Paris was being overwhelmed by Eastern European refugees with terrible stories. What if her parents had survived, or if there were people who had heard of them? Day after day, she had been going to the railway stations of Paris where the refugees came in, scouring their faces, asking, "Has anyone come from Kielce? Has anyone heard of the Bielawskis?"

"There are so many refugees," she argued with her aunt and uncle now. "And there's a huge demand for volunteers. I want to help. Besides, I may meet someone who knows about my parents or my brother."

"*Chérie*," her uncle had said, gently putting an arm round her. "If your parents had survived, they would have been in touch by now. Someone would have let us know. You must learn to accept they are no longer alive. We did make enquiries, you know."

"And Ethan?" Vera had barely become familiar with her brother's name before they were torn apart. "Isn't it possible that somehow Ethan survived?" Some kind person might have rescued him from the thugs that day at the railway station; battered and bruised, yes, but alive – and perhaps they brought him up. How old would he be now? Ten years old? Miracles happened. Until she knew for sure about all their fates, Vera knew she would never find peace.

"Ethan." Uncle Victor spoke her brother's name softly and with respect. "We'll always keep making enquiries – I promise you, Vera. If Ethan is alive; if *anyone* is alive, we'll find them."

Vera had then shut herself away in her room and wept and wept; a shuddering outburst for all the years she hadn't truly grieved.

As evening fell, she emerged. Aunt Minnie was dressing to go out. Vera lingered silently in the doorway of her aunt's dressing room, just as she had done ever since she had been delivered to them ten years ago – a grief-stricken, silent, unattractive, grubby little girl. She would never forget the look of horror and revulsion on her aunt's face when she had seen Vera. It had taken the next few years of living with them for Vera to accept that she represented everything her aunt had run away from: the loathsome pallor of poverty; the crushing, demeaning lives they'd endured in the *shtetl* in Poland.

She was always a reminder to her aunt of their origins, and because Vera was the sort of child who always asked questions, she was a source of great exasperation.

"You should have been a boy," her aunt had once complained. "Questions, questions, questions; and for every answer, more questions! Analyse, reanalyse, always pestering! What's the meaning of this, you ask, or the implication of that? Why did you make that statement? Can you back it up? You're just like your grandfather." And Aunt Minnie mimicked him in Yiddish, wagging her finger mockingly, just as he would have done: "'*You can't just make statements without evidence supporting them. Show me the evidence. You always have to have a reason for your beliefs and actions,*' he would have said. '*Reasons, reasons, reasons.*'" Aunt Minnie's voice would rise higher and higher. "You could be standing in the *shtetl*, up to your knees in filth – and ask for reasons."

Vera had accused her bitterly: "Do you have no feeling whatsoever for your parents, your sister – my *mother*? I know the *shtetl* we lived in was poor and wretched compared to this, but it was home, Aunty – *home*. My home and your home. It's where you were born; it's where you went to school and where you had friends. Your father was a rabbi and so was mine. Doesn't it mean anything to you? And it wasn't all bad. Even I remember the dances and celebrations, the musicians and singers, the fun and joy of the markets. There was love there, and friendship. Why do you choose to forget? If I can remember these things when I was only a child of six, so can you. You must be able to remember our community, which always helped when there was a need. I need you, Aunty. I need your memories – don't you understand?"

Vera had faced her aunt with tears streaming down her face. But her aunt had turned away, muttering, "Pointless nostalgia, pointless sentimentality; pointless, pointless, pointless. It's gone, forget it."

Later that evening, when she had calmed down, Vera crept out of her room to lean in the half open doorway of her aunt's boudoir, and wondered, just as she had always wondered, what her aunt was thinking about as she dressed to go out. Like a painter, Aunt Minnie applied her make-up: massaging in her skin cream, delicately powdering the contours of her face, adding touches of blusher to her cheekbones, outlining her eyes with mascara and adding her lipstick. Did she ever look deeper into herself, behind the mask she had created? Did she ever penetrate her own soul; could she face the truth about herself and who she really was?

Unaware of being observed, her aunt leaned forward, inches away from the surface of the mirror, and stared at herself straight in the eyes. Vera suddenly smiled: not with derision or contempt, but an unexpected surge of admiration for this woman who, against all the odds, had created her own image and was preparing to go out and face the world as the person *she* wanted to be. Wasn't it heroic? Heroic.

Aunt Minnie had erased her entire life before Paris. She lived for the present, in the present, in the charmed life her husband had given her. She had put the past behind her. She loved her life; she loved being the gracious wife of Victor Moskowski, the famous art collector. They were known throughout Parisian society for their collections of artworks, and people were thrilled to be invited to their soirées, or to be on their dinner-party list. She felt safe.

Aunt Minnie continued to scrutinise herself in her dressing-table mirror, as if she too was a work of art. Barely taking her eyes from her reflection, she reached for a pair of pearl and gold drop earrings and held them against her skin, then put them down to take up a matching necklace.

"Jeanne!" she called. "You may do my hair now."

And Jeanne, who had been assembling her mistress's outfit in the dressing room, emerged with an armful of clothes which she laid out on the bed: delicate silk lingerie, silk stockings, a beautiful cocktail dress, and a brocade jacket. She picked up a brush and examined Aunt

Minnie in the mirror. Somehow the angle revealed Vera in the shadows. Their eyes briefly met before Vera stepped out of sight.

While far away in America Fred Astaire was dancing and singing in 'Top Hat', here in Europe Vera could only imagine the terror of people displaced and transported across Europe: separated from their children and families, shot and murdered arbitrarily, no longer deemed human beings. The disabled, the homosexuals, the Roma, the communists, the anarchists, the trade unionists; and there were the Jews – the Jews above all. Denied food, denied rights; starving and dying on the streets. New laws were being passed by the Third Reich to deny Jews their citizenship, their very humanity. Above all, there was the fear: not just the fear felt by the victims, but the fears of good, ordinary, decent people. To help the victim was to condemn yourself to the fate of the victim, and your family too, or even your entire village. Fear stalked in the wake of the Nazis like a hideous and contagious disease, and made cowards of everyone. "Idiot! How rash! What folly!" some cried. Others reacted with anguish and despair.

If, in future generations, citizens were asked, "What did you do?", so many might shudder and say, "I was afraid, and did nothing," and they might also admit, "I was ashamed of my fear." And where was God, the great Judge over all, as the Nazis moved relentlessly across Europe?

There was another mood since Kristallnacht: an entitlement, a permission to bring out the ugliest of attitudes, threatening and cruel. People felt freer to be openly anti-Jewish. Gwen and Dodo would have recognised the casual taunts and sneers and the petty acts of hatred. Vera felt it every time she passed the window of Madame Boucher, their concierge, who smirked and barely bothered with the customary *"Bonjour."*

She wondered if her aunt and uncle ever noticed. If so, they never said a word.

Vera had been playing the piano when her aunt and uncle emerged from their dressing rooms, looking so polished and chic and ready for their evening out at a restaurant with friends.

"We're off now, *chérie*," said Uncle Victor.

"Have you made any contingency plans in case war is declared?" Vera knew they would hear the sarcasm in her voice. "If Germany invade Poland, we'll be at war, won't we? And if they invade France?"

"Oh really, Vera! This obsession you have with war! It's that wretched synagogue feeding you with ideas and fears," snapped her aunt. "Why can't you just go out and have a good time like other young people? Go to parties and concerts; go to the theatre. You're mixing with the wrong types."

"They won't dare to go to war with France, or England. Be assured," said her uncle earnestly. "France is strong, and well-guarded against invasion; the Maginot Line is impregnable. We don't need to overreact. And you forget we are French citizens. We are not aliens, or refugees. I am more French than many French citizens. My family has been in France for hundreds of years and your Aunt Minnie's papers are being regularised right now. She's lived here long enough to qualify as a citizen. We must do the same for you, just to be sure. But we have nothing to fear, even, *even* if the Nazis walked in – which they won't. What's more . . ."

Her uncle paused suddenly, as if he had misspoken. She heard Aunt Minnie's sharp intake of breath.

"What?" asked Vera.

"We're not Jewish any more. We've converted. We are Catholic. Louis too," said Uncle Victor quietly.

Vera stared in disbelief.

Her uncle gently took her arm. "I know how you feel about your faith and race, Vera. But I earnestly advise you to convert for your own safety. After all, our Jewish God is the same God as the God Christians worship. We share the same heritage as Abraham and Moses. Let me take you to our country house. We know the *abbé* there. He's a good man. He can instruct you in the church and have you baptised. It would be of such reassurance to us if you did."

"You never told me," she whispered. "You did it behind my back when I was in England."

"We knew you wouldn't approve, and we didn't want further friction with you. But now, it isn't any longer a question of nationality, faith, or assimilation; we aren't blind and deaf to what's going on. We have to consider Louis – and you too."

He put a hand on her shoulder. Her aunt and uncle didn't often touch her except in formality, and Vera recognised his genuine concern.

Aunt Minnie stood silently, half turned to the windows, looking out into the street below, her fingers twisting the curtain between her fingers. Her face showed no emotion, but for the first time, Vera felt her fear.

"We're going to be late," said Uncle Victor, taking Aunt Minnie's arm. "We'll talk further tomorrow, *chérie*."

Jeanne had bathed Louis and tucked him into bed when Vera appeared to say goodnight.

"I've got a good bedtime story for you, Louis," she said with a smile, sitting down on the side of his bed.

He threw his arms round her neck. "Veroshka," he whispered tearfully. "I wish you weren't going back to England."

"Your parents are worried about me, *chéri*," she answered gently. "They only want what's best. Now don't worry. If I have to go back to England, I'll write to you, OK? You're almost reading now."

"Am I in danger?" he whispered.

"No *chéri*! You're a Christian now. You'll be all right."

He held her tight. "I wish you wouldn't go."

She soothed him gently, laid him back down on his pillow and began to sing quietly: "*Il y a longtemps que je t'aime, Jamais je ne t'oublierai.*"

Never shall I ever forget you.

CHAPTER 18

Daniel Returns

The next morning there was a letter from Daniel to say he was back. Vera felt a surge of joy. *I'll be at the Café Rigaud*, he wrote. She went looking for him.

A bitter wind with specks of snow swept up the Boulevard Saint-Michel. She buttoned up her coat, tucked her chin into her scarf and strode out, smiling into her collar.

He was sitting at the Café Rigaud surrounded by his student friends. She paused, leaning into the dappled trunk of a bleak, leafless, horse chestnut tree; out of sight but within earshot, she drank in his image and quietly relished a few moments of joy at seeing him alive.

His face was gaunt and his cheeks hollowed out, just like the Catalan they heard speaking last summer; his face was browned like a walnut from the fierce heat of Spain, except for the new jagged white scar from his brow to his cheek. He sat awkwardly as if in pain, and eased himself from time to time beneath his thick khaki overcoat. He was talking passionately. He had returned wounded but alive and burning with activism. His thin, long-fingered hands shaped his emotions in the air as he spoke. Vera almost smiled. That was Daniel. Only death could extinguish that spirit of his.

"The war isn't over," he was insisting. "We can't let the fascists win. Refugees are fleeing to every corner of the earth. But for how long will any of us be safe?"

Vera was about to step out and make herself known when Simone appeared from inside the café. She was unbearably thin; her face was pale, and she walked with difficulty. Gently, their friends made way for her next to Daniel as if it were her natural place.

"Simone! At least your beautiful face is unmarked, eh?" they joked with her ironically.

"Brave woman," cried Daniel admiringly, leaping up to give her an affectionate embrace. "You should see the way she carried on, even after she was shot. We need more like her."

Vera shrank back behind the tree, suddenly wishing she was anywhere else but there. When the waiter appeared to take more orders, she slipped away unseen. Somehow, her tears of last night had not been completely drained, and they poured down her face again as she hurried along the boulevard, grateful for the biting wind which dried them as fast as they fell.

She pulled her scarf across her face, and just walked and walked. She found herself going to the synagogue in the Marais district. It was teeming with refugees and volunteers parcelling clothes, distributing food, and handing out information as to where they could find accommodation. In their midst was Rabbi Rosenthal.

"Can I help too?" Vera asked him.

"Ah Vera! Good that you've come. Yes – Madame Cohen over there is short-handed. She'll have something for you to do for sure."

The rabbi waved her in the direction of a rotund bustling woman standing behind a trestle table sorting through a mound of clothes. So Vera packed clothes, distributed rations, made coffee, comforted children separated from parents, and parents who had lost their children, often asking the question, "You didn't happen to hear of Ruth and Eli Bielawski, did you? They had a baby called Ethan."

She saw Madame Blumstein who lived on the floor above them in the same Rue d'Assas apartment block. They caught each other's eye.

"Ah! Vera!" Madame Blumstein cried with a broad smile. "Good to see you here." She was a dark, pretty, elegant woman with three young children – the oldest, Samuel, was the same age as Louis, and they often played in and out of each other's apartments.

Vera went over and kissed her on both cheeks. She hadn't noticed the Blumsteins coming very often to the synagogue and was therefore surprised to see Madame Blumstein here, chicly dressed as always with her red-painted fingernails and beautifully cut hair, as if meeting in a stylish coffee shop on the Champs-Elysées rather than as a volunteer at a refugee centre. But here she was, pitching in with the rest of them.

"I'm afraid I don't often come to the synagogue," Madame Blumstein confessed, "except when someone has a bar mitzvah or something. But I really wanted to help in some way."

For a while they worked side by side, making small talk. Madame Blumstein asked what it was like to be at an English boarding school. She had obviously had enough coffee and cakes with Aunt Minnie to know a good deal of information about Vera, so she spoke tactfully and with sympathetic curiosity.

"There you are, Veroshka!"

Their chat was interrupted. Vera whirled round to see Daniel loping across the hall.

"Where were you? I waited ages at the Rigaud. Didn't you get my note?" He clasped her shoulders and kissed her thrice on both cheeks.

"I . . . er . . . " To her mortification, tears welled in her eyes again. "I'm so thrilled, relieved, full of joy to see you," she managed to stammer.

"You need a break – you've done a lot. Go on, *ma chère*," Madame Blumstein urged her affectionately. "Get some air. I'll manage here a little longer."

Daniel ushered Vera out while she desperately struggled to control her emotions. They found a small coffee shop nearby and sat at a table deep inside.

"Why didn't you come? Don't tell me you were

going to leave for England without welcoming back your conquering hero?" he teased.

"Of course not . . . it's just . . ." Her emotions threatened to overwhelm her again: joy, love, doubt; doubt that her love could be returned. She lowered her eyes helplessly.

"Aren't you pleased to see me?" he asked gently.

"Daniel!" She looked up, aghast at being misunderstood. "I'm so pleased to see you back; so relieved. I've been following events – and it all looked so bad. The Republicans haven't been doing well, have they? And look at you – so thin and limping around. What happened? Were you seriously wounded? Look at that scar, how did you get it? Tell me everything. Are you properly better? Thank God you're safe."

"Safe?" He almost sneered, and she recoiled. "We're Jews, Vera. Jews are never safe. That aunt and uncle of yours, do they really feel safe, or have they got a suitcase packed and ready by the door? Thank God you're leaving Paris and going back to England."

"I'm not going."

Daniel frowned. He looked almost angry. "Don't be idiotic. You must go."

"How can I leave Paris? I feel like a coward."

"Surely your aunt and uncle don't agree?"

"No."

"Then you can't disobey them."

They can't make me go," muttered Vera, hating the way this conversation sounded more like a quarrel than a reunion of friends. "They wouldn't want to drag me kicking and screaming to the Gare du Nord. I want to stay here and help. I couldn't possibly leave Paris just to sit in the safety of the English countryside, twiddling my thumbs. Even if war doesn't happen, there are still enough bad things going on which means we have to be ready to fight. And look at you; already wounded!" Her voice was passionate.

"Simone too. Got a bullet through her thigh. She could have died."

"Ah, Simone. She's brave. And don't you need more like her?" asked Vera, unable to resist the sarcasm.

If Daniel heard it, he ignored it. "Yes – we do. And we need more like *you*. Many more like you." He clasped her hands and pressed them to his lips. "Don't you understand the difference between her and you?" So he had heard the sarcasm after all. "Some people are helpful and brave short term. You, Vera, you are long term. We're going to need you long term."

"But there's still a chance of peace, isn't there?"

"If they don't invade Poland," muttered Daniel. "If they do . . . then we'll be at war – unless the British and the French are complete liars. But we have the Soviet Union on our side. The fascists would be mad to take them on too."

"I'm not going back to England, Daniel," Vera said firmly, removing her hands from his lips. "So, you'd better get used to it."

They kissed their *adieux* formally when suddenly he pressed his lips near her ear. "I never knew you were so incorrigible," he whispered affectionately. "Be patient. Please. Will you wait?"

She nodded and briefly leaned into the curve of his neck.

"Emotional involvements must be set aside for the moment, but our time will come," he murmured. Then they separated.

Vera returned to help Madame Blumstein for a little longer before walking back with her to the Rue d'Assas. "I think Samuel is playing with your Louis upstairs," said Madame Blumstein. "I'll come up with you and get him. It will soon be supper time."

Aunt Minnie and Uncle Victor were just pouring a cocktail when they arrived. They greeted Madame Blumstein warmly, making her sit down, pressing a glass into her hand.

"Let the boys have five minutes more," Aunt Minnie cried. "They're having such a good time."

"Vera, play the piano for us, will you, while we chat with Madame Blumstein?" Uncle Victor requested. He often liked to show off his niece. *"Elle joue du Chopin très bien,"* he would say with pride.

"I expect you miss Vera when she's in England," remarked Madame Blumstein.

"Naturally, we do – especially Louis. He adores her," replied Aunt Minnie. "She's leaving next week – though she doesn't want to go back," she declared, as if expecting to find an ally in her neighbour.

Madame Blumstein expressed surprise. "Is she not happy there?"

"Of course, she's happy."

Vera stopped playing.

"You're happy aren't you, Vera?" Aunt Minnie called over to her.

"Yes," answered Vera simply. "It's just that I'd rather be here in Paris helping out with the refugees."

"Very laudable, Vera!" exclaimed Uncle Victor jovially.

"It is indeed," agreed Madame Blumstein. "I'm told she has been a remarkable help at the synagogue. They all speak so highly of her. What a shame she's leaving. I for one wish she would stay. As a matter of fact, I was going to ask if Vera could teach the piano to my eldest girl, Mireille."

"Oh yes, I'd love to teach Mireille," exclaimed Vera enthusiastically.

How strange, that an accidental remark of a neighbour should have been a turning point, and that, by the end of the evening, Aunt Minnie and Uncle Victor had agreed that perhaps Vera need not return to England.

Like fate, the very next day Jeanne announced that she must go back to her village as soon as possible as her mother had fallen ill.

"Well, that settles it, I suppose," said Aunt Minnie. "Vera, you'd better stay and look after Louis – at least till Jeanne returns – and give Mireille piano lessons."

Later Vera hurried to Jeanne's room to find her packing a suitcase. "Oh Jeanne!" she said. "You will come back, won't you? We'll miss you horribly. I don't know how Louis will bear your absence. I don't want you to go. Please come back."

"I will. I promise," Jeanne reassured her. "You know how much I love Louis."

That night, Vera stood on her balcony and stared upwards. The clouds seemed extra white and luminous against the dark sky. People had been overwhelmed with reassurances that there wouldn't be a war, yet everyone was on a war footing: gas masks had been allocated, instructions for air raid shelters sent out, and advice given about what to do in the event of an attack. Many parents had already sent their children out of Paris.

Although she felt triumphant that she wasn't returning to England, beneath her contentment lurked a terrible presentiment for the future. All Paris felt it. How could they not? But the mood in the city turned especially nasty, lashing out at the foreigner and refugee, and – the Jews.

For the next two or three months, Paris seemed to hover in a strange no man's land. People no sooner dared to think everything would return to normal than all their hopes came crashing down. Would it be war? Would it be peace?

Then came news that the Germans had entered Prague.

"So that's Czechoslokavia done for," exclaimed Vera to her aunt and uncle. "Do you still feel safe?"

Vera wrote to Noor.

I miss you all so much. But I know I'm where I should be – here in Paris. I'm looking after darling little Louis. I'm sure I would love Ethan in the same way. How I dream that he is alive. There is much unease and fear here in Paris – especially for we Jews. The stories we hear are terrible. Now the Nazis have gone into Czechoslokavia. Where next? It's the uncertainty that is so hard.

Daniel and I – we love each other. We do, Noor. There – I've said it. I haven't said it to anyone else, not even Daniel, though I know he loves me too. It doesn't need saying out loud. But he won't even discuss the future. He says we mustn't. We can't. There is no future; not while Hitler and his jackboots march across Europe. How I wish I could see you again. I send you all my love and deepest friendship. Tell Noor, Gwen and Dodo the same.

It was 23 August when Daniel came to the Rue d'Assas looking for Vera. Her aunt and uncle were out, so it was she who opened the door in response to his urgent ringing and knocking. He looked agitated.

"Daniel! What's happened?"

"We are betrayed!"

Vera couldn't understand what he meant. "Betrayed? How? By whom?"

"Let's not talk here."

"I'm looking after Louis – we're going to the Jardin du Luxembourg. Louis!" she called over her shoulder. "Are you ready? Get your boat we'll sail it on the lake!"

"Oh yes, yes! My boat, my boat! I want to sail my boat," Louis sang, and rushed to his room to find it. He appeared, his eyes shining, bearing the glistening white and red sailing boat under his arm, the sail folded to the mast. Vera helped him put on his navy-blue blazer and suggested he wore his sailor's cap. Then she flung a jacket on herself, fixed a hat to her head, and out they went.

Daniel was waiting by the outside door. "*Bonjour* little fellow!" He bowed to Louis.

That was another reason she liked Daniel, thought Vera. He always acknowledged everyone – even children. But his face was stricken.

They crossed the road into the gardens. As soon as Louis had raced ahead towards the lake, Vera asked, "What is it?"

"I can hardly believe it. We're lost, Vera – lost."

"What, for God's sake?" begged Vera.

"Stalin and Hitler have made a deal with each other, that if Hitler marches into Poland, Russia will do nothing to stop him."

Vera was bewildered. "I thought things had improved." She had been following the news, and seen all those headlines: a pact between France, Britain and Germany promising never to go to war with each other again. Germany agreeing not to invade Poland. The British Prime Minister meeting Hitler. "Didn't Chamberlain come back to London waving the contract proclaiming 'Peace in our Time'?"

"It's just a piece of paper! And the Russians have betrayed us. How could they? After all we've sacrificed in Spain! I can't believe it." And Daniel allowed a torrent of swear words to pour from his mouth in fury and anguish.

Louis came hurtling into them. "Help me with the boat, Daniel!" he cried.

"Which way is the wind blowing?" Daniel licked a finger and held it up. "Follow me, *monsieur*," he declared, marching round to the east side of the lake with Louis behind him. Vera followed, grateful for the interruption to absorb the news.

Daniel set the boat in the water and a wind filled the sails. Louis shrieked with delight as the boat began a steady path across the lake, and dashed round to be on the other side.

Vera reached Daniel's side. His face was now stony – and utterly grim.

"And do you know what else it means?" he said, as if they hadn't been interrupted. "It means that we French communists – we, loyal to France – have been made enemies in our own country."

PART 2

WAR

CHAPTER 19

If The Beauteous Day
Did But Reflect The Times

LONDON, 3 SEPTEMBER 1939

An English September morning gleamed as mythologically golden as the apples in the Garden of Hesperides. After the violent storm of the night before, London was washed clean; the sky was like a shining blue eye gazing down, it seemed to me, with the utmost benevolence. I felt poetic.

And yet – all eyes and ears were waiting for the clock to chime eleven across the city.

Two days earlier, before dawn had broken, in the sleeping fairyland twilight of a full moon and a star-scattered landscape, Germany had pounced into Poland with outspread claws, like a merciless tiger after its prey. And what had we done – we British and French? Nothing. And Russia did nothing. For two days we had bleated about broken promises, forgetting that this was not about boy scouts, or county cricket. It was about the Nazis fulfilling their secret pledge – to take Poland and destroy it forever.

But we had done nothing. Shame!

Britain had finally issued an ultimatum that unless Herr Hitler withdrew his troops immediately, it meant war. The Prime Minister had given him till today at 11 a.m. to respond.

How I relished being in London. Many girls had wept when their school lives came to an end – but not us: oh no! Dodo, Noor and I somehow got through our school Leaving Certificates, and decided to come to the great capital of the empire. We had arrived in June like Gilbert and Sullivan's 'Three Little Maids from School': so merry and fancy free, and full of expectation.

Noor and I had decided to do a Red Cross training course. It seemed sensible while there was this threat of war hanging over us. Dodo was ecstatic, because she had got into RADA to train as an actress. We rented digs three floors up in a narrow twisty building in Orange Street, just off Trafalgar Square. I'll never forget the day we moved in, giggling and gasping as we heaved our bags and baggage up three flights of stairs, or Noor with her precious veena.

Our landlady, the fierce Mrs Antrobus in her flowery cotton overalls, stood guard on the first landing with broad strong arms clasped across her stout body, cigarette clenched between her lips, supervising our arrival and warning us repeatedly not to lean into the walls and mark her freshly painted stairwell as we struggled upwards.

Despite Mrs Antrobus's rules for a 10 p.m. curfew, no loud wireless, and no gentleman callers, we loved being in central London. Dodo was in seventh heaven as we were surrounded by the theatres. Of course, there I was again, Dodo's gatekeeper: charged with making sure she could get in, and not be apprehended by Mrs Antrobus, as it was always way after 10 o'clock at night before she returned from the theatre or – just as likely – a rendezvous with Charles. We had already found a way of opening and shutting the front door as silently as burglars and had identified which stairs creaked. So far, we had got away with it.

With talk of war even louder, London was tense. People milled about anxiously. Everywhere were signs of war preparations: sandbags piled in shop doorways, people with their gas masks slung over their arms as routinely as their brief cases or handbags, and barrage balloons hanging in the sky like sentinels. Everywhere were public messages and notices about where to go and what to do in the event of war, and where the air-raid shelters and first aid posts were located. People had already got used to all kinds of instructions: how to drive during blackout at night without causing accidents; making sure all windows were properly blacked out. Londoners were used to stern air-raid wardens patrolling the streets after dark, and wagging a finger if they saw even the tiniest chink of light.

However, Dodo, Noor and I were only a threesome for a couple of months. After we had completed our Red Cross course, Noor made a shock announcement.

"I've joined up!"

"You've WHAT?" Dodo and I chorused with astonishment.

We couldn't believe it. This princess – this daughter of a non-violent Sufi philosopher – had decided to join the army; she, who had been brilliant through her Red Cross training, who could do dressings for all kinds of wounds, set broken bones, treat fractures, administer injections, and drive ambulances – it had seemed ideal work for this tender-hearted girl with such non-violent feelings. Even so, she had joined the army.

We were disbelieving.

"Isn't it a bit soon? We may not even go to war!"

"It's coming," said Noor. "I know it is. So, I've joined the ATS: the Auxiliary Territorial Service. I'll only be a clerk or something, or they'll teach me to drive – nothing violent. We won't be in combat roles. But at least I'll be doing something."

Noor's face was pale and sombre, and I realised what a crisis she had been through. The one thing her philosophy embodied – non-violence – was being unbearably threatened. What demons had she fought this past year which had led her to make this decision? What silent, anguished dialogues had she had with her absent father?

"I know I'm not supposed to believe in violence," she said, her eyes lowered, "and I don't. I don't! Though I know I'm supporting others who will be violent. But I do believe we have no choice but to fight evil in any way we can."

How mysterious. There she was, living with us, and we hadn't seen her drifting into this other space, driven with a resolve which Dodo and I had been completely unaware of.

Noor received a letter a week or so later; a letter in a brown envelope with an army seal on the back. A letter summoning her to barracks. By the next day, she was gone – begging us to take care of her veena and to hang on to any letters that came for her, especially those from India. She had stopped talking about her father, and letters from him were fewer.

The next time we saw Noor – two months later – she was in army uniform.

"Noor! Your hair! What have you done?" wailed Dodo.

She had cut her long thick plaits almost as short as a boy's, leaving just a few dark curls to flow from beneath her cap. Yet despite looking so grown up in her khaki uniform, brown stockings, and brown leather lace-up shoes, Noor was still the gentle, mysterious girl we knew.

Over that weekend, we all became schoolgirls again. We cooked, ate, laughed, teased and talked in depth, the three of us; good friends that we were.

"Have you heard from Vera?" I asked Noor. "Is she all right?"

"She's helping the refugees in Paris. There are thousands and thousands of them you know, coming in from all over Europe. She hopes someone may have heard news of her family. Poor Vera. I wish I was there with her. It sounds terrible."

Then Dodo put a Glen Miller record on the gramophone to cheer us up, and we jiggled and giggled around to 'Little Brown Jug' until Mrs Antrobus came storming up the stairs to complain that we were making too much noise.

Later, Dodo and I could laugh about how Noor nearly missed her train the next day. "Still the same old scatty Noor!" She had been so intent on taking the opportunity to play the veena that she had played long into the night and overslept, so we had a terrible dash next morning to make her train, racing across Trafalgar Square to Charing Cross, Dodo and me fumbling for change to buy platform tickets, and she hunting for her pass.

"Oh, get on with it!" The ticket collector shook his head with exasperation. "Go on – you'll miss it."

The guard was blowing his whistle and waving the green flag, and the giant wheels had begun to screech and spark as they slowly turned. Noor raced towards a still open carriage door and pitched herself inside as the guard, too, leaped aboard and slammed it shut.

I can see her now, leaning out of her train window waving, and calling out, "See you again soon!"

"Oh Dodo!" I sighed. "How on earth do you think Noor copes with the discipline of army life?"

"Bet they don't know about her fairies," Dodo sniffed. Was she close to tears?

I had woken very early that radiant September morning and decided to go to the Sunday service at St Martin-in-the-Fields. I left Dodo asleep. Knowing her, having come home late as usual, she'd sleep well into the morning.

When I arrived at St Martin's, people were streaming up the stairs into the church, hardly talking. I made my way inside and sat down at the back. The organ was playing softly. People acknowledged each other, fiddled with their hymn books, then stood up as the vicar entered with his entourage, and men and boys of the choir in their white surplices. He climbed the pulpit steps and stood ready to start the service. The organ stopped. The vicar opened his mouth to speak. Outside, we could hear the clock striking 11 o'clock.

"Dearly beloved brethren, we are gathered together here in the sight of God . . ."

Suddenly, the vestry door at the side flew open. A young curate ran in, up the pulpit steps and whispered to the vicar. The vicar threw his head back, looking up to heaven. He gripped the lectern.

"I have just been told that the Prime Minister will broadcast to the nation at eleven fifteen this morning on the BBC."

For a second there was silence; then a gasp; then a quiver as though each member of the congregation had been struck by a bolt of electricity. Everyone got up and, in one silent exodus, fled the church. The clock had barely finished striking eleven as I too raced back to Orange Street, up the three flights of stairs, and over to the wireless.

"Dodo! Where are you?" I gasped, as I heard the announcer, Alvar Liddell, introducing Mr Chamberlain's voice.

"This morning, the British Ambassador in Berlin handed the German Government a note stating that unless we heard from them by 11 a.m. that they were prepared to withdraw their troops from Poland, a state of war would exist between us. I have to tell you now, that no such undertaking has been received, and that consequently this country is at war with Germany."

I realised I had held my breath throughout the Prime Minister's announcement. I exhaled and felt faint, completely uncertain of what to do in the next two minutes, let alone tomorrow or tomorrow or tomorrow. Waves of panic swept over me. It had finally happened. War.

"Dodo!" I called again. Where the hell was she?

All over Britain people must have paused. Workers must have downed tools, teacups poised mid-air, ears pressed to the wireless as the Prime Minister's solemn voice came over the air. Millions must have looked at each other in dread, and held their children closer.

But where was Dodo?

"Did you hear it?" Mrs Antrobus stood in the doorway.

Her face was ashen, her whole body trembled and she looked as if she was going to cry. Outside, sirens had already begun to wail. "It's war. Oh my God!"

We stared out of the window. Down below, the streets seemed to turn into a multitude of rivulets all running in different directions as people raced to their own destinations and priorities. Some had already found their gas masks and were struggling to put them on. Shop keepers came out to check their sandbags, and shutters of their windows; taxis were being hailed, people leaped on to buses. A sense of panic gripped everyone as though the Germans were already on our doorstep.

"What are we going to do? Should we head for the shelters? The nearest is in Leicester Square, isn't it?" Mrs Antrobus, her chest heaving for breath.

It had the effect of calming me down. "I think we should have a cup of tea, Mrs Antrobus," I said. "Here, sit for a moment." I took her arm and led her to the sofa, then put on the kettle. "They're just practising. We should sit tight and listen to the radio. They'll tell us what to do."

Mrs Antrobus rocked to and fro, wringing her hands in her lap. "We've hardly got over that last war. The Great War took my husband – now another war? I can't believe it. My boys! They're both in the army. It could take my boys." Her voice quavered. She wiped her eyes with her overall.

"Oh Mrs Antrobus," I sat down next to her, "I'm so sorry. My brother's in the air force. I'm scared too. What are your boys called?"

"Billy and George. Twins – they're only twenty."

The kettle whistled shrilly, and I hurried off to make the tea. "I don't know where Dodo's got to!" I called. "I left her asleep to go to church. I'd only been away about fifteen minutes, but when I got back, she'd gone."

"A young man came by in a fancy car. A soldier, in uniform. Tooted the horn, he did – and she was out in a flash!" Despite her anxiety Mrs Antrobus managed to sound disapproving.

"A soldier! Oh, I wonder who that was?" I cried. "She might have left me a note."

After we'd drunk tea together, Mrs Antrobus insisted on taking me down to her flat on the ground floor. I needed her company as much as she needed mine. All her petty, inquisitive, picky, prying personality, which had sometimes made us want to move somewhere else, had vanished; suddenly she was just a lonely, frightened widow and mother, worrying about her sons.

The tobacco smoke was overwhelming and seemed to colour everything as she took me into her over-cluttered living room, with its fawn carpets and fawn curtains and fawn sofa and chairs, the only colour were three green and brown china ducks flying across her browny, wallpapered walls. She led me to an alcove where, in an almost revered and sacred space on the wall, was a sepia photograph of her husband, Bernard: upright, moustachioed, in a khaki army uniform, staring with pride out of the brass frame.

She lit another cigarette. It dangled from her lips as she

rummaged in a drawer of her Welsh dresser and pulled out a photograph album.

"Sit down, ducky." Mrs Antrobus patted a place next to her on the sofa. She laid the album across her knees and opened it up. I watched the end of her cigarette drooping longer and longer as she took me page by page through the album, flicking the ash off into the ashtray at the very last minute. She named and described the circumstances of every photograph over the last twenty-three years of her life: her wedding day, her husband, first as a grocer in overalls, in his shop behind the counter, then as a gunner in the Great War. Bernard had been shot just a few days before armistice was declared, and she still pregnant with the twin boys who would be born six months later. She wailed at the injustice.

"They're very handsome, Mrs Antrobus," I said, trying not to let my mind wander as her hopes and fears streamed from her. She clutched the album to her bosom, and stared into space.

"I'd better go now," I whispered, after a while. "But please let me know if there is anything I can do." I don't know if she heard me, and I gently let myself out and climbed the stairs back to the third floor.

CHAPTER 20
Meeting Ralph

I opened the window and gazed down at the scenes of chaos below, feeling hollow and unbearably lonely: a child again – wanting comfort, wanting my mother, wanting Aunt Madge and Uncle Harold. I wanted the sounds and smells of India; I wanted my ayah. I wished Eric hadn't gone into the air force. How was Noor feeling? Was she terrified? *Where was Dodo?*

The voices of paper boys rang above the sound of traffic that was building up: "Special latest news! It's war! England at war with Germany!"

I had an urge to hear dearest Aunty Madge and Uncle Harold. I must telephone them. We should leave London immediately, and go to Wales, shouldn't we?

Dodo and I had built several towers of pennies especially set aside for phone calls. There was a bank of telephone boxes in the square. I swept one whole tower of coins into my purse and, grabbing my gas mask and keys, ran downstairs and out into the commotion: police cars with sirens screaming, air-raid wardens in their uniforms pointing out the nearest shelters, Red Cross ambulances and lorries packed with soldiers summoned back to barracks. Drifting high above in the skies were the barrage balloons. People gazed up fearfully, wondering how soon they would hear the roar of German bombers.

I wasn't the only one desperate to make a phone call. Queues of shuffling, anxious people stretched away from the red telephone boxes, all with their gas masks hanging from their arms. I chose a queue and waited. In all that bedlam, London suddenly seemed to be the loneliest place on earth.

It was ages before I finally reached the phone box, aware of the impatient people behind me, desperate for me to hurry up and make my call. I set the coins on the ledge, took out two pennies and pushed them though the slot to make the initial connection. I dialled the number, my finger poised over button A to press when someone answered. Far away in Wales, I could hear it ringing and ringing and ringing. The next person in line was staring at me through the glass squares of the phone box. I determinedly let it ring for nearly a minute.

"Please, someone be home," I begged. But on and on it rang; unanswered. Sadly, I pressed button B and got my coins back. I left the phone box, barely able to get out of the door before the next person shoved me aside to get in.

A young man in a soft brown suit, shirt, tie and trilby hat only two away from his turn muttered "damn!" as he fumbled in his pockets. "Excuse me!" He caught my eye and held out a florin. "I'm out of pennies. You couldn't be a sport and help me out?" He couldn't have been much more than my age. "I can't believe I'm such a clot. I could have sworn I had coppers left in my pocket. Must have used them all up last night talking to my mother."

"I've plenty," I said. "Anyway – my people aren't at home, you can have them." I gave him my pennies, and almost instantly it was his turn.

I left him to it and walked over to a bench in a pool of sunlight, and sat, overwhelmed with misery. I couldn't bear to go back to the empty flat. I got up and began walking aimlessly. The news had woken the city as if from a dream straight into a nightmare. The pavements were jostling with panic, urgency, bewilderment; people all going somewhere or nowhere. I bought a newspaper and sat down, trying to read it – but could barely focus.

Footsteps came running up behind me. It was the young man in the brown trilby. "I say! I'm glad I caught you!" he said. "That was really sporting of you. I just didn't have any change, and I was desperate to talk to my little sister. She's in a boarding school in Surrey and in a bit of a flap. Not surprisingly. Look, can I give you a cup of tea? Then I'll be able to change my florin and pay you back. There's a Lyons over in Piccadilly. They'll be open on a Sunday."

To my surprise, I nodded. "All right." Was this was what Dodo would have called a 'pick up'? But he reminded me of Eric. He was not especially tall, though taller than me; not especially handsome in any film-star way, though he looked interesting and intelligent. He was thinner than I thought he should be; his suit hung on his frame, and beneath his trilby was a rather gaunt, angular face with very dark brown eyes and a stubby nose. But I liked his face. They say you can't judge a book from its cover, but if a face can reveal anything, this young man's face seemed open and honest, and his eyes twinkled as though everything had a funny side – even war.

Taking my elbow, he ushered me across the square, past Eros and into Piccadilly's Lyons Corner House. The nippies, in their starched white waitressing pinnies and little white bonnets, were flustered and distracted. The word 'war' buzzed in the background conversation as they led us to a table and took our order.

"Pot of tea for two," the young man began to order – "or would you prefer something else?" he asked me, removing his trilby hat to reveal an unexpected mop of reddish-brown curly hair.

"Tea would be lovely." I hadn't eaten breakfast or lunch, but didn't dare say so.

"How about some scones or a toasted teacake?" he asked, as if reading my mind, or perhaps hearing my tummy rumble. "I'm starving. Mr Hitler quite made me forget to eat."

He made the order without further consultation before he pushed back his chair, grinned and stood up. "I thought it best to order straight away. First things first, eh? But now, it might be an idea to introduce ourselves. I'm Ralph

Penbury, otherwise known as Rusty – you know – the red hair, et cetera!" He held out his hand. "I'm very pleased to meet you, and thank you again for making it possible for me to phone without losing my place in the queue. It was very good of you." He shook my hand vigorously.

"Not at all!" I cried, laughing, because he spoke with such comic gravity. "I'm Gwendoline Atkins, otherwise known as Gwen."

"Well, Miss Gwendoline Atkins, otherwise known as Gwen, may I know a little more about you? In India, if you walk more than seven paces with another person, it makes you a companion, and gives you some rights of friendship – did you know that?"

I looked up with delight. "Do you know India?"

"I was born there," said Ralph. "Lived there till I was six, in Lucknow. Then of course, was ditched into school here. It quite broke my heart. But we're not meant to say that, are we? Got to be strong, little soldiers for the empire! But I'll never forget India. It's the land of my birth, my home; and I'll always remember the stories my ayah used to tell me. Can't wait to go back!"

"But that's the same as me," I cried in amazement. "I was born there too – Dehra Dune actually. I was lucky not to be sent over when I was four or five, but there was a good school in Mussoorie, up in the foothills of the Himalayas. Then my father was posted to Poona. I was eleven before they brought me and my younger brother over to England. My older brother, Eric, came over here much earlier – and now – he's joined the air force. I was just getting to know him all over again when . . ." I trailed away, suddenly wanting to cry.

"Mr Hitler's somewhat upset my plans too," interjected Ralph quickly, enabling me to gulp back my emotions. "I have just had a year doing medicine at Edinburgh, and had all these plans to return to India to be a doctor when I had qualified. But now I'm going to join up. It's going to be all hands on deck, I reckon. That's why I'm here in London. I'm joining the navy. Always did love the sea. Any idea how you will spend the war?"

"I had been planning to go to university," I replied. "Wanted to read History, but decided to postpone and do a Red Cross training course. More useful in the circumstances, don't you think?"

And so, we talked and talked and talked about India, managing to sip tea and eat the scones and teacakes in the miniscule gaps in between. Then we walked and walked, enclosed in our own bubble, impervious to the agitation all around us. We took a bus to Hampstead Heath and walked some more, and talked as if we had known each other all our lives.

"It's very noble of you – I'm sure your mother would say 'rash' – to be walking alone with a strange man who you've only known a couple of hours," murmured Ralph. "I'm very grateful, you know. I couldn't have borne this terrible day on my own. I've only been in London a day or two and don't know anyone."

"I too was dreading the day alone," I confessed. "My roommate Dodo – my best friend from school – we share digs, but Lord knows where she is, and what with me failing to talk to my aunt and uncle on the phone, I was feeling very sorry for myself. Sometimes you just have to follow your instinct – and if you're Jack the Ripper, then you're very clever at covering it up."

We both laughed – and it felt comfortable and unforced. From our high point on the heath, we stared out across London and tried to imagine what war would mean to our capital.

"She's a magnificent city, isn't she?" commented Ralph. "Not beautiful like Paris, but with such strength and energy."

"From here, she looks indestructible," I said.

"Let's hope so."

"Isn't it amazing," I pointed at the sky, "how this morning was a perfect summer with not a cloud in the sky. But look how murky and dark it has become; it feels quite sultry. I think it's going to rain." Even as I spoke, we heard a rumble of distant thunder.

"War drums! We'd better head back," said Ralph, taking my elbow and guiding me across the gloomy heath and back to the bus stop.

It was as if the heavens now reflected our anxiety. The sky was turning a strange yellow, and getting darker all the time, and the thunder rolled ever closer with distant vivid forks of lightning.

"My God!" exclaimed Ralph. "Has the war started

already?" Even from this distance, we could hear sirens wailing, and the clanging bells of police and fire services. "We'd better hurry, before the blackout. I hope you know where your nearest shelters are."

Never did a storm seem more ominous than now. Before our eyes, it seemed that London was sinking like a huge liner into an ocean of darkness, as the thunderous skies blotted out the afternoon. Night fell early; our first night of war, our first night of fear, wondering if all those preparations which had been made throughout the past year, would come into play.

The blackout had started two days before. No street lamps, no vehicle lights, no interior lights of any description were to be glimpsed from outside, whether domestic or commercial. Notices on billboards had appeared all over the country with instructions that every single building was blacked out with black curtains or black paint. From now on, we could expect bombs to fall, air-raid sirens to make our blood run cold; from now on, we would be creeping down to the shelters in complete darkness with whimpering children and stumbling adults and all with the dread that perhaps this time, the Germans would be strong, enough to invade our islands.

We arrived back at Leicester Square. The sirens had stopped. Ralph held my elbow. I liked it; I liked feeling close. I liked feeling another human being breathing beside me, transferring his breath into me through his fingers. There was a great murmuring of a populace as they shuffled along in the darkness. Only the piercing tring-tring of bicycle bells reminded everyone that it was light that alerted the enemy, not sound.

The first drops of rain fell heavily. Clusters of people grouped together, talking in distracted whispers. The dark shapes of trucks rolled by, piled high with sandbags for stacking in doorways, and crowded with personnel. War was going to affect us all – and bombs wouldn't discriminate.

Every now and then, great flashes of lightning illuminated the sky as Ralph walked me to my door. He said my name softly – "Gwen!" – and removed his hand from my elbow. Before I quite realised that this was goodbye, he tipped his hat and took my hand. He held it for a moment, before it turned into a handshake. "Thank you for sharing this day with me. I'll never forget it. I join my ship tomorrow."

"Oh no!" I couldn't help my cry of dismay.

"Watch out for bombs," he murmured, then doffed his hat, and hurried away to be almost instantly swallowed up in the black void.

I felt an unreasonable sense of desolation and abandonment. I stood awhile, just staring, as though my whole life and everyone I had ever known had been sucked away with him into a drizzly void. I turned to climb the stairs. Mrs Antrobus's door was ajar – and I glimpsed her, sitting in the gloom, almost exactly where I had left her hours earlier. The glow of her cigarette stub hung in the darkness. Her curtains were wide open.

I stepped into her room. "Are you all right, Mrs Antrobus? Shall I draw your curtains for you? Don't want those blackout wardens to see your cigarette!" It was raining hard now.

"Did you hear the thunder?" she said. "I thought it was them bombs going off already!"

"No, Mrs Antrobus. We'll hear the sirens if the bombers come." I drew her blackout curtains, pinning them together with a couple of safety pins, then turned on the light.

She blinked, and I saw the photograph album still lying across her knees. A pyramid of cigarette stubs in the ashtray beside her looked like a miniature city in ashes.

"Are you sure you'll be all right?"

She nodded sadly. "Yes, ducky. Your friend's back."

"Call me if you need anything," I cried, already out of the door and dashing upstairs to find Dodo.

Our door was also open. I burst in. "Dodo?"

I saw her outline in the gloom. She too hadn't closed the curtains and was sitting on the sofa in the dark as if turned to stone.

"Dodo!" I cried again.

She looked up at me, and suddenly came alive, as if some puppeteer had shaken all her strings. She got unsteadily to her feet. "Where the hell have you been? Haven't you heard? They've gone and done it. We're at war, Gwen! It's war! And where were you? Sipping tea with your church friends?" She was babbling, and I wondered if she'd had too much to drink.

"Dodo! For God's sake," I cried. "You were asleep in bed when I left for church. I rushed back for Chamberlain's broadcast, but you'd already upped and gone. No note, nothing." I ran to the windows and drew the curtains tightly before turning on the light.

"Oh heavens, Gwen, I'm sorry," moaned Dodo. "It's Charles! He's joined up." She burst into tears. "I'll die if anything happens to him!" And she collapsed back on to the sofa, weeping.

We sat a long time together. If Dodo was weeping outside, I was weeping inside. What on earth was going to happen to us?

As the storm broke over London with loud thunderclaps and torrential rain, I said, "Dodo, it's obvious what we have to do. We must join up like Noor, and Charles; like my brother Eric, and like Ralph."

Dodo stopped crying. "Who's Ralph?"

As I went into the kitchen and to prepare some supper, I told her about Ralph.

That very evening, as thunder shook London, the BBC reported that a German U-30 submarine had sunk a British passenger ship, *Athenia,* in the Bay of Biscay. She was carrying over a thousand refugees, mostly women and children. One hundred and seventeen were killed.

The captain later said it was a mistake.

"We'll join up tomorrow," said Dodo.

CHAPTER 21

Meeting Max

Dodo was dreaming.

It started well. She was playing Juliet on stage at the Old Vic. She felt the swish of her silk costume, the smell of paint and make-up, the warmth of stage lights, the mysterious throbbing darkness of the auditorium stretching away into infinity. She felt ecstatic; she was doing what she had always wanted to do: act. She was playing the part she had always wanted to play, and doing it well. But suddenly there were sounds rolling in through the darkness from the audience: a low whispering, growling sound which grew and grew into a roar. The audience started booing, louder and louder. Voices were yelling at her, "Traitor, traitor! Hitler lover! Get off the stage!"

Dodo woke up shaking, whimpering and mortified. She stared into the pitch darkness. Everything had gone horribly wrong. One minute, she had been with her best friends, Gwen and Noor – the next, everything had changed.

On 4 September, the day after war was declared, Dodo and Gwen had heroically joined up, even though Gwen had a place at university, and Dodo had been admitted to RADA. But they agreed, such ambitions should be put on hold. Like Noor, they too would join up.

Gwen had only one thought: to fly aeroplanes. The army was her best chance. She might at least learn to service planes. "You know how mad I am about them. I may get a chance to fly," she said excitedly.

Dodo wasn't sure where to go. "I don't just want to be a general dogsbody. That's all they think women are good for – typing and making tea. But RADA can wait! I'll join the army too."

Both went for interviews.

A week later, each received an official brown envelope with a Home Office stamp on it. Mrs Antrobus was awestruck. "That's patriotism if ever I saw it," she cried, giving them both a smacking great kiss.

"No more than your two boys," said Gwen, warmly returning her hug. "We've all got to do our bit."

They had opened their letters upstairs in their flat. Like Noor, Gwen was taken on by the ATS, like Noor. But Dodo gave a cry of mortification.

"Rejected!" she wailed. "They've turned me down!"

Gwen tore the letter from her hand. "That can't be right."

But the letter stated quite clearly that because Dodo's parents were still on enemy territory, she couldn't enlist until all security issues had been investigated.

"Oh Dodo!" Gwen was aghast. "I'm so sorry. That's really mean."

All over Britain, so-called enemy aliens were being rounded up. But Dodo's British parents were being treated as enemy aliens in Germany, and enemy sympathisers by their own country. "Merely a formality," her parents reassured her, after a desperate phone call on a bad line. When all procedures had been gone through, they would soon be home. "Not to worry, sweetie!"

"Then you'll be able to apply again," Gwen was sure.

But Dodo worried. She knew – and her dreams confirmed it – that she felt guilty and confused because her own parents really did admire Hitler, and that they were Nazi sympathisers in thought, if not in deed. 'Nazi sympathisers'; the term was chilling.

"What will you do with me and Noor away?" Gwen was concerned. "You can't stay in London on your own." And she had begged Dodo to go to Wales and stay with Aunt Madge and Uncle Harold.

"No offence, Gwenny Penny, I love your aunt and uncle, but I'd die being so far from London," Dodo had declared. "I'll stay on here in Orange Street, and carry on with my course at RADA. I'm a big girl now, aunty! Though I'll miss you like hell!"

But after Gwen left, Dodo did indeed miss her like hell,

wishing she was there to confide in and advise. And she hardly heard from Charles at all.

With a deep breath, Dodo bucked herself up and leaped out of bed. She unpinned the blackout curtains and let in the grey dawn light. At least RADA had stayed open. There was to be a casting audition that morning for a part in 'Lady Windemere's Fan', an Oscar Wilde play. She went out on to the landing and peered over the banister. The shared bathroom on the lower landing was vacant, so she tossed in her towel and inserted her three pennies for hot water. The geyser choked and steamed but washed away her gloom and the hateful dream.

After swallowing a slice of toast and a cup of tea, she went downstairs to where her bicycle was propped in the hallway.

Mrs Antrobus popped out and nodded inquisitively at the letter rack. "Got a letter, I see Miss Brid-ges-Smi-th." She always relished extending Dodo's surname as far as it would go. "From Switz . . . er . . . land." She extended that too. "Got friends there, have you?"

"Yes," said Dodo with ultra sweetness, though it wasn't true, and she had no idea who had written to her from Switzerland.

"If you don't need them yourself, could I have the stamps? My boys are great stamp collectors."

"I'll give them to you later." Dodo stuffed the letter into her jacket pocket and wheeled the bike out into the bright sunlight. Thank God it wasn't raining. "Bye, Mrs Antrobus!" And she pedalled off muttering, "Nosey Parker!" under her breath.

She cycled hard until she reached Bloomsbury Square. Then, laying down her bike on the grass, she sat on a park bench and slit open the envelope. The letter was from her mother with an added note from her father. It was dated 9 September 1939, and it was now the end of October.

Darling Dodo,

We can't believe that Chamberlain declared war. Chamberlain is just a ridiculous, little man compared to Hitler. We do hope you haven't done anything silly like joining up with Gwen.

We are now in Zurich. All the British were advised to leave Germany immediately, so here we are until we are free to go back to England. There's some paperwork to deal with.

We do so wish you were with us, but I suppose RADA is where you want to be. Better there, out of trouble training to be an actress.

I'm sure you will be pleased to know that Charles's parents, Mavis and John Brandon, both say you must treat them as your own parents, and that you are welcome to stay with them in Ramsgate any time. They are very fond of you. So is Charles. I think he's a bit besotted, don't you? Nice boy.

We don't like the idea of you living alone now that Gwen and Noor have moved on. (Whatever happened to that little Jewish friend of yours? Vera, was it?)

Dodo cringed to hear her mother's edgy, prejudiced voice in her ears.

We have asked our friend Maxine King to look you up. She's very nice, and has kindly offered to let you have the top floor of her house, until we get back . . .

"Oh Mummy, what the hell have you done?" Dodo exclaimed out loud. She skimmed the rest of the letter with outrage. Her father had emphatically added:

Dodo, be a good girl and do as we say. Missing you very much, honeybun.

No, you aren't, thought Dodo bitterly.

Can't wait to see you.
   Your loving Papa
   xxx

She sat in tears, full of self-pity and loneliness. "Blasted war!" she moaned, wiping her nose. "Stinking, blasted war!"

It had been wonderful living in Orange Street with her best friends. Now it had all gone wrong; not just because of the war, but because of her parents and their stupid Nazi friends. And now *this*.

Anyway, who was Maxine King? Dodo had never heard

her parents mention her – but then they had so many friends. She loved her independence after years of boarding school, and absolutely did not want to move.

But the next day, on returning from RADA, Mrs Antrobus popped her head out at the sound of Dodo's key turning in the front door. "Oh, Miss Bridges-Smith! So glad you're back. You have a visitor." And she opened her door further to let Dodo into her rooms.

Dodo was dumbstruck. A tall woman stood there: a charismatic presence, larger than life, filling the space, commanding attention, and seeming to enhance even her landlady's brown, dull, unprepossessing space.

She was smartly dressed in a yellow, black, and red checked suit, with red leather gloves, and a hat with a pheasant's feather. She was not young, yet had the tanned gauntness of someone used to a lot of physical exercise and fresh air. She could have been in her forties. Her skin was finely wrinkled, although that was probably a result of outdoor weathering more than age. Dodo looked up into sharp sapphire blue eyes which returned her stare with unblinking scrutiny as if, at a glance, she knew everything about her. Dodo felt disconcerted.

"I am Maxine King." Her voice was tobacco rich. "I believe your parents have told you about me. I've heard so much about you." Removing her glove, she extended her hand. Dodo stepped back but shook the outstretched fingers.

"I'm so pleased we meet at last," said Maxine King. Was that a shred of a foreign accent in the gushing, breathy voice?

Dodo glanced at Mrs Antrobus, but she just stood rubbing her hands subserviently on her overalls.

"How do you do, Miss . . . Mrs . . ." Dodo stumbled.

She laughed. "*Mrs* King. Maxine King. But just call me Max. I was such a tomboy when I was young and made everyone call me Max! So, it stuck even though I decided that being a woman was all right after all. May we go up to your room? I've held up Mrs Antrobus far too long."

Dodo obediently led the way upstairs.

While Dodo made her tea, Max lit up a cigarette and chatted like an old friend. She didn't accept the offer to sit down, but followed Dodo around the flat and into the kitchen, as if checking her out. Dodo was now sure there was an accent, although she didn't dare ask. But when Mrs. King told her that her husband was an Ulsterman, Dodo thought – oh that's it! Must be an Irish accent!

"We used to live in Belfast," Max continued, "where my husband had a business; something to do with manufacturing aircraft parts. We have two girls – you must meet them – Lotte and Caroline. But we decided to move to London as Peter's business grew. We love London, and we love the opera and theatre. It's where I met your parents. Such lovely people. But I'm afraid you won't meet Peter; he's in America at the moment on business. Even war doesn't make him stop."

Dodo brought in the tea tray, and set it down.

Max sat next to her on the sofa and leaned towards her a little too closely. "Tell me all about yourself. How exciting that you want to be an actress and studying at RADA! You must be talented. They don't let in anybody."

Dodo changed her mind. That slight guttural roll of the 'r's in Max King's pronunciation of RADA didn't sound Irish.

Dodo poured. Max leaned over to tap her collapsing ash into the ashtray on a side table. Dodo solicitously moved the side table round nearer to Max, then sat herself down in the armchair opposite. She told Max about her course; about how there was a shortage of men as so many had all joined up. But still, she was learning so much, and studying all the major roles in theatre literature – male and female.

"I love it, but it's mainly tights for movement, scripts for learning, and bone props between your teeth for diction!" she exclaimed with a pealing laugh. "Of course, I really wanted to join up. But they wouldn't have me because my parents were in Germany when war broke out." She stopped, swallowing hard against that feeling of rejection.

"I know about that," Max murmured almost to herself. She leaned forward and patted Dodo's hand. "But maybe you are where you should be; where you always wanted to be – training to be an actress. After all, the war has barely started, and it may just fizzle out, and you won't have wasted all that time on boring drill, and being a general dogsbody. No, dear girl! I think you are doing the right thing." She smiled reassuringly. "But your parents . . ."

Dodo braced herself as Max subtly changed tack.

"Your parents are unhappy about you living alone. It's not wise for a young woman, and you are far too young to take on that kind of responsibility."

Dodo felt a surge of resistance; she knew what was coming.

"So dear girl," continued Max. "Your parents have agreed that you must move in with us as soon as possible. Tomorrow if you like?"

Must?

"Oh Max!" Dodo lied brightly. "That is *so* kind of you, but what my parents don't know yet is that Griggy, my nanny – Mrs Grigson – might be able to come and live with me for a few weeks. That would be *so* much better, as, here, I'm within cycling distance of RADA. Of course, if Griggy can't come, that would be different. May I let you know? The war has disrupted the post, otherwise I'm *sure* I would have heard by now."

Max's blue eyes narrowed. She got up and walked to the window. "I really think your parents' wishes should come first," she said sternly.

"Griggy has always been like another mother to me. She's been my nanny since I was born, so I'm sure my parents wouldn't object if they knew it was a possibility," replied Dodo in a steady voice.

Max turned abruptly. "Very well," she said, slightly

affronted. She then softened and smiled. "Now look! I want to invite you over for a little lunch party on Saturday. Dinner would have been so much better, but with the blackout, it's not really easy – unless of course you stay overnight?"

"Oh, lunch is fine, thank you!" cried Dodo cheerfully and emphatically, in case Max changed it to dinner.

"There'll be other people, some of whom know your parents. Oh – and Roger, my nephew," added Max. "His health stopped him from joining up, but he got a job in some Home Office department doing German translation and I thought you and he would get on like a house on fire. Please come!"

"I . . . I'd love to. Thank you," said Dodo, cursing her inability to say no, and feeling the woman's claws pressing a little deeper into her skin. "What time?"

"Roger will fetch you in his car. Around twelve noon. Is that convenient?"

"Oh – but I can easily take the bus or cycle!" protested Dodo.

"Tch tch!" said Max. "Don't want you finding your way unaccompanied – not these days. I mean what if there's an air-raid alert? We are at war after all. Now, I must be off!" She embraced Dodo, pressing her hard to her bony chest, and scooping up her handbag, gloves, and brolly, made for the door.

Dodo stood on her upstairs landing, listening to the click clack of heels as Max descended. When she reached the bottom, Mrs Antrobus emerged. Dodo peered discreetly between the banisters.

"Is she moving out then?" asked Mrs Antrobus in a low voice.

"She's asked her nanny to move in with her. Did you know?" asked Max.

"Hasn't said a word to me about it."

"Her parents want her to live with me, but she seems unwilling. Well, she may have to if her nanny doesn't come. Here's my card. Drop me a postcard, or phone any time. Goodbye Mrs Antrobus."

The front door closed. Dodo silently withdrew into the flat in case Mrs Antrobus spotted her. She felt outraged. How dare Max King discuss her affairs with her landlady? She peered from her window at the street below to be sure Max was really leaving, and was relieved to see her striding away towards Leicester Square.

A man over the road got up from a bench and opened his umbrella, although it hadn't been raining. Dodo watched for a moment with casual curiosity as he then refolded it and, using it as a walking stick, strolled towards Leicester Square behind Max. But her mind was composing a letter to Griggy, so she barely gave it a second thought.

Darling Griggy,
I won't beat about the bush. Gwen and Noor have both joined up, and Vera's in Paris, so at the moment, I'm living alone in our London flat. I don't think I told you that I tried to join up too, but

they refused me because of Mummy and Daddy. I've been doing fine on my own, but my parents want me to move in with friends of theirs, Maxine and Peter King, and I really don't want to. Have you heard of them? I hadn't. Mrs King has just called in. (She made me call her Max.) She wanted me to move to them tomorrow – would you believe! She's very bossy, but I put her off by saying I had asked you to come and stay with me. But she'll be back.

So what I'm asking Griggy is, PLEASE consider coming to live with me here for a couple of weeks – at least till my mother and father return? PLEASE Griggy, save me! Stay with me awhile, if it's not too horribly inconvenient, until I sort things out? I just don't want to go and live with strangers. She may be a vampire for all I know!

Write back like the wind,

Your loving,

Dodo xxxx

PS Anyway – I'm not totally alone. There's always my landlady, Mrs Busybody Antrobus downstairs, who watches every coming or going.

Holding her shoes in her hand, Dodo crept soundlessly downstairs, let herself out, and raced for the letterbox.

Griggy replied like the wind. I'll be with you by next Monday. That was only five days away.

"God bless you, God bless you, God bless you!" Dodo almost wept, and immediately sent a postcard to Noor asking if Griggy could use her room for the moment, knowing in advance the probability of her answer. She dropped a further postcard to Max, and smiled as she did so.

CHAPTER 22

The Aryan Fellowship

The doorbell rang at exactly twelve noon on Saturday. It was autumn now and distinctly cooler. Dodo had chosen to wear a green, long-sleeved, thin woollen dress, with a black velvet neck, and black court shoes. If these were friends of her parents, then she should dress more formally. She put on her camel brown coat, and a green beret which matched her dress, with tan leather gloves, and her red umbrella. Not forgetting the compulsory gas mask.

She peeped out of the window. The branches of the plane trees were almost stripped bare. Gold, yellow and purple leaves were gently spiralling down. The sky was the brightest of blues, but even so, the chill outside had penetrated the loose-fitting sash windows. A bright yellow and black MG was parked outside, with its hood back in the midday sunshine. She wasn't sure whether to feel excited or nervous about the driver she was about to meet.

Turning off the gas fire, she went downstairs and

opened the front door just as the bell went. Mrs Antrobus nosily opened her door as well.

"Hello! Are you . . . ?" Dodo asked, expecting someone looking frail and in ill health, and, instead, surprised to see a jolly, broad, plumpish, rosy-cheeked young man beaming at her.

"I'm Roger." He had a flop of light brown hair beneath a green plaid driver's cap, and looked as if he had squeezed himself into a brown and fawn tweed jacket. He exuded a gentlemanly charm as he doffed his cap and bowed. "Miss Bridges-Smith, I presume?"

"Yes," agreed Dodo, smiling back. "I'm Dorothy – though everyone calls me Dodo."

The Kings' apartment was a grand affair, full of plush furnishing, with thick flowery satin curtains that hung from tall windows overlooking a garden square. Even the blackout curtains were beautifully made. There were rich carpets on shining, oak parquet floors, and gilt-framed English landscapes on the walls. In a bay window stood a shining black grand piano covered with a deep, orange chenille throw, and a large vase of freshly cut flowers on top.

A young man hovered over a gramophone, obviously in charge of the music. A record of sparkly dance music was playing: a solo clarinet displayed tuneful acrobatics, and a rhythmic trumpeter set the feet tapping. Guests jigged around together. The atmosphere was more that of a night club than a lunch party.

"Hey Max!" someone called out. "Tell your young man to change the music. Too Jewish sounding, eh? It grates on my ears."

There was a trill of laughter. Dodo stiffened in astonishment.

"Oh *Gott*!" laughed Max and waved at the boy. "Put on a Zarah Leander," she called.

The boy dutifully took off the 'Jewish-sounding' music, riffled through a pile of records and extricated one from its sleeve. He rapidly rewound the handle of the gramophone, and placed the needle on to the surface of the record.

"Aryan enough for you?" inquired Max with a laugh, as Zarah Leander's husky voice coiled its way into the blue haze of cigarette smoke and the dancing changed mood.

"That's better," shouted Roger.

"Some wine, madam?"

A maid offered Dodo a silver tray bearing glasses of Reisling. Others homed in on her, bearing platters of little sausages on sauerkraut, and finger-picking crêpes stuffed with cheese.

"Ah! Dearest Dodo," exclaimed Max loudly across the room. "So good you have come. How nice you look. *Sehr sehr schöne, nicht wahr!*"

Heads turned, and Dodo blushed. She could have been in one of the drawing rooms of Munich, rather than in central London. Max had spoken German – *schöne*. Was it a *German* accent she had detected before?

Max clasped her arm as if she owned her. "Come! Let me introduce you to some of my friends. They are also your *parents'* friends, so you must consider them your friends too. Lady Carter!" She hailed a tall, angular, austere woman, smoking a cigarette on the end of a long ivory cigarette holder. "You must meet Dorothy Bridges-Smith – Veronica and Anthony's girl!"

Introductions were made and pleasantries exchanged. Still firmly holding her arm, Max whirled Dodo round the room, introducing her to a lord and lady here, an honourable there, and even a Rumanian princess from Bucharest. The accents were English, of the highest order.

"Roger! Dear boy!" someone drawled. "You're in the know. We're at war – but we'd hardly know it. What on earth are the British up to?"

"That sinking of the *Royal Oak* was a rum deal. Doesn't look like England is ready for war at all!"

Dodo remembered the headlines. Earlier in October, a German U-boat had sunk a British warship, and everyone thought war had started. But it hadn't; not properly. Not in England.

"Sorting out their armaments I expect," chortled another.

"Bit late, I'd say! The Germans are miles ahead of us. Armed to the teeth."

"The whole world lags behind Germany!" quipped an English voice. "Here, we're barely ready to gather the harvest."

"You British are behaving like dolts; *idioten*!" That was German. "But your government will realise their mistake and make a deal. You mark my words. They'll wish they had agreed a peace deal as soon as they see the might of the German army. Poland is dying in front of their eyes; serves them right; damned foolish for anyone to think the British will lift a finger to help those lower orders – Slavs, gypsies, and Jews. Anyway – what weapons have the British got: ploughs and scythes and farm horses?"

"They're counting on the Americans to get them out of trouble."

"I wouldn't bank on it," drawled another English voice: aristocratic and authoritative. Everyone turned to look at a tall, stooping, sleek, man with dark brown hair slicked back and parted down the middle, and thick horn-rimmed spectacles. "The Americans don't want to be drawn into another European war." He wandered up to Dodo like a swan stretching out its neck for attention. "Max, dear! I don't think you've introduced me to this young woman?" He had an indolent voice, in contrast to his eyes, which were penetrating.

"Oh, Hubert! Yes – you must meet Dorothy Bridges-Smith. She's Veronica and Anthony's daughter," enthused Max. "Dorothy, this is Sir Hubert March, an under-secretary in Parliament. He is working so hard to bring peace between us and Germany."

Sir Hubert's grip was too tight. Between him and Max, Dodo felt imprisoned.

To her relief, he let go after he had murmured, "How do you do, Miss Bridges-Smith?"

"Dorothy's going to be touring England this winter, entertaining the troops and factory workers, aren't you dear?" cooed Max, as if she was proudly showing off one of her daughters.

Feeling more confident, Dodo engaged in small talk about RADA, and how they were preparing for a Christmas show.

"I hope we'll see more of you, Miss Bridges-Smith," said Sir Hubert. "Can you bring her to Fotherington Hall, to one of our concert parties, Max?"

"What a splendid idea," exclaimed Max. "And now, Dodo – better get you back to Roger." The Zara Leander record had given way to Glen Miller, and people were tapping and jogging again. "Dance with her, Roger! You're both young, and you've got to enjoy yourselves despite what's going on in the world."

Roger was a good dancer. Although Dodo knew the basic steps, he was an expert, and whirled her around, gliding her across the room, and making her laugh as he tipped her this way and that like a pair of professionals. After a while, he slowed it down so that they could chat as they bobbed gently to the music.

"I see Max has introduced you to Sir Hubert March."

"Do you know him?" asked Dodo.

"He's very keen on Anglo-German relations. In fact, he founded the Aryan Fellowship. Haven't your parents mentioned it? We meet about once a month to try and oil the wheels, you know. We have lectures about Schiller and Goethe, and concerts of German music."

"Why is it called the Aryan Fellowship?"

"Because we believe Germans and the English – most of us anyway – come from the same ethnic roots as the Aryans, from thousands of years ago. We share the same stock and ethnicity. We believe evolution has advanced us beyond other races."

Dodo murmured inaudibly. Roger spoke with such panache she wasn't sure if he was joking.

"You should come to one of our gatherings and see for yourself. They have talks and recitals. If you'd like to go, I'll take you. They hold them at Sir Hubert's place in the country."

"Yes Sir Hubert mentioned the parties at Fotherington Hall now."

"Oh, you've been invited already, have you?"

"More a suggestion than an invitation," replied Dodo with a laugh.

"They are lunchtime affairs these days, as people need to get back before the blackout. I could drive you, if you decide to accept," said Roger. "It's quite a way out in the country."

Dodo laughed self-consciously. "That's terribly kind of you but I'm not sure that I can. In any case," she dropped her voice to a theatrical whisper, "they might not find me Aryan enough. I'm told my nose looks a little too Jewish."

Roger laughed uproariously. "I hear you want to be an actress?" he said, changing the subject.

"Yes – I love the theatre. It's always been my dream to act. That's why I'm at RADA."

"Max tells me that you and your fellow actors will be touring the bases to cheer up the soldiers?" said Roger approvingly. "How lucky to be doing what you love." He sounded wistful.

"Nothing's been organised yet, and it still hardly feels like war," said Dodo. "But yes – that would make me feel useful." She was aware of Roger studying her closely. "What about you? Are you joining up?"

"Not exactly," he answered a little evasively. "I've a bit of a dicky heart." He smiled, and patted his left top pocket. "But I do my bit. I work for a government department publishing house, translating messages et cetera. My German is good, so they thought I was more use to them in civvy street."

Max had wandered over with their glasses, and was hovering close by as if eavesdropping. "Isn't it wonderful, Roger, that these drama students will be giving up their precious spare time to go around bases entertaining the troops?" she said now as she handed them back their drinks. "And factories too, didn't you say, Dodo? What good practice for you. Do let me know if I can ever attend an event. I'd love to see you perform, dear!"

Suddenly, someone brought out an accordion and began to play the kind of knee-slapping dance music Dodo remembered from parties in Munich. The mood rose, becoming almost raucous, with slapping thighs and knees, in time to the music. Roger and Dodo were soon clapping and whooping along with everyone else.

"Very German," yelled Roger. "Don't suppose Churchill would approve!"

"Not sure I do either!" panted Dodo, giggling from a mixture of wine and feverish rhythms. "Better not dance like that for the soldiers!"

Dodo was pretty tiddly by the time Roger said, "Well, better get you home before the blackout."

"Oh . . ." Dodo mumbled. "Is it getting dark already?"

"We have an hour. Let's get going." And Roger brought her coat.

Dodo thanked Max for "*such* a lovely lunch. I had *such* a good time," her voice slurring a little.

"You must come again! We love having these get-togethers, don't we Roger?" gushed Max. "*Auf wiedersehen!*"

"Absolutely!" agreed Roger jovially.

At Leicester Square, Roger parked the car and said, "We still have about fifteen minutes before sundown. How about a cocktail? Look, there's a place open over there."

Later, Dodo only had a blurred recollection of their

cocktails. She knew she was drinking more than she should and babbling stupidly, telling him all about her friends: Noor, Vera, and Gwen, and what they were doing. When finally, Roger escorted her out and back to Orange Street, it was pitch black, and she was barely steady on her feet. She felt Roger's hand firmly on her arm as she opened the door.

Thank goodness for nosey Mrs Antrobus, who appeared the instant she heard Dodo's key.

"That you, Miss Bridges-Smith?" she exclaimed. "You're back at last! I was just beginning to get worried."

"Sorry Nosey P— I mean, Mrs Antrobus. I'm afraid I've drunk too much."

"It's my fault. We did have rather too much of a good time," said Roger. "We have to live for the moment. Who knows what tomorrow will bring, eh? I'll call round in the morning, Dodo, to make sure you're all right."

"Don't go to that trouble," mumbled Dodo. "Griggy's coming and then I'll be in good hands."

"Thank the Lord for that," muttered Mrs Antrobus. "And you, young sir, better go careful in this blackout. Good job they painted the kerbs white."

"I will, Mrs Antrobus," Roger called, disappearing into the blackness.

Dodo started up the stairs, clambering on her hands and knees.

"Careful how you go now," cautioned Mrs Ambrose.

"Nearly there," Dodo burped. Groping through the

darkness, with just a cloudy night sky casting ghostly slivers of light through a skylight, she reached the bathroom on the landing and pushed open the door in time to vomit into the lavatory bowl.

CHAPTER 23

Griggy Saves The Day

D odo set her alarm for 11 a.m. to give her enough time to get dressed and meet Griggy at Victoria bus station at 2 p.m. She would have slept till God knows when if the alarm hadn't gone off, bringing her awake with as much brutality as a bucket of water. She still felt queasy after last night. Not daring to lie back on her pillow, she threw off the blankets and braced herself against the cold morning air in the unheated room.

She washed and dressed, then checked Noor's room, which Griggy would use, and gave herself a pat on the back for remembering a pretty bunch of flowers she had bought on the street which now stood in a suitable, dark blue vase on the mantelpiece. The bed was made up with one of Noor's Indian bedspreads and looked pretty. Noor's room was always pretty anyway.

At 12.30 she glanced round the room for a final check. Housekeeping was not her forte. Snatching up her Swiss stamps for Mrs Antrobus – she was bound to ask again – Dodo put on her coat, hat, gloves, brolly, grabbed her gas mask, and stepped out on to the landing.

Out came Mrs Nosey Parker as Dodo reached the bottom.

"Good morning, Miss Bridges-Smith! Off to fetch your nanny? That'll be nice. I look forward to meeting her. Hope her bus is on time."

One day, Dodo thought, she would come and go by the drainpipe at the back. Mrs Antrobus was like a prison warden. "Here are the stamps I promised you, Mrs Antrobus!" she said aloud.

Mrs Antrobus beamed with huge pleasure, and Dodo felt guilty about thinking such mean thoughts. As she headed towards Trafalgar Square to find a bus to Victoria, she noticed the same man she had seen when Max had visited: sitting on a bench over the road, same hat, same brolly, with his head in a newspaper. He obviously lived round here. Lord Nelson came into view at the top of his column as Dodo hurried along, gazing down Whitehall. How noble and confident he looked; so reassuring. The bus stop was in Cockspur Street.

It was funny to think they were at war. Even though Charles had dropped her a card to say his regiment has been moved to Belgium, there still seemed little to be overly alarmed about.

"Charles." Dodo breathed his name out loud. Her stomach lurched briefly with how much she missed him.

The last time he'd been on leave, he had kissed her full on the lips as if to plant a seal on their relationship. It had felt different from all the bumptious hugs and squeezes he had done before, when she had met him secretly out of school to go to the theatre or a cinema, and they had often got a bit tipsy and silly. This time he was stone-cold sober, and had held her closely, still and long; almost with foreboding. "Darling," he had murmured, "I'm really fond of you, but I don't think this is the right time to start making plans. Let's get this blasted war over with, shall we?" When she had murmured, "I love you Charles," he hadn't replied, but just kissed her again, and they had clasped each other very tightly.

She had relived that moment over and over again, but wondered if he really did love her at all.

CHAPTER 24

The Phony War

I'm at an ATS training camp. It's harsh. I'm here with twenty other women for six weeks.

They're determined to turn us into battle-hardened combatants. So, it's drill every morning come rain or come shine, marching up and down till our feet blister, and our muscles scream. Left right, left right, up and down, round and round, being bawled at by sergeant majors. "No talking, chins up, shoulders back, eyes left, eyes right!" Every yell is an order which must be obeyed at the double: marching orders to clean the latrines, scrub the floors, wash the windows: left right, left right. Instead of rifles we carry mops; march to the latrines and clean them; left right, left right; march to the kitchens to peel mountains of potatoes; left right, left right. After six weeks of this, when they've knocked off any softy, home-comfort edges, they will send us off to be trained in all those non-combatant jobs which men usually do, like transportation, truck driving, mechanical engineering – including the maintaining of aircraft. I wonder how on earth Noor coped with this.

Finally, they issue us with our khaki uniforms and all our kit, pile us into trucks, and send us off to various camps across the country.

It's November now. Nothing has really happened yet, and people even grumble, saying, "Where is the war?"

But everyone is in a state of constant readiness. Even when going into our little town where I am stationed, we never go without our gas masks, and always know where the nearest air-raid shelters are. The blackouts are hellish. Every night there is some kind of accident – whether cars, or bikes crashing into each other, or people getting knocked down crossing the road; or pedestrians tripping over pavements, or simply getting lost. Worst of all are the night wardens, who go round inspecting homes and properties to ensure the blackout. They are like little dictators; and give you hell if they see even the tiniest speck of light anywhere after dark. "Put that out!" they thunder, at the dimmest glow of a cigarette. "Want to bring them bleeding German bombs raining down?"

Needless to say, pickpockets, robbers, and rapists have a field day. Perhaps it will all go away. Nothing has happened. Perhaps everyone will come to their senses and see how ridiculous it is to have wars.

"The whole thing's phony," people jeer. "It's boredom what's killing us, not Hitler's bombs."

But you only have to go to the railway stations to see hordes of arrivals from Europe. More unaccompanied children with placards round their necks bearing their names, like the ones that had come to Barrowfield; desperate parents sending their children out into the unknown, hoping that England would take care of them, not knowing when or if they would ever see them again.

Eric is with 139 Squadron of Bomber Command. He is already in the air going out on missions. I listen to the news bulletins on the wireless. Yes, we are at war, even if they haven't yet dropped any bombs over England. British ships are being sunk at sea, the Russians have attacked Finland, the Germans have attacked Norway; that is a disaster for us, if we did but know it. Already, individual families are receiving telegrams with the news of a missing relative; the death of a father, husband or brother killed in action.

I'm glad to have joined up. Best of all is driving out on supply missions – out into the countryside. Deep inside, my foreboding is growing.

My joy at having joined up has turned to fear. Where is Eric at this moment? The airmen seem to be in the greatest danger. We occasionally arrange a phone call. He is always cheerful – but that's Eric. In one letter he writes: *When I'm up, up, in those skies, flying above the clouds,*

I feel so free, Gwenny; so liberated. Odd isn't it, when the only reason I'm up there is to protect our freedoms – but I know I'm killing people for that purpose. I feel almost guilty to find such utter joy in flying higher than the birds.

Letters from our parents in India take such a long time to arrive now that the Suez Canal is closed, and longer for me, because Dodo then has to forward them to me.

I'm feeling orphaned. I wonder about Ralph. He hasn't been out of my mind since we met. If he had been killed or wounded on one of those ships attacked in the North Sea, how would I ever know? Each time there is news of a ship being sunk, I scour *The Times* for his name among the columns of dead, wounded or missing. I wish he would drop me a card. But then, he probably never even thinks of me. Why should he? We'd only spent a few hours together.

After my initial training, I had to sit a series of written exams for the War Office so they could deploy me to the most suitable department. I was mortified to do terribly badly in my practicals. You had to have brilliant eyesight, very quick reactions and good coordination, not to mention climbing walls and swimming across rivers in full kit – and I thought I was good at sport! But then, my self-esteem rose when I was told I was being sent to the Locations Section. They had realised I was good at puzzles and problem solving. But it's classified work. I wish I could tell Uncle Harold, but I've had to sign the Official Secrets Act.

I can't tell anyone. I have already sectioned off my brain into compartments with different bits of information. My fellow trainees think I've been deployed into an administration department for Industrial Output, which is what I've told Aunt Madge and Uncle Harold – and anyone else who asks. I have to get used to lying – or rather, avoiding the truth. I hate lying, especially to my nearest and dearest. I hate this war and what it makes you do.

The Locations Section is claustrophobic work. We're stuck in a room with no windows. It's like living in a prison with locked doors and codes for keys. In fact, there are codes for everything. When troops or an expeditionary force are being flown off to France or North Africa, their kit is stamped with letters and numbers. Only a small group of officers know these destination codes; even the sailors don't know which country they have been sent to, and won't know till they land.

Then I got a shock much closer to home. Dodo was on a surveillance list. I couldn't believe my eyes when I saw her name. It wasn't the red list, which contained the names of people considered to be a major security threat, but the green list, the lowest list: the question-mark list. I'm overwhelmed with guilt. I'm spying on my best friend.

What a relief it was to hear I'd been given a few days' leave over Christmas. I went back to Orange Street first, before going to Wales. I would have time to think, and get my feelings and values in order.

Griggy's gone home for Christmas – quite happily when she knew I was coming. And I think she'd had enough of London; it made her nervous. Everyone's nervous. I almost wish the Germans would hurry up and start bombing us instead of leaving us in this uncertainty. We all seem to be in a no man's land this Christmas.

Dodo and I had a couple of days together before we parted. At the sight of her, all my fears melted away. She was my oldest, dearest friend; I was so thrilled to see her again, and she was so cheerful and upbeat about performing at factories and military bases all over England. She didn't know that I too was touring, only on a map, and I knew where she'd been. I suppose I too was an actress. I was able to chatter normally to Dodo about everything – except my secret work. I felt treacherous as she chattered to me about RADA, and how she might even go over to France or Belgium. Every now and then she would mention Peter and Max King, and make some passing reference to their nephew, Roger. I was attentive.

"Thank goodness I managed to avoid living with them," sighed Dodo. "Max is a bully in a charming, glitzy sort of way – a bit like a prima donna, ruling the roost through sheer force of personality."

"And where is her husband?" I inquired.

Dodo shrugged. "On business in America. I haven't met him yet. Do you know what Max and her friends call themselves?" She chortled. "The Aryan Fellowship! I'm invited to their New Year's Eve party in some country house or other. Thank goodness I've got those dresses we bought for Munich! Honestly darling, when I think of you slaving away down in some ghastly War Office cellar, I'm almost glad the ATS turned me down. I'm having a whale of a time."

As I listened to her burbling on about the lunch parties she went to – the high jinks, dancing, and even German slap-dancing – a suspicious worm niggled inside me, and I felt my training kicking in. Dodo, for all her worldliness, was yet such an innocent. What was this Aryan Fellowship?

"And Roger?" I asked.

"Oh Roger! Well . . ." Dodo proceeded to tell me that he came most weekends to take her out in his MG sports car. He even, occasionally, drove her to a barracks or a factory where she might be doing a performance for the troops with her fellow students. I sighed. Dodo had the knack of attracting dashing young men in fast cars.

"And what does Roger do, when he's not whirling you round London or driving you to entertain the troops?" I asked. "It's a wonder he isn't lynched, when we're all being asked to tighten our belts."

"Gwenny Penny! You're as nosey as Mrs Antrobus."

I grinned. "Oh? Is he a secret agent or a spy?"

"If only," sighed Dodo with a peal of laughter. "That would be so much more interesting. He's actually rather boring! He works in a translation department of the

Ministry of Labour or some such. He speaks fluent German, so he's always useful. But the only thing that gets him excited is this Aryan Fellowship thing!" She mimicked him: "We should learn from Germany! Hitler's doing wonders, modernising Germany with *Autobahns*! The trains run on time and . . ." she mimicked a Nazi salute – "we will save the Aryan race from being contaminated by poor blood."

The colour must have drained from my face.

"Joke, darling!" said Dodo, laughing. "Joke!"

As if on cue, there was a toot tooting outside. Dodo rushed to the window and threw it open. "Speak of the devil! It's Roger!" She waved madly. She seemed delighted to see him, even if she did find him boring.

"Are you free now?" I heard Roger shout up. "I've got three matinée tickets for 'Cinderella' at the London Coliseum. Wanna come? If so, we have to leave right away."

"I've got my friend Gwen here!" Dodo called down.

"I told you – I've got *three* tickets. One for Gwen as well! You told me she'd be with you."

"Oh Gwen!" Dodo turned to me with shining eyes. "Are you up for it?"

"Of course, darling!" I cried, curious anyway to meet this Roger.

"Now look here, Gwenny," said Dodo coyly as we put on our hats and coats. "You won't go all aunty on me, will you? No political arguments with Roger. Don't go spoiling our afternoon."

"Wouldn't dream of it, Dodo," I said, somewhat icily.

But I don't think she noticed as she was already opening the door and heading downstairs.

It was wonderful! We laughed, we sang, we yelled. We were like children. "Look behind you!" We loved the spectacle: the costumes, the magic, the comedy. Then Roger suggested Grantleys for a bite to eat.

I could see why Dodo liked him. He certainly had lots to say about German pride, and the conversation over supper was a mixture of funny, odd, and disturbing – especially after two glasses of wine, and I had to bite my lip several times – such as when he said it was the loyal duty of every Aryan woman to have lots of beautiful babies to preserve the master race. Another joke? We all laughed uproariously.

"Dodo says you work in the ATS," Roger said to me.

"We're strictly on the ground typing, nursing, secretarial stuff; this and that. They give women all the boring jobs." It wasn't strictly true, and I shrugged with practised evasion. "But I'm desperate to fly, and am going to try and move across to the ATA, which would be as close as I can get to the RAF."

"Don't tell me you want to be flying spitfires in battles against German Messerschmitts?" he quipped.

"No such luck. But someone has to deliver the planes! That's why they're bound to teach us to fly. I hope one day, it will be me," I said.

"Well, you girls are certainly doing your duty to your country, eh?"

"I'm trying to persuade Gwen to join your Aryan Fellowship," giggled Dodo.

I looked at her askance. Was she serious?

"Excellent," said Roger looking me, unsmiling, straight in the eye. It flashed through my mind that we had an instant flicker of mutual suspicion of each other.

"Darling, do you mind if I leave you now and go back to the flat?" I got to my feet. "I must get my stuff together. I have an early train to Swansea tomorrow."

"I'll come with you," said Dodo, also getting up from the table.

Roger escorted us back to Orange Street. Thank goodness, he declined a nightcap and, after handshakes, and "thank yous," we let ourselves in. Mrs Antrobus had her blackout curtains firmly shut, and she didn't pop her head round the door.

"Any chance of your parents being allowed back by the new year?" I asked Dodo, as we finally sank back into our own sofa with a cup of bedtime cocoa.

"Not yet."

"What news of Charles?" I asked tentatively.

Dodo blushed fiercely. "Not sure. He's in Belgium, I think. It's hard for him to write. What about your Ralph?"

It was my turn to blush. "He's somewhere over the North Sea on patrol. Anyway, he's not *my* Ralph. We only spent about four hours together, and he's barely dropped me a couple of postcards."

Dodo put on one of her faces that always made me laugh. "Romeo and Juliet only knew each other for about a week before they got married."

"And look what happened to them!" I quipped.

We sipped our cocoa companionably.

"Isn't this war thing strange?" I murmured, suddenly serious and confidential as only best friends can be. "Somehow it changes even the way Time works: compresses it, makes us do more, in a shorter space of time than ever before. The four hours I spent with Ralph were more like four days, considering the intensity, the lack of small talk. Whatever we talked about was important; we got straight to the point – and I feel as though I know him as well as I know Eric. Well – of course I don't, but . . ." I trailed off. "Do you still care about Charles?"

"I think about him all the time," said Dodo quietly.

"And Roger?"

She threw back her head and laughed frivolously. "I don't encourage him – but as he keeps wanting to take me out for supper or dancing, I go. What else is there to do?"

"I think you're using him!" I chided – though actually, I thought the opposite.

"How? I never ask him for anything. It's terribly hard to have a social life with these blackouts and this uncertainty," Dodo pointed out. "And a girl needs a bit of fun, doesn't she? The company of a young man with a car is so useful. You should get yourself one."

I shrugged. "Just haven't met the right person."

"You're too choosy!"

"And maybe you should be a bit *more* choosy," I retorted. I wagged my finger dramatically. "You be careful, Mis Bridges-Smith. We live in a dangerous world."

"Yes, aunty," she teased.

"Dodo?" I was suddenly deadly serious. "I mean it. We're at war. What might seem normal and innocent during peace time, can be very different in war." I wanted to say, *like the Aryan Fellowship,* but I didn't. Not yet.

"Gwenny Penny!" She put her face right up to mine. "Lighten up!"

It was nearly Christmas. Noor couldn't get leave, and Dodo was due to go touring with her RADA friends. So I caught the train to Wales alone. Paddington was milling with troops being allowed Christmas leave and there was a lot of jollity, as if no one really believed in this war.

I hated leaving Dodo in the hands of Max and her friends. She saw my anxiety as I leaned out of the train window to say goodbye.

"Don't worry about me, aunty!" She squeezed my arm affectionately. "I'll be fine."

Darkness fell. With the blackout, it was like being on a

ghost train with no lights anywhere – just an astonishingly bright white moon keeping pace, casting a vast shadow of the great iron beast, pounding and hissing across the land, its clickety-clack wheels echoing through copses, over bridges, and across the fields, its whistle screaming a warning from time to time. Snow was falling across the empty, frozen fields. Like last year, it was going to be a white Christmas.

They were all there to meet me at the pitch-black station. Aunty Madge waved a white handkerchief, Uncle Harold waved his scarf, and Archie sang Gilbert and Sullivan at top speed – *"I am the very model of a model major general"* – having learned it to perfection since we'd last met. Then the shriek of the engine's whistle drowned him out as it churned its way onwards through the night. How we raced towards each other.

This time, we weren't expecting Eric. Uncle Harold thought he might be on runs over the North Sea to protect our navy. He sighed heavily. "Things are going on out there which I don't think they're telling us about."

"Are you flying Spitfires yet, Gwenny?" teased Archie. "I do hope the war lasts long enough for you and me to become fighter pilots!"

"Oh Archie, that's damned immoral," I cried, putting out my arms and whirling round him making aeroplane noises.

It was a short but jolly Christmas: just three days. But this time, I didn't mind. I was worried about Dodo, and anxious to get back to base and do some checking. I was scared that she was being drawn into something over her head. Back in my windowless cell in Wiltshire, I searched fruitlessly for information about the Aryan Fellowship. It barely took a day for me to discover that Peter King was not in America after all.

Friends or Enemies

When Dodo got back to Orange Street after touring the RADA Christmas show with her fellow students, a letter had arrived for her. It was the first letter of the New Year, 1940, and embossed with the seal of the Home Office.

Dear Miss Bridges-Smith,

You are aware that your parents, Anthony and Veronica Bridges-Smith, are unable to return to the United Kingdom while their status is being investigated.

We would like to meet you and discuss a way forward. I would appreciate it if you could come for a meeting with us at the above address at 3 p.m. on Wednesday 3 January.

Yours sincerely,

D.M.H. Brown Esq.

Dodo presented herself at the address in Baker Street on the day and time requested and rang the bell. The doorman told her Mr Brown was two flights up, and then a door on the left.

The door was opened by a stocky, military kind of man, wearing a dark brown suit with a black stripe and silver-rimmed spectacles behind which surprisingly large, saucer-like blue eyes scrutinised her. He had a sharp black moustache, almost like Hitler's, and his sleek hair seemed similarly smoothed over a balding head. He managed a slight smile as he shook her hand and indicated a chair before his desk.

In the far corner, a plump middle-aged woman sat at a small desk with a typewriter and notebook. She flashed Dodo a swift, reassuring smile.

"My name is Duncan Brown," said Mr Brown with a clipped voice as he settled into his own oak-backed swivel chair. "And you are Miss Dorothy Bridges-Smith." It was a statement not a question.

"That's right," said Dodo nervously. It felt like the start of an interrogation.

"Miss Bridges-Smith, I see your parents have been refused entry back into the United Kingdom."

"Yes," said Dodo.

Pause

"On the grounds, it seems, of having sympathies for Nazi Germany."

"I don't think that's fair at all!" exclaimed Dodo indignantly. "They have very great friends in Germany, it's true. But that doesn't make them Nazis."

"And what about you?" said Duncan Brown. "Do you have sympathy for Nazi Germany?"

"Of course not!"

"Or friends who are sympathetic?"

"No!" protested Dodo. "Well, yes. Some. Some friends of my parents think Hitler's a jolly good thing."

"Peter and Maxine King?"

Dodo suddenly realised that Mr Brown knew quite a lot about her.

"The Kings kept an eye on me at the request of my parents," she said. "But they're not *my* friends. They're *their* friends."

"And Peter and Maxine King think that Hitler's a *jolly good thing*?"

"In a way. Partly," Dodo procrastinated. "They think he's strong; a better leader than we have. He gets things done. Most Germans seem to admire Hitler a lot too. Well, maybe not the Jews." The image of the Jewish shopkeeper being beaten up in the street in Munich flashed through her mind.

"Do you have any Jewish friends?" asked Mr Brown.

"One. Vera. We were at school together. That's how I know about the way they're being treated by the Nazis. She lost her family. Dreadful."

"Has Mr Roger King met Vera?"

Dodo looked up, startled. He knew about Roger? "No. Vera returned to Paris."

"Roger is the Kings' nephew, isn't he?"

"Yes. They introduced us. Well, Max did. Her husband, Mr Peter King is in America on business."

"What kind of business?"

"I don't really know. Something to do with aircraft engineering I think."

Pause

"And what does Roger King do?" asked Mr Brown.

"He's a translator somewhere. He's bilingual in German and English." Dodo's voice trailed away, as she realised that her description sounded more like an indictment than a qualification.

"Very useful," murmured Mr Brown dryly. "What does Roger think about the Jews?"

"No idea," Dodo said. "Although he jokes about them not being of the Aryan race."

"Ah! The Aryans," said Mr Brown. "Your friends – I beg your pardon, your *parents'* friends believe in the superiority of the Aryans, do they not?"

Dodo nodded.

"Roger too?"

She shrugged.

"I imagine Roger thinks Aryans should have lots of babies to ensure the strength and continuation of their race, doesn't he, Miss Bridges-Smith?"

"Not with me, that's for sure." Dodo laughed, taking his remark as a joke, but then saw he was unsmiling.

"Would you say your parents are loyal to England?" asked Mr Brown.

Dodo flushed angrily. "Of course they are."

Pause

Mr Brown's blue eyes suddenly lifted from his notes and he stared at her as if her life depended on the answer she gave.

"Are you loyal to England?" he said.

Dodo met his eyes defiantly. "Yes. I wanted more than anything to join up. I'd be ready to die for my country."

"And Roger?"

"I can't speak for Roger. I hardly know him – except he has a dicky heart and was refused admission into the army, so he did try."

"What kind of war work will you do when this situation with your parents is settled?" asked Mr. Brown.

"I've already done a Red Cross course. As I'm sure you know, I tried to join the ATS but was stopped – by *you*, presumably," she replied with heavy irony.

"I have to remind you, Miss Bridges-Smith, we are at war with Germany. We have to know who our friends are. Sensible, wouldn't you say?"

Pause

"What if you were able to continue your drama training, but worked for the war effort too?" asked Mr Brown softly.

"How can I do that if I'm not allowed to join up?" said Dodo. "Right now, all I can do is entertain."

"Very commendable. And your friend Mrs King –"

"She's a friend of my *parents*," Dodo repeated.

"What kind of interest did Maxine King show as regards your entertaining the troops?"

Dodo pondered the question. She realised that Max had casually asked a number of what had seemed totally innocent questions: where the bases were, what was going on there; had Dodo noticed personnel movements, the location of the factories and what they produced. All had been threaded through conversation, so that it was only now, by being asked to remember, that Dodo understood what she had told her. "She was just curious," she said a little weakly.

"Curiosity killed the cat," remarked Mr Brown. He sounded almost menacing. "Are you a member of the Aryan Fellowship?"

Dodo blinked. "You know about that?"

"It's our business to know. They hold meetings in the apartment belonging to Peter and Maxine King, do they not?"

Pause

"Are you a member, Miss Bridges-Smith?"

Dodo rubbed her forehead. "I've been to a couple of their gatherings: a concert, a lecture – that sort of thing. Does that make me a member? Roger likes to take me, that's all."

"So, Roger is a member?"

"He thinks it's important to keep up cultural bonds with the Germans. Sounds to me like a very good thing," Dodo replied defensively. "Better than dropping bombs on each other!"

"Perhaps you don't understand," said Mr Brown, "but

societies such as this passionately believe that Hitler is their salvation. They are very happy to drop bombs on anyone who stands in their way. They believe that as the master race, they have a right to rule the world. This is the future they believe in, and want people like you to believe in."

His voice had got quieter, yet so intense Dodo felt it could be heard three streets away. She bowed her head. She felt her cheeks flush red, and she wanted to cry.

"Mrs Donaghue, I think we could do with a cup of tea," said Mr Brown. "Do you mind?"

The lady who had been taking notes got to her feet. "Of course, Mr Brown."

"Miss Bridges-Smith, you say you are loyal. I'm wondering what you understand by *loyalty*." His voice became suddenly conversational. Dodo looked up and found herself staring again into Mr Brown's large blue eyes, which refracted and filled the lenses of his spectacles.

"Loyalty to your parents and your parents' friends?"

"Yes. Up to a point. Without always agreeing with them."

"Can you be loyal to your parents and your country at the same time?" asked Mr Brown.

Pause

"I'm going to come to the point." He leaned forward, his eyes suddenly hard. "I remind you again: we are at war, Miss Bridges-Smith. It may not feel like it to you, but we are, and it is deadly serious. Your parents have been severely compromised by the company they keep; as have you."

Dodo looked into his face, which was expressionless even when he was being sarcastic. *I hate you*, she thought.

"You have already given Max King some very useful information. As she is an unashamed Nazi sympathiser, it follows that you have been giving information to the enemy, does it not?"

Dodo jumped to her feet, angrily. "How can you say that?"

"I can, Miss Bridges-Smith, and I do. Please sit down and hear me out."

He handed her a handkerchief as tears began rolling down her cheeks. She took it and sat down, feeling like a rabbit caught in a trap.

"At this very moment, there are English people – British citizens – preparing for the possible invasion of this country by Hitler," he said. "Yet your friends – your *parents'* friends – are organising themselves to create a pro-Nazi British government, a Nazi civil service, a Nazi BBC and a Nazi press. They are collecting information from every quarter that they feel will be of use to the Nazis. They are recruiting people like you: some naïve, and some passionate adherents to the idea of the master race. They are of the gravest danger to our country; do you understand?"

Dodo felt faint.

"You probably think you weren't giving them very

important information, but I assure you, my dear, it is exactly the kind of information our enemies like: locations of military bases, factories and their output. Useful targets, wouldn't you say?"

"I'm sorry," whispered Dodo. "I didn't know."

Mr Brown's stern expression suddenly shifted. "However, I think you could be of use to us."

"Really?" sniffed Dodo.

"You could report back to us from time to time about your – your *parents'* – Aryan Fellowship friends. It would be an arrangement which would be of great help to your parents, as well as to yourself. You can carry on giving the Aryan Fellowship information about your theatrical tours, but I would like you to give *me* information as well."

"What?" Dodo whispered. "How?"

"Keep a notebook, and write down every person you meet in this Aryan Fellowship. Give me their names, addresses and occupations. Anything that you hear, no matter how trivial, could be of vital use to us. Demonstrate total loyalty to them, but be working for us."

Dodo flinched. "You're asking me to spy?"

"I'm asking you to serve your country. So far, you have been helpful only to the enemy. As such, you are already a spy and a traitor."

Dodo felt the blood draining from her face, and a descending darkness. She was aware of Mrs Donaghue bending over her, saying, "Do have a cup of tea, Miss Bridges-Smith."

Pause

Dodo sipped the tea. It was hot and burned her tongue.

"By the way," Mr Brown finally continued, "you said Peter King is not in the country at the moment?"

"He's on business in America. I told you." Her voice was small; almost inaudible.

"No, Miss Bridges-Smith. Peter King is not in America. He's in Brixton prison for helping our own home-grown Nazi, the fascist leader, Oswald Mosley, to organise demonstrations, riots and insurgency."

Dodo shut her eyes.

"Do you see who you are involved with?" Mr Brown asked.

Dodo nodded.

"Do I take it you will cooperate with us?"

Dodo nodded again, unhappily. "You want me to spy on the Kings, Roger and the Aryan Fellowship."

"I do."

"And, as they want me to give *them* information too, it makes me a double agent, doesn't it?" She gave an ironic laugh.

"Whatever you like to call yourself, Miss Bridges-Smith. But the one thing that must have no double meaning at all is your loyalty. You can only be loyal to one side, not both. Are you clear about that?"

"Totally."

Mr Brown opened a drawer and pulled out a form. "This form declares that you will abide by the Official Secrets Act.

By signing it, you will be agreeing to confide in no one about your work for us. No one, Miss Bridges-Smith: not parents, boyfriends, best friends, priests, or anyone. Everything stays between you and me. If you breach these terms, it will be a criminal offence, and you could find yourself in prison. Read it please. And if you agree, then please sign it."

Dodo put down her half-full cup and took the form. She read it slowly, absorbing the information. Then she took the fountain pen he held out for her. It felt as if she was signing away her soul.

"We will itemise what sort of things we want you to do," said Mr Brown, passing the signed form to Mrs Donaghue. "You will never communicate with us. Once you leave this office, you will not come here again until this war is over. You and I will not meet again. You will be approached in the next few days and you will hear the password 'Ophelia'. You will reply 'Rosemary'. You will then be passed an envelope, in which there will be instructions about where to leave any information. We do not risk the post or the telephone. We have secret drop-off points. You will be told of them as and when. We will trust you to guard your notes scrupulously and destroy them when completed.

"We will want to hear from you every week. If you have nothing to report, just write NTR on a page, fold it into an envelope and leave it at the designated places."

"What about the Kings, and Roger?"

"Keep giving them the usual kind of information, as if nothing has changed. As an actress, Miss Bridges-Smith, this should be right up your street?" He looked at her with raised eyebrows – almost kindly.

Dodo nodded.

Mr Brown got to his feet to indicate the interview was over. "You'll get a message soon from an intermediary using the code name 'Ophelia' – for which your answer will be . . .?"

"Rosemary," whispered Dodo.

"You will be passed on to a man you will only know as the Bard. He will be your handler and trainer, and your main line of communication. Goodbye Miss Bridges-Smith."

Mr Brown held out his hand. She shook it, and Mrs Donaghue opened the door for her.

Dodo was halfway through the door when she turned. "By the way, Mr Brown, you didn't mention Sir Hubert March. Does that name mean anything to you? He's a member of the Aryan Fellowship – or rather, the founder, I believe. I'm told he is some kind of parliamentary under-secretary?"

A look of utter consternation crossed Mr Brown's face. Before Dodo had reached the bottom of the stairs, she heard him on the telephone:

"Put me through to the Prime Minister, please."

CHAPTER 26

The Bard

A week or two later, Dodo heard a whisper at the newspaper stand from where she regularly bought the evening paper.

"Ophelia."

She automatically replied, "Rosemary."

There was a note inside the paper, pinned to a library ticket. Her instruction was to go the next day to the reference section of the Russell Square library, and wait near the Oriental section.

She felt intensely nervous; afraid even, as she walked through the doors, showed her library ticket and asked for the reference library. The woman on the desk waved her through. It all felt so unreal that she, Dodo, once a stage-struck fool of the Lower Fifth, should now be meeting her own spy handler. She hadn't really thought what the Bard would look like: perhaps a stone-age Druid, with a long white beard, painted in woad, wearing a cloak of animal skins, with laurels round his head.

She walked round studiously examining dusty volumes

about Oriental culture. The library was mainly empty except for few students sitting at tables, heads down. She was scrutinising a shelf of books about the Afghan Wars when a man approached, slightly bent, walking carefully with a stick. He came and stood beside her. His face was in shadow as he leaned forward, peered closely at the titles and took one down.

"Ophelia."

Amazed by her own self-possession, Dodo instantly replied, "Rosemary."

With a swift, youthful movement, he opened a door in the wall marked 'Staff Only' and ushered her into a claustrophobic, windowless office, with a wall of filing cabinets which could only be opened with codes.

The moment the door closed behind them, the 'elderly' man flung off his coat and straightened up to reveal someone much more like her young dialect coach at RADA. His long fluid limbs were barely contained in loose, brown corduroy trousers, cream shirt and tie, and a green jacket. But despite his casual appearance, he regarded her with a stern formality. It made her nervous.

He indicated a chair for her, while he sat behind a small table on which was a typewriter, ink pot, blotting paper, notebook and telephone.

How do you do?" He shook her hand formally. "Let's start at the beginning: you know me as the Bard, I shall know you as Guinevere."

Dodo beamed. "Oh! I'll remember that. My best friend and flat mate is Gwendoline – Gwen for short."

He didn't smile back. "I know. That's why I chose it. I'm told you have a good memory?"

"Well, I'm at RADA. Actors have to have good memories."

"Then I hope you will be able to remember all the details I shall now impart to you. Let us begin."

On that day and in the days that followed, Dodo learned to memorise and destroy all her instructions. She was taught how to encrypt messages and how to select and use dead letter boxes. She learned how to be an effective observer, what characteristics to look out for in people she met: their physical appearance, their mannerisms, way of speech, how to assess the usefulness of any information she might come across.

"Don't assume anything is unimportant. Far better to pass on what might seem trivial than to miss something of vital importance."

The Bard already knew the pattern of her movements, and she wondered if one of them was the man she had often observed sitting on the bench in Leicester Square. Had he been an operative checking her out and reporting back to him? By the end of the session, the Bard was impressed with her: she was praised for being a good student, which was not something she had been used to hearing at school. He was pleased by her good memory and powers of observation.

Over the months it became routine that whatever information she gave to Max, she also passed to the Bard, keeping her notes meticulously in a series of small thin pocket notebooks which the Bard provided, and which tucked neatly into her handbag or coat pocket. Once used, they were destroyed.

She found out that there were sub-groups of the Aryan Fellowship which had sprung up outside London and in the provinces. The Bard wanted lists of names: those who had joined the Aryan Fellowship recently; those who had just as suddenly left. Dodo found out their jobs and professions. They were teachers, clerks, journalists, businessmen, lower class, upper class, aristocrats. They had positions of authority in the post office, on the railways, at the waterworks and electricity boards. Some were just wealthy landowners who moved easily round the country and round Europe. She graded their names out of ten to indicate their level of interest in Anglo-German relations.

She and the Bard always decided the amount of information she would give the Aryan Fellowship about her movements such as which barracks and factories she was due to visit to entertain the troops and workers.

The Bard agreed that she should continue in the company of Roger King.

It was early May, and the war still didn't seem real; no bombs had fallen on English soil. Dodo reported that Max declared Hitler would be welcomed with open arms if he decided to invade England. She rather enjoyed playing her part as an enthusiastic member of the Aryan Fellowship. When letters came from her parents in Switzerland, she shared their gossip with the King family as well as the Bard, and always gave Mrs Antrobus the stamps.

Max still tried to persuade Dodo to leave Orange Street, but failed. Dodo was relieved that the Bard didn't force her to accept the invitation. He thought there would be more danger of giving herself away.

Roger became her regular companion to country house parties, hunt balls, and numerous dinners and soirees with the Kings. Finally, the Bard said it was time Dodo learned a few more tricks of the trade; she was to go to an address he gave her.

W.G. Hildevelt: Theatrical Costumes, Jewellery, and Props, Marylebone Mews. It was a fifteen-minute cycle ride away from Orange Street, taking back streets, and wiggling down alleys to the High Road. After some searching, there it was: a small, shabby establishment with a peeling sign. The shop looked dark, dingy and unlit; the windows were protected with wire netting, and the panes were dirty. She cautiously pushed at the door. A bell rang fiercely.

Dodo paused. The smallness of the shop front was deceptive; the interior stretched away deep into a cavern filled with endless piles of tables, chairs, cabinets, and every kind of furniture for any period in time you might desire. It was a stage manager's dream.

At first no one appeared. She walked hesitantly inside. "Hello? Is anybody there?"

"Ophelia?"

A nasal, high-pitched voice from close behind made her jump. She turned to face a man rather shorter than she was, in a knitted woolly grey jumper and grey trousers covered by an overall. He had dusty, flattened, greasy brown hair, a small, brown moustache and blotchy skin. Dodo instinctively took a step back.

He squinted at her. "I thought you were Ophelia. Sorry to have made you jump, miss. Can I help you?" His accent was Cockney with a trace of something else.

"Rosemary," Dodo replied awkwardly.

He sighed with satisfaction. "I've been expecting you. Just a moment." He left her to lock the shop door, turned the notice from 'Open' to 'Closed', and returned to her. "Now, what is it you want?"

"A pendant on a chain to wear round my neck with an eighteenth-century dress," replied Dodo, using the exact words she had been instructed to say.

"Follow me," he said, and led her through a narrow canyon of furniture which looked as if, at any minute, it could topple down and crush them. He opened a door to a small, dark staircase. Switching on a dim light, he led her to an upper floor. Dodo was faced with rails and rails of costumes, and shelves crammed with hats, gloves, cravats, stockings and shoes. At the far rear of the store room were glass cabinets filled with costume jewellery.

"Something like this?" He unlocked one of the cabinets and drew out a finely engraved pendant on a silver chain.

"Goodness!" exclaimed Dodo. "It seems a bit large for a pendant. Is it a locket?"

He opened it up. "Take a look."

Instead of a small portrait or lock of hair, as Dodo would have expected, there was a strange object, with what looked like the pupil of an eye, embedded inside.

"It's a camera," he said. "All you have to do is open the locket. With practice, you will be able to take photographs without removing it from the chain, but it easily unhooks. At the back here," he turned the locket round, "there is a small button which you press, and the picture is taken." He showed her a miniscule compartment near the eye of the camera in which lay a tiny roll of film. "We will give you a number of rolls of film which you can store inside a lipstick container like this." He produced a lipstick to fit inside her make-up bag. "You can only take six pics per roll, so be discriminating. There is a slim compartment in the lid, in which you can place a suitably-sized minature or image, just in case an inquisitive person wishes to look inside. Try and change the roll within twenty to thirty seconds."

He smiled. "Just in case you've been followed, here is an eighteen-century costume blouse which I've folded into a carrier bag. Return it when you next come."

He led her back downstairs to the front of the shop and let her out.

CHAPTER 27

Noor's Loss

What a surprise! I've been posted back to London. I'm tracking troop movements in the maps department of the War Office, and listing aircraft sorties too. I suppose that puts me a bit nearer to aeroplanes.

It means I can live in Orange Street again. How pleased we both were, Dodo and I! At least, I think Dodo was pleased. I hated my suspicions. I knew which side I was on; did she?

True, we were both leading our own lives, sometimes barely seeing each other from one day to the next. She was invariably asleep in the morning when I would creep round the kitchen to make a cup of tea and breakfast, and I would be asleep when she returned late at night after a show. It was normal, yet not normal.

She was seeing a lot of Roger and Max, to my surprise. "I think Max is trying to get us together!" she told me with a big grin.

"You don't seem to mind," I replied somewhat tartly.

"You're as bad as Nosey Parker downstairs!"

I was home on a full day off when Noor turned up unexpectedly. How we fell upon each other with joy!

Dodo and I never knew when we would see Noor. She would just arrive out of the blue, saying she needed to shop, and off she would go to Selfridges, or the Army and Navy Stores to buy a jacket, or a skirt, or lingerie. We loved it when she came. It was like being schoolgirls again, laughing, teasing, and fooling about as we ever did – and sometimes being entranced when Noor would play the veena for an hour or so – "Just to restore my soul," she would say with a smile.

This time, she didn't even take her coat off, and seemed almost glad that Dodo was at RADA. "Please Gwen, have you the time to come to Kew Gardens with me?" She sounded desperate.

We took the train from Charing Cross across the Thames over Kew Bridge. It was wonderful to be out of the centre of London and breathing in clean air.

We walked for at least an hour, happy and at peace with each other. We admired the copses of azalea, and rhododendron, the flowering trees of cherry and magnolia. She stopped often, as if to commune with the blossoms, but I noticed her mood becoming more and more forlorn.

We had entered a flower garden, filled with roses when she stopped and bent forward, staring into the layered depths of a pale, yellow rose. She suddenly crumpled into a heap and broke out weeping.

"I can't see them any more. They've gone. My beautiful fairies have gone. And I don't know why. I've looked for them everywhere. I haven't seen them for months. I thought here at Kew, at least one would show itself to me – but not even here! It's like losing your faith; like God no longer existing. Without my fairies, Gwen, I feel abandoned."

I led her to a bench where she sobbed quietly, "Do you think it's because I've joined up? Do they hate me, and shun me for joining the army?"

"I think it's because you are missing your father, and we're at war," I said gently. "Look what a life you're leading now in the ATS. I honestly don't know how you've coped with it. The fairies of your childhood need to reemerge as fairies in your adulthood. For the moment, you can't see them; but they are there. I'm sure of it. They are affected by the same things that affect you. They feel the fear and anxiety of war and conflict. You are a child of peace, but you are fighting *for* peace. Maybe you won't see your fairies again until peace returns."

"But Gwen, it's now that I need them most!" Noor cried. "If only my father was in touch. Where is he? No one has heard from him since he took the road into the mountains. If he had died, we would never know."

We sat for a while, her sobs decreasing.

"You're right," she sniffed at last. "The fairies in Paris told me they were feeling threatened by the trolls. They were very afraid. Perhaps all over Europe, the fairies have gone into hiding. The most terrible things are happening over there; the Nazis have stopped being human. What more can I do?"

"Don't despair; don't give up. Your father would hate that," I begged her. "I'm sure your fairies will come back."

She wiped away a few tears. "I've heard nothing from Paris – have you?" she asked. "I worry so much about Vera. It's awful not hearing from her."

"No," I replied sadly.

"I cannot concentrate in my training at all," said Noor sadly.

We sat silent and pensively for a while. To divert her mood, I asked, "What are they making you do these days in the ATS?"

"Field training, endurance exercises, climbing, that sort of thing. I'm hopeless really." She paused, then said, as if ashamed, "They've taught me how to handle a gun."

"What? You?" I gasped.

"Everyone has to, though I'd never ever use one." She clasped her hands together like a pledge. "Besides, they know I'm not very good. So, they moved me to secretarial. I can now operate my typewriter at about fifty words a minute. Pretty good, eh? Though I need to get to at least eighty to be truly competent."

I laughed. "Sounds as fast as a woodpecker to me."

With her mood lighter, we got to our feet and continued our walk.

Dodo was back in the flat when we returned. As we cooked our supper, we chatted and joked, and Dodo told us hilarious stories about her tours, and the dreadful boarding houses they were forced to stay in.

Yet, somehow, despite all our laughter and wisecracking, it was as though there were glass walls between us. We were affectionately together yet strangely apart. We were reserved; we told each other about our lives, but in very small portions. When certain questions were asked, they were not always answered. We were secretive about what we did. We cooked, following war-ration menus, and invented amazing concoctions. Later, I realised we didn't talk about the war at all.

Noor returned to her barracks the next day.

CHAPTER 28

An Unexpected Visitor

It was mid-afternoon when I staggered upstairs to the flat after a day in the dungeons of the War Office, plotting troop movements. There had been extra activity, and it kept us on our toes till we were dropping.

I dumped my bag and turned on the radio. A motherly voice was giving advice about how to make oatmeal sausages with shredded suet, or bubble and squeak using leftovers; and apple crumble made with powdered eggs. Good. I need some inspiration for supper. It was my turn to cook.

I hadn't even changed out of my uniform when the front doorbell rang. I ran on to the landing. "It's all right, Mrs Antrobus, I'll get it!"

As usual, Mrs Antrobus had already opened the door to reveal – Charles Brandon.

"Oh my God! Charles!" I screamed. "How wonderful. I can't believe it!" I clattered downstairs to greet him in the hallway and embraced him heartily. "What are you doing in London? Come up, come up! You don't mind, do you, Mrs Antrobus? He's not just an ordinary gentleman caller but one of our oldest, dearest friends."

I think it made a difference that Charles was in his army uniform, which impressed Mrs Antrobus no end, so she didn't object.

"Dodo will be thrilled," I cried, leading him upstairs. "She's not back yet – but she'll be over the moon at seeing you."

"Where is she?" asked Charles. "Gadding about as usual?"

"No! Serving her country; using her talents. She's a real *trouper* rather than a trooper – if you see what I mean!"

"Glad to hear it. Can't wait to see her." Charles cheerfully plonked down his duffle bag, and took off his cap.

"What are you doing here, though?" I asked. "I thought you were with your regiment in France?"

"Got a quick bit of compassionate leave; my mother's been ill," he said. "I've been down to Ramsgate to see them. Just four days, then back again to France. Had to reassure my ma and pa! They think it's still about trench warfare! But I was desperate to see Dodo. You're expecting her back, are you?"

I beamed at him. "Any minute now. I've got to get supper going. You will stay and have some, won't you? Do have a cigarette – there's some on the table. And help yourself to a sherry over there. Pour me one too. My uncle had a bottle sent to us. Feels very indulgent when there's so much rationing."

Charles lit a cigarette, then poured two glasses of sherry, watching the rich dark golden liquid glimmer in the crystal. "Cheers!" he said.

We clinked glasses and sipped.

"How splendid you look, Gwen. That uniform rather suits you!" He circled me teasingly, and wolf whistled.

"Oh, shut up!" I laughed. "Now tell me what you've been up to while I get on with what's supposed to pass for a dinner. Dodo always comes back starving." I began peeling potatoes and chopping onions. "I must say, it seems awfully quiet for a war – not that I'm complaining. I'd love it if they called the whole thing off and did away with all the sandbags and blackouts and air-raid warnings. Half the time, I don't know whether to laugh or cry; be happy or scared stiff."

"Don't be fooled," said Charles, suddenly deeply serious. "The Huns haven't been building up their armaments for nothing. It's just *when*, not *if* they come crashing down on us."

I shuddered. "Now you're frightening me. My brother Eric's been doing some sorties over Norway. He says those German Stukas are deadly. We've got to be ready for them, I suppose."

"What use is the army making of you, anyway?" Charles asked.

"I'm not on the frontline, that's for sure," I said dolefully. "Not that there is any frontline here yet. I'm in the map room down in a basement in the War Office. It's like being in a prison – worse – no windows – and everyone smokes like hell. At least I can sleep here in the flat."

"Is Dodo all right?" Charles asked tentatively. "She was pretty fed up at being rejected by the army because of her parents."

"She was upset." I tipped my onions into the stock. "Humiliated. It felt like a slur on her and her parents. But it's really good for her to be touring and learning her trade on the hoof. And, of course, her parents' friends have been cheering her up." My voice must have sounded unenthusiastic.

Charles wandered over to the window and looked down on the street below. "Who are these friends? She never really told me – except for some woman called Max she doesn't seem to like too much."

I grunted. "Maxine King. I've never met her. Dodo says she's rather bossy, but knows how to handle her."

"Well I hope she's not too much of a Nazi-lover," said Charles. "Let's face it, Gwen – Dodo's parents are pretty admiring of that lot. I hope she's careful about the company she keeps. Remember that summer in Munich when we all met up there?"

"I'll never forget," I replied quietly. "It still makes me shudder. Dodo was shocked too. Genuinely shocked. I'm not sure why she spends so much time with Max and her friends." I shook my head, perplexed. "Perhaps they just don't see what's going on."

"I doubt it," said Charles sceptically.

"I'm worried," I said. "Dodo always disagreed with her parents and their pro-Nazi sympathies. She thought they were all far too keen on Aryan superiority and saying what a jolly good chap Hitler is. Yet she seems to be seeing more of their friends these days, rather than less."

Charles was frowning. "I hope she realises we're at war. Socialising with Nazi-lovers is folly, if not downright treasonable."

"Warn her, Charles. She'd take it from you." I urged. "But I can't believe . . ." I hesitated. "She's surely not changed her views?"

"Of course not," said Charles firmly. "We know our Dodo. But she sometimes talks without realising the consequences. I say . . ." he exclaimed, leaning forward to see better out of the window. "Who the devil's that? Dodo's just pulled up in some fancy car. Who's the driver?"

I ran over and looked out. "Damn. That's Roger, Max's nephew. He chauffeurs her around sometimes."

"Oh, he does, does he? And does he add kissing to his duties?" There was a chilling edge to Charles's voice.

"Oh Charles! Don't sound so jealous," I said lightly, peering down to the street below. Inside, I was cursing Dodo. "Damn, damn, damn!"

"Perhaps *that's* why she's seeing so much of Max and her friends," sneered Charles.

"I won't have that," I said defensively. "But you know what she's like – what all these theatre people are like.

They're all lovey dovey and kissy kissy – it doesn't mean a thing. Oh, damn and blast. They're both coming up."

"Is there another way out?" Charles spun round like a trapped animal.

"For heaven's sake, Charles," I scolded. "Don't go thinking the worst. No, there isn't another way out, unless you're a cat burglar and go down the drainpipe. Really – don't be an idiot. She worships you. I should know. I live with her. Anyway – too late. You'll just have to face it."

We could hear two sets of footsteps racing up the stairs.

"Gwenny!" Dodo burst into the room, followed by Roger. "Roger's dropped me home, and he's inviting us out to eat. I hope you haven't started cooking." She tossed her travel bag into a corner, then saw Charles.

"Oh! Heavens! Charles!" Her face turned red and pale, then red again, and her eyes filled with tears. "Oh my God!"

"Hello Dodo." The chill in Charles' voice made even my heart freeze. "Sorry. I should have let you know I was calling in. I wanted it to be a surprise."

There was a split second when Dodo looked as if she was on stage and had forgotten her lines. She then gave a theatrical squeal and came back to life. "Oh Charles! It *is* a surprise. A wonderful surprise!"

She ran up to him and threw her arms round his neck. When he didn't respond, she took a step back, her voice edgy and horribly polite. "Charles, this is Roger King, a friend of my parents. Roger, meet Charles; he's –"

She hesitated, and I thought she would weep openly. ". . . a very old friend." Her voice trailed away.

"Yes, Roger," I reiterated, trying to give her courage. "Dodo and I have known him for ever."

Charles stared at Dodo and she stared back; both of them were in shock.

"How do you do?" said Roger.

Charles slowly took Roger's hand but didn't take his eyes off Dodo. He slung his duffle bag over his shoulder and put on his cap. "I don't want to hold you up," he said stiffly. "I was only popping in for a few moments. Back to France again with the British Expeditionary Force, don't you know? I'll drop you a telegram next time. Must be off now."

"You're not going yet? Please? Charles?" Dodo reached out desperately and held his arm.

"Love you darling," murmured Charles. He lightly kissed her brow and left.

"Stop him Gwen," begged Dodo. "Oh, stop him!"

She ran out on to the landing, peering down over the banister. I joined her, and listened to his feet clattering down the stairs; the front door opened, then shut with a firm click.

I turned on Dodo with an overwhelming rage. "Dodo! You really are a blithering idiot. What the hell are you up to, messing about with Roger? Are you in love with him? Is it all this Aryan stuff you're mixed up in?"

Dodo's face was expressionless. "Mind your own business, Gwen. Don't get involved."

"Involved in what?" I demanded.

"Get a move on, you two," Roger called from inside the flat. "We'll lose our table."

"I just hope you're not playing with fire," I hissed at her. "Haven't you heard of the fifth column? It's bad enough, your parents being known as Nazi sympathisers without you being one too."

As I heard the terrible words falling from my lips, Dodo's eyes flashed with the kind of fury I had never seen in all our years of friendship. "My God, Gwen!" It was almost a growl that escaped her throat, and she raised her hand as if she would strike me. Then turning on her heel, she strode back into the flat. "Roger, darling! I'm ready. Let's go!" With an expert change of mood, she danced towards him, full of dazzling warmth. "So sorry Charles had to go."

"Pity. I'd like to have got to know him," Roger murmured.

I was still full of jumbled feelings of anger and puzzlement over Dodo's behaviour. "Yes," I said, trying to reduce the emotion and bring things back to normal. "A pity, yes. It was a really quick visit. Look, I've got some stew on —"

"Keep your stew till tomorrow, Gwen," said Roger jovially. "We'll be late for the Criterion. No more long faces."

"It's really sweet of you, Roger; I'll stay. But you two, please go. I mean it, Dodo," I said, firmly shepherding them both towards the door. "I'm absolutely pooped, and I have some reports to write. Go on – off with you!"

They went – with Dodo glancing over her shoulder at me with a look of utter despair.

I listened till I heard the front door close. I felt confusion, anger, and a feeling of unutterable sadness. What was happening to Dodo? This wasn't two competing boyfriends; it was two competing ideologies. We were at war, and for all I knew – for all *Dodo* knew – Roger might be the enemy.

I stared at Dodo's travel bag, lying where she had tossed it. Then I went back to my stew, sniffed it, stirred it, and replaced the lid. I couldn't eat. I turned off the gas. Something came into my head; something I wanted to do. I went to my room and changed out of my uniform. My eyes were drawn again to Dodo's travel bag.

I decided to take a walk to think things over.

Grabbing my hat and coat, I went out into the glowing, early evening. I walked for an hour, across Trafalgar Square, into the Mall and across into St James's Park. I sat on a park bench; stared at the ducks, moorhens, and coots squawking in the pond. Prim, uniformed nannies pushed their charges in large black hooded prams past the deep trenches which had been dug in the event of a bombing raid, scarring the grass as though giant claws had ripped the turf apart.

I thought about Ralph through waves of emotion. How many times had I relived our encounter that day war was declared? Our walk and talk; how he held my elbow; the closeness; the strongest feeling I had ever had that I was in the company of someone I'd known all my life, even though it had just been a couple of hours. Dodo was right to tease me. I thought about him incessantly.

It was almost dark when I walked slowly back to Leicester Square. No one was queuing for a phone box. On an impulse, I rummaged for pennies and went into a kiosk. I dialled the number in Wales. It rang and rang. I had almost given up when Aunt Madge answered breathlessly.

"Aunt Madge!" I stammered into the phone, then burst into tears.

I talked and wept, and talked again, and fed the telephone until I ran out of coins. Then Aunt Madge rang back, and we talked further, and I told her of all my fears and concerns. I told her what had really torn me apart: my anxieties about Dodo's connection with the Aryan Fellowship; about Roger, and Charles; about friendship and loyalty, and about my feeling that something was wrong.

"What shall I do? I feel so lonely, Aunt Madge."

"You must do your duty," said Aunt Madge gently.

Duty. The word hung heavily. "Yes. But she's my best friend."

"Darling, come and visit us in Wales. Can you get permission? You can but ask."

I did ask. I spoke to my superior and managed to negotiate three days.

CHAPTER 29

Rosemary for Remembrance

The atmosphere was still icy when Gwen announced she was going to Wales for a few days, Dodo wasn't surprised. Their friendship was on the line, and she knew it. Yet Gwen looked guilty, and Dodo wondered what on earth Gwen had to feel guilty about. Was it her outburst of anger over Charles? Dodo was mortified.

It's me, she thought to herself. She was the guilty one. Spying, pretending, double-dealing. Lying to her best friend; betraying her parents. And now Gwen thought she was betraying Charles. The Bard could praise her for being a good actress – but he was wrong. That wasn't what acting was about. Acting was about truth, not duplicity. She felt bereft and helpless about how to put things right.

The day she left for Wales, Gwen politely asked Dodo what she would be doing while she was away. Dodo lied as usual; it was now routine to lie.

"I'm committed to a tour round Norfolk with the troupe," she said, as easily as if she had told Gwen she was going shopping, when, in actual fact, she had an appointment with the Bard.

The message had been passed to her just the day before, when she had stopped to buy a paper.

"*Star* and *Standard*!" the newspaper seller was yelling. "Where's the war then, Mr Hitler? Read all about it!"

"*Daily Star* please," Dodo said, handing him her coins.

"Ophelia," the newspaper seller muttered as she took the paper.

"Oh! Rosemary," she returned in a startled whisper.

"Check page three, Miss. *Star* and *Standard*! *Star* and *Standard*!"

Dodo hurried back to Orange Street to pick up her bicycle. With her book bag and newspaper in the front basket, she headed towards Bloomsbury Square and RADA. She first went to the bench in the square and read the words scrawled across page 3. *Urgent. Meet contact at Foyles Bookshop, Charing Cross Road, theatre and plays department tomorrow. 5 p.m.*

She found it hard to concentrate all day until at last, classes were over. It was 4 p.m.; ample time to get to Foyles. She went to get her coat – and glanced out of the window.

"Damn!" she groaned out loud. There, parked opposite the entrance into RADA, was Roger, lolling in his yellow MG.

Dodo raced upstairs to the costume department and rifled through the wigs which lined a shelf. She picked a black straight-cut bob wig with a fringe and put it on; it looked right. She took off her own fitted, tweedy green coat and velour hat, and swapped them for a dark blue, saggy coat and red woolly hat which she pulled over her ears. Not very elegant; not very Dodo. The finishing touch was a pair of spectacles.

A crowd of students was now pouring through the front door. She saw a girl she knew. "Hey! Joyce!" Dodo grabbed her arm. "Joyce, it's me – Dodo!"

"My God!" Joyce exclaimed in a shriek of giggles. "You had me then. Didn't recognise you at all. What are you doing in that get-up?"

Dodo's explanation flowed through her lips like oil. "There's a chap out there who's sweet on me. I'm trying to avoid him because I'm about to meet someone else – you know!" She shrugged with a sheepish grin. "Please Joyce, can I take your arm and walk out with you?"

"Of course, ol' thing. I don't think even your own mother would recognise you looking like that. Here! Grab my arm."

They pushed into the thick of the other students. Down the steps. Roger was immediately opposite.

"Turn left," hissed Dodo.

No one called out or came after them. When they reached Charing Cross Road, Dodo said, "I'll be fine now, Joyce. Thanks. I'll buy you an iced bun with your tea tomorrow. You're an absolute brick." And they parted.

"Ophelia?" The shuffling, old woman didn't even look

at her as she browsed the shelves in the theatre section.

"Rosemary," Dodo answered, moving closer.

The woman spoke in a low but totally clear voice: "We are in a state of emergency. We are getting reports of German troop movements along the borders with Belgium, Holland and France. We need more information on Sir Hubert March; he's working in the heart of government. We're sure he's drawing up a blueprint which states who will be assigned to every single position in the British Government: local authorities, libraries, schools, hospitals; every post of administration and law. They will replace one of their own from the Prime Minister down to the smallest post office clerk. If you glean anything about this plan, let me know using the RED alert code. There's a code book at the desk downstairs. Paid for. Just say it's for Rosemary. From now on, you must only use these codes for communication.

"Wait five minutes to give me time to leave, then be on your way. Do not open the book till you are at home and strictly private. I believe your flat mate is away."

Dodo was always amazed at how much they knew about her life.

"Do not delay; this is of extreme importance." Her contact straightened, turned abruptly and made for the stairs, spritely descending them, not in the least like an old woman.

CHAPTER 30
Fotherington Hall

BEFORE 10 MAY 1940

There had been many informal gatherings with the Aryan Fellowship over the winter. When she wasn't fully taken up with Christmas shows for the factories and troops, Dodo attended quite a few talks, mostly at Max's Dolphin Square flat, mostly about German culture, always reporting back to the Bard.

It was now May, when a formal invitation to Fotherington Hall came in the post from Sir Hubert March.

It was to a dinner on the Saturday night, staying over for a lunchtime piano and song recital on the Sunday. Max and Roger were both invited, of course, and they pounced on Dodo, entreating her; almost compelling her to accept. "You MUST go. It's wonderful there. You'll love it! Roger will drive you."

She reported the invitation using a DBS, and was summoned to see the Bard back at the Russell Square library.

"You must get as close as possible to the Aryan Fellowship," said the Bard. "We need every scrap of information we can lay our hands on. Don't assume that anything is too trivial to report. And continue your liaison with Roger King."

Liaison! What a horrible word to use. It made her feel grubby. But she was already grubby – most of all because of her perceived disloyalty to Charles and Gwen, but to Roger as well.

She liked Roger, she told the Bard. "I like him enough to hate deceiving him."

"Good," said the Bard when she protested. "Like Roger all you want; the closer the better. Nothing like pillow talk, you know." He had the grace to bow his head as she looked at him with disgust. Then he sighed, and lit up his pipe. "We think there's someone at the very top of society playing a major part in the Fellowship. Someone titled; like a duke perhaps. We'd love to find them."

Back at the flat, Dodo got in the bath and scrubbed herself hard till it hurt, as though some how she had been dirtied by the whole conversation.

As Roger drove her cheerily to Fotherington Hall, singing loudly at the top of his voice, Dodo felt she was acting the part of her life. She was fully competent now with the locket-camera, which she wore round her neck as a permanent accessory. Dodo joined in the singing enthusiastically, but was plagued by the image of Charles's face when she had turned up, disastrously, with Roger. How often she had wept and cursed at that unexpected turn of events. She hadn't heard from him since. She had lost him forever, she was sure. Yet she loved Charles – though he would never believe that, or trust her again.

Keeping her misery at bay, Dodo braced herself for her first visit to Fotherington Hall, preparing herself for a weekend of deceitful hob-nobbing, artificial smiles, and brittle repartee.

"Quiet, darling?" Roger patted her knee, as he drove them out of London. "Penny for your thoughts."

"Everything's wonderful!" she exclaimed. Yes – she was a good actress, and flew into her part with gusto and conviction. "Tell me more about the other guests I'm going to meet. I like to be prepared!"

Roger rattled off names of people who were almost certainly going to be at the recital, and what kind of things they did. When they stopped at a pub for a break, she excused herself and went to the ladies' room. Here she hurriedly made a note of all the names Roger had mentioned and whatever bits of information she had learned. When she rejoined him, she was light-hearted, hoping he wouldn't detect any treachery in her smile as she looked up into his face.

They drove a further half an hour, before turning off through great wrought-iron gates, and down a long beech-tree-lined avenue towards a magnificent classical Italianate country house. Dodo gazed with apprehension at its grand edifice, with flights of stone steps, and pillars that seemed to herald a temple rather than a home. This was Fotherington Hall, and here she had to act as never before. Here she had to pass the test of everyone's scrutiny – especially Sir Hubert's.

It was a curious moment, arriving at this most grand of houses in this most English countryside. What a stage for her to perform on. Dodo felt a surge of bravado in the face of the enemy. Her fear of failure dropped away and she swept up the steps like a diva.

There was Max, acting as a hostess, gushing profusely as she introduced lord and lady this, and princess that, and countess from heaven knows where – while all around wafted the beautiful people in their chic clothes, with their scintillating chatter and ringing laughter. The German and English languages mingled – so superior, so confidently Aryan; so sure, of being members of the master race.

But it was Sir Hubert March Dodo dreaded: coming under the scrutiny of those strangely translucent, hazel eyes and their forensic gaze. She could hear the sneering voice of Mr Brown in her ears: "As an actress, Miss Bridges-Smith, this should be right up your street."

Yes, she was an actress, she told herself firmly, and maybe she would never play a more important role in her life. So, she had packed her best day dresses, and jackets, and the ball gown which she had last worn in Munich, where she had danced with heel-clicking Nazi officers in the company of beautiful Aryan debutantes.

Brave and upright, Dodo allowed Roger to take her arm and lead her into Fotherington Hall. Sir Hubert March approached her immediately with his neck outstretched and extended right hand. "My dear Miss Bridges-Smith! Welcome!"

A further flurry of arrivals meant that, thankfully, he soon had to direct his attention to his other guests, leaving Roger and Dodo to be greeted by a maid who led them up a grand staircase, up two further floors, and along a corridor to their rooms.

"This one is yours, madam," said the maid stopping outside a room with the name 'Primrose'.

"See you later," Roger breathed into Dodo's ear, with such tenderness that she suddenly felt a frisson of attraction and flushed bright red. For an instant, they looked into each other's eyes; then Dodo quipped: "If I can find you. I forgot to leave a trail of crumbs."

"Then I'll have to find *you*," he replied, as he followed the maid further down the passage.

Dodo's room was indeed as yellow as primroses: from the yellow drapes which hung around a small four-poster bed, to the curtains in the windows. She breathed a deep sigh. Alone at last. Her windows overlooked the front drive. She could see the length of the avenue they had driven up, and the front lawns sloping away down to a small lake.

She took her time unpacking and hanging up her clothes. She washed, redid her make-up, and changed into a light but stylish navy and white summer dress and jacket, adding the locket round her neck. With a last glance at herself in the mirror, she admired what she saw – nose or no nose – and, adjusting her locket, she took a deep breath, and went downstairs to join the proceedings.

Roger was already deep in conversation with a group when she entered the Music Room where the lunchtime song recital was to take place. Briefly alone in the doorway, Dodo slid open the locket and discreetly took random pictures of guests. But the one photograph she must get was of Sir Hubert March, as she had failed to take one at previous gatherings in London.

Roger looked pleased to see her and beckoned her into the group. She paid attention when he introduced her to everyone, committing to memory their names and what they did. At a suitable break in the conversation, she excused herself to go to the ladies' room, where, in the locked privacy of a cubicle, she quickly wrote down all the names and details. Then, flushing the lavatory, she powdered her nose, and went back to the proceedings.

"Ah, Dodo! Have a nibble before we go in for the performance," Roger urged, and Dodo took the glass of champagne she was offered and a couple of cheese straws.

"Ladies and gentleman!" Sir Hubert brought everyone to his attention. "Do take your seats. The recital is about to begin."

Dodo dutifully sat down, with Roger on one side and Max on the other, among the rows of gold-gilt and scarlet chairs.

Max murmured, "What a pity Peter can't be here for this. He does so love German song. I would love you to meet him."

A man in Brixton prison would not be sitting on a scarlet and gold chair waiting to listen to a piano recital, Dodo thought, as she nodded sympathetically and expressed a hope that war wouldn't stop him from returning home, as it had her parents.

Sir Hubert escorted the singer and pianist on to a slightly raised dais and introduced them to the audience. Dodo clicked her locket. Got him!

An elegant young woman with shining blond plaits coiled round her head like serpents took her place before a shining black Steinway grand piano. Her blue eyes gleamed as she acknowledged the applause. Gunter Meyer, the soloist, was a sturdy young man with a sensitive face, who looked strangely uncomfortable as he stood before the audience with clasped hands, staring into the middle distance.

Schumann songs filled the room with aching beauty, as if the singer wished the music could erase the horrors of the war. Many sighed, and even wept. This was high art;

this spoke to the Germanic soul, to what they believed was the very essence of the Aryan spirit.

The buffet lunch after the recital was under a marquee on the lawn. There was croquet and tennis on offer, and walks in the garden. Sir Hubert mingled among his guests, engaging them with conversation, and drew Dodo and Roger into a group discussing German philosophy. Hit by a curious sense of euphoria, Dodo chatted easily, even cracked jokes. After all, the conversations were all on topics she was used to hearing with her parents, and these were her parents' friends.

"Anglo-German relations have never been better – despite the fact we're supposed to be at war," someone said.

"We are getting more interest in the Aryan Fellowship," agreed Max. "And we're hoping Dodo will bring in many more recruits. What do you think, Dodo? Have you friends who would like to join us? What about your friend, Gwen?"

Did she think before she spoke? Dodo wasn't sure; the words just tumbled from her mouth. "Most of my friends think anyone who fraternises with the Germans must be a spy!" And she roared with laughter – except she was the only one laughing. The silence made her feel as if she had suddenly gone deaf, until Roger came to her rescue with a hoot of amusement. Everyone joined in, except Sir Hubert, whose dead eyes stayed fixed on her.

At that moment, three cars came down the drive towards the house.

"Ah! They've arrived," said Sir Hubert. "Some more guests. Excuse me."

He hurried away to greet them. They were too distant for Dodo to get any sense of them, other than there were three men and a woman, and they were greeted like royalty.

"How lovely you look!" Roger said admiringly when Dodo appeared later for dinner in her evening gown. "And you're wearing the same locket again. What a charming thing it is; most unusual. Where did it come from?"

Dodo smiled, fingering it in a way she hoped had become a noticeable characteristic. "It was my grandmother's. I have a lock of her hair inside, see?" Without demur, she opened the locket in which she had laid a coil of her grandmother's rich, brunette hair. "I believe the locket is early Victorian. Pretty, isn't it?"

Sir Hubert didn't appear for dinner. Nor did the four 'guests' who had come in the cars. Apologies were announced, but no explanation. This time Dodo was careful to blend her conversation with the general tone of everyone else: how wonderful the singer had been, and wasn't Schumann divine, and what did you think about the latest essay by Alfred Baeumler on Nietzsche, and wasn't that philosopher, Martin Heidegger, a wonderful proponent of National Socialism, and how the Third Reich had restored Germany's self-esteem.

After dinner all the ladies left the table, so that the men could smoke and drink brandy without the presence of the opposite sex. The ladies mostly went to the withdrawing room where they, too, would gossip over another glass of wine or a sip of brandy.

Dodo headed again for the privacy of the ladies' powder room. She would have passed the heavy dark oak door, as she had before, without taking particular notice of it – but for a slit of light which came from under the door and fell across the floor in front of her. She paused, hearing a soft murmur of voices. Was this where Sir Hubert was ensconced with his latest visitors? She calculated that there was likely to be a window which overlooked the front, exactly below her bedroom. Then she continued to the ladies' room to write up her notes.

While she was in the privacy of her cubicle, the powder room door flew open, and she heard a bevy of young women come in.

"Have you ever had a chance to see our beloved Führer?" asked a German woman. "*Mein Gott* – it is like seeing our Saviour."

"You're so lucky to have Mr Hitler," exclaimed an English voice. "Our politicians are clowns in comparison."

"You can be sure that all of Europe will benefit, once everyone realises his greatness and value."

Dodo flushed the lavatory and let herself out. The women stared at her curiously. She gave a genial smile. "Good evening," she said, and washed her hands.

"And what position do you have in your work?" asked someone of another, carefully applying some more lipstick.

"I am a secretary in my local authority tax office. You'd be amazed what I learn by working there."

"Ah yes!" The other nodded approvingly.

Dodo dried her hands, then took out her make-up bag. She fiddled with the locket and, as they giggled and chattered, absorbed in themselves, she took a photograph of their reflection in the mirror – just before they all flooded out.

Alone, Dodo looked at herself in the eye of her mirror image. What the hell was she doing in a place like this? What the hell would Gwen think – or indeed Charles? For a moment, she felt the blood rush up her neck and flood her cheeks; her chest tightened; she couldn't breathe. She had an urge to flee; to run away into the darkness; and run and run till she got back to Orange Street.

Instead, she went outside and walked across the grass and down to the lake, darkly glistening under a rising moon. Water birds splashed and squawked to each other among the reeds; a late flock of ducks circled in the evening sky before gliding down into the lake to settle for the night. Reflections of the willows and alder trees quivered with the impact.

Dodo sat on a stone bench and lit up a cigarette, inhaled deeply and exhaled slowly, watching the smoke coil up into the darkening sky. She felt calmer, and even smiled. Perhaps some officious little blackout warden would appear out of the lake, to reprimand her for taking the risk that enemy aircraft might see the glow of her cigarette.

She swivelled round to scan the front of the house, which was covered in Virginia creeper. She was certain her window was the one to the left on the second floor, where an ancient tangle of wisteria twisted up the walls, its deep blue flowers hanging like bunches of grapes.

Yes, it was as she thought. Sir Hubert had taken his guests into the library, two floors beneath her bedroom. The curtains were not quite drawn, and a strip of light gleamed through the gap. It seemed the occupants weren't overly bothered by the blackout either.

Dodo smoked her cigarette right down and stubbed it out with her heel, then crossed the lawn back to the house. Sounds of a Strauss waltz, mingled with laughter, drifted around as she walked towards the lighted window and peered carefully between the curtains.

She could see parts of faces: Sir Hubert, three men with their backs to her, and a fashionable, angular woman, whose face she only partly glimpsed but whose red-painted fingernails rested intimately on the arm of one of the guests. All were listening intently to Sir Hubert.

Dodo fiddled with her locket, pointed and clicked. Someone high up in British society, Mr Brown had said. A duke perhaps? She clicked again, trying to pick up identifying features. If only she could hear what they were saying. Out of sight, a typewriter was tapping rapidly, taking down the conversation.

There was movement; they were getting ready to leave. She clicked again and again – then, not risking her luck any further, went back into the house.

CHAPTER 31

The Library

In the ballroom, dancing was in full swing when she re-entered the proceedings. A young, vigorously playing quartet of string players were seated in an alcove flanked by two potted palm trees. In the doorway, Dodo stopped dead, seeing Sir Hubert with Max and Roger. There was no sign of the new arrivals.

Sir Hubert saw her and immediately advanced. "My dear! I was looking for you. Before we become too frivolous with music and dance, allow me to show you my library. It's just down the passageway. Come – let me take you. You can't really know a person till you see their bookshelves, don't you think? And I'd like you to know a little more about me!"

"How kind!" Dodo enthused.

But as Sir Hubert escorted her to the library, she felt a surge of panic. Had he somehow known she had been in the garden, lurking outside?

"After you," said Sir Hubert with a bow.

He opened the great oak door to reveal shelves from high ceiling to shining polished oak floors, stocked to the gills with books. There was a table in the window and four deep red padded chairs where Dodo had glimpsed the visitors. The room was empty now, though the typewriter was still there, and a waste-paper basket nearby was filled with discarded blue copy paper. A smell of cigarettes lingered in the air.

She gave a polite gasp of appreciation. "Oh, my goodness! Don't tell me you've read all these?"

"Most of them," Sir Hubert replied with pride. "These are my gods; my mentors." He ran his fingers along the titles on the shelves. "They speak of inner truth and greatness. I think philosophers should rule the world, don't you? And scientists too. Do you love science? German science and technology, combined with German philosophy, will lead the Aryan people to their great spiritual destiny."

He spoke with a simmering passion, and yet, when Dodo looked into his eyes, they were cold. Was he testing her? Was she one of them, his scrutiny questioned?

"Here is my shelf of philosophers: Nietzche and Heidegger."

Dodo's eye caught the name *Adolf Hitler*. "Hitler! I didn't know Hitler was a philosopher."

"Oh yes! His book, *Mein Kampf*, has become like a Bible to the Third Reich. It means 'My Struggle'. Everything of importance in this world has been gained through struggle – I'm sure you'll agree." He handed her the book. "Bedtime reading? It's in English. I'm sure you'll find it most inspiring. I take it you enjoy reading?"

"I'm afraid I'm terribly ignorant," Dodo responded with a feeble giggle. "I'm too busy learning my lines to be able to do much other reading."

"But you won't be learning lines this weekend I hope, Miss Bridges-Smith, so you'll have time to read a little bit of *Mein Kampf* – yes?"

"Yes. Indeed," murmured Dodo, clutching it to her chest. "I'll be most interested to know what Herr Hitler has to say."

"Life is all about struggle. No greater struggle than your hope to go on the stage. I believe you are quite an actress?"

"I don't know about being *quite* an actress!" Dodo tried to sound amusing and light-hearted. "But I do love the theatre and hope I can be sufficiently good to get work on the stage one day."

"And your friend who shares your flat, is she an actress too?"

"Good heavens, no. She's in the ATS – but they've put her in the map department of the War Office for the moment."

"Moving little toy aeroplanes around, eh?"

He laughed. She laughed.

"Oh yes! Gwen's in the know," Dodo boasted. "Though she never breathes a word to me!"

"Interesting woman. I wish you'd bring her to Fotherington Hall one day. I should like to meet her. We have Aryan members in the theatre world, you know – and in the War Office. I'm not sure we have any in the map department."

"Probably not," said Dodo. "I wouldn't think the Aryan Fellowship is quite their thing."

"We find people who are interested in us in the most surprising places. Perhaps you and your actor friends could perform for one of my weekend parties. I'd love to see you act."

"That might be a while off yet," replied Dodo carefully. "I'm afraid we have our time cut out entertaining at the factories and bases, while also continuing our courses and preparing for exams."

"Well, you must let me know where you will be performing next, so that I can see your talents for myself. I don't think I've ever been on the factory floor." He laughed as though it was a joke at his own expense. "I suppose you actors have to be like a kind of Janus; you know – show one face to one set of people, and another to others. Do you perhaps have a doppelganger?"

"You mean a double?" asked Dodo, feeling an icy chill in her stomach. Did he know she was a double agent? "What a funny question! Not that I know of."

"But you're an actress!" he said, with a faint smile. "Do you actors sometimes forget who you really are, being so busy being someone else?"

"I think I know exactly who I am," replied Dodo quietly. "Good actors are not fantasists, and always know exactly what they are doing and why."

She must have sounded a bit defensive, as Sir Hubert responded with a light wave of his hand: "Forgive me. We in the Aryan Fellowship are perhaps over-sensitive. Having friendly contacts with German culture is not exactly popular at the moment. They misunderstand that all we want is for Germany and Britain to be friends. We are working to stop this idiotic war."

He paused, looking hard at her, but she avoided his eye.

"Well," he said. "I'm depriving you of your young man, Roger. He'll be eager to take you on to the dance floor. Why not leave *Mein Kampf* here on the table, and pick it up later, on your way to bed.

Back in the swirl of the ballroom, suddenly there was Roger coming eagerly towards her. "May I steal her back now, Sir Hubert?"

Sir Hubert bowed graciously, and kissed Dodo's hand. "We've had a most interesting conversation, Roger. Do remind Miss Bridges-Smith to collect her bedtime reading from the library."

It was past midnight when people finally dispersed in trickles to their various rooms in the house. All around were end-of-evening exhortations: "Goodnight, *gute nacht, schlafen sie gut*, sleep well, sweet dreams, see you in the morning."

At Dodo's bedroom door, Roger took her hand, clicked his heels and bowed low. He kissed her fingers, then drew her tenderly into his arms. "Dodo," he murmured, pressing his face into her hair. "I've become really fond of you."

If he hadn't clicked his heels, she might have . . . succumbed; surrendered, yielded – what were all the terms they used? God knows she felt her body yearning, leaning, desiring . . . She was on the very brink of falling; and if she had returned his embrace, she would have fallen – plunged out of her depth, out of control. But he had clicked his heels as he kissed her fingers; like all those young men in Zürich who, while clicking their heels, turned a blind eye to shopkeepers being savagely kicked in the street. She remembered it; and also heard Gwen's warning voice – "You will be careful, Dodo" – and Mr Brown saying she could not have divided loyalties; and that Germany had plans, not only to take over Britain, but the whole of the British Empire. Not least, she saw Charles's face of anguish – Charles, whom she had loved for so long, and still loved, but who now thought she had betrayed him. As Dodo hung over the precipice, almost letting go, her feet found a footing and she stopped her fall.

"You're such a sweet, boy, Roger. I really like you. But be good chap and let me get some beauty sleep otherwise I'll look such a hag in the morning!" She loosened his fingers from her shoulders, kissed him lightly on both cheeks, and went into her bedroom, shutting the door firmly behind her.

She wept, she bathed, she brushed her hair a hundred times, she got into bed, switched off her light, and tried to sleep. She felt unbearably lonely, unbearably unloved, and tried to sleep again; perhaps did sleep. Till something awoke her. Something outside.

She hurried over to the window and peered through the curtains. Three limousines were lined up before the front steps. In the light of the portico, she saw Sir Hubert escorting his visitors into their cars with a swift, low, obsequious bow. Then, with astonishment, she saw him give the Nazi salute to each vehicle as it pulled away.

CHAPTER 32

Mein Kampf

Dodo checked her watch. It was 2 a.m.

Her brain sprang into focus. *Mein Kampf* still waited for her in Sir Hubert's library.

She waited a further hour, reading through her notes to keep awake, hoping that was time enough for the household to settle into sleep. At 3 a.m. she put on her dressing gown and silently opened her door.

Confident of her excuse – retrieving her so-called bedtime reading – she descended the staircase, her way lit by night lights at regular intervals. The library door was unlocked. She didn't turn on the light but pulled out her torch which, though barely larger than a pen, had a powerful beam.

The book was still there.

Dodo ignored it and began systematically to examine the room. First, the wastepaper basket. It hadn't been emptied, and she retrieved discarded sheets of paper, some of it blue carbon paper imprinted with typewritten words, which she tucked inside her dressing gown.

She slid open each drawer of the bureau, took out the contents, photographed them, then replaced them. Her eyes scanned book by book along the shelves. One book was slightly protruding, and caught her attention. She pulled it out. *The Selected Poems of Hanns Johst*, the title said. She had never heard of him, though the poems were translated into English.

The book was hollowed out, as though a rat had been trapped and gnawed deep into the heart of the book. In the hollow was a piece of folded paper. Dodo opened it.

The first line was in English. *Whenever I hear the word 'culture', I release the safety catch of my Browning*. Was it a code message? There were further sentences in German, and a list of names. Dodo spread it across the desk. Angling her torch, she used her locket camera to photograph it from every angle: click, click, click. She then replaced the book exactly where she found it, even remembering to leave it slightly protruding.

Finally, she tucked *Mein Kampf* under her arm and went back upstairs. Packing away her camera and film inside a secret inner base of her handbag, she fell into bed and slept deeply.

Despite her disturbed night, Dodo wasn't the last to arrive at breakfast the next morning – though Roger was already there.

"Why don't we leave early?" he whispered conspiratorially. "We can have a pub lunch on the way and have the afternoon to ourselves."

They found Sir Hubert, and Roger genially made their excuses. Sir Hubert was courteous. He bowed and kissed Dodo's hand. "I hope you enjoyed your bedtime reading, Miss Bridges-Smith?"

She smiled disarmingly. "I did try to make some headway with it, but I'm afraid I couldn't keep my eyes open. Perhaps I can try another time. I returned the book to your study this morning."

"Indeed," replied Sir Hubert, graciously. "You must come again. Oh – and bring your friend, Gwen."

Roger and Dodo went through all the niceties with the other guests, resisting Max's entreaties to stay a little longer. Before they left, Max drew Roger aside for a quiet word.

"Phew!" exclaimed Roger, returning and helping Dodo into the car. "I've had enough of Fotherington Hall for one weekend. I hope you agree. It's a bit stuffy for my taste."

"Can't say I mind at all!" she agreed truthfully.

"I know an excellent pub by the river," Roger said. "And after, we can drop in to a dance at the Lyceum in Hammersmith. We could do with a bit of boogie woogie after those stuffy waltzes and ländlers – don't you think?" He looked boyishly rebellious. "By the way, Max thinks you should come and stay with us at Dolphin Square for a few days. As Gwen is away, she thought you should have company."

Dodo was taken aback. "Good heavens no! I'm used to Gwen going off."

"Please Dodo," Roger begged. "Max would really love it. It's her birthday tomorrow, and we'd love you to celebrate with us. If you stayed over, you wouldn't have to worry about the blackout and getting back in the dark."

"Look – can we get going?" Dodo laughed lightly, trying to avoid any further coercion. "I'm longing for a good old knees-up!"

So, here they were, in the Lyceum ballroom, under the revolving light ball. All kinds of men and women – soldiers, sailors, airmen and civilians, many in uniform – circled the ballroom in a great joyful whirlpool of movement. Roger held her close and brushed her hair from time to time with surreptitious kisses, his lips on her cheek, or her ear, or the top of her head. She leaned in to his arms. It wasn't difficult; he was tender, gallant, caring. Despite his somewhat weighty figure, he was a smooth and elegant dancer, moving with lightness and practised footwork, and he treated her as respectfully as one of King Arthur's knights.

The atmosphere in the dance hall was getting more and more raucous. The orchestra played Glen Miller, and people broke into irresistible foot-tapping, body jiggling to *In the Mood*.

Then came a dread sound.

An air-raid siren ripped through the air. The music faltered to a halt. People reluctantly stopped dancing.

The lights went out; organisers yelled instructions and begged everyone to stay calm. The exit doors opened. A ripple ran through the darkness as everyone surged outside. The horrible wailing went on and on, until it seemed to engulf them. The surge accelerated into a stampede.

"I've dropped my bag!"

"I've lost a shoe!"

"Oh forget your silly shoe – let's get out of here."

"Margie – where are you! Bertie!"

People were calling to each other; some stumbled, others fell; hands were loosened, friends separated.

"Hold on to me," Roger murmured in Dodo's ear as they were jostled and pushed towards a side exit by the weight of bodies behind them. "Probably just another practice."

Dodo clasped her handbag tightly to her chest. Roger swept his arms round her waist so as not to lose her until, at last, they stepped outside into a side alley. The siren was still howling. Shades of darkness folded and inter-folded as a moon appeared and disappeared behind tumultuous clouds. They breathed deeply, relishing the sharp night air, until they reached a wall and used it as a guide to move further and further away.

The siren stopped its wail.

"Listen!" said Roger.

"What?" asked Dodo fearfully.

"No aeroplanes!"

Dodo looked up into the vast ocean of black sky, and

listened. In between the luminous white clouds were spaces like oceans; empty and silent.

Roger kissed her full on the lips.

"It was a practice," he murmured into her ear as the all-clear sounded.

But over the Channel in France, it was not.

CHAPTER 33

The Archangel

PARIS, 10 MAY 1940

Sirens were wailing in the middle of the night.

Vera was wrenched from her sleep. There was a rumpus on the stairs and a loud frantic rapping going from door to door.

"It's happened, it's happened! The Germans are invading France. Listen to your radio. They've gone into Holland, Luxembourg, Belgium – all at once! They've reached the Ardennes!" Voices were shouting down the stairwells and across the courtyards. "They've stormed the Maginot Line! The boche are in France!"

Uncle Victor got out of bed and opened the door. His neighbour from across the way was turning in circles, breathing hard and clutching his chest. "Calm down, man!" cried Uncle Victor. "You'll give yourself a heart attack. Come in and have some rum."

Aunt Minnie came out, clasping her dressing gown, as Uncle Victor led their neighbour into the apartment.

"What's happening?"

Vera scrambled from her bed as Jeanne rushed in weeping, "Oh my God, what's going to happen?"

"They've done it!" panted the neighbour. "The boche have invaded. I heard it on the BBC."

For the first time, Vera saw her aunt's cool veneer shatter. She ran into Louis's room and knelt by her sleeping son as though he were her little Christ Child, and the only one who could save them.

More and more people appeared in their doorways, huddling into tight clusters. Voices rang up the stairwells. What to do? Where to go? What had happened to the French army? Although war had been declared eight months earlier, and thousands of Parisians had fled the city for the coasts or the Spanish border, when nothing happened they had returned home, deciding that, somehow, the whole thing was a dream.

Now fear tore through the city all over again.

By noon the following day, the whole of Paris was seething with the news. It spread from one neighbourhood to another and another, and another. People rushed into the streets, gathered on corners, and shared newspapers filled with headlines: *Invasion!* The streets and boulevards became great rivers of vehicles: barely functioning old bangers, chauffeur-driven limousines; small cars, battered cars, large and sleek cars; the rich, the poor, the in-betweeners; those with hand carts, prams, bicycles, horse-drawn carts, piled with whatever they could carry – suitcases, bundles, mattresses, prams, toys, pet dogs and cats and birdcages. It seemed the entire populace was on the move – heading westwards to Normandy or Brittany, or south towards Spain – the Pyrenees – or anywhere – just getting out. The railway stations were teeming: trains pulling away with doors still open, people hanging out, and families getting separated.

"We've been invaded! The boche are really coming this time!"

Vera cycled across the city, taking the back streets but hardly able to avoid a distraught populace, their cries filling the air like panicked birds in the face of a storm. She arrived at the door of the Alkans' bookshop. Would Daniel be home?

It was a while before it was opened – just a crack. Daniel's mother peered through with a look of terror, as if Vera was a German already on her doorstep. "Oh, it's you, Vera! I thought you were the *flic*." She was even more afraid of the French police than the Germans.

"Is Daniel here?" Vera asked urgently.

Madame Alkan pulled her inside. "He vanished three days ago – we haven't seen him, and now they've invaded." Her voice splintered with fear.

Daniel's father appeared and put his arm round his wife. "They're after communists. I told Daniel he should have resigned from the party after that dirty deal with the Nazis. But he wouldn't. Stubborn as ever! With luck, he's hiding out somewhere safe. He told us not to worry, but if you should hear anything –"

"Of course, of course!" Vera reassured him.

"They've invaded, Vera! Can you believe it?" cried Madame Alkan. "The boche have broken through the Maginot Line just like that – as though it were a mere ribbon. They're coming. What are we going to do?"

Impulsively, Vera kissed them both, then grabbed her bike and cycled on.

A police van cruised slowly down the Rue des Rosiers, beeping hard on its horn to make people jump out of the way. One lad didn't move quickly enough. The van stopped. Two *gendarmes* leaped out, grabbed him and they flung him into the back of the van.

Vera headed for the Café Rigaud.

The awnings were raised, the tables cleared and Georgie was heaving in the chairs. She rushed over to him in horror. His face was bruised; his chin red, his eyes black and blue.

"They're after the communists!" he said. "Now that those bastard Russians have made friends with the boche, all commies are seen as enemies. They raided us last night. Picked up a bunch of students: commies, anarchists – you name it. They took Antoine and Yvette. They picked up Levi. Trust them to start with Jews."

"Levi?" Vera felt sick; Daniel's best friend.

"You lot better watch out."

"And Daniel?"

"*Non*. Not Daniel." Georgie grasped her arm and lowered his voice. "Daniel was hoping you'd call by. He's making himself scarce these days; left you a note." He pushed a piece of paper into Vera's hand. "If you see him, tell him to lie low. They've got his name on a list as a ringleader and troublemaker." He jerked his head behind him. "They would have got Simone if she hadn't been in the ladies' room. She had the sense to stay put when she heard the rumpus."

Vera saw Simone in a far dark corner, stirring a cup of coffee with a blank expression on her face.

"She won't go home," said Georgie. "Get the hell out of here; take her with you if you can. And don't come back. I tell you, I'm lucky they didn't snatch me too. If they catch any more commies here, they'll shut me down."

"I'm sorry, Georgie," Vera said, kissing him. "Let's go, Simone. I'll walk home with you."

Simone didn't move.

"Scram, *mademoiselle*," Georgie yelled roughly. "I'm closing up now."

Simone drank the last of her coffee. "It's fine. I can see myself home," she told Vera sullenly. "I'm not a child." And determinedly, she limped away down the boulevard.

Vera opened Daniel's note.

I've left home. It's not safe. I'm staying at this address.
Ask for Marianne. Just give your name. You'll be let in.
You must keep this a complete secret from everyone – even from
my parents.

Marianne? Could she be Noor's Marianne? Vera took up
her bike. It would take her at least twenty minutes.

She skirted the east side of the Jardin du Luxembourg,
cycling against the flow of people and vehicles, and crossed
the river towards Parc Monceau. She was unnerved by
the contrast: the empty streets, the silence, the sense
of desolation. She cycled slowly, and arrived before an
elegant wrought-iron gate, behind which stood an ornate
house shaded by plane trees bursting into leaf. Crossing
a front garden lined with beds of flowers, she climbed a
flight of stone steps leading up to the front door, rang an
unpolished brass bell and waited.

"Who is it?" asked a female voice from within.

"Vera Bielawski. I'm to ask for Marianne."

The door was opened by a young woman, who admitted
her into an elegant hallway facing a staircase which curved
away to the next floor.

"Wait here," said the woman, shutting the door and
indicating a chair.

It was so quiet Vera could hear the clock ticking. She
glimpsed a figure, a shadow, as a person of barely any solid

substance glided noiselessly past the living-room door. The breathless silence was broken by the sound of hurried footsteps from beyond. A rear door opened and – her heart jolted.

"Léonie told me it was you! Oh Vera!" Daniel clasped her in his arms. "It's fantastic that you've come." He kissed her very tenderly, then led her along the passage to some dark stairs leading down to a windowless lower room.

Her friends rushed over to greet her: Antoine, Tibor, Yvette, Paul and Yvonne Barrault, all busily putting packs of identity papers together.

"Georgie told me the police picked up Levi," whispered Vera to Daniel. "Is he all right?"

Daniel's face creased with anxiety. "No one's heard from him since they nabbed him for doing nothing at all. All we can do is wait and hope."

At least a dozen men and women crowded round a central wooden table. Vera recognised some of them from her synagogue, but there were also immigrants and refugees from Poland, Czechoslovakia, Rumania, Hungary – from all over Europe. They had fled to Paris – but now where were they to go? There was an atmosphere of quiet agitation and deep fear.

In a far corner of the room was a desk with a powerful lamp angled over a box of inks, pens, paint brushes, rulers, and rubber stamps. Nearby was a printing machine. An angular, intense young man holding a magnifying glass crouched over a sheet of card, working so closely that his nose nearly touched the paper. Standing behind him was an old man who passed him different pens and inks, and read from a list of names. As each document was completed, it was taken to the printing machine.

"You've arrived just in time, Vera," said Daniel. "We need go-betweens, messengers, and dogsbodies to fetch and carry. We're creating identity cards, travel passes, ration books – anything which may be required. We need couriers to take to them to a list of names I've put together. Do you have your bicycle?"

"Outside," Vera said.

"The Germans will reach Paris in a few days, and then believe me," said Daniel, "the net will start to close. But we've been preparing for this ever since war was declared. We must get as many immigrants, Jews, and refugees out of here as possible, with all the documents they'll need. Walter over there, he's a professor in the art college. The young man is Jacques, his student. He's a brilliant forger." He laughed ironically. "My God, he could have a great career in crime one day!"

"What about your parents, will you make papers for them? Where is everyone going to go?" Vera felt a wave of panic. "And my aunt and uncle, and Louis –"

Suddenly a woman appeared at the bottom of the cellar steps. People stopped talking and looked up respectfully. "*Bonjour, madame*," rippled softly round the room.

Vera stared at her with awe; this was the Marianne whom Noor had talked about with such love and concern;

the same person Noor had pointed out to her that evening at the Café Rigaud summer before last, when they had attended the talk given by the Catalan. Her hair was drawn back by combs, her pale face very lightly made up; she had dressed with sufficient care to give her an air of competence and authority.

She spotted Daniel and embraced him heartily. "Good to see you, *mon chèr!*"

Daniel put a hand on Vera's back and nudged her forward. "Marianne, please meet Vera. She would like to help us."

Marianne shook her hand warmly, and kissed her on both cheeks, looking distracted. "Thank you, thank you," she muttered, her eyes looking beyond Vera. "We shall need all the help we can get."

"I'm Noor's friend from school in England," Vera blurted out, to stop Marianne from turning away.

Marianne's face lit up with joy. She clasped Vera again. "You know Noor? My beloved Noor? Ah! Of course! You're *Vera!* She told me about you. She stayed with you the summer before last, *n'est-ce pas?* How is she? I haven't heard from her – not since she wrote to tell me she had joined the British Army. I couldn't believe it. Our pacifist, peace-loving, non-violent Noor is in the army? Tell me how this happened! When did you last see her? How is she? You don't have to leave just yet, do you . . .?" Her questions fell from her lips with no space to answer them. "You will stay – stay overnight. I do so want to hear more of Noor, and her family. Her father – how is her dear father?"

Vera looked helplessly at Daniel. "There is so much to tell –"

"Marianne," Daniel said gently. "You can talk to Vera tomorrow. You will have time to hear all her news. But not tonight. We must deal with these people here. I need Vera to collect documents from a list of addresses I'll give her, and she must return to her family, or they'll worry."

Marianne shook her head, her face brimming with smiles. "This young man – we call him the Archangel, Vera. We rely on him completely. He's so level-headed and calm. I do everything and anything he asks. But I rely on you, Daniel, to allow me time with Vera – very soon, mind, or else I'll explode with impatience." She laughed and moved away.

"She's wonderful," said Daniel, "and for someone who isn't a Jew, she is taking the most incredible risks to help us."

"I shall always think of you as an archangel now." Vera smiled lovingly. "It describes you perfectly."

Daniel hugged her. "So long as I can be your guardian angel, I don't care what I'm called. Now look, after you've delivered these documents, the addresses are mostly in the Marais – please go to my place in Rue des Rosiers and tell my parents I'm all right. Ask them to give you their passport, travel cards, and identity cards. You must bring the documents here tomorrow so we can alter the details.

Do the same for your aunt, uncle and Louis. Bring all the documents together. We've got to stay ahead of the game; we've got to assume the worst will happen. But on no account tell them of this place."

Daniel gave her an innocuous cloth bag which had an inner lining sewn into it for the documents in case she was stopped and searched, and a clear set of instructions. As he led her up the stairs and back to the front door, he called out to Léonie to bring a small amount of fruit and vegetables to put in the bag. "If they ask, you've been at the market. Deliver to these addresses first, then finally to my parents."

As Vera wheeled her bike on to the road, she glanced back at the house, and saw the pale face of a man in a dressing gown, watching her from the window. She wondered who he was as she cycled away.

The streets in the Marais were a heaving flood of people. She made her deliveries, knocking with a special knock on each door which had been agreed. She finally reached Rue des Rosiers.

"He's safe. Don't worry," she reassured the Alkans. "He'll be in touch as soon as possible." And she asked for the documents which Daniel had requested.

"We shouldn't have to do this." Daniel's father shook his head despairingly as he handed them over. "We are French citizens."

When Vera returned to Rue d'Assas it was to find more distress: her aunt weeping, her uncle adamant that nothing could happen to them.

When Vera told him the plan to forge them new documents in case they were needed, Uncle Victor was overcome with uncharacteristic fury.

"It's ridiculous," he spluttered. "I refuse to hand over my papers. My God – if they should ever find false documents in our possession we would be done for! No. We will carry on and obey the law. I have no intention of running away like a rat. We are French; we are Catholic," he ranted. "We have demonstrated in every way our loyalty to France. My father was a major in the French army during the Great War. He fought with honour and was decorated. My family have died for France. We are as French as anyone."

"What about me?" murmured her aunt fearfully.

Uncle Victor snorted. "Your papers are in the system, and you are married to me, and the mother of my son who was born here. We have nothing to fear. But you, Vera – you are a different matter. We insist . . ."

Insist . . . insist . . . The word rebounded through Vera's brain.

"This changes everything. I *insist* you leave for England immediately, Vera! How dare these student dissidents and communists involve you in counterfeiting forged documents – my God! These fellows are hot-headed and dangerous. It is you who could be in danger. I forbid you to see them again! Your aunt was right. I shouldn't have let you stay instead of returning to school.

"We've been talking it over. I have already booked your train tickets to Bordeaux. You will be met by my colleague, Mathieu Printemps. He thinks he can get you on to a boat to England, or to the Channel Islands. If that fails, he swears to keep you safe. You'll be safer there than here in Paris. Take this money. It will cover you back to England, till I can send some more. You must return to Barrowfield."

They forced her to pack; hurrying her along. "The train leaves in two hours. You just have time to make it," said Uncle Victor. "The concierge has got us a taxi."

This time, Vera didn't dig in her heels. She said goodbye to her weeping aunt, and clasped Louis, who was clinging to her legs, begging her not to go. She covered him with kisses. "Just remember," she whispered in his ear, "I'll never forget you."

Vera and her uncle climbed into the taxi together. There was a massive movement of people heading for the train stations, and they were pressed for time. Vera's uncle was prepared to carry her bodily on to the train if she resisted, but she didn't resist.

"*Au revoir, mon chèr oncle,*" she whispered tenderly.

He clasped her tightly. "*Au revoir, chérie*; stay safe. Forgive me. It's for the best – for you and us all. We'll be in touch somehow."

Vera followed the porter on board and leaned out of the window. Uncle Victor was standing there – and for all his fine clothes and confident poise, he suddenly looked unbearably vulnerable, and tears trickled down his face which he didn't bother to wipe away.

"Stay safe, Uncle," she called, her own eyes springing with tears. "Don't trust anyone. Jews are no longer safe. Look after Louis."

The train pulled slowly away with grinding wheels and screeching whistle. As soon as her uncle was lost in the swirls of steam, she opened the opposite door and flung out her bag.

"*Mademoiselle!*" A voice called out in alarm. "*Non!*"

But lowering herself towards the track, Vera let go before anyone could stop her.

CHAPTER 34

Operation Dynamo

So, this is it. The war for us has finally arrived. Day after day the news is terrifying. Our troops advance and are then forced back; battles rage on the ground, sea, and in the air.

I had been in the Locations Section, but am now in the heart of London, back in the depths of the War Office with the tele-prompters rattling night and day. The Germans are on the move. I don't know when I'll next get back to the flat. I ask a colleague to drop off a note for Dodo at Orange Street.

Every day, I lean over the map table like a billiard player, holding a long pole. Before me stretches the map of Europe and, like some dark game, I move the pieces around, representing the armies. The Germans have already gobbled up Czechoslovakia and Poland – they didn't have a chance. Now it's Denmark and Norway and – a shiver goes around the room when our radio operator calmly says: "They've crossed into France. The Maginot Line is broken."

The swoop carries on into Belgium, Luxembourg and Holland.

Around me I can hear a buzz of anxiety and consternation. It is hard to conceive that the pieces I move on the board represent real men: fighting, fearing, wounded men; dying, calling, weeping, remembering, hurting. A veritable Babel's Tower rising into the firmament, a tower of lamentation; millions upon millions of people calling out in all their different languages.

It'll be England next. We aren't strong enough to stop them. Everyone knows that. But Winston Churchill says no; no, no, no. Never, never, never.

The very day after the Germans burst into France, Chamberlain resigned, and Winston Churchill became joint Prime Minister with Clement Attlee of the Labour Opposition. It was to be a special War Coalition. Logic said we hadn't a chance, but Churchill continued to insist: "We must fight. We will never surrender," and all of us in the map room couldn't help cheering.

My mind flew to Vera. If she was still in Paris, then she would be in mortal danger. If only she would leave. It was not for want of begging her; endless letters, telling her to get herself to Bordeaux, where there were still Red Cross boats leaving for England.

Nowadays, my heart and brain are like separate entities.

One bit is in utter dread for Eric up in the skies, Vera in France, and Aunt Madge, Uncle Harold, Archie and – yes, silly, isn't it – Ralph too. The other part is me, myself. Who am I, what am I? A mere cog in the war machine, carrying out orders, removing any human feeling from the theatre of war. But I know I'm needed – every single cog and screw is vital. If one piece fails, the whole machine could fail. A battle won here, I move a piece; a battle lost there, I move another piece. The tele-prompters rattle on.

The battles rage in Belgium and France, on land and in the air; our troops are being pushed back and back towards the coast. The German war machine seems unstoppable. We whisper to each other: "What's going to happen to our troops?" There is now a real danger that even the British Expeditionary Force, the *crème de la crème*, are in danger of being wiped out. Isn't Charles among them? Dodo will be worried sick. Or will she? I remembered our last encounter.

I shuffle the military positions round with my pole. Calais has fallen, Boulogne has fallen; now, there is only the small port town of Dunkirk which they are smashing to smithereens.

Dunkirk, where the land runs out. There is only the sea. All eyes scouring the skies for those tiny black specks topping the horizon like screaming harpies, nearer and nearer; bombs dropping, machine guns firing. The horrible scattering of men across the open beaches, rushing into the sea, floundering with all their kit, many to drown. Our troops are trapped in their thousands with nowhere to hide.

Battleships, cruisers and destroyers come to the rescue but dare not get too close to the shore and be trapped in the shallows. They watch helplessly as soldiers try to swim for it, or get into wobbly inflatable dinghies and capsize.

Churchill warns that we face a colossal military disaster. We could lose over 400,000 troops – our finest troops. If they are lost, the war will be lost. Surely that means surrender? But Churchill says again and again, with utter conviction, "We will never surrender."

Panic-stricken ideas pour out. How can we evacuate our troops? The battle ships, medicine ships, the cruisers and destroyers have already been deployed; the air force has flown inland, to keep the enemy at bay. I think of Eric. He has been training with newly adapted Spitfires. But now, with barely any time to get to know the new planes, they are being sent out into combat. What should we do; how could we help? Why were we so outclassed by the Germans? Weren't we supposed to be the strongest nation on earth?

At last, I was sent home.

I entered the flat and, through a haze of unbearable fatigue, saw Dodo scrabbling round for pennies for the telephone.

"I must phone Charles's parents in Ramsgate," she cried.

I hardly heard her, let alone responded. I grunted

something like, "Must sleep. Talk to you later," fell into bed fully clothed and was immediately unconscious.

God knows how long I slept. When I finally awoke, the flat was in pitch darkness and the blackout curtains were closed tight; nothing to tell me if it were night or day. Just a feeling of utter emptiness.

"Dodo?"

I sensed absence.

I stumbled into her room. The air was cold. I drew aside the curtains and daylight poured in. She was gone.

No time to think. I had to get back for the afternoon shift.

The pressure at work was intense. We were going to evacuate Dunkirk. They called it 'Operation Dynamo'. For the next few days, we weren't allowed home but were given camp beds to sleep on. They needed us on hand every hour of the day and night. We hardly saw daylight; daytime and night time were as one. We snatched sleep whenever we could.

We knew that thousands of soldiers were pouring down on to those vast exposed beaches at Dunkirk with nowhere to hide from the Stukas and their rattling machine guns. The whole operation seemed absolute folly. Already the casualties were appalling: bodies scattered across the sands, floating face-down in the sea.

A call for help was put out for anyone with a shallow-bottomed boat to go and help with the evacuation. And they answered the call. The shrimpers and crabbers, the dinghies, the motor boats, the holiday cruisers, the paddle steamers, the small yachts, the sailing boats, the fishing boats; all the little craft that the people of England owned for messing around in had set off across the Channel.

On the beaches of Dunkirk, the astonished soldiers saw a ghostly sight: hundreds of small boats emerging over a misty horizon with chugging engines and fluttering sails. It must have seemed like an armada of angels. I heard the word *miracle*. It *was* a miracle. Desperate soldiers rushed into the sea to greet them.

But soon, the mist turned to smoke, with explosions and machine guns. The toll was awful. Shell fire, bombing; air attacks, sinking of ships packed with troops. And still the small craft plucked bedraggled and half-drowned soldiers from the sea and struggled back to England.

On 4 June, ten days later, Operation Dynamo was declared over. The evacuation of Dunkirk was completed. An unbelievable 338,000 troops had been rescued; the British Army was saved.

Our defeat felt like a victory.

I was exhausted, euphoric; but fearful. This was not the end of the war, but the beginning.

It was after midnight. I drifted up a ghostly Whitehall to Trafalgar Square. Above me the barrage balloons floated silently, translucent-grey guardians of the skies. Emptied of thought, I sat on the edge of the fountain, relishing the soft silky air of a summer's night before carrying on to Orange Street.

No Mrs Antrobus popped her head round the door as I quietly turned the key. Poor Mrs Antrobus. I hadn't even had time to enquire after her boys. Might they have been caught up in Dunkirk? I needed to check. How I hoped Dodo had been sympathetic. I removed my shoes and noiselessly climbed the stairs. Another gentle turn of the key and I entered the flat.

I was about to turn on the light when I saw the curtains were wide open.

"Oh God, Dodo! How can you be so irresponsible!" I rushed to close them. "Dodo!" I shouted, so exasperated I didn't care if I woke her up. I ran to her room bursting with annoyance and yet exhilarated with my news. "Operation Dynamo is over! Most of our army has been rescued. Dodo! Wake up."

There was no reply. Her bedroom curtains, too, were open wide, and her bed empty and unslept in.

"Where the hell are you?" I said, pulling the curtains closed.

I stood there; remembering. I hadn't seen her since before Dunkirk, when she had been scrabbling round for telephone money, and I'd been too exhausted to talk to her. I remembered, too, how on waking the following morning, she had gone.

This absence was different.

Emptiness hung around the flat.

I had a bad feeling. Why wasn't I being rational? Surely she was just on one of her entertainment tours. She was always going somewhere; always apologising for not letting me know, or leaving a note. But this time, everything told me Dodo had truly gone. This time I felt frightened.

"Dodo?"

I spoke her name out loud as if, wherever she was, even if she were on the moon, she would hear me. But there was no reply.

I went back into the living room and put on the reading lamp to see if my note was lying around, and whether perhaps she had left me a message.

My note was there, lying so carelessly near other unopened letters which were neatly piled up. Someone had been in. Mrs Antrobus, I supposed. But nothing for me from Dodo: no message, no postcard.

I went back to her bedroom. What was I looking for? I didn't know. I opened the drawer of her bedside table and rummaged among odds and ends, and uncovered her notebook – one I'd seen many times with her drama manuscripts. I'd always assumed they were rehearsal notes. I picked it up and flicked through it.

I felt the blood draining from my face as I saw the lists of names, addresses, venues, factories, bases – information of value to the enemy.

"Oh Dodo!" I whispered. "What the hell have you been up to?"

"She's been working for us."

The unexpected male voice – a stranger's voice – froze me in terror. I fled for the door. He blocked it. He was speaking quietly, as if trying to calm me down, but my panic deafened me. I backed away, but he caught my arm, and forcibly held me. I opened my mouth to scream; he put a hand over it, while speaking softly and reassuringly:

"It's all right. Listen. Sorry to shock you. I'm Home Office." His face was in dark shadow. I struggled to free myself. "Don't run again – and I'll show you my identity. Please?"

I nodded. He took one hand away, and from his inside jacket pocket produced a card. It read: *Duncan Brown MI5 Special Operations. Home Office.*

He released me. I leaned back against the door.

"I think I'd better have this," he said, taking Dodo's notebook from me. "That's why I'm here. I came to collect it. Forgive me for frightening you like that."

"Is she a traitor?" I asked with dread.

"No. She was a patriot."

I shook my head as though I hadn't quite heard. "Is she not *still* a patriot? Is it because of that wretched Aryan Fellowship she got mixed up in?"

"She left a letter for you. I was going to take it as evidence." He held out a white envelope addressed to me in Dodo's writing.

I hardly understood what he was saying. "How dare you take my letter! What evidence?"

"Miss Atkins," Mr Brown said. "I believe some time ago, you reported anxieties about your friend, because of her association with the Aryan Fellowship, with Sir Hubert March and Mr Roger King."

"Yes! But not to you," I exclaimed angrily. I shook my head with guilt and remorse. "And not to betray her. I mean – I just wanted you all to know that this Aryan Fellowship existed. I thought that was important."

"It was indeed, Miss Atkins."

"And I was worried!" I insisted. "Dodo is naïve, warm-hearted – and these people were friends of her parents. But I've known her for years – since we were at school together. I would pledge my life that she is as loyal as can be. Her parents . . . well. They are a different matter. I can't tell you how much it grieved her. But they are just sympathisers – not traitors. There's a difference, isn't there? Oh God – I suppose now you think Dodo is a traitor."

"I don't think you quite understood me, Miss Atkins," said Mr Brown gently. "Miss Bridges-Smith was no traitor. She was a patriot, working for her country; working for us."

"Dodo?" I shook my head. "She wasn't even accepted in the ATS. How could she have been working for you? Where is she now?"

Mr Brown walked across the room, then back again, and looked at me very directly.

"Where is she?" I repeated. "Is she in prison?"

"I'm so sorry Miss Atkins. I'm afraid I have some bad news for you. Will you sit down?"

I didn't.

"Miss Dorothy Bridges-Smith was killed at sea while trying to rescue soldiers trapped on the beaches of Dunkirk."

I gasped in disbelief.

"I'm afraid she's dead."

I couldn't breathe.

"She died in the service of her country, helping at Dunkirk," Mr Brown continued. "She put out to sea with a Mr Clive Brandon – father of her acquaintance, Captain Charles Brandon? I believe you know him. An officer with the BEF? Captain Brandon was among those trapped on the beaches. His father had a small yacht, and responded to the call-out. Miss Bridges-Smith joined him. They rescued dozens of soldiers, ferrying them to the ships anchored further out. But on one of their sorties, I'm afraid their yacht took a direct hit. We only know about Miss Bridges-Smith because Captain Brandon's father was picked up safely by a hospital ship. He reported that she had been killed instantly."

My breath finally released in a terrible moan. I sat down.

This was the kind of bad news I had been rehearsing in my head ever since Vera told us her horrible story; ever since war had broken out. I had been preparing myself to receive the worst possible news that one could ever receive: the deaths of parents, siblings, husbands, lovers; Eric – even Ralph! Always wondering: how would I react?

How would I cope? What would it feel like? Now it had happened. This was no rehearsal. I was receiving real news. Dodo, my very best friend from school, was dead. I didn't know grief would be so physical.

Mr. Brown walked over to the sideboard. "May I pour us a drink?"

I stared at the window; at the curtains, and the orangey-brown patterns, remembering how Dodo always thought they were hideous, and that one day, we should change them.

"And Charles?" I finally managed to ask.

He handed me a sherry and indicated a glass for himself. "May I? Officially, Captain Brandon's missing. We haven't yet got a full list of dead, injured, or missing. I can't tell you one way or the other about the fate of Captain Brandon. We must wait till all have been accounted for."

He sat down in the armchair and sipped his sherry. "I think you should read the letter your friend left for you. I came for the notebook in case anyone came in; particularly the King family, Roger and Max."

I shuddered, repelled by the thought of strangers – enemies – contaminating our little Orange Street home.

"They've been looking for her as intently as we have," said Mr Brown. "They even got hold of Miss Grigson's address, and paid her a visit. Fortunately, we had already warned her that Miss Bridges-Smith was missing. We alerted her to the possibility of strangers turning up, making enquiries. When Roger King did indeed turn up, she reported them immediately, as instructed. It was Miss Grigson who told us about the Brandons in Ramsgate. We were hard on your friend's heels, but sadly, just a day too late to stop her putting to sea."

"Oh poor Griggy! Dodo was like her own child." I was beginning to sob. "I presume she knows now?"

"Yes," said Mr Brown, "I went to see her myself."

"And what about her parents?" I felt a sudden surge of rage. They were the cause of all this – of their daughter's death. She would never have got involved with the Aryan Fellowship if it hadn't been for them.

"They'll be receiving a letter," said Mr Brown curtly. "Of course, the Aryan Fellowship also questioned Mrs Antrobus. But we had already recruited her. She may be a gossip, but she isn't stupid, and she's loyal. You were right: the Kings and their Aryan Fellowship are the enemy.

"Miss Bridges-Smith gave us invaluable information. She was at Fotherington Hall the day Germany invaded France. That day, at great risk to herself, she obtained very important information which would have affected the security of our country. It led to the arrest of the leader of the British Union of Fascists, Oswald Mosley, and several hundred of his followers – many of whom were in the Aryan Fellowship. She also identified others: people who were extremely high up in society with immense influence, about whom we had suspicions but no proof. Her service to us was unique.

"Forgive me, but I did read your letter. It's my job. But I'm happy to say I can leave it with you for your own reassurance." He swallowed the rest of his sherry and got up. "Thank you for the notebook." He tucked it into an inside pocket of his jacket. "Pity your other school friend, Miss Khan is away."

I looked up, surprised. "You mean Noor?" Of course, he'd know about Noor. "She's somewhere in Surrey on an ATS training course."

"Yes, we have her details." He sounded apologetic for this invasion of our privacy. "Would you like me to ask Mrs Antrobus to come up and keep you company for a while?"

"No. Thank you. I'd rather be alone."

"I'm so sorry for the loss of your friend." His voice changed from being official to human, and he said gently, "We were all taken by surprise at her decision to help with the Dunkirk evacuation. It was an impulse. She told no one. We will miss her valuable contribution."

I stared at him with watering eyes.

"I think I can trust you to say nothing to anyone about me, or who I am?" he said.

I nodded tearfully.

"Goodbye Miss Atkins."

I tried to get to my feet, but Mr Brown said, "Please don't get up, I can see myself out." He held out his hand. I shook it. He put on his hat and, pulling the brim over his eyes, left, closing the door softly behind him.

I read the letter.

Darling Gwen,

I hardly know who I am any more. I seem never to be able to speak the truth. I wonder if I'll ever speak Truth again. I can't even tell you what I'm talking about. I can't bear knowing what you think of me; I can't bear knowing what Charles thinks of me – that I am the child of my parents, and believe what they believe. All I can say is, I've tried to do the right thing; tried to do my duty; but I've felt torn apart. I don't think I can bear it any longer. I'm weak. I'm a coward. I don't feel trustworthy.

Please forgive me for deceiving you.

I've gone to Ramsgate. All hell is breaking loose over in France. Well, you'll know that already. Charles's parents are desperate with worry. I am too. Our soldiers are trapped in Dunkirk, and Charles is surely among them. I can't just sit here knowing he's in deadly danger.

The big ships can't get close enough to the shore so they're calling for anyone with a boat to go and help. The Brandons have a small yacht and are bound to help with the evacuation. With Mrs Brandon ill, I must join them. How could I ever live with myself if I didn't try to save Charles? I'm taking the next train to Ramsgate.

For once, I'd appreciate you going to church and praying like hell. (Can you pray like hell in church?)

In haste.
Dodo

P.S. In case you weren't sure, it was always Charles I loved.

CHAPTER 35

Never, never, never, never, never,
NEVER, NEVER, NEVER, NEVER, NEVER

I dream, intense dreams, like a fisherman hauling up nets out of the ocean, leaping dreams like silver fishes from the darkest deep of my subconscious; sounds I thought I'd forgotten. My Indian ayah's soft singing in the shade of the veranda, fanning me to sleep with a banana leaf; the rhythmic clipping of the gardener's shears, horses' hooves in the road, or the creak of bullock carts. My mother drinking tea with her friends; she turns, smiles at me and waves. "Come and say hello, darling!" Then I dream of my father sitting at his desk, plotting his next tour round the district: handing out orders, distributing wheat, flour, and rice to the villages, mopping the sweat from his brow. I feel the heat of the day; hear the endless cooing of doves, the voices of children, the mixture of languages: Punjabi, Hindi, Urdu, and English. My brothers laugh and playfight.

Tied to the earth's orbit, I rotate among the stars, and over the ocean, and tip into England; into school. I dream of my friends, I dream of Dodo, I see her loving, mocking face, and hear her taunting me:

"Yes, Aunty Gwen," when I beg her to be careful as she goes off on a daring escapade with Charles which could get her expelled; and I hear her grateful sigh when I, always her gatekeeper, let her back into school after the gate has been closed. "Thank you Gwenny Penny."

I wake up laughing and crying. She can't be gone. I remember King Lear repeating and repeating over the body of his beloved daughter, Cordelia: "Never, never, never, never, never see her more." Dodo had longed to play Cordelia – now she never would.

CHAPTER 36

The Fall Of Paris

14 JUNE 1940

Vera sat up in bed; something had woken her. Her first instinct was one of fear. She had been sleeping – deeply – and with a new sense of security knowing that Daniel was nearby in another safe house. Better for everyone in their small organisation, to stay as separately as possible in case of a raid.

Marianne had willingly taken her in, after she had jumped the train which was supposed to take her to the boat to England. She had been given a mattress on an upper landing. There was barely a square inch of the house that wasn't a space for a refugee staying, while a safe route was organised to get them out of Paris. Vera easily became an integral part of the network: identifying a chain of safe houses for Jews and stateless foreigners, who were being helped to escape from the ever-increasing roundups and arrests.

The sound from outside came again. She stepped to a window, peering out between the shutters into the grey light. A dark green truck drove slowly past their house. A Nazi flag fluttered on the bonnet. A grey-uniformed German soldier picked up a megaphone: his metallic, disembodied voice obscenely shattered the sleeping neighbourhood. In heavily accented French, he decreed over and over again: *Paris is now under the occupation and control of the Supreme German Military High Command. Tonight, there will be a curfew starting at 8 p.m. Anyone seen out after this hour will be severely punished.*

"They're here!" Vera screamed, rushing out of her bedroom. "The boche are in Paris."

Wanting to be in control before Paris awoke, the Germans had poured through eerily empty suburbs in the grey twilight, along silent, sullen boulevards, where the shops and cafés were boarded up, and the curtains drawn in the apartment windows. When the citizens awoke, they immediately knew who was in charge. "We are here!" the red, black and white swastikas proclaimed, as they replaced the French tricolores on public buildings. "We are the victors!" yelled the posters everywhere showing the Nazis' own V sign.

Sleeping bodies stirred in alarm. Marianne and Léonie appeared on the landings below, struggling into their dressing gowns. They flew into the living room and Marianne opened the doors on to the balcony overlooking the street.

Vera clutched the curtain to her mouth to control her terror.

"So! They've arrived," a voice said softly. It was the man in the dressing gown she had seen before, who had appeared silently at her side to gaze out of the window. "We tried to stop them in Spain," he muttered sadly, "but we were nothing against their war machine. Now, they're here."

"Yes," said Vera, thinking him to be one of those in hiding here in Marianne's house.

"What do you think, *mademoiselle*? How should a Nazi invader enter Paris with any dignity? How should he claim this beautiful city, this golden prize, this jewel of Europe?"

Vera shook her head helplessly. "I have no idea."

"Here they are," he said, "in the very epitome of culture, resistance, freedom, philosophy and the arts; everything that is worth living for. *Non?*"

Vera nodded, feeling his grief. "The Germans – they have culture too," she reminded him: "music and philosophy, Beethoven, Schubert, Goethe, Kant. But what use is culture and civilisation if they behave like bandits?"

"Perhaps they never learned enough about *liberté, égalité, fraternité?*" He shrugged. "But how humiliating if they came in like marauding barbarians – like Attila the Hun, or Genghis Khan. In Paris of all places, Hitler wants to be seen as civilised and noble, not as a vandal. But you see, they will soon show their barbarism: they will be bombing and scattering thousands of panic-stricken citizens; the old, young, infirm, disabled, women and children fleeing Paris in whichever way they can."

"Where will they go?" Vera murmured. "Look!" She pointed. "The sky over there is pink. Is that the dawn?"

The man at her side, gave no reply. And when she turned to him, he had gone, as silently as he had come.

Later more and more of their friends came to Marianne's door. The pink of dawn had become Paris on fire. They heard more stories. The Parisians were burning oil tanks ahead of the enemy's arrival, and flames were shooting out of government buildings as official papers were burned. The populace plodded on, listening for the next distant whine of German fighter planes, swooping across the open skies, dipping low over the endless winding trails of exhausted families, with no food, water, or shelter – disastrously exposed to the deadly, rattling machine guns.

Parisians had crammed the railways stations to overflowing, crushing children and fainting women, bringing the trains to a standstill until, at last, the madness stopped. It finally dawned on them that flight was useless; there was nowhere to go. And after the defeat at Dunkirk, England would surely be next to be invaded; no one would be coming to their rescue. So, they turned around despairingly, and headed back home, leaving behind them abandoned cars in ditches, scattered belongings and, along the roadside, the bodies of men, women, and children, some entangled with each other in death, others separated, maimed, wounded, and dying, while dogs howled helplessly; birds tipped over in their cages, flapping and fluttering.

Before the sun was up, Yvette arrived on Marianne's doorstep. She was shaking, crying, and ashen-faced: "They're here!" Vera sat her down and put a blanket round her, while Marianne ran into the kitchen and came out with hot bowls of coffee and bread.

"I was trying to get home," stammered Yvette.

She had stayed in Marianne's cellar late into the night working on some urgent travel passes and identity cards. Then she had set off with the documents hidden in a secret section of her handbag, ready to hand over to a family in danger of being rounded up. It was just before dawn when, after delivering the papers, she was making her way back and heard something. Instinctively, she hid in the shrubbery of an apartment block. "I saw them!" She shook uncontrollably as she described the German soldiers: some stalking the streets, others on motorbikes and tanks, others in jeeps mounted with machine guns, on the lookout for any attackers. "I couldn't move," she said. "Heaven knows, they would have shot me for sure. They seemed to come from every direction."

Vera thought of her aunt and uncle and of little Louis.

Why were they still in Paris? What folly. She leaped to her feet. "I must see my family!" she cried.

Marianne restrained her. "No Vera. This is not the time for rash acts. You'll endanger them, yourself, and us. Stay calm."

Daniel arrived. "Thank God you're safe," cried Vera, throwing herself into his arms.

"Calm, calm dearest." How tender he was with her these days.

And while Paris came to terms with the German occupiers, Marianne and the team continued their work with more intensity and urgency than ever: forging identity cards, railway and travel passes, ration books, letters proving intent and identification. They sent people on their way, dodging patrols and curfews, to be passed secretly from one safe house to the next.

One late night Vera, unable to sleep, quietly descended the stairs to get a drink from the kitchen. She passed Marianne's door. It was slightly open, and she couldn't help but observe a figure propped in bed while Marianne gently administered a spoon of medicine. By the light of an oil lamp, Vera saw it was a man – the pale man she had talked to earlier. His eyes gazed into Marianne's, his mouth open as trustfully as a child's.

"It'll soon work, darling Pascal," she said. "The pain will ease, and then you'll get some sleep."

So, this was Marianne's husband.

CHAPTER 37

Deadly Rain

LONDON BLITZ: 4 SEPTEMBER 1940

"We heard this noise," Mrs Antrobus would tell me afterwards.

It was 4 September, a year and a day since war had been declared.

She had gone over to see her sister Molly in Canning Town, East London, where Molly lived with her husband Reg and their three children.

"We looked at each other, all of us puzzled," said Mrs Antrobus.

"What the heck's that?" Molly had asked.

Reg had shaken his head. "God knows."

They had all gone outside to see, and so had the whole street. The noise was getting louder and nearer: a dark, deep rumble. Was it tanks? Motorbikes?

Now everyone was looking up into the late evening sky. It was empty except for a few isolated birds flying madly by as if in a dash for cover. What they saw, transfixed them.

"We'd only once seen such a sight," Mrs Antrobus said. "We were in Blackpool one year, and the sky was filled with wave after wave of migrating geese, honking and beating the air with their wings: vroom, vroom, vroom, coming and coming and coming like a rising tide."

"This ain't no geese," Reg had muttered as the first bombs began to drop like rain: iron rain, needles of rain, deadly rain; a deluge, hurtling down, on and on and on; wave after wave of German bombers flying in formation, coming nearer and nearer; explosions and flames shooting into the air; the ground bursting open. Even the sky was on fire.

"Get to the shelters," someone yelled as the air-raid warning sirens began wailing.

There was a mad dash to the public shelter three streets away. Mums and dads scooped up their children and ran – stumbling, gasping, crying; panic-stricken. Molly and Reg grabbed their two eldest, Ivy and Gordon. Mrs Antrobus was already holding baby Florrie in her arms, and they, too, ran for it. No one looked over their shoulders, so they didn't see or hear her cry. They didn't see her stumble, falling on to her knees and elbows as she desperately protected the baby.

"Flat on my face, I was – and little Florrie screaming blue murder. Old Mr Belling was at the gate. He'd lost a leg in the last war so he wasn't going nowhere in a hurry."

"Oi, missus," he'd called out to her. "Come in here. I've got a cellar. Bring the littl'un!"

"I hauled that baby up like a bundle of laundry," Mrs Antrobus said, "and rushed inside this bloke's house and down into the pitch darkness of the cellar.

"All night long, them bombers and Stukas swooped over the city with machine-gun fire and incendiaries. You should've heard them ear-splitting bangs and booms, as if they would blow the universe apart. Oh Gawd; it went on and on and on. We thought it would never end. The noise made your whole body shake like it would tear your heart out. I thought it was the end of the world.

"Then it stopped."

They had waited; just listening. In that long, frightening silence, no one called out, no child cried, no dog barked, no sirens sounded. Then finally they heard the jangling, clanging bells of police, ambulances, and fire engines rushing into the scene.

"It took us a while to open the door – what with the rubble – what with Mr Belling with his one leg, and me with the baby. But when we finally clambered out of that cellar, we must have looked like ruddy ghosts – all covered from head to foot in fine white dust, wondering if we were really alive. The front of the house had come down. Half the street was flattened; fires were burning; smoke and ash swirled through the air. We thought we'd died, Miss Atkins; died and gone to hell."

Mrs Antrobus told me all this two days later, when they finally found me. I rushed straight over after my duties were finished, to find her in a makeshift bed in a church hall in Islington, white-faced and in shock. She still had little Florrie cradled by her side; she wouldn't be parted from her.

"Florrie's all that's left, you see. Molly, Reg, Ivy and Gordon all made it to the communal shelter in Canning Road, only to get a direct hit from a ten-ton bomb. Hit the lot of them. No one survived."

I was working all hours in the map room, often sleeping there on a camp bed, and not returning to Orange Street for days on end. Anyway, it was still too painful to walk into the Orange Street flat with Dodo gone.

Mrs Antrobus took Florrie to Basingstoke to live with her brother. She was too terrified and traumatised to stay on in London. Night after night, the bombs kept falling; the sirens screamed. By day, survivors emerged to discover who of their families and neighbours were alive, injured, or dead.

Yet the post got through – even if delayed. I even got a letter from Eric.

Gwenny –
I've never seen such a sight in my life. I don't know how I can admit this – but instead of feeling horror at what was happening below me, I was awestruck. It was like seeing some kind of cosmic creation happening in the universe; a wondrous beauty. Incredible

colours from flames and smoke, orange, yellow, red, blue, purple and white, mixed and merged and swirled as if on some kind of vast palette. And though I dived into the fray with my machine guns firing, and watched my enemy plunging earthwards like falling candles, I was untouched; I felt invincible, exhilarated; God was on our side! It was only when we were counted back in, I realised my mates Makepeace, Gibb, and Courtney were blown up, and Rowley – my dear friend, Rowley – was terribly burned – but alive.

The blitz continued relentlessly. Eric went back up again and again. Even though the average lifespan for a young pilot was ten days, it was as if Eric had a shield around him – though I tried not to fool myself. It was luck, and Lady Luck is fickle. Eric said, "If your number's up, then it's up. Nothing to be done, old thing!"

I routinely searched the casualty lists to see if Ralph or Eric's name was among the lost, wounded, or killed in action.

On his next leave, Eric and I met for a day and walked down Piccadilly arm in arm. We talked softly about our childhood: nothing too deep, nothing much about the future – except – maybe – one day – a determination to return to India.

"If they'll let us," I said with a laugh. "Noor says they're going to kick us out as soon as this war's over!"

One day, the blitz stopped. London was eerily quiet. For days, people walked in a daze, past shattered buildings with their innards hanging out, revealing bathrooms and kitchens; staircases that ended abruptly, leading nowhere; a living room intact, with sofa, two armchairs, radio on the mantlepiece, and even the table set for supper: everything untouched, except with the walls sliced off.

But it was true. After fifty-seven days and nights, Hitler had stopped bombing London.

Orange Street had got a battering but, amazingly, our building stayed standing, and I had been able to creep back from time to time, to wash clothes and replace underwear.

With the announcement that Hitler had turned his attention to Russia, I decided to move properly back to the flat. How strange it felt, to sleep there, entirely alone. No Dodo; no Mrs Antrobus.

Then one day, I came back to find Noor.

I looked at her as if she were a phantom. I hadn't heard a word from her since the start of the Blitz. She was thinner; looked, more fragile; she said she'd been on a training course somewhere out in Norfolk. They had been allowed no contact whatsoever.

"I can't believe you're safe," I cried, as we joyfully hugged each other. "Where have you been? I thought you might even be dead."

She was back in London to appear before a board. "I'm being interviewed for a new position," she said, but was vague about what it was.

With dread, I brought myself to ask, "You know about Dodo?"

No, she hadn't heard about Dodo. I told her. Her tears rolled down silently while I explained.

She found the veena and, in a rippling of strings, invoked everything: her memories, her friends, her grief; stripping her sorrow down to her tangled aspirations for all that was loving and hopeful. She didn't talk about her fairies; only about how she wanted to fight the forces of evil which were trying to destroy us. She talked philosophically, hopefully, about life and death. Everything had meaning.

That night, I lay in bed listening to Noor. Long into the night she played – with an intensity and ferocity I had never heard before, reaching low notes which seemed to growl and howl through the darkness, her fingers tugging so fiercely at the strings it was a wonder they didn't snap. The veena reverberated like voices calling across the divide between those here and those thousands of miles away, between the living and the dead.

As I finally drifted away, it was to the sound of a single string being plucked. It was comforting, soothing, simple; like a lullaby. "Sleep now," the music murmured. I slept.

The next morning, she talked about her father with more love and understanding than I had ever heard before. All her resentment and bewilderment about how to balance peaceful action against violence seemed to have vanished.

"At last, my father sent me the reply I needed," said Noor. She showed me his letter. "It took months to arrive. At last, I know what to do."

4 September 1939

My darling daughter,
You must have felt I hadn't answered your question properly in your last letter. I realise how futile and inadequate it must have sounded. That's because I dreaded giving you the true answer. I needed courage to put it into words. You will remember the story of the Buddha and the Hare. Read it again, my dearest one, and you will know what to do.

Your ever-loving father

He had repeated this ancient story in his letter.

In a previous incarnation, the Buddha was born as a hare. He lived on the outskirts of a forest with three friends: a jackal, a monkey, and an otter. All three looked to the wise hare as their leader. It was he who taught them the importance of keeping moral laws, observing holy days, and giving alms. If they saw an empty bowl, then it was their duty to fill it – especially if it was the bowl of a holy man.

From on high in his heaven on the peak of Mount Meru, Lord Indra watched the four friends, and one day decided to test them. That day, they had gone their separate ways in search of food. The otter found seven red fish in the river; the jackal found a lizard and an abandoned vessel of milk; and the monkey found a small pile of mangoes from the nearby mango grove. But the hare had only the green, green grass.

Lord Indra transformed himself into a holy man, and approached each one with an empty bowl.

"Holy man, are you hungry?" asked the otter.

"I am indeed, kind sir," said the holy man, and the otter immediately gave him all his fish.

The holy man approached the jackal, who saw his bowl was empty.

"Are you hungry, holy man?" asked the jackal.

"I am indeed," replied the holy man, and the jackal gave him the lizard and the milk.

The holy man approached the monkey.

"Your bowl is empty, holy man," said the monkey. "May I fill it? I have a pile of mangoes."

"That would be most kind," replied the holy man.

Finally, the holy man approached the hare. The hare noted that his bowl was empty, but what could he give him? The hare looked at the grassland which no human could eat.

"Oh blessed holy man, light a fire," said the hare.

So, the holy man lit a fire.

Then the hare laid himself in the flames, crying out, "I have nothing but grass to offer you, and myself. Please eat me."

The holy man then revealed himself as Lord Indra. He quenched the flames before any single bit of the hare could be burned. "Because you were willing to sacrifice yourself, you will never be forgotten. Your virtue will be remembered through the ages.

"Every time a full moon rises, everyone will see the image of a hare on its face – an image that will be an everlasting reminder of your sacrifice."

Dodo was like the hare.

CHAPTER 38

A Hiding Place

Vera was now acting as a courier and a go-between, escorting terrified groups of people to secret rendezvous to be collected and taken towards safety by Daniel. They never knew how long each rescue would take, and there was always the risk of betrayal. Once, Daniel hadn't returned after two weeks. Vera was in a frenzy of anxiety, and even Marianne looked white and almost resigned. Then one morning they awoke to find him asleep on the kitchen floor. He had accompanied his parents and several other Jewish families to safety, first through the Unoccupied Zone, then onwards via a secret chain of contacts till they reached neutral Spain and safety. At last, he was back, exhausted but triumphant.

If only Vera could do the same for her family.

One of her missions took her near the Rue d'Assas. She was overwhelmed with a desire to see her home, her aunt and uncle and, above all, Louis. What did it matter if her aunt and uncle were hostile? They could no longer order her about – and maybe she could persuade them to leave. They must have heard of the increasing disappearances, round-ups and arrests.

She walked boldly up to the open window of the concierge, Madame Boucher. This was the first test of her disguise. "I'm here to visit the Moskowskis," she called out, waving her forged identity card which named her as *Aimée Badoit*.

Madame Boucher glanced at it, then looked up at Vera. She narrowed her eyes as if struck by something; but nodded her through. Vera was glad to enter the apartment block and hurried upstairs. She reached her door, and rang the bell, while at the same time taking out her key and letting herself in.

It was Jeanne who came hurrying towards her. *"Qui êtes-vous?"* she asked, with distinct fear in her voice at the sight of a stranger.

"Jeanne! *C'est moi*, Vera!"

They hugged, Jeanne weeping with joy – at the same time as Vera exclaiming in dismay. A scene of desolation stretched before her eyes. Gone were the paintings and mirrors, the elegant side tables with vases of flowers in the passageway.

"What's happened?"

"Terrible things," cried Jeanne. "The Nazis have been robbing Paris of all its treasures. The art galleries, people's homes and businesses. They came here and took everything – and they've arrested *madame*."

Vera stared at her in agitation. "My aunt? Arrested?"

"They said she wasn't a French citizen – her papers hadn't come through. Lost somewhere in the machine."

"My uncle, where's my uncle?"

"*Monsieur*'s been going from pillar to post trying to get her freed. He's at the Prefecture now."

"And Louis? Did they take Louis?" Vera's voice rose in panic.

"It's all right, he's here. Don't worry," Jeanne soothed. "Louis! *Viens vite!* We have a surprise visitor!"

"Louis!" yelled Vera.

Louis came tearing out of his room. He had heard Vera's voice – but stopped dead in his tracks at the sight of her. "You aren't Veroshka . . ." he stammered.

"I am, my darling boy. Look!" Vera stripped off her hat and glasses, and shook out her hair. And he flung himself into her arms and she held him tightly, as if she would never let him go, kissing and hugging him and crying, "You're safe, you're safe!"

"They took everything!" cried Louis indignantly. He dragged her from room to room, their feet echoing on the bare floorboards: the living room, dining room, study, bedrooms all stripped bare. Miraculously, the piano remained.

"Probably for some boche who loves music," muttered Jeanne scornfully. Many apartments had already been appropriated by German officers. "There are rumours that they're out to get all non-citizens; and it's sure to spell trouble for the Jews, citizens or not. The French police are appalling. They've been raiding the homes of communists and Jews, and immigrants – even those who are legal – arriving at dawn, hauling people out of bed, pushing them into vans and just driving off who knows where?"

"Oh, why didn't my uncle leave?" cried Vera. "He's so pig-headed!"

"*Monsieur* is adamant that they will be safe once they know who he is."

"I know," muttered Vera with furious sarcasm. "'We're French through and through'," she mimicked him, "and he proudly wears his military medals as if they have magic powers."

"*Monsieur* was so sure that it was only the new arrivals," wailed Jeanne. "His family have been here for generations. But then they came and took *madame*, as her papers weren't in order."

"We are *catholique* now," cried Louis with outrage. "Why did they take Maman away?"

"Papa will sort it out. Don't you worry," whispered Vera, kissing him again and again. She turned to Jeanne. "Jeanne, you could leave right now! Go back to your village. You are a typical French girl from the countryside. You could just go home. No one would stop you. Why don't you?"

"Because . . . *madame* and *monsieur* have been so good to me. Much better than my own family." Jeanne gathered the child up in her arms. "How could I abandon them now, how could I leave Louis? No, no. I have to stay. I can help them."

Jeanne and Vera studied each other. They had both changed. Vera was no longer the grubby little girl from a Polish *shtetl*, nor the wilful adolescent who argued so much with her aunt. She was a young woman: authoritative, and mature. She had become beautiful. Jeanne was thinner and her usually fresh, vivacious face was pale and lined with anxiety.

"Thank God for you!" Vera embraced Jeanne with relief and gratitude. "That's all I can say, Jeanne. Thank God."

"And I thank God for you, Vera. You stayed too, when you could have gone back to England. Between us, maybe we can save this family."

"Where are the Blumsteins?" Vera nodded her chin at the apartment ,upstairs.

"They left a month ago without telling anyone. Pfft! Gone! Leaving everything. Monsieur Blumstein was sacked by his bank even though he'd worked there for twenty years. One morning we awoke to find they had left. We don't know where. I hope they got out."

"Papa says nothing will happen to us. He'll bring back Maman," said Louis confidently.

"Nothing will happen to you, Louis," said Vera as Jeanne put Louis down. "But – just in case – you must have a plan." She knelt down and took his hand. "This is very important. You have a secret hiding place, don't you?"

He nodded.

"Does Jeanne know it?"

"No!" he said proudly. "No one knows it. It's my secret hideaway. You'll never find me. No one has yet. Not even Maman."

"He's a little devil!" Jeanne wagged her finger.

"I bet I could find you," boasted Vera. "Go and hide now, Louis, while I count to a hundred. Let's see if I can find you. Come on Jeanne. Shut your eyes too."

As soon as Louis ran off, Jeanne almost broke down. "*Monsieur* is almost mad with worry," she sobbed, shaking and tearful. "I hear him in the night, raging round the apartment; weeping and kicking chairs and hurling his precious books against the wall. By day he sits at the kitchen table writing letters to all his influential contacts, begging them to use their influence to free *madame*. He sends me to deliver them by hand. Then he walks and walks round the Jardin du Luxembourg, weeping in despair. Some friends have promised to do what they can to help; others are deserting him – very politely, of course. What's going to happen? I'm so afraid."

Vera put her arms round her. "Tell my uncle I called. Tell him I'm sorry I disobeyed his wishes by not going to England. I'm safe, living in a good household, and helping refugees. Tell him I can help him too – and Louis – and you, if you need it. He must stop being so stubborn. Listen! Do you remember that chestnut tree in the Jardin du Luxembourg, where we used to sit and have picnics in the summer with Louis? On the Boulevard Saint-Michel side?"

Jeanne nodded. "I remember."

"Do you remember the hollow at the base of the tree – quite deep? Louis hid my handbag there once, and it took ages to find."

Jeanne nodded again.

"If ever you need to contact me – or if I can help – leave me a message there," said Vera. "I'll check as often as I can. I can't tell you where I am. I too need a secret hiding place. The less you know, the better. And watch out for Madame Boucher."

Jeanne nodded in agreement. "Thank you, dear one."

"We'd better go and look for Louis." Vera breathed deeply and adjusted her face to a carefree smile. "Coming, Louis!" she sang. "Ready or not!"

Vera was determined to find him; but at the same time she didn't want to. This was no longer a game. She and Jeanne went systematically through every room: under beds, inside wardrobes and cupboards; the pantry, the utilities room; the kitchen and bathroom where there seemed no conceivable hiding place; the balconies outside; even the room from which he had set off – but there was no sign of him.

"*Vraiment!*" Jeanne exclaimed, "it's like he vanishes into thin air. He found this place at least three years ago, and I still haven't worked it out."

Vera shouted, "Louis! You win. We can't find you. Come out now."

After about a minute, Louis appeared, flushed and triumphant. "I told you, told you! It's my own private, secret kingdom."

Vera got down on her knees and held Louis by his shoulders. She looked into his eyes. "You're right, Louis," she said. "It is your own private secret kingdom, and I shall never again try to find it. And don't ever tell anyone where your hiding place is. No one: not Mummy, or Daddy, or me, or Jeanne. If bad people come, people you don't know, you must hide; quiet as a mouse. Understood?"

Louis looked excited at the thought. "Even bad people won't find me!"

"Good," said Vera. "Now run off and hide again; but somewhere else. I'm only going to count to fifty this time, so you'd better be quick."

Louis fled. When Vera was sure he had gone, she whispered rapidly to Jeanne, "Just in case the concierge mentions it, I am now called Aimée Badoit. Oh God! I sometimes feel such a coward. But this is the only way I can stay in Paris and help." She hugged Jeanne tightly. "Thank you, thank you for your love and loyalty." Then she yelled out to Louis – "Coming! Ready or not!"

This time they found him after a mere five minutes of looking, hiding in a kitchen cupboard among the brooms.

"I must go now, *chéri*!" Vera said, holding him tenderly. "Whatever you do, don't tell anyone I came here. Keep my secret; promise?"

"I promise, Veroshka," said Louis solemnly.

"Darling Louis. I hope to see you again soon. But however long it is – don't ever forget me, will you? *Il y a longtemps que je t'aime,*" Vera sang.

Louis joined in. "*Jamais je ne t'oublierai.* I'll never forget you. Never," he whispered. "Never."

CHAPTER 39

Noor's Quest

What can the tiger catch in the dark corners of his own lair?

"So, your name is Noor Khan."

She nodded.

She was seated in front of a board of three men and one woman having an interview to get a commission – so she hoped. Her CV showed her training with the ATS in signalling, coding and wireless operation, but she was frustrated. Despite having attended many training courses, and demonstrating her resourcefulness and intelligence, they only seemed to see a rather timid, well-meaning young woman, whom they had confined to backroom work.

Noor felt under used, especially with her fluency in French. She had mentioned it to her superior officer more than once.

She stared at the pinstriped man before her, flanked on either side by two further men, one in military uniform, the other plain clothes. Further down the table was a neat woman with iron-grey hair, who looked as if she could have been anything from a headmistress to a company secretary. She felt a superior coolness coming from them, bordering on hostility.

"You are Indian."

"My parents are Indian; I was born in India, then lived in France and England. I dream in French."

"Oh really."

Noor couldn't interpret the tone of his reply.

"Aren't you happy with the ATS?"

"I just felt I had more to offer, which is why I . . ."

Even to her own ears, her voice sounded high, child-like, inexperienced, lacking depth and conviction.

"Yes, yes." He sounded sceptical. Perhaps he thought she was a butterfly, fluttering about, not settling on anything. "I suppose you found the signals training beneath you as well, being a princess."

"No sir! Not at all!" The jibe was cruel. "The ATS is wonderful; essential. I was honoured to be there. But I feel I have more to offer. I'd like a commission, sir."

"What does it mean to you to be loyal?" The major, who had been bent over his notepad, looked up and fixed her with a forensic eye.

Noor paused before answering, but held his gaze without blinking.

"*Who* are you loyal to? *What* are you loyal to?" He articulated carefully as if she were stupid.

"I'm loyal to mankind . . ." she stumbled, knowing that

she only added to their impression that she was nothing but a privileged flibbertigibbet.

"You're an Indian, lived in England and France; you dream in French and speak pretty perfect English and presumably an Indian language too. I just wonder which country you are loyal to; a reasonable question isn't it?"

She still made no reply.

"Do you love India – your *Mother* India?"

"Yes," she replied quietly, while inside she silently screamed in protest. "Of course I do, and not just because it's my motherland. It's my blood country; it's the land of my father and mother and family. My ancestry."

". . . and related to Tipu Sultan, I see according to my notes," said the major. "He's the man who fought the British, eh – albeit a couple of hundred years ago. Would you fight the British too? Don't you want to kick us out like your ancestor?"

"Yes. No. Of course not!" she exploded angrily. "Not right now."

"But why not right now? There are many of your countrymen who want to fight against us *right now*; they want to join the Nazis. Tipu Sultan would have joined the Nazis to get rid of us, wouldn't he? Surely *right now* is the best time to kick us out."

Time stood still. How long did it take to remind herself of the letter which had finally come from her father after months of waiting, when no one knew if he was alive or dead; written a day after war had been declared?

"Well?" demanded her interviewer with exaggerated patience. "Why not fight your enemy – the British? Is not your enemy's enemy your friend? Perhaps you are not brave enough? Your reports say you have a terror of violence."

Noor found her voice. Anger and outrage surged through her. "I don't know if this is also in your notes," she said passionately, "but I have been brought up a Sufi. We believe in non-violence. When I realised the extent of the suffering around me brought about by the evil of Nazism, I didn't know how to react. To do nothing was unthinkable."

"Why not work for the Red Cross; isn't it non-violent enough?" asked Plain Clothes.

"Because . . . look . . . I feel I can be of far more use to you. With my radio training, you could send me to France. I won't be killing people. I don't ask for a gun. But I could be helping you. I speak French; I pretty well pass for French. I know Paris like the back of my hand. I don't know if you're swamped by people like me but –"

"Thank you, Miss Khan. We'll let you know."

Flushed and feeling utterly dismissed, she saluted, spun on her heel, and left the room.

Outside, an air-raid siren was wailing its warning.

"I don't think she'll be of much use to us," said the military man. "We'd never be able to trust her; not just her loyalty to Britain, but her character. She's will-o'-the-wisp, unreliable; her supervisor finds her scatty, and her performance reports," he held out a sheaf of papers, "show that she was fearful during physical training, and has a low pain threshold. If she was ever captured, she wouldn't last five minutes under torture. The only thing she's good at is her wireless training . . ."

" . . . and of course, her French," said Plain Clothes.

"So, leave her where she is?" Pinstripe looked round the table.

"She'll do less harm here."

"Well – I think all those qualities you mention could benefit us very much," said the grey-haired woman thoughtfully. "She breaks the mould of our usual agents. She's not the sort of person the enemy expects."

"Hmmm . . ." Pinstripe lit a cigarette. "It can't hurt to give her a try. We won't give her any information of value so if she's caught, she'll do no harm. It could benefit us."

"Maybe even give her misinformation; now that could be of help to us," said Plain Clothes. "What do you think, Mabel? You train the women."

"You mean she's expendable. Use her – and let her take the consequences?" She looked grim.

"Miss Khan offered herself. I think we should take up her offer."

THE FIRST JEWISH LAW

3 OCTOBER 1940

The French government of collaboration under Marshal Philippe Pétain passed its first widespread anti-Jewish legislation. This included even stricter definitions. Someone was Jewish if he or she had three Jewish grandparents, or two Jewish grandparents if his or her spouse was also Jewish. The first Jewish Law also called for the drastic cutback of Jewish involvement in French society. Jews were to be excluded from the army officer corps and non-commissioned officer posts, top government administration positions, and any other job that influenced public opinion. Jews were only allowed to hold low-level public service jobs if they had fought in World War I or distinguished themselves in battle in 1939-1940, and they were limited within liberal professions such as teaching.

Up above the sea's grey flatland, wind is gathering the clouds.
In between the sea and clouds proudly soaring the Petrel,
reminiscent of black lightning.

THE SONG OF THE STORMY PETREL
MAXIM GORKY

CHAPTER 40
Paris Armistice Day

11 NOVEMBER 1940

A cold winter was approaching. Life was dominated by food shortages. The rationing system hardly worked; people trudged from shop to shop, spending hours and hours queuing for basics, squabbling over diminishing stocks of eggs, milk, bread, cheese with even fights breaking out. People had taken to growing vegetables in their cellars. As for meat, you might as well have asked for the moon. It got colder and colder; fuel became an obsession. By November, everyone was bracing themselves for a freezing winter.

With all these hardships, the once liberal, gracious, tolerant French turned on their foreigners, and Jewish compatriots, and blamed them for everything – even the outbreak of war itself.

Every night, after hours of work, Daniel, Vera, and all the other helpers would collapse in Marianne's kitchen – the warmest place in the house. Despite putting on layers of clothing and huddling into blankets, keeping warm had become a major struggle. Fuel was so low that people had resorted to burning their furniture.

Each day Marianne and Léonie prepared bowls of hot vegetable soup, using their small rationing of food and fuel allowances as creatively as possible. But even the thin soup contained nothing but cabbage leaves, radish tops, and small amounts of carrots and potatoes – when they could get hold of them. Meat or fish was now unimaginable.

Barely five months had elapsed since the Germans entered Paris, but the hardships had only deepened and showed no signs of picking up. They said the Germans had taken most of the food for themselves. Worst of all, more and more people were disappearing; Jews especially. They were losing their jobs, being banned from professions and public places.

Everyone knew that the newspapers about the glories of the new regime and the Third Reich were just propaganda, yet so many were prepared to believe it. As ever, people believed what they wanted to believe.

On Armistice Day, there was a commotion. It wasn't clear how it started. An outburst in a students' café perhaps. But suddenly there was a state of feverish revolt among the children and students of Paris.

Voices shouted, "There's a protest taking place! The students and school children are protesting. Can you imagine!"

They must be crazy! Vera thought. The Germans would go mad. But suddenly it was like chains bursting apart. Was it madness to feel hope? Hope brought by children? Could they demonstrate? Be French again; cry freedom?

"Today is Armistice Day," the students cried. "We must go and lay flowers at the tomb of the unknown soldier – just as we've always done."

They walked out of schools and university and some of their teachers joined them. Word spread.

"We must protest. The boche can't walk into our city without consequences. Are we so feeble? Do you remember Bastille Day this year? What did we do? Nothing. We didn't lift a finger. We didn't shout and scream. We stayed mute; we didn't protest; we obeyed the curfew, we obeyed orders. We peered like frightened old women from behind our shutters. We betrayed our Revolution. We betrayed France. How can we talk about *liberté, egalité, fraternité* – aren't we just timid hypocrites? We must take to the streets!"

"We've got to join them!" exclaimed Daniel, and the others all agreed.

"You'll get arrested; please don't go," begged Marianne. "It's folly. You'll be shown no mercy. I need you. Daniel!" She clutched his arm.

But the rallying cry had gone out, and it was spreading like wildfire.

"Come out, come out! Show yourselves! Protest! Citizens of Paris, we must defend our values, our principles, our future! We have stayed quiet too long. It's time to protest!"

"We have to go!" Daniel declared. "We need to show solidarity!"

Daniel, Vera, Yvette and Antoine joined dozens of other young people in a café assembling near the university. "It's Armistice Day! Was the sacrifice of millions of our fellow French soldiers in the last war all in vain?" they shouted. "Remember the barricades of the Great Revolution!"

Nervously, the authorities proclaimed a curfew to head off the demonstrations. But all through the day, more and more school children and students poured on to the streets.

"All for one and one for all," proclaimed Daniel, holding Vera closely.

They were hustled and jostled down the boulevards, singing the Marseillaise – *"Allons enfants de la patrie"* – at the tops of their voices, even though it had been banned, heading for the Arc de Triomphe with banners proclaiming '*Libération, Résistance*, down with Hitler, down with war. Never Again!' Their blood was up; they felt like warriors.

Wave after wave of young protesters surged down the Champs-Élysées, carrying bouquets of flowers and waving red, white and blue flags. It was joyous and brave. The police tried to break them up, linking arms to create a barrier; to no avail. The young people swept them aside with shouts and jeers and sheer force of numbers.

Just when it seemed that the students had successfully occupied the Place de l'Étoile and the Arc de Triomphe, shrieks of alarm rippled through the throng. Armed German soldiers had appeared from nowhere. They charged into the crowd with fixed bayonets, punching and lashing out; hurling children to the ground and beating them with their rifle butts. Shots rang out.

"My God – they're shooting at us!" gasped Daniel, trying to protect Vera, but not knowing which way to go. Neither did the young crowd. They surged and collided and pushed and shoved. More shots rang out. There was panic and confusion; people fell, were trampled, shot, wounded. Daniel slumped to the ground, groaning. Vera threw herself on top of him, trying to protect him from a forest of stampeding feet as live bullets whistled overhead. He was bleeding.

"Help me, help me!" Vera pleaded, but children were being dragged away by the police and soldiers and no one did.

In all the frenzy she suddenly saw a face she knew; a face staring blankly in a crowd of thousands. Simone.

"Simone! Help me!" Vera cried. "Daniel's been shot!"

Simone's face took on an expression of cold hatred before she simply disappeared. More shots ricocheted round the Étoile; more students fell. "Child killers! Filthy boche!" The students became like a pack of wild dogs, punching and kicking and bringing down soldiers as if they would tear them to pieces.

Vera crouched over Daniel, protecting his head, when thankfully, there were their friends, Stefan and Antoine, dishevelled and bleeding.

"Come on, come on!" they yelled. "Get him up!" Heaving Daniel to his feet, together with Vera they half dragged him away to a side street.

"Oh God!" exclaimed Marianne, full of admiring reproof when, barely half an hour to go before the curfew, Vera, Stefan and Antoine arrived at her door carrying a wounded Daniel. It was brave; it was folly. "Who do you think you are? The child crusaders of the Middle Ages?" She hugged and kissed them profusely. "Yvette – go and fetch Doctor Priaulx. Quickly, before the curfew. You've got twenty minutes."

"I saw Simone there," Vera told Daniel quietly as he lay on the couch with his eyes closed.

"That was brave of her." He didn't open his eyes. "I hope she's all right."

"Yes . . . well . . . I don't know. She vanished in the crowd." Vera didn't say that Simone, instead of coming towards them, had backed away. She didn't say Simone had looked at her with the utmost loathing.

Dr Priaulx came in the middle of the night, risking the curfew. He removed a bullet from Daniel's shoulder. "You'll be fine now," he said. "Keep it clean."

"Could you check on Pascal now that you're here?" Marianne asked.

Marianne took the doctor upstairs. Vera stayed with Daniel and asked him about Pascal.

"He joined the French army after fighting in Spain," said Daniel. "I met him briefly when I was out there. Great guy! But when the Germans invaded France, he was wounded at Calais. Marianne managed to get him home, God knows how! That woman is a witch. He'd be dead if it weren't for her – but he is still very much an invalid. Had a bullet in his lung."

"Do you think this will ever end?" asked Vera, laying her head on Daniel's chest. She could hear his heart thumping as he stroked her head with his good hand.

"These things always end," he murmured, and drifted away into sleep, his hand still tangled in her hair.

Now the general public understood what Occupation really meant. Any dissent would be met severely. They would make an example of anyone caught acting in opposition.

All through the night and the next few days, the army and police spread through the city. They stormed into the schools, colleges, and the university, hauling suspected students out of class. They turned up at their addresses, pushing aside stricken parents, bundling them into police vans. They would punish, and punish severely. Rumours spread of torture. They prohibited walking down the Champs-Élysées; anyone caught was arrested and forced into cold, dark cells where they were beaten and starved. Some were kept in solitary, alone for months, no one knowing if they were alive or dead. It was rumoured that at least twenty students had been killed. Nonsense, said the authorities – maybe two, who got in the way.

Late one night there was a frantic hammering on Marianne's door. These days it took courage to answer such a summons. But the knocking persisted. "I'll go," said the faithful Léonie.

On the doorstep stood Marcel, and Raymond, in a dreadful state, along with student friends Philippe, Julie, and Marguerite, with whom they had often met in the Café Rigaud. They were all in a miserable huddle, weeping and sniffling. Léonie and Marianne pulled them inside and shut the door.

"Tibor's been shot!" groaned Marcel. "Right there on his own doorstep. Just trying to enter his own house. For what? He hadn't broken the curfew. So why?"

"You mean that Hungarian student?" said Vera. "He was at the protest."

Marcel shrugged. "Yes – he was at the protest. But why him? His parents had been refugees years back, but he was born in France. Did someone report him for being a Hungarian?"

"You should have heard him howling!" cried Julie. "There was blood everywhere. He was calling for his mother and father to open the door. But the soldiers stood there with their machine guns pointing and yelled, '*Whoever opens that door will be shot!*' It was unbearable. We didn't know what to do. We were hiding. If they had seen us, we would have been shot too."

They had seen Tibor's door open slightly; how could any parent not risk all to save their child? The soldiers started shooting, and soldiers yelled out their warnings again. The door closed. Tibor was beating at the wood. "Let me in! Mama, Papa! Don't leave me to die."

The street had emptied; curtains fluttered as people peered out in horror. After a few minutes, with Tibor screaming in agony and calling for help, the door opened again, and a hand reached out. Tibor had stretched to take the hand. "Papa!" they heard him cry. The soldiers opened fire; the machine guns rattled mercilessly, puncturing holes in the door; the hand fell limp and withdrew. Tibor was killed instantly.

"He was just a kid, I tell you!" wept Raymond.

"We want to join you," said Philippe, white-faced and furious. "We want to kill those pigs. The more of us that fight, the better."

CHAPTER 41

Birdsong

11 MAY 1941

One morning, I awoke. It was extraordinarily quiet. I left the cellar and went up to the flat. I opened the curtains; the skies were empty; the air-raid sirens hadn't gone off. I could hear a dawn chorus in the square, and the unusual piercing whistle of a blackbird. I couldn't believe it; the bombers hadn't come. For months, we had been bombarded night after night. Thousands of people had been killed, and parts of British cities and ports reduced to rubble.

I turned on the radio. I heard birdsong outside my window; the rest of the world was in turmoil.

I clattered down to the front door. Miracle! A letter from India. I snatched it up, and almost missed the note lying next to it. I raced back upstairs two at a time, and ripped open the letter first.

It was from my parents, dated 17 March. It had taken two months to arrive – but arrive it had. God bless the Royal Mail.

Darling Gwen,

We think of you and Eric unceasingly – our beloved, brave, and loyal children fighting for England and empire. How we love you, admire you and pray for your safety.

All this time, since war was declared, we wished we had never sent you away to England – and especially when we heard of the horrors of the Blitz. You can't imagine our relief when your letters trickle through. But though we thought we were safe in India, now we watch Japan with alarm. They have invaded China – horribly – and have their eyes on Singapore, and the rest of Asia. But though Indian regiments are fighting for the empire across the world, the movement for Independence here in India is very strong. Many ask, "Why are we fighting our enemy's enemies?"

I felt a new fear. Were my parents not safe, even in India? Almost indifferently, I unfolded the second piece of paper. It had been hand-delivered; probably a note from the milkman. It had today's date. The words scrawled in pencil came into focus. I blinked; I read the words. Disbelief. I felt my feet lifting; wings sprouted and, for a moment, I swear I levitated.

It was from Ralph.

I'm over the road. Lyons Corner House in Piccadilly. Remember? Join me? Have a few hours of leave. Don't know anyone else in England, so thought I'd see if you were free.

He'd added the time: at least an hour ago. Was I too late?

Panic-stricken, I grabbed my coat, ran out, then in again, checked my face in the mirror, shook out my hair, dabbed on a bit of powder and a touch of lipstick, put on my hat, then dashed out again.

I stumbled and twisted my way through the debris and mountains of rubble, crunching over glass and rubbish to the Lyons Corner House. It was barely recognisable under an outer shell of sandbags, but I found the door and went inside.

He was sitting at a table reading a newspaper, facing the doorway – yet I saw him first. I paused for a moment, to take him in and dispel my disbelief that it was really him. A last he glanced up, and saw me. He rose to his feet as I made my way over to his table.

"Good morning Gwendoline, otherwise known as Gwen." His face was breaking into a thousand smiles.

I felt my expression mirroring his. "Good morning Ralph, otherwise known as Rusty."

Somehow, it was the most natural thing in the world to fall into each other's arms and hug and hug, as if to make up for all the hugging we had never done before we ever met.

Even when we finally sat down and ordered some breakfast, and we could hear the nippies giggling, we could hardly stop touching each other: clasping hands, entwining fingers, and stroking cheeks, as if we had been lovers forever.

Afterwards we walked, our arms clasped round each other – it was like the first walk and the last walk, as if it had to contain all our past and future. We went to St James's Park and finally, we kissed.

"I don't have much –" we both said simultaneously, then laughed.

"Time?" he asked gently, finishing off the sentence.

"Time."

"Neither do I. My train goes in a couple of hours. Back to my ship."

"So soon?" I clung to him desperately. Then I said, "I've applied to be moved to the ATA to fly aeroplanes."

"What? Now look here! Don't you go taking extra risks with your life. It's my life too, don't you see?" Ralph looked upset, and held me at arm's length. "Don't you see?" he repeated with anguish.

"Oh! Is this to be our first lovers' quarrel, so soon after our first kiss?" I teased. "I wouldn't be going into battle. They'll never allow women to go into battle. I'd just be delivering aeroplanes from factory to base. It's the only flying they allow women to do. And I've always wanted to fly."

We sat down on the grass and he held me close, and we didn't speak for a few moments. Then I said gently, "Darling? We can't go around thinking there's a magic formula to ensure our survival. We have to live and live and live; make every second count. I feel buried alive down in my coal cellar, and down in the map room, hardly ever seeing the light of day. I long to be a bird, and fly up and away, as high as I can. As I'm not flying in battle, I don't see that I'd be any safer on the ground than up in the air. You're going back to your ship. You are in far more danger with those U-boats than I would be!"

Day in day out, I heard news of U-boat attacks, the biggest danger to Ralph.

"What can I ask *you* to do, to survive?" I said. "All you can do is your duty – and if duty is combined with something that you've always passionately wanted, then how lucky is that? You always wanted to go to sea, and I've always wanted to fly."

"Just you wait Miss Gwendoline Atkins, otherwise known as Gwen. When we are married, I will not put up with this insubordination," Ralph murmured into my neck.

I laughed with joy. "Just you wait, Mr Ralph Penbury, otherwise known as Rusty. You'd better be clear now. IF you ask me to marry you, and IF I say yes, you won't be marrying an obedient little girl."

"Hmmm," sighed Ralph sorrowfully. "I might have to get used to it."

STATUTE DES JUIFS
(THE SECOND JEWISH LAW)

2 JUNE 1941

The Statut des Juifs *made the definition of a Jew even more rigid, and called for the removal of Jews from industry, business, and liberal professions. Only a few Jews were exempted from these cutbacks.*

Now almost all Jews were allowed no professions and were banned from public places. They faced penury and ruin.

What shall I think? What shall I do? – two things which are interrelated very closely. What use is thought without action, or action without thought?

MESHE FLINKER
Children's Wartime Diaries

Ever darker, clouds descending ever lower over the sea, and the waves are singing, racing to the sky to meet the thunder.

THE SONG OF THE STORMY PETREL
MAXIM GORKY

CHAPTER 42

Cover Name: Geneviève

APRIL 1942

They have waited for a full moon; an April moon.

A small black speck, a high-winged Lysander, moves steadily across the sky, grateful for the mountainous, glistening white clouds into which it disappears, and reappears, as inconspicuous as a solitary bather in a wide, wide sea. Below is the Channel; tips of waves catch the reflections of stars like fishes in a net. The low dark land looming ahead is France. The pilot shifts his goggles, staying high to reduce the sound of the engine, scouring the moonstruck ground for signs of enemy activity.

The young woman behind him is sitting in a separate cockpit, stiffly upright, as she has been ever since they left the little airfield near Dover in England. Quiet as stone, her face is still; her eyes open, yet not taking in the immense night sky. She is dressed the French way, in a brownish flared check skirt and matching jacket, white blouse, and sensible brown shoes. Her hair is tucked back under a small plain brimmed hat, and on her knees, she clutches a modest holdall. By her side is a leather suitcase.

My name is Geneviève Bisset, she repeats silently inside her head. *I am twenty years old. I was born in Céret, in southern France, but I have a position as a piano teacher in the 6th arrondissement in Paris.* She has been assigned to this mission with hardly any notice at all.

"You all right?" the pilot asks, through the intercom, briefly looking round.

She fixes her eyes on him. They gleam in the darkness. "Yes," she replies without emotion.

"We'll be at the landing in about twenty minutes."

She glances out of the window. They are flying over woods: the fields, woods and farms of France. The pilot checks his instruments, then stares into the shadowy darkness below, praying that the clouds, while giving him some protection, don't totally block out the light of the moon; he will need it to identify the landing strip which the partisans will have marked out for him. He hopes they've positioned a light correctly – not too near the trees like last time, when one of his wings was struck by a branch and nearly grounded him.

The plane starts its descent. At first there is no sign of life, nor of anyone waiting in the shadows to receive them. Even the cattle in the fields stand like statues, their moon shadows cast behind them. He drops lower and lower, then whistles with satisfaction. There it is! A dim torchlight! It waves at him in intervals: three seconds on

. . . ten seconds off . . . He aims for it. Down, down he drops.

"Be ready to leap off as soon as we touch down and come to a standstill," he shouts to his passenger. "I won't even turn the engine off. Get out as fast as you can. Eduard should be there to meet you. If not, find the road and wait – at least an hour – inconspicuously of course. If he doesn't arrive, you must walk northwards to the village. One of our contacts from the Maquis – the French Resistance – should be looking out for you. From there, do your best to make your own way to Paris. You have your story worked out, and you know the address. Understood?"

"Understood," she shouts back.

The pilot is heading for the intermittent light; it's barely brighter than a candle.

The wheels of the light aircraft hit the ground; they bounce. She's on her feet; crouched; one hand gripping the holdall, the other, her suitcase. She nearly loses her balance as the plane bounces again and again. Then it stops: the propellers are whirring.

"Out, out," he shouts.

She grasps the handle of the door and presses with all her weight. It doesn't open.

"Get out, for God's sake!" The pilot sounds panicky.

She lets go of her bags, and with both hands, throws her weight on to the door handle. The door flies open; she instinctively falls backwards. The door is like a gaping hole into the darkness. Then suddenly there is someone below on the ground, calling softly, but urgently, with outstretched hands. She hurls out her suitcase. It's caught – thank God – otherwise it might have burst open and damaged its precious contents. She flings out her holdall; then, sitting on the edge, drops into the arms of a stranger waiting for her. He drags her away, ducking their heads beneath the wings. The aircraft is moving again; bumping away into the darkness. There is a rev of engines as the Lysander rises into the sky. There are no gun shots, no shouts; nothing. She is pulled away.

"*Venez, venez vite*! Come on!"

They run. She follows the torch leading them further and further away from the tell-tale runway. Gasping, her lungs fit to burst, the stranger slows down and finally stops. The noise of her heart and panting breath are the only sounds. All is silence.

She can't see his face but smells him: Eduard. He smells of the farm, and cows and manure and country, as they crouch in a shallow ditch on the edge of the country road. "*Ça va?*" he grunts.

"*Ça va,*" she replies.

"*On attend, Bertrand!*" he whispers, then breaks into a flurry of swear words which she understands: "Where the hell are you? Idiot. Pigdog. What are you playing at? Late – always late – just like the last time. Trying to get us all killed?"

She says nothing but sits on her suitcase. What were her orders? If no one comes after an hour, walk north towards the village, six miles away. But keep off the road; walk in the ditches; be ready to hide if a car passes.

After half an hour, they hear a distant sound of a car's engine. Relief! A small beaten-up Renault without lights pulls up. They scramble on to the road.

"Not bad going for the time of day," the driver whispers in English.

"Especially when the wind is blowing in from the north," she replies, finishing off the password.

"Get in!" orders Eduard, opening the car door and flinging her bags inside. "Late again, Bertrand! You'll get us all shot."

"I'd like to see you do any better, getting through those controls! The *flic* are like bloodhounds. Worse than the boche. I hope your papers are in order, *mademoiselle*," he hisses as she slumps into the back.

"In order!" she confirms. "*Au revoir*, Eduard! *Merci!*" she whispers into the darkness as their car pulls away, and she sees him hauling a bicycle out of a ditch.

She must have slept. Frightening how sleep can grab you like an assailant, catching you unawares and plunging you into unconsciousness. But suddenly she's awake – just at the point the car pulls up before a stone farmhouse. Bertrand gets out without a word. He opens the car door and lifts out her suitcase. She follows with the holdall. Shapes of sheds and barns loom in the darkness. A dim, swaying storm lantern squeaks from a hook. Somewhere, a dog is barking ferociously; his chain grates as he lunges forward.

Bertrand takes her case to the top of a flight of stone steps.

"This is where you'll stay to be processed and checked before you go on to Paris to meet your cell. When I've gone, knock three times. You will hear the code sentence before they open. You must reply with your password. Got it?"

"I understand. Thank you."

"*Au revoir. Bonne chance.*" He leaves her. She would have preferred that he hadn't wished her luck. It feels like a bad omen.

The sound of his car fades down the lane and is gone. The dog is still barking wildly, yanking at his chain. She pulls her suitcase to her chest as if in defence, then knocks on the door three times. She doesn't hear approaching footsteps, but a voice from the other side of the door says: "*A la claire fontaine,*" and she replies in French, "*Il y a une rose . . .*"

The door opens. A shadowy figure grips her arm and pulls her inside. Her bags are taken from her, and she follows a figure down a dark passage to a closed door with a slit of yellow light spilling from beneath. It opens.

She blinks with wonder. It's like stepping back into normality. There is a kitchen table, with five people sitting round with glasses of red wine, and bowls of stew and hunks of bread. A dog – not the dog which barked outside – drowsily gets to his feet from his place before a glowing fire; he comes over to her, sniffs, inspects her, then ambles back to flop on his paws.

"Ah! César! He's just checking you out," someone says with a laugh. And suddenly she is surrounded by men and women welcoming her, shaking her hands, kissing her on both cheeks, saying, *"Bienvenue, mademoiselle!"*

They introduce themselves, all of them surely giving her their fake names except for Jean-Pierre and Sabine Verney, a middle-aged farmer and his wife. This is their farm. The others, Emile, Denis and Auriol, are in the Maquis. It's their job to receive agents from England, and vet them before sending them on their way.

"Geneviève," she says. "I am Geneviève."

They sit her down, give her a glass of wine, and put a platter of sausages, olives, tomatoes and bread in front of her. "Soup?" asks Sabine, gesturing towards the great pot of stew on the fire, and she nods eagerly.

But, despite the cheeriness, no one is relaxed; their senses are alert. It's always dangerous when a plane comes in with an agent – especially when there is a full moon. Having extended their friendship, it's down to business, all the time someone listening; checking.

The dog outside barks again. They stop, look at each other questioningly. Emile goes to the door, then returns with reassuring hand gestures. Probably a fox.

Instructions ring in her head.

"You will stay here for two days for orientation. We'll check your papers, and give you all the passes and documents that you need."

"We'll make sure you have your story correct and consistent."

"We'll tell you what's going on in Paris; who to look for, what to do, what not to do. You must be rigorous with security. Always check passwords; don't trust anyone – not even one of us."

The dog outside begins barking again. César gets to his feet, agitated, with a low growl rattling in his throat, the fur along the ridge of his back on end. They hear a chugging car pull up.

As one, they jump to their feet. Jean-Pierre draws a revolver from his belt. Geneviève feels sick. The others leap into action, heaving away the kitchen table, rolling back a rug to reveal the bare floorboards. Someone fetches a wrench from the fireplace and levers up four floorboards, which have been stuck together to make a trap door. Steps lead down into pitch darkness.

"*Descendez! Vite!*" Emile urges her, and thrusts a torch into her hand. It pierces the blackness, creating giant swinging shadows. She stumbles down; they hurl her suitcase, holdall, and coat after her; Emile, Denis and Auriol follow. Above their heads, the trap door is lowered; they hear the table being moved back into place. The whole well-rehearsed manoeuvre is performed within forty-five seconds.

Light footsteps – Sabine? Shuffling footsteps – Jean-Pierre? And heavier, unknown footsteps tramp down the passageway into the kitchen. Male voices greet each other; French voices, with the same regional accent.

"*Salut*, Albert!"

"*Salut, salut!*" Albert's rough tobacco-ridden voice replies. "Did you have visitors? I saw a car in the lane earlier; didn't recognise it. Thought it might have come from your place."

"*Non*! Probably one of the boche from Rive Bouton. They're always getting lost."

"No wonder, with the signposts being constantly vandalised. Idiots, whoever it was – they'll get us all shot."

Down in the darkness of the cellar, they look at each other anxiously by the light of their torches.

"Did you need something, Albert?" they hear Jean-Pierre ask evenly.

"*Oui*! One of my storm lamps is broken. Can you spare me one of yours? Clarabelle is calving. I'll probably be up half the night."

"Sure thing. Come on out to my shed. I expect you need oil as well."

"Have a glass of wine before you go," Sabine calls out. Geneviève imagines she has already whisked away the tell-tale dishes from supper. "Take a seat, Albert. You might as well get some strength for the night ahead. The lamp can wait."

Wine is poured, and Albert and the Verneys chatter about the state of the war. Down in the cellar, they too relax.

"The boche are everywhere," grumbles Albert. "You know they've commandeered Jacques' farm, and billeted a platoon on us. We have two corporals staying with us, would you believe? They got word of a plane landing last night over by the Bouton Rouge farm. Some piece of scum reported it."

Below in the cellar, Geneviève feels alarmed.

Denis shakes his head. "Not us," he mouths.

"Well, everyone knows when there's a full moon . . ." declares Jean-Pierre for them all to hear.

Sabine changes to the food shortages in Paris with a cynical laugh. "We peasants have become popular! They treat us with respect when they need our produce."

Below in the cellar, they hear the scraping of a chair. At last, Geneviève hears the Verneys' neighbour get up to leave. "Well, I'd better get back to Clarabelle. Wouldn't do for her to start calving when I'm not there."

"I'll fetch that lamp for you," Jean-Pierre says.

The door shuts as Jean-Pierre and Albert go out into the yard, and the dog starts barking again. In the cellar, they wait, listen, and say not a word.

Geneviève looks around. The cellar has been converted into a workshop. There s a broad table with pens and inks, and rolls of paper; a tray of lead letters for printing.

If the enemy ever comes across this, they will be executed.

Suddenly, she is overcome with terror, as if Death himself has entered the cellar, and thrown a net around them.

A scream hurtles up her throat; her mouth opens. She clamps a hand over it, and bites into her palm. Silently, her body shakes with the reality of what she's doing. Waves of panic weaken her muscles and limbs; dry her throat. She thinks of all the things that could happen, especially torture.

She remembers the time when she caught her foot in the bicycle spokes and took all the skin off her ankle, nearly to the bone. That was the worst pain she'd ever known. How she screamed when her mother dabbed it with near-boiling water to kill any infection. Oh God! she doesn't think she could stand pain. What if she is captured and they torture her?

Her breath is coming out in short bursts; she is panting loudly.

"Hey!" Auriol grips her arm with concern. "You all right?"

She looks at her through a terrified haze. "Sorry! Just tired."

"It's being down here. Makes you panicky. Calm down. We'll make your identity papers and train pass tonight."

"Tonight?" says Geneviève. "But you must be exhausted!"

Auriol laughs. "Yeah – but then nothing may happen at all tomorrow, and we'll sleep all day! We'll do you a ration book as well. Don't worry. It'll all be done by tomorrow. You're the one who needs some sleep."

She sits on the bottom step, holding her head in her

hands, seeking the inner voice of her father. *Father! I'm afraid of death.*

Child, comes his answer. *Don't fear the road to annihilation. It's an easy road, so easy, that it may be travelled sleeping.*

The door at the top of the cellar steps opens. A weak, electric light trickles down through the dusty darkness.

"You can come out now," says Sabine. "He's gone."

CHAPTER 43

Code Name: Hare

Geneviève stayed for two nights, by which time she had been thoroughly briefed. They had a forged letter confirming her employment as a music teacher to a young child at an address in Paris in the 6th arrondissement, but no information about the cell she was joining, nor where she would be living. She would receive that later. "We give and take information in tiny portions so that if any of us are caught, we can't give too much away. Safer that way."

She had her cover name, Geneviève Bisset, for her identity cards and travel passes, and she was told her code name: *the Hare*. She smiled. The Hare was appropriate.

They brought out a bicycle from the barn, and helped her to strap her suitcase to the seat, and sling her holdall across the handlebars. The holdall was stuffed with fresh produce from the farm: potatoes, carrots, cabbages and swedes. "They're starving in Paris, so it would be natural for you to be bringing in vegetables."

A satchel slung across her body contained her identity papers, which she would, for certain, be asked to produce, and, of course, her train ticket to Paris. At some point on her journey, she would be contacted by a man called Marc Nadeau.

"Don't look for him, he will find you. He will give the password, and you must answer. He'll take you to the address where you will be based. You will get further instructions on where to meet your resistance cell."

It was a hushed noon; farmers and fieldworkers paused for their midday meal. Jean-Pierre and Sabine said their goodbyes inside, each giving her a warm embrace, and that dreaded whisper: *"Bonne chance!"*

Geneviève wheeled her bicycle out of the farm, and cycled off down the long straight road to the little station, three miles away. The road was long and straight, dappled with leafy shadows cast by long lines of poplar trees, straight as a guard of honour. She tried to take comfort from the rippling green and brown wheat and barley fields, stretching, so normally, away on either side.

The small rural station was silent and empty when she arrived. As instructed, she abandoned the bike against a wall to the side. Clutching her holdall and suitcase in each hand, she wandered on to the platform. The train was due in fifteen minutes. A blackbird was whistling his head off, as if there was an eternity of tomorrows.

She sat on the wooden bench; utterly still; waiting. The sun, which was now at its zenith, threw hot stripes of dazzling light between the black slatted shadows of the station roof, and enveloped her like a cloak of gold, as if her father were sitting next to her. His voice entered her head, unbidden: *My daughter, we are waves, whose stillness is non-being.*

"Papa!" she murmured. She slid her hand along the empty bench, looking for reassurance, feeling for her father's hand; that remembered, warm, broad palm she used to hold when she was a child.

Her SOE trainer in London, Jack Court, knew from her performance record how easily frightened she was. "It's not too late to pull out," he had told her. "No one would despise you, or call you a coward. On the contrary, they would respect you for understanding yourself and your own limitations. It's no crime to admit your own weakness and doubt yourself. There is only one crime, and that is to betray your comrades."

"I won't let you down. I promise," Geneviève had said.

Remember, you are the Hare, said her father.

There was a distant shriek of the whistle, and she saw the puffs of smoke as the train approached round the bend. It came to a spluttering standstill, and she was startled to see a station master appear as if out of nowhere, carrying a flag. The engine driver leaned out of his cab, barely visible in the swirling clouds of steam, and they greeted each other warmly.

At that moment, a slight, male figure appeared in a loose, brown raincoat and fedora, carrying a bag, with floppy dark brown hair falling over his eyes. She caught a brief glimpse of his face. It was surprisingly young, boyish even, though with a whispery moustache. He pushed his unruly hair beneath his fedora, and she noticed a black mole on the lobe of his right ear. Was this Marc Nadeau?

As he sauntered away from her along the platform and boarded the train near the back, Geneviève opened a carriage door and heaved her bags inside. To her astonishment, the carriage was packed with women, old men and children, their bags crammed with produce from the countryside; their faces were sun-beaten, lean, and gaunt. All eyes turned on her.

"*Bonjour,*" said Geneviève, pulling the door shut.

One or two nodded courteously, but for the most part, they just continued to stare. Geneviève leaned out of the window, as if to say goodbye to no one in particular. The station master blew his whistle, the engine driver waved and the train tooted a warning of departure.

She turned to look for a seat, but although there was a token shuffle, they barely made room for her, and she was forced to sit on her suitcase. A child whispered audibly, "Is she a Jew?" No one bothered to answer the question. It was her pale olive skin and dark hair; of course, she could be Jewish. Then before the child could ask again, her mother said, "She's probably Italian."

That was the first shock. It took her breath away. She had been told what to expect in France after nearly three years of Nazi occupation, but nothing had prepared her for this reality.

Is Truth the same as Reality? she remembered asking her father once.

There is no proof of true reality, he had told her. *Only the reality inside yourself – self-realisation. That is true reality.*

The fields gave way to the factory roofs and industry of a large town. She felt disembodied, passing through a beloved country which was no longer the country she had known. It felt like a parallel world. The French *tricolore* of red, white, and blue flags were nowhere to be seen. Instead, post offices, town halls, municipal and public buildings fluttered with Nazi flags: a red background with a white circle, and a black swastika in the middle. Poor beautiful France had been captured by an ogre and, like a fairy princess, thrust into captivity.

They pulled into a wide echoing station. Some of the passengers prepared to get off. She leaned out of the window, wondering if she could spot anyone who might be Marc Nadeau; but soon the train was off again, heading for Paris.

From the window, she saw the roads teeming with German troops: lorries, motorbikes, staff cars, and infantry in their grey uniforms – the colour of wolves – and every now and then, the dread sound of an aeroplane patrolling the skies. Geneviève sank back into a now empty seat, hugging herself to contain her panic.

An old woman was looking at her with curious concern. "*Ça va?*"

Geneviève steadied herself. She was an idiot, giving herself away already. She wouldn't last five minutes like this. She had to pull herself together. She managed to smile back at the woman with a nod of appreciation. She remembered her trainer's concern that she hadn't got it in her to be an agent. Yet, of all the people who had trained her in England, Jack Court was the only one she felt was on her side. I won't let you down, she told him in her head.

The train stopped at the last suburban station before Paris. A group of German soldiers milled around on the platform, looking for a carriage. Two of them decided they would try and squeeze into Geneviève's.

"Move!" they ordered monosyllabically, trying to cram themselves in. *"Bouge, bouge!"*

No one did. Geneviève stayed in her seat, and the other passengers sat sullenly, with lowered eyes; so, the soldiers got out again, and slammed the carriage door with displeasure. One of the women spat out of the window after them. *"Boches sales! Cochons!"* she declared, and everyone shuffled uncomfortably, scared of her scathing contempt.

Paris. Gare d'Austerlitz was heaving with German soldiers, all armed with packs and guns. They mingled uneasily with the locals spilling off the train, who tossed their bundles ahead of themselves on to the platform, and quickly dispersed. Geneviève wondered where they were going.

"They've all been on a mission to find food," a voice explained in her ear, as though he had been inside her head throughout the journey. She swung round to face a rather shabby man in a grubby coat with dandruff scattered on the collar. He had an oddly lop-sided face from an earlier wound. He was of indeterminate age, wearing a maroon beret pulled over his ears. He had a small black moustache, and spectacles. He wasn't the man she had seen getting on the train . . .

He pulled her into his arms as if she belonged to him, and kissed her on the lips. She felt repelled and pulled away, but he held her tightly. "*A la claire fontaine,*" he whispered, nibbling her ear.

"*Il y a une rose,*" she replied stiffly.

"*Je suis* Marc Nadeau."

"*Moi,* Geneviève."

"Don't pull away from me; it looks less suspicious like this," he muttered, with a 'don't you dare resist' expression. "Believe me, *mademoiselle,* this is no time for niceties. We have to trust each other. Everyone is suspicious, and the boche have eyes everywhere."

Marc released her, picked up her bags and walked a little ahead, winding his way through the crowd. "Did you get potatoes?" he asked loudly, affecting a southern drawl. Mingling among the reflections in his glasses, she felt his gaze appraising her.

"A couple of kilos maybe," she replied equally loudly. "But I got plenty of swede."

"Ugh!" he almost spat. "See what we've come to? Horse food."

Geneviève gave a Gallic shrug.

"*Très bien*. Your French is perfect!" he praised her softly. "Play the game, like this, and you'll do all right. But be prepared. You can be stopped at any time and asked for your identity papers. Now follow me. Hardly anyone can afford a car these days, petrol rationing is impossible. But I got hold of a horse and cart; better than nothing."

They boarded the cart outside the station together. The little horse trotted along with Marc holding the reins, and Geneviève sitting alongside him.

"At any other time, I'd rather enjoy this," he said.

"Until it rains," jeered Geneviève, getting into the spirit.

The cafés along the boulevards were thronging with people, just as they'd always been: drinking, talking animatedly, gesticulating, laughing, arguing; lovers leaning into each other, clasping hands, their foreheads touching. This was the France she knew; and yet it wasn't. The cafés and restaurants along the boulevards were full – but with German soldiers, and their girlfriends. The sound of German filled the air.

The 18th arrondissement of northern Paris was a great muddle of a district, with Montmartre crawling up its steep streets, and Sacré-Coeur gleaming like a Madonna at the top. To the side were the poor, mundane, undistinguished dwellings, with rundown blocks of flats going up four or five storeys, housing mainly immigrants and refugees from all over Europe and North Africa. Playing on the grubby stretches of brown grass, hordes of children dodged lines of washing, watched from balconies by mothers, aunts or grandmothers.

"Hey *garçon!*" Marc shouted to an Algerian boy. "Look after the horse. Here's twenty centimes. I'll double it when I leave."

The boy looked pleased.

Geneviève and Marc walked through an arch into a courtyard and climbed four dark, smelly flights of stone steps in the far right-hand corner. They entered a dingy landing, on which there were two doors into two separate apartments.

"You'll be staying here. They're expecting you." Marc dumped her baggage before number 23, a door on the third floor. "I'm off now."

"Will I see you again?" she called after him.

"Perhaps." And she heard his footsteps diminishing down the stairs.

She rang the bell. The door opened cautiously; a bosomy, late middle-aged woman peered out. *"Bonjour?"*

"Je suis Geneviève Bisset, your new tenant. Are you Madame Courvet?"

"Ah! *Entrez, entrez,*" said the woman without confirming her name.

Geneviève stepped through the door into a scene of disarray. The living room was more like an untidy office, with filing cabinets and drawers overflowing with books and documents and papers, papers, papers. A shortish, wiry, balding man with a brown, sharply edged moustache was intently shredding a pile of documents at the far end of the dining table.

"Our tenant's here, Mademoiselle Bisset," announced the woman who had let her in.

"Ah! *Mademoiselle!*" The man at the shredder straightened to greet her but didn't smile or hold out his hand. There was an uneasy pause.

"*Bonjour*," said Geneviève politely, suddenly wondering whether she had come to the right place. She looked round uncertainly. No one had offered the password. Perhaps she should speak first? Her mind suddenly went into a whirl of uncertainty about how to proceed.

From another room came the sound of someone whistling a familiar tune. *A la claire fontaine* . . . A door opened and the whistler appeared: a strangely nondescript man who would never stand out in a crowd. He was of moderate height, with a lean, almost scrawny body, wearing a beret with a scarf slung round his neck, as if ready to go out. Narrowed, brown eyes stared hard at her as he continued to whistle.

The penny dropped. "*Il y a une rose*," Geneviève offered.

Everyone broke out in smiles, and the tension dissipated.

"I'm so sorry! I was waiting for you to speak first," Genèvieve explained, embarrassed.

The whistler came forward with outstretched hand. "Welcome! I'm known as Raymonde Gilles. It is my cover name. We are part of the British cell, Avalon, which you have come to join. Forgive our awkwardness. We needed to hear your password. The Gestapo are everywhere. The slightest suspicion can bring them to our door."

"Welcome, *mademoiselle*," said the bald man at the shredder. "I am Laurence Courvet, and this is my wife, Denise." He indicated the woman who had let her in, and she reached out to shake both their hands.

"Please sit down," said Madame Courvet, somewhat curtly, and took her suitcase. Geneviève stiffly obeyed. With an apologetic nod, Laurence returned to shredding documents.

Raymonde said, "You must regard this as your home, but you will go each week to an address in the 6th arrondissement, Rue Racine, to give piano lessons. It is where you will meet other members of the cell."

"Will I meet Merlin?" Geneviève asked.

"None of us knows who Merlin is," replied Raymonde. "He gives orders; we carry them out – but the less we know about each other the better."

Madame Courvet bustled off to serve a meal. "You must be hungry," she said, sounding kinder, and Geneviève realised she hadn't eaten since breakfast time and yes – she was starving.

"Contact London and let them know of your safe arrival," said Raymonde Gilles, and led her to a back room.

"This is your room for the time being."

She was relieved it was uncluttered: just a simple bed, a chest of drawers, a wardrobe, a book shelf with French classic novels and travel books. A sash window with shutters opened to the back of the apartment block with a view of more roofs and chimney pots. Nearby was a writing desk, with inkpot, pen, and a blotter.

"You can set up your radio in here, and fix an aerial from this window," said Raymonde. "You are not overlooked, and being at the back of the building, your signal is unlikely to be picked up by a wireless detector. The boche patrol all the time."

Geneviève nodded, hoping she looked calm and competent.

"Can you manage?" asked Raymonde.

"Yes," she murmured, and he left her to it.

She opened her suitcase. After storing her clothes, she loosened the base to reveal two packs: one contained her medical kit, the other, a pack with her shortwave Morse transceiver of sockets and dials for receiving and sending messages. It was inside a small grey metal box disguised as a book, but which contained a set of dry batteries, knobs and dials, a pair of headphones, and a coil of wires attached to an aerial. Also included in her pack were detailed maps. Exactly as she had been taught, she took everything out and assembled her radio on a table in front of the window.

Her hands trembled with tension and fatigue, but she had to send her message to London to confirm her safe arrival.

Taking a wire, she plugged one end into the radio set and fed the other end to the aerial.

Opening the window, she leaned out, looking for an innocuous place to position the aerial. Ah! The chimney pot. She took off her shoes and stockings for better grip and, barefoot, climbed out on to the tiled roof with the aerial, a wire trailing behind her. Sitting on her bottom, she edged down the slope and up again to reach the chimney. Standing on tiptoe, she managed to place the aerial securely on the ledge, before crawling back.

Inside her bedroom once more, she extricated the all-important encrypted code book from the hidden pocket in her suitcase. Selecting the right combination of letters on her transmitter, she began to beep out her simple Morse-coded message to London to say she had arrived: *The hare is ahead of the hounds.* After a while came the reply: *The tortoise is slow and steady. He will arrive when the moon is high.*

With a sigh of relief, she packed everything away and went for supper.

Raymonde Gilles had gone.

CHAPTER 44

Instructions

"Today you will go to the Rue Racine in the 6th arrondisement to meet your piano pupil Sylvie," said Madame Courvet the next morning. She handed Geneviève a leather music case.

The table had been cleared of documents; the shredder was out of sight, and everything looked normal. But both the Courvets appeared harassed and exhausted, as if they'd been up all night. After a perfunctory exchange of pleasantries, Madame had put coffee and croissants on the table for breakfast.

Geneviève too had barely slept. London had sent her instructions along with coordinates for an aircraft landing with a delivery that very day. She had written them on a fine piece of muslin and stitched it into her petticoat with needle and thread from her sewing kit.

Breakfast was a silent affair. Afterwards, Monsieur Courvet excused himself to go into his study, while Madame Courvet showed her a bicycle.

"Thank you, Madame," Geneviève said, trying to be friendly.

Madame smiled wanly. "I hope all goes well."

With her music case strapped to the back rack of the bicycle and a shopping bag hanging from the handlebars, Geneviève cycled nervously off to Rue Racine.

The streets teemed with German soldiers on and off duty, seemingly impervious to the frantic bustle of ordinary Parisians hunting for the bare necessities of life. The air was tense and surly. She felt exposed, as if voices accused her: *spy, spy, spy*. Every time she passed a German, she almost expected a shout – "Hey you! Let me see what's inside your bag!" They would have found some groceries in her shopping bag. A cursory glance inside her music case would have revealed her jacket and scarf, under which was a volume of music. A more determined search would have uncovered the book which wasn't a book. But despite the constant danger of being stopped, Geneviève had already decided she would be fanatical about never being parted from her radio transmitter.

She arrived at a grey stone apartment block, entering the courtyard through a broad, high wooden door. She politely acknowledged the concierge, whose eyes swept over her with that same scrutiny Geneviève knew from the past.

"I'm visiting the Lejeune family," Geneviève announced. "I'm here to give piano lessons to their daughter, Sylvie."

The concierge nodded. She was expected. "Second floor," she said, indicating the stone steps she should use to the right of the building.

Propping her bicycle on the wall near the steps, Geneviève took her shopping bag and music case, and climbed the broad, cool, echoey stone staircase to the second floor, feeling the eyes of the concierge piercing her back. She knocked on the door with the name *Lejeune* over it. It was opened by a woman of indeterminate age, with sleek brown hair smoothed back into a bun into the nape of her neck. An expressionless face looked her up and down.

"*Bonjour*. Can I help you?"

This time, Geneviève didn't hesitate. "*A la claire fontaine*."

The woman nodded. "*Il y a une rose*." She opened the door wider to let her in. "Our piano teacher has arrived!" she called out as she led Geneviève into a conventionally furnished sitting room with a sofa and armchairs.

Within a blur of cigarette smoke, four others in the room got to their feet. The atmosphere was tense; almost as unfriendly as at the Courvets. Why? She had given them the correct password.

A middle-aged man in check shirt and corduroy trousers stepped forward with outstretched hand. She shook it, feeling relieved. "*Bonjour*. I am Geneviève Bisset, come to give young Sylvie music lessons." She looked round for any sign of a child or a piano.

"Bonjour, *mademoiselle*," he said politely. "I'm Leo Masson. Let me introduce you to your colleagues. These are Hermine and François Lejeune, the parents of your piano pupil, Sylvie. And this is Claude Janvier, and Christine Martell. We and the Courvets make up our cell. And Raymonde Gilles; I believe you met him too. We are the British team, code name Avalon. We take our orders from London. Forgive our suspicions. You are unknown to us, and we understand this is your first mission so things will be new to you. We welcome you." Yet he was unsmiling.

She nodded, and shook hands with all of them.

"I must get straight to the point," said Masson. "We were betrayed last night. The Courvets didn't tell you?"

"Betrayed?" The word struck Geneviève like a blow. "They didn't tell me. Even London didn't tell me." It explained the confusion she had found, and the frantic shredding of documents.

"Three of us have been picked up, including our radio operator, Armand Barrault. It's a disaster. Armand was a very experienced radio operator. His arrest is a terrible loss for us – and a danger. We don't as yet know what the consequences will be. He was taken to the Gestapo headquarters on the Avenue Foch for interrogation. We don't doubt his total loyalty, but the Nazis boast that their methods of torture can get anyone to talk. Who knows what they'll get out of him. We had a cell member picked up by the Gestapo three days ago, who may have betrayed Armand. If he breaks, they will come for us." He struck a match and lit his pipe.

If he breaks.

In her medical bag, Geneviève had a small silver pill box in which were two cyanide pills. She had transferred them to a secret pocket stitched inside her blouse. She might prefer death to torture and betrayal. "Everyone has a breaking point," she had been told when given the pills. How strong was Armand? What would they get out of him?

"Can you inform London right away?" said Leo.

She nodded.

He took her on to the landing, slid aside a trap door in the ceiling and pulled down a ladder. "This leads to the roof. There should be good reception. Armand's code name was 'Le Roncier': the briar patch. Tell London 'the Briar Patch has been picked'."

Geneviève nodded calmly. "What is Raymonde Gilles' role? How does he fit in?"

"He is a coordinator," explained Masson. "We know very little. That's how it works. You have to trust. I'm sorry. Bad luck you've arrived in the middle of a dangerous emergency."

"Emergency is all around us," she murmured, stepping on to the ladder.

This was the first test of her competence. She scrambled up into the dusty loft, where there was a skylight looking out over the roof, and assembled the radio. Taking the aerial, she reached outside and fixed it to a hook which Armand must have used many times. Then she sent her message: *The Hare has met the Lion and his Pride. The Briar Patch has been picked.*

She waited for the reply.

It came quickly in code. *Hare must join the Pride. You must pick the Briar Patch.* Further instructions followed.

Back down on the landing, Leo was waiting.

"Message received by London and understood," Geneviève said, coming down the ladder. "I am instructed that the drop tonight must go ahead. I am to take Armand's place. For the moment, I am the only contact with London, and will pass on further information to you when it comes."

Leo led her back into the living room. "Meet our replacement radio operator," he said.

The others looked at her without enthusiasm.

"London says we must go ahead tonight at three a.m." Geneviève tried to sound authoritative as she scanned their faces. Was one of them a traitor? Was one of them Merlin? "This drop is important. Tonight, they are dropping supplies of sabotage equipment. "Ammunition, fuses, detonators and radio batteries. I need to be there to verify the success of the drop. I have the coordinates." She laid them out on top of a map of Paris and its environs.

Leo took up his protractor, and quickly identified the location of the drop. "Ah! Here, in the Forêt Montmorency: about sixteen to twenty miles north of Paris. There is a factory on that side that is producing engineering parts for the Third Reich. Members of the Maquis will collect the equipment and sabotage production at the Forester's House. Claude, Geneviève, and I will go for the drop tonight. We'll meet up here." He prodded a location on the map. "We'll go separately." He wrote out the address for each of them, and instructions where to meet.

"Avalon must disband from tomorrow," said Geneviève. "But I shall continue to come here and teach Sylvie, as I am unknown to the Nazis. London will inform me and Merlin on further instructions."

Madame Lejeune brought in a tray bearing a china teapot, a jug of milk, cups and saucers. She placed it in front of the sofa on a low table, still unsmiling. "Will you pour?" she asked Geneviève.

Geneviève took the milk jug and poured milk into the cups, then took up the teapot.

"*Mademoiselle!*" Madame Lejeune interrupted her quietly but sternly. "In France, we never pour the milk first into a cup. Only the English do that. You give yourself away instantly. In France, it's tea first, then milk."

Chastened, Geneviève put down the teapot with a clatter.

"And," said Madame Lejeune once more, "forgive me for being personal – it is for your own safety – but your dark hair and olive skin give you a Jewish look. These days, it could be enough to have you stopped by the police or the Gestapo. I suggest you dye your hair, make it lighter – more brown. Luckily your eyes are light brown."

Geneviève nodded, feeling embarrassed and amateurish.

"I'm glad you were wearing a headscarf when you arrived, so the concierge will perhaps not have noticed your hair. I will buy the dye for you, as I too dye my hair.

One can't be too careful; there are spies and informers everywhere. I will have it here for you by tomorrow."

"Madame Lejeune is a stickler for detail," said Claude, smiling. "Pay attention – it could save your life."

"I understand," replied Geneviève. "I'm grateful."

They heard footsteps at the door.

"Ah! Your pupil!" exclaimed François Lejeune, and hurried to let in his daughter.

A slender girl of about eight years old with almost white-blonde hair drawn back in a blue ribbon, wearing a blue checkered school smock over her dress, came in shyly. With a slight curtsey, she shook Geneviève's hand as her mother introduced her.

"First Sylvie must have her snack, and then – a piano lesson," Madame Lejeune said with a smile, and the child was led away to her nursery.

The piano was in a room overlooking the courtyard. Leo opened the window. "Just to confirm to those beyond these walls, that our newly arrived piano teacher is doing her job," he said wryly.

While she waited for her pupil, Geneviève sat at the piano and played quietly: a piece of Debussy, enigmatically rising and falling, its melody tranquil, then agitated. It brought back emotions and memories too dangerous to express, of places and people that she hardly dared hope she would see again.

The cell had been betrayed. Already, she had stepped into the greatest danger possible. The music controlled her nerves; her heartbeat steadied, and her fingers were firm on the keyboard. She could hear her father's voice in her head: *On whichever instrument you play, each note, each scale, and each phrase has its own life span as you do, yet like you, will be an everlasting inspiration.* The music said there was still hope.

Sylvie crept in quietly, waiting for the music to end. Geneviève turned to greet her.

"I wish Mademoiselle Goldstein was here," murmured Sylvie mournfully.

One day, her Jewish teacher had failed to turn up to give Sylvie her lesson. It had been a month since she disappeared.

"I'm so sorry," replied Geneviève. "You must have been very fond of her. Come, play for me – something that would have pleased Mademoiselle Goldstein."

Sylvie sat at the piano and gave a spirited performance of a Bach gigue.

"Bravo!" exclaimed Geneviève, delighted. "I think we'll get on like a house on fire."

After the lesson was over, Sylvie returned to her nursery, and Geneviève joined Leo Masson and the Lejeunes. "You teach well," murmured Madame Lejeune with a smile.

Geneviève cycled back to the Courvets. She needed to snatch some sleep before the rendezvous. It would be a long night.

CHAPTER 45

The Drop

Taking a train from Gare du Nord, Geneviève arrived on the outskirts of the Forêt Montmorency just before the 9 p.m. curfew. She needed to rendezvous with the others before the curfew began.

Across the road was a shrubbery, and a bicycle. Following instructions, she cycled along a narrow road to a small safe house with a vegetable garden owned by an old man, Henri Le Brun, who lived alone. Dogs barked from household to household, as if passing on messages: "Stranger, stranger!" She swerved down a narrow lane just as the curfew sounded. A small gate led her into Monsieur Le Brun's allotment. She moved silently enough for humans not to notice, but not quiet enough for dogs, whose sharp ears could even pick up her breathing. A dog close by barked furiously; a voice bellowed through the darkness, "Shut up!"

Tentatively, she opened the shed door. Leo and Claude greeted her with relief, and indicated a bale of straw for her to sit on. Bread rolls of cheese and tomatoes were passed round, along with a bottle of red wine.

"He's good fellow, this Monsieur Le Brun! Even provided a puncture kit with pump in case of mishaps," whispered Leo. "Can you whistle, *mademoiselle*?"

"Pretty well," answered Geneviève.

"Like this." He whistled a single note, then slid up to a top note which he repeated four times. "Then repeat until you hear an answering whistle."

"Got it!" she said.

Claude had three pistols to hand out, just in case – but Geneviève declined. "I hate the things. I'll take my chances."

Claude forced it on her. "It's for our safety too."

She took it.

"If for any reason we have to separate," Leo said, "we meet back here. We will wait until the end of curfew at 5 a.m. If any of you don't show up, you're on your own."

They set off cycling down the dark tunnel of the country road, well spaced from each other but within earshot. Only once did Claude whistle in alarm, and they pitched themselves into the roadside ditch. Three armed German motorbikes, with bright-as-suns headlights, roared past, the soldiers singing lustily at the tops of their voices. For a few seconds, everything was lit up as bright as day – the light swept over the bikes and the four of them cowering in the ditch before they were plunged back into darkness. With relief, they continued on their way.

The drop was taking place as near as possible to an extended clump of woods near a small area of ploughed fields. Geneviève and Claude left the road and waited for Leo to arrive. Then they followed a dirt path for a further twenty minutes until they reached the shelter of the trees, beyond which lay the clearing. They dismounted, tucked their bikes into the dense undergrowth and prepared to wait for the drop.

Time extended deep into the night. They didn't talk; just listened for an approaching aircraft. Geneviève was to learn that, for every lightning-speed action that took place, she would calculate hours of waiting.

"Listen!" hissed Leo. They heard a distant drone. "It's coming." They got to their feet, looking up at the sky, as a speck emerged through the clouds. Leo left the shelter of the trees and stood just where the edge of the woods met the field. He flashed a signal.

On off; on off on off; on off; on off on off . . .

The plane flew over, turned, and came back, tipping its wings to acknowledge contact. Like grey-green jellyfish, three parachutes billowed silently, slowly – infuriatingly slowly – down, down, down through the sky with their cargo. One, two . . . "Damn!" The third drifted into the trees and got tangled up. They all rushed forward to collect several boxes of cargo and the two acccessible parachutes.

The plane turned, heading back to England.

"Geneviève, hide these parachutes and boxes into the undergrowth," ordered Leo, "then go to the farm and tell the farmer, Monsieur Melot, that we have the drop but we must retrieve the third. Wait at the farm till we come."

Geneviève cut free the cargo and hid the parachutes. She decided to carry what boxes she could to the farm. Speed was of the essence. Everyone knew the peril they had put the farmer and his family in. Should their participation ever be known, it could be instant execution.

There he was, Monsieur Melot the farmer: an elderly man, beginning to stoop with age, patiently waiting by his horse which was already harnessed to a cart of hay bales. His widowed daughter was making space to hide the contents of the drop. Both women ran back to carry more boxes and gathered up the harnesses.

It took an agonising twenty minutes for Leo and Claude to find the third parachute, cursing the moon for disappearing just when they most needed her. When they returned to the farm, everything had been hidden in the hay wain, ready for collection by the sabotage team the next day. The farmer voiced his appreciation for Geneviève's initiative.

"I must contact London," said Geneviève.

She had already spotted a suitable apple tree in the nearby orchard, and climbed up with her radio transmitter. She fixed the aerial and started tapping. *Hare calling Tortoise. Hare calling Tortoise. Jellyfish.*

It was pre-dawn when Geneviève returned to the Courvets'. Everyone was sleeping. All the untidiness of the apartment had been cleared away, and there was an air of domestic normality. But there was more to do. She climbed out of the window and rigged up her transmitter, ready for further instructions from London. In the distance, the Sacré-Coeur struck 5 a.m. Her transmitter became live.

Jack Court coming Paris tomorrow. Meet at Café Bijou 11 a.m. Do not acknowledge. Go to Metro Pigalle. Wait by entrance. He will approach you again. Acknowledge with password.

She was sure that the noise of her Morse code tickety-tack tapping on the telegraph keys echoed all over Paris. Putting away the transmitter, she laid her gun on the bed. She stared at it with loathing, then hid it along with the transmitter.

She managed to get a few hours' sleep; a tangled sleep full of fears, and shadows. In her dreams, she held a gun as an enemy approached.

Oh Father, I am constantly afraid, and if this is noticed, I will be shamed and condemned.

My child, came the answer. *Bring your right hand to your right lung. Say out loud: "I believe; I trust." Believe in Trust and Hope. Trust will help you release the uneasiness of hope. Trust follows from hope.*

CHAPTER 46

Jack Court

Geneviève arrived at the Café Bijou off the Champs-Élysées in good time for her meeting with Jack Court. She ordered a coffee and sipped it, feeling nervous and unsettled about meeting her trainer. She had wanted to prove herself to him; to make him feel they had been right to trust her. Now with betrayal, everything was in disarray.

He arrived at the café on the dot of 11 a.m. It only took one glance to recognise him; despite his very un-English coat, and trilby, he seemed to her quintessentially English. As instructed, she barely raised her eyes when he brushed past her to a table nearby, whistling, *"A la claire fontaine,"* to which she murmured the response.

After a while, she paid and left the café, heading purposefully towards the Pigalle metro station as instructed, where they were finally to connect. Suddenly she had a clear intuition that she was being followed – and not by Jack Court. She reduced her pace to a stroll, then, as if on impulse, went to the kerbside, looking both ways, waiting for an opportunity to cross the road.

Was it her imagination? Was someone following her? She leaped into a gap in the traffic and picked her way through the cars, doing a final skip to the other side, where there was a boutique.

She stared into the glass, as if window shopping. In its reflection she saw a man in a belted raincoat with a fedora cocked to the side, crossing the road. He lit up a cigarette and strolled along the pavement, passing her slowly. Geneviève had a feeling she'd seen him before.

A taxi stopped to let out a passenger. Swiftly, Geneviève jumped in. *"Trocadero, s'il vous plaît.* As fast as possible – I'm late for an appointment?"

As they sped off, she didn't risk glancing out of the window to check on the man who had been following her. She glimpsed Jack on the far side going in the opposite direction, towards Pigalle metro station. How long would it take for him to realise something was wrong? How long would he wait?

The address she'd given the taxi driver took her down small side streets, winding to the right and left. Looking out of the rear window, she was sure she hadn't been followed. She stopped the taxi, paid him off. She was now twenty minutes late. She had a headscarf in her bag. She stood in a doorway, took off her hat, put on the headscarf and a pair of glasses, and hurried on.

Jack was still at Pigalle. "It's all right. You're fine," he said reassuringly, kissing her flushed cheeks the French way. "I saw you crossing the road. I guessed you might be followed and was prepared for it. Good for you to notice."

"My intuition." She smiled. "My father always said it never let me down."

"Whatever it was, it was spot on. You lost him. Had you seen the man before?"

"Not sure. Maybe on the train when I came into Paris? A man got on at my station. This could be the same man. I'd have to see his left ear."

"Oh?"

"The man on the train had a noticeable black mole on his left ear."

"Intuition plus observation makes you a good agent," he said approvingly.

They took the metro, then a bus going out to the Bois de Boulogne. "Many cafés are now bugged. It's best to have conversations outside," said Jack.

The Bois de Boulogne was like a tranquil walk in the gardens of Paradise. A horse rider trotted along a track, dipping in and out of the dappled shade. Jack was measured and gentle; no longer the strict instructor, assiduously making sure she was fully prepared for her future as an operative with the SOE. He was more like a friend, wanting to know how she was coping. She relaxed and even began to laugh at some of his jokes. He became more intimate, tucking his arm into hers; they walked as old friends, but he quickly became serious again.

"Armand lasted three days," he murmured. "They tortured him. When it got too much for him, he managed to bite on the cyanide pill hidden beneath a fake crown in his back tooth."

"So he is dead," murmured Geneviève with a deep sigh.

"And none of us knows if he divulged anything before he died," said Jack. "We can't take any chances. Since my arrival, I have reconvened the cell. They have a new code name, Pegasus, and the head of the cell is no longer known as Merlin. From now on, messages will come from Hummingbird. Just follow instructions."

"Are Merlin and Hummingbird the same person?" asked Geneviève.

"I'm sorry. I can't tell you. The less you know the better, for your sake as well as everyone else's. But Hummingbird knows everyone in the cell, including you, and will always let you know where meetings are to be held, and alert you to any information that is relevant."

"And you can trust him?" asked Geneviève.

Jack stopped and turned, looking her full in the face. "Who – Merlin? Or rather, Hummingbird? Why do you ask?" When she hesitated, he frowned. "Is this," he joked, "your intuition again?"

"Intuition," she confirmed. "I just . . . Well. I don't know. I don't suspect anyone, yet I suspect *every*one. The person following me; is he the enemy, or on our side?"

"Didn't we train you to think like that and observe like an eagle?" asked Jack with a laugh.

"Your nurture adds to my nature, I suppose," she said with a wry smile.

"I didn't know we had a philosopher in our ranks."

She grinned. "I can't help it."

"I'll check on this black mole. That's what we can call him from now on: *Black Mole*."

They walked on in companionable silence. Then Jack said, "There is to be another drop of sabotage equipment tonight. The same plane will take me back to London."

"Oh! So soon?" Geneviève couldn't help the disappointment in her voice.

Jack suddenly, almost tenderly, held both her arms and gazed into her eyes with such familiarity it took her breath away. "You only have to say the word, and we'd get you out of here in a jiffy. Things have got much more dangerous, more quickly than we thought." He spoke as if he cared.

"It's all right, Jack," she said. "I know I spend most of my time in a blind terror – but I'm not leaving here. I know my job. Besides, it's because I'm new, uncontaminated, and unknown that I can still be of use to you."

"For the moment," retorted Jack caustically. "Remember something else we taught you? Never underestimate your enemy."

"I know, and I don't," she said. "But even so, I think the cell trusts me – as much as any of us can trust each other. So long as I can still be of help to you, I'll stay."

They looked at each other deeply. Oh God, Geneviève thought. Another time, another place . . . ? Then he let go of her arms.

"Keep up your cover as Sylvie's piano teacher, but the cell will no longer meet there," he said. "Continue to stay at the Courvets for now; they haven't been compromised yet. But I'm afraid we are beset with collaborators and informers. You must always be prepared to move. Keep up the radio contact. Where do you keep your transmitter?"

She indicated the large-ish handbag slung over her sholder. "I always keep it with me."

"Good," said Jack. "I knew you were an excellent pupil, even if you were a quivering, shivering little mouse."

"Squeak, squeak!" She laughed, and he squeezed her arm.

"Get in touch any time you need to, no matter how trivial," he whispered earnestly. "And, if the Courvet address becomes unsafe, you will be given alternative safe houses to go to."

They walked on. Geneviève questioned him about the state of England, and how people were bearing up.

"You know us!" he said with a laugh. "We bungle around, and somehow pull through."

"Are we going to win?"

"I truly don't know. But if we don't . . ." He sighed deeply. "God help us all."

They reached a road. "We'll get a bus from here," said Jack. "We shouldn't look as though we're together now. We mustn't speak and be identified as 'those damned English'. Some here hate us as much as the boche. But we have good friends too."

He lit up a cigarette and offered her one. She declined. A coil of smoke rose into the air.

"Before you go," she said, delving into her bag, "would you get a message to my mother in India? Let her know I'm safe?"

"I will," he said, tucking her letter into an inside pocket. As they parted, he murmured, "Don't take silly risks. We want you back in one piece."

They were no longer together. A whiff of cigarette smoke drifted her way. She breathed in the smell of the tobacco as if she breathed in his presence, trying to retain it inside herself.

The bus came. He jumped on to the back platform; she felt a dreadful longing as he went inside.

CHAPTER 47

A Black Citroën

The sight of the black Citroën one morning worried Geneviève greatly.

She was content living with the Courvets and felt an instinctive trust in them. She felt comfortable in this district as well; with so many different ethnic groups, her own skin colour didn't stand out, and there was a general solidarity for the outsider. But ever since Avalon had been blown, she had been on edge, and was constantly vigilant.

So far, her life had been passing radio messages between London and the Maquis, who were increasing their acts of sabotage. But the German military and the French police had become more alert and ferocious. There was a frantic increase in spot raids taking place at any time of day or night. No one could drop their guard. Worst of all, the German command was taking revenge. For every act of sabotage, there were arrests and torture; for every death of a German there were sometimes ten French citizens who would be executed – mostly Jews and communists, already rounded up and held in detention camps; and there were the random on-the-spot executions to deter resistance.

That morning, early, Geneviève had crawled out of her window and placed her aerial on the roof to receive her daily message from London before going to the Lejeunes to give Sylvie her piano lesson. She had noticed the black Citroën through the gaps between the chimney pots, parked on the other side of the estate, surrounded by inquisitive gaggles of children.

It was a large car for this area, and looked out of place. She delayed her radio contact. The Citroën could be a radio interceptor, although she saw no telltale aerials protruding from anywhere.

After weeks of living with the Courvets, she had become familiar with the vehicles on the estate. Most of them rested on bricks, rusting, as no one could afford the petrol. She had never seen this car before. It was a powerful vehicle – 15CV. In this day and age, who could afford to run that, apart from German officials or collaborators? Most people could barely afford more than a 2CV – and even they lay mouldering in garages or along the road.

She flew round tidying up her room in case they were raided, removing any incriminating evidence. Instead of a radio transmitter, all an intruder would find was a metronome and a volume of beginners' piano music.

She mentioned the Citroën to Madame Courvet over breakfast. Her landlady was alarmed, and ordered Geneviève to tell Leo Masson. Geneviève was due to meet him in an hour, for the first time since the cell had been renamed Pegasus, in a café just off Boulevard Saint-GermainPrès.

Geneviève set off on her bike, managing to avoid the black Citroën. What had brought it there? Would she need another safe house? She hoped not, but had to tell London.

She cycled down the Boulevard Saint-Germain, casting a nostalgic glance at the Café Rigaud as she flew past. Turning into a narrow alley off the boulevard, she came to the Café Chat Noir. It was a shabby, dark place; not very salubrious for a rendezvous. A gaunt old man was serving and, for a while, took no notice of her.

"Excusez-moi!" she said. *"Un café, s'il vous plaît!"*

"Je viens, je viens!" he said grumpily. "I'm coming."

He brought coffee over, slopping it into the saucer. She tipped the coffee in the saucer back into the cup, and drank a little. It was good. She waited. The clock ticked by. Leo didn't show up.

Her anxiety built. She had to tell him about the Citroën, as well as the instructions she had received in a late-night transmission from London: instructions that Pegasus was to blow up a railway bridge over a track which took transport eastwards. It would kill two birds with one stone, destroying both a road and a rail link.

She ordered a second coffee and sipped it slowly, flicking through a magazine which she always took with her. She felt sick inside. Where was Leo? The black Citroën concerned her even more now. They had already been betrayed once. Had the same traitor betrayed the rest of them?

No one ever waited more than half an hour, to avoid suspicion. So Geneviève paid up and left, wheeling her bike back up to Boulevard Saint-Germain, unsure what to do. She came to the Café Rigaud, and couldn't resist going in. Its familiarity was comforting. It was close enough to the Café Chat Noir, and she might just see Leo passing by.

Georgie was there as she had remembered him, lazily wiping glasses and replacing them in the rack above his head; pausing for a puff of his cigarette; relaxing after the early morning breakfast rush. Her disguise meant that he showed no sign of recognition as she entered, though she longed to greet him like a friend from the past. She sat down at a table facing the street. Georgie came over immediately, wiping his hands on his apron.

"Un café, s'il vous plaît," she said.

A young blondish woman entered and glanced round the café. Her eyebrows lifted questioningly when she saw Geneviève, and she caught Georgie's eye. Georgie gave a slight shrug as if to say, 'I don't know who she is.'

A young German officer strode in next, jovially calling out, *"Bonjour!"* and asked for a schnapps. Georgie poured a surly measure. Leaning against the counter, the officer's eye fell on Geneviève. He put his schnapps down and marched sternly over to her.

"Your papers, *mademoiselle*," he demanded, stretching out an officious hand.

This was the first time she had been asked for them. She hoped he didn't see her hands shaking as she delved into her handbag and brought out her identity card and work permit. He scrutinised the papers, squinted at the photograph, and studied her closely.

"Geneviève Bisset?" he asked loudly.

She nodded. Prayed he wouldn't search her.

He flipped through the papers a second time, then handed them back more politely. "*Pardonnez-moi*, but you look Jewish, and Jews are not allowed in cafés here."

So much for dyeing her hair. Finding her courage, Geneviève looked up at him, smiling sweetly. "It always happens! It must be because my grandmother is Italian. She lives just outside Milan. I'm often told I look like her."

"Ah! That's it. Italian. They are good friends of the Germans. Please excuse me. Just doing my duty," said the officer, and returned to his schnapps at the bar. With no conversation forthcoming from Georgie, he tossed back the remains and left.

"Good riddance to bad rubbish!" snorted Georgie. "*Ça va, mademoiselle?*"

Geneviève smiled shyly. "I've known worse," she remarked, but her heart was thumping, and all she could sense was that something had gone wrong. Leo hadn't turned up.

The young woman opposite was studying her closely. Their eyes met. It took all Geneviève's self-control not to cry out. But her training kicked in and she lowered her head for a further sip of her coffee. She avoided any further eye contact and, after flicking through the magazine for a few minutes longer, she finished her coffee, paid her bill, and left quickly. There was nothing for it but to return to the Courvets and radio London as soon as possible.

She cycled as fast as she could – a full fifteen minutes back to the apartment. The black Citroën had gone. But something was wrong. The children weren't playing as usual, and the brown grass was thronged with residents milling about in disturbed groups, glancing up constantly – to the third-floor apartment where the Courvets lived.

The Algerian boy who had looked after Marc Nadeau's horse and cart when they had arrived ran over, his black eyes wide with excitement. "The *flic* came. You should have seen them! Three cars and a police van. A whole bunch of them jumped out and dashed inside. They raided your apartment and took the Courvets away in the police van. They've gone. You should have heard the shouting and screaming! They'd have taken you too, if you'd been there."

Geneviève propped her bike against the wall, and raced upstairs. The door was wide open; the police hadn't bothered to close it. The flat looked as if a tornado had ripped through it. Doors, cupboards, drawers, bedrooms – everything had been turned over and stripped. Her metronome on the piano was ticking slowly down as it ran out of spring.

Geneviève leaned weakly against the wall. She saw the

telephone. She had to ring the Lejeunes and warn them. She dialled the number. It rang and rang – and just when she was about to give up, the receiver was lifted.

"Hare," Geneviève said, using her code name.

"I'm afraid *madame* is out." François Lejeune sounded stiff with warning.

"I'm sorry to hear that," said Geneviève. "The Lion didn't turn up for the meeting."

"That's a pity. I will confer with my colleagues and ring you back in a few minutes." François' voice cracked as if about to burst into tears.

Geneviève put down the phone.

"Wow! Look what they've done!"

The Algerian boy was staring round at the mess in the apartment.

"Who did they arrest?" asked Geneviève urgently.

"All of them. I told you. They'd have nabbed you too. Lucky you weren't there."

"Perhaps you ought to go home," she said. "Go on, get out of here."

He stared at her. "Are you a Jew? Did you dye your hair? I can always tell. They're after Jews you know." And he drew a finger across his throat.

She ignored him and went into her bedroom. That too had been turned over. Thank God she'd taken everything with her. Her instincts had been right.

The phone rang. "It's the telephone," said the boy, unnecessarily.

"I can hear it," replied Geneviève. "Go on – scram!" She lifted the receiver. "Hello?"

"François Lejeune again." His voice seemed to have shrunk, and she struggled to hear. "I have a message for you. Leo was delayed. He wants to meet you in the Café Alma near the George V cinema in half an hour. Can you be there?"

"Yes," said Geneviève. "Of course. I'll be there."

"*Mademoiselle*! Leo –" François was about to say something else, she was sure of it – but the line went dead.

The Algerian boy was sitting at the top of the stairs as she left the apartment.

"I've got nothing against Jews you know," he said. "My granny was Jewish, back in Algeria. Luckily she's dead; otherwise, they'd have been after her." He looked her in the eye with a strange wisdom and challenge. "Are you with the Maquis?"

Geneviève laughed uneasily. "You've been reading too many comics. I'm a piano teacher not a resistance fighter."

"I hate the boche."

"Really?" said Geneviève carefully. "Who looks after you?"

"I live with my mum. She's works over in the 8th arrondissement; gets back just before the curfew. Sometimes she doesn't get back. I'm used to it. My dad was with the French army, but we haven't heard from him since the invasion. He's probably in prison somewhere. Or dead," he said flatly.

"What's your name?"

"Bobbi."

"Bobbi, you could do something for me? It may take an hour or two. Will anyone worry about you if you do this errand for me?"

"Nope."

"You seem to like spy comics. Are you good at keeping secrets? It would be a bit like being a secret agent."

The boy's eyes lit up. "What do I have to do?"

"I have to meet a man in the Café Alma, next to the George V cinema. Do you know it? It's in the Champs-Élysées, not far from the Arc de Triomphe. He's tallish, bulky, got a moustache . . ." Geneviève described Leo Masson. "Take my bike and cycle to Pigalle. Leave the bike there. Make sure you chain it up – here's the key. Take the metro to Place de l'Étoile. When you get there, walk down to the cinema."

"Then what?" said Bobbi.

"I want to know if the man is there. Don't approach him; just notice everything about him. Also – and this is important – look around. Look down the boulevard both ways, and over the road; look out for anyone else also hanging about; a couple of men maybe. Anyone who looks suspicious." She used the word *suspicious* as it would make the boy even more perceptive.

Bobbi's eyes brightened. "Sure, sure!"

"The clever thing is for *you* not to look suspicious!" emphasised Geneviève.

The boy grinned and tapped his nose. They went

downstairs and stood just inside the doorway to the apartment block.

"See that bike over there – the dark green one with the basket in front, leaning against that wall with all the other bikes?" she said. "That's mine. Take it. I'll follow on the metro. I'll get off at Place de l'Étoile and wait for you there above ground."

"Are you sure you're not with the Maquis?" the boy asked mischievously.

She shook her head with mock exasperation. "I want you to be able to describe the man as exactly as you can. Will you do that?"

The boy looked excited. "Sure thing! I always wanted to be a spy."

Geneviève held him by his shoulders and looked into his gleaming brown eyes. "Yes – and I *am* asking you to be a spy. But this is real – not make believe; not Tintin. There may be German spies watching this man, and if they become suspicious of you, they could just haul you off. They wouldn't care that you were a kid. It could be dangerous. Do you understand?"

He nodded enthusiastically.

"Let's go then! Here – take a metro ticket." She took out her book of tickets and gave him one. "I'll meet you at the metro by the news stand, so come back there when you've done what I asked."

413

Bobbi was waiting for her, looking very pleased with himself, when she emerged from the metro half an hour or so later. She walked past him and muttered, "Follow me. We'll go down that side street."

He followed her to a narrow alley. They came to a small square with a children's playground, and a bench. It was empty. They sat side by side.

"Right, *mon agent secret*," said Geneviève. "Was he there?"

Bobbi described Leo exactly. "He was walking up and down on the pavement between the cinema and the café; he kept looking around. Does someone want to kill him?" he hissed with excitement. "Two guys turned up: one was wearing a black leather jacket, the other a brown raincoat and a fedora pulled down – dead giveaway." He snorted derisively.

"Any guns?" Geneviève asked.

"I didn't see any guns. One of them spoke to your *monsieur* – the one in the grey raincoat. Then he went off down the boulevard. The other one – the guy in the brown raincoat – pretended to look at the cinema posters. Didn't fool me. After a while, he went over and asked for a light. They said something to each other. They both went into the Café Alma. That's where I left them."

"Hmm . . ." Geneviève was troubled.

"But you know what?" exclaimed Bobbi. "The brown-raincoat guy was the same guy who brought you to the Courvets. I looked after his horse, remember? He's in the café now, sitting with your *monsieur*."

Geneviève was astonished. "Are you sure?"

"Of course I'm sure. I never forget a face. I told you I'd make a good spy."

"Did he see you?"

Bobbi shook his head.

"Right," she said. "Let's walk together. They'll be looking out for a woman on her own. Do you think he'll recognise you?"

"Nah!" said Bobbi confidently. "He barely looked at me when I said I'd mind his horse and cart. Anyway, don't we Algerians all look the same?" He chuckled cynically.

So Bobbi had seen Marc Nadeau. Geneviève's brain was ticking off all the possibilities. How did Nadeau fit into the picture? Was he a double agent? Could he be both Hummingbird and a traitor?

"Do you mind tucking your arm into mine, as though we are related?" said Geneviève. "Let's go and check out what's on at the cinema."

They arrived outside the café, and Bobbi said, "Your *monsieur* – that's him, isn't it? The one with the pipe?"

Geneviève glanced through the café window. There was Leo Masson. Sitting with him was indeed Marc Nadeau. They weren't talking. Why hadn't Leo kept the rendezvous with her? Was he in the café under duress?

Then her eye was drawn to another man at a nearby table, leaning back with his legs sprawled out, and reading a newspaper; supposedly not with them. He lowered his paper to light up a cigarette. As he turned to fumble in his pockets for the matches, his right ear was clearly visible. It was Black Mole.

A car drew up outside. Marc Nadeau stood up decisively, slapping some money down on the table. He got Leo Masson to his feet with a sharp prod, and nudged him out of the café. The car door opened, and Leo was bundled into the back, while Marc Nadeau. got in next to him. The car sped off.

"Now what?" exclaimed Bobbi with disappointment. "It's over."

"No, it's not," she murmured.

Geneviève was watching Black Mole. He put out his cigarette, folded his newspaper and called for the waiter to pay. Geneviève bent down to tie Bobbi's shoelace as Black Mole left the café and headed down the boulevard.

"Bobbi, follow that man as far as you can," Geneviève instructed. "Do you understand? He may be even more important than the *monsieur*. If he gets into a car, we'll lose him and it will be over. But if he gets on a bus or a metro, then you must too. Can you do that? Don't let him see you; he mustn't suspect anything. I need to know where he goes. Here's some money – it should be enough for the moment."

Bobbi took the money eagerly.

"I'll have more money for you tomorrow," Geneviève promised. "Give me the key to the bicycle lock."

He rummaged in his pocket and brought out the key.

"Everything understood?" asked Geneviève.

"Understood!"

"We'll meet at Pigalle metro tomorrow morning."

The boy grinned, and sprinted off to catch up with Black Mole.

Geneviève took the metro to Pigalle and found her bicycle. She felt despairing. Everything was falling apart. She had no home to go to: the Courvets had been raided, Leo had been picked up, and the Lejeunes were in trouble. The traitor had been busy. She had to contact London as soon as possible. But how?

There was only one place she could go.

YELLOW STAR JEWISH
LAW IN OCCUPIED FRANCE

7 JUNE 1942

All Jews over six years of age to wear, on the left side of the chest, a yellow star the size of a person's palm, with the inscription Juif inside.

Jews must go to the nearest police station, be registered, and issued with the yellow star. Any Jew caught without the star will be arrested and detained on the spot.

The badge is attached to our coats but has not touched our consciousness. We now possess so much consciousness that we can say we are not ashamed of our badges.

YITSKHOK RUDASHEVSKI
Children's Wartime Diaries

So he dashes, like a demon, — proud, black demon of the tempest, — and he's laughing and he's weeping . . . it is at the clouds he's laughing, it is with his joy he's weeping!
In the fury of the thunder, the wise demon hears its weakness, and he's certain that the clouds will not hide the sun — won't hide it!

THE SONG OF THE STORMY PETREL
MAXIM GORKY

CHAPTER 48

Beating the Curfew

Vera was on a mission to deliver papers.

She arrived on her bicycle in the early evening at the address of the Rubins, a Jewish family, with instructions and papers for getting them out of Paris and, ultimately, the country. There was no time to lose.

The authorities were hotting up. It had started with arresting foreigners, illegals and refugees without citizenship, including Jews whose citizenship hadn't been regularised. But then it became all Jews: Jews who had been in France for generations, Jews who were regular citizens in jobs across society, including those who fought in the French army, and even those at the very top of French politics and the establishment. All were in danger, and all were being rounded up. There was a deep and growing terror, which must have been as great as for those aristocrats during the French Revolution.

There was a new law: all Jews – men, women and children – had to wear a yellow star with a J in the middle which stood for Jew. *Juif*. Every other day there were more restrictions, more suppression, more tales of arrests, torture and brutality. No Jew could simply merge with the crowd, but had to go to the nearest police station, be registered, and issued with the yellow star. Any Jew caught without the star was arrested and detained on the spot.

Vera sat with Monsieur and Madame Rubin and their six-year-old daughter, Rebecca, round a small table covered by a pristine but barren white tablecloth. There with nothing to eat or drink; the whiteness of the cloth only emphasised the paucity of their circumstances, and there was evidence in the grate of furniture having been burned in a desperate attempt to keep warm. It had become ferociously cold, and they were all bundled up in woollen clothes and blankets as if they were at the South Pole. They stared at her with darkly troubled eyes, already exhausted by the thought of yet more flight. They were not French citizens, but part of the ranks of hated immigrants. It was barely two years since they had fled from Rumania; dodging the fascist Iron Guards, Nazi soldiers, police dogs and collaborators, sleeping rough, walking mile upon mile, daring to take the odd bus or local train, till they finally reached what they thought was the safety of France.

They had registered as refugees, and managed to find a one-roomed apartment in the 18ᵗʰ arrondissement. Then the Nazis came; so, yet again, they had packed suitcases by the door, ready for flight.

Daniel had asked Vera to deliver forged papers for the family: identity documents, photographs, travel passes, and proof of address. How exhausted he had looked as he handed her the package. He had turned into a night owl, with dark rings round his eyes from working through the night,

"You will be careful, my darling?" he had murmured. Then he kissed her with such intensity, it made her feel afraid. He hardly ever kissed her on the lips, as though it would weaken his resolve. He had refused to allow themselves to enter a fool's paradise of false hope. Yet today, he had kissed her as if he never wanted to let her go. He may have feared his own feelings, but she wished he realised what courage that kiss gave her. Swearing she would do nothing rash, nothing to attract attention to herself, she had set off, cycling with deep joy.

"Your surname is now Vallée," she told the Rubin family and spread their papers on the table. "Your first names are Christophe, Renée, and your daughter is Lys. Will you remember that?" Vera leaned forward and looked at the girl. "You're not Rebecca any more. You're Lys Vallée. It's easy isn't it – Lys?"

The child nodded, her eyes wide with years of terror.

"All your instructions are here. Read them carefully. Don't talk loudly in French; your accent will give you away," Vera advised. "And for heaven's sake, don't speak to each other in Rumanian anywhere in public. If all goes to plan, you will be picked up in a van and driven fifteen miles out of Paris. *Monsieur*, you will be deposited at a rural train station with your forged travel pass and identity card, heading for Marseilles. You must be prepared for constant checks, so have your story ready. The van driver will have your tickets to Marseilles, then on to Perpignan. Your wife and daughter will be taken to another train station, and will take a different route to Perpignan, where you will all be met and driven to the Spanish border."

The family nodded unemotionally. They'd been through all this before. They knew not to get their hopes up too high. So much could go wrong. Even the child was utterly composed; not clinging fearfully to her mother or father, but holding herself a little apart. Vera saw herself in the little girl. Fate would dictate whether Rebecca – now Lys – like thousands of other children would be separated from her parents as she herself had been; whether they would live or die.

"If this plan doesn't work out, we'll try again. We must never lose heart. We won't abandon you." Vera got to her feet and shook the hand of each parent. She picked up the little girl. "What is your new name?"

"Lys Vallée," the girl said clearly.

"Lys Vallée, look after your mother," Vera said, kissing her on both cheeks, and putting her down.

With much hugging and hand shaking, Vera finally left. Cycling hard to get back before the curfew.

CHAPTER 49

The Reunion

Darkness had fallen when she returned to Marianne's. Every muscle protested with fatigue as she lugged her bike up the steps. She fumbled for her door key just as the curfew went off, its ugly sound a daily reminder of the fear people lived with: the injustice, the hopelessness. What had created these monsters? How dared they march into other people's countries, creating havoc? How dared they cause beautiful families like the Rubins to flee like criminals; how dared they terrify little children like Lys and Louis?

She turned the key and entered.

It was as if some divine ear had heard her furious grief. A glorious sound reached her ears; a magical sound, fairylike, haunting, soothing. It enveloped her; lifted her away from the hatefulness of the outside world as she entered Marianne's house. It was a sound she knew.

She leaned her bike in the hallway and wonderingly entered the living room. The room was in blackout; not even a candle glowed to identify who was making this music. She only knew one person it could be. After today, perhaps it was no surprise. "Noor?"

The music stopped. "Vera?" A figure rose, propping the instrument against the cushions. "Marianne told me you were living here. I couldn't believe it," said Noor.

They rushed towards each other and embraced. Vera switched on her torch, and enveloped her friend in a pool of light; then they rolled around giggling like schoolgirls.

"Good gracious! Look at you! Almost a blonde," shrieked Noor.

"And you with your *Italian* grandmother?" Vera chortled.

"I knew it! I knew it was you in the Café Rigaud!" Noor exclaimed. "I was terrified you'd give me away. You'd better get used to calling me Geneviève Bisset."

"And I'm Aimée Dubois," said Vera.

"How do you do Aimée." Noor held out her hand formally, the English way.

"How do you do, Geneviève," replied Vera, and they shrieked with laughter all over again. How good it was to laugh.

Marianne entered carrying a storm lamp, beaming with pleasure at the reunion. "Even in such cruel times, friendship overcomes everything, *n'est-ce pas*?" She put an arm round her beloved Noor. "Come, I've prepared supper."

They allowed themselves one evening of reminiscence and sociability. Geneviève could be Noor again, and Aimée could be Vera. They talked of their schooldays in England; what news of Gwen, and was Dodo still at RADA?

This was the moment Noor had to break the news which she knew would cast a blight over their joyous meeting; that Dodo had died at Dunkirk.

Vera stared out of the window into the black night. She had been so obsessed with the possibility of a war breaking out, and her worst fears had been realised. Now, of their group of friends, Dodo was the first to be sacrificed.

Vera's voice was small in the darkness of the room. "Each one of us has become a victim of this war," she said. "I hope I can be as noble as she was."

With the mood now sombre, Marianne said sadly that she would prepare a bed for Noor in the garden shed.

While the house slept, Noor sat on the swing beneath the moon-struck heavens, and allowed herself to wonder about her fairies. She pushed herself to and fro, the bolts squeaking in the wood of the old chestnut tree, just as it had always done. A breeze as soft as butterfly wings brushed her face, and the rustling sounds of leaves seemed to tingle with fairies breathing.

"You're there, aren't you?" whispered Noor. "The trolls didn't chase you out."

"No, no! We're here, Noor. And do you know? One night, Marianne came and sat on the swing and wept; she wept for her poor Pascal – so badly wounded during the invasion – and she wept for her children and their future; and she wept for France. We had to comfort her. We blew soft perfumed air through her hair, and sang songs in her ear, and suddenly – it was as if she saw us. She became calm. When she walked back into the house she whispered, '*Bonne nuit, mes petites fées.*' So, we knew we couldn't leave. Welcome back, Noor. So long as you live, we have life."

"How that pleases me," whispered Noor. "Thank you." She got off the swing. It was time to contact London before sleeping.

Her fairies tinkled. "Be brave, Little Hare."

She smiled. They knew her code name.

She hoisted herself up into the tree and found a clear high point to set her aerial and began transmitting.

Hare calling Tortoise. Hare calling Tortoise. Has Leopard changed his spots? Hare needs a burrow.

The next morning, each was back attending to their own plans. Noor became Geneviève again, and Vera, Aimée.

"I wonder if we'll see each other again," sighed Vera with tears in her eyes, as Noor took her bicycle down the steps.

"We will, darling Vera. We will."

They embraced one more time before Noor, Geneviève once more, set off to meet Bobbi at Pigalle.

CHAPTER 50

Raymonde Gilles

He was there, as arranged.

"Good man," said Geneviève. "You've come. Anything to report?"

"That *monsieur* – the one you told me to follow yesterday? He went to the Avenue Foch – number eighty-four," said Bobbi in awe.

"He did?" Geneviève felt faint. "On his own?"

"Totally. The guard just opened the gate for him as if he were a regular."

"You're a master spy, Bobbi. What's more – you're a hero. Now get off home before your mother gets worried. Here!" She pressed some more money into his hand.

He tapped his nose. "Don't forget. Any time you need me!"

"Go, go! I won't forget."

Geneviève felt cold as death. Bobbi had seen Black Mole going into a building on Avenue Foch: number eighty-four. Everyone knew that was the Headquarters of the Gestapo.

Marianne had said Geneviève couldn't stay in her shed more than a day or two. The detector vans were always prowling round the suburbs. If her signal was picked up, they would be in great danger and their whole escape network jeopardised.

By the end of the day, London had given her the address of another safe house where she could bed down, but she would be moving every two or three days. She told Marianne and Vera that she would leave regular notes in the shed when she could, so they would know she was all right.

She left a small sprig of leaves and flowers to say goodbye.

Geneviève became obsessive about checking every time she went out. She noted who was around when she left a building; she altered her routes, crossing roads. She continued to explore every café and shop window. She changed her appearance, alternating between headscarves and hats; hair up, hair down; hair blonde or brown or even chestnut red. She found a pair of spectacles she could wear from time to time – and she never went to the same safe house within three days. It was exhausting carrying a basic bag around as well as her transmitter. With little food, and poor sleep, she was beginning to look thin.

Once when she was in a safe house, trying to rig the wire to her aerial from her window to a ledge on the roof, the door was flung open and a Nazi soldier burst in. They were going block by block, looking for Jews and illegals. "Your identity card please!" barked a German voice.

Half in and half out of the window with the wire in her hand, Geneviève closed her eyes for a second or two before turning with a great beaming smile. "Oh *monsieur*! You've come just in time to give me a hand. I was trying to rig a washing line from my window to that ledge. If I hold this end, could you kindly crawl out and attach it to the nail on the chimney breast?"

He was a young lad, all puffed up with authority and duty. "Of course, *mademoiselle*." He took the end of the wire and climbed out of the window. Hurriedly, Geneviève scooped up her codebook and any other signs of her transmitter, and shoved them under the bed.

The young soldier fixed the line to the chimney and scrambled back.

"*Merci, merci!*" she sang. "You are so kind – *très gentil*."

"*Pas de quoi*," returned the soldier with a click of his heels, and left.

It was another safe house she had to abandon as soon as she had radioed London. Out of other options that night, Geneviève headed for Marianne's.

In a state of utter exhaustion, she let herself into the garden shed and switched on her torch. Even before her mouth opened to scream, a figure stepped into her torchlight. "*A la claire fontaine.*"

"*Il y a une rose,*" she replied faintly.

"I am Hummingbird."

"You!" exclaimed Geneviève. "Raymonde Gilles?"

"You have an excellent memory for faces," Raymonde observed.

He made her sit down, and poured her a small glass of wine. They stayed for a while, discussing the fate of the Courvets and the Lejeunes. They had been arrested and sent to a concentration camp.

"And Sylvie?" asked Geneviève, filled with dread.

"She was at school when they came. We rushed her to safety." He got to the point. "London thought it time we met, Geneviève. There is only you and me who remain from our cell, and we are barely one step ahead of being captured ourselves. Jack Court suggests you return to London. You are exhausted, and they can replace you with someone else."

"No! Tell Jack I'm fine. I want to carry on," said Geneviève. "I have all these contacts now. Someone else would have to start from scratch. I must stay."

"Sleep on it," Raymonde advised. "You know how to make contact if you change your mind. I hope we meet again in happier times, *mademoiselle*." And, opening the shed door, he slipped away into the night.

CHAPTER 51

Future Passed

If I shall exist eternally, how shall I exist tomorrow?

Vera went to the Jardin du Luxembourg. A few days had passed since she had been able to check the secret hollow of their tree for a message from Jeanne. There had been nothing since the note telling her that Aunt Minnie had been sent to a concentration camp outside Paris called Drancy.

This time Vera found a crumpled paper bag looking like a piece of lazily discarded rubbish. She extricated it and unfolded the creased brown paper. *Your uncle is distraught. Can we meet? 3 p.m.*

Vera felt a surge of frustration. Jeanne hadn't dated the message, or put a time. It could have been written five minutes ago or a week ago. But she couldn't hang around. She always felt nervous about being in a public space which was forbidden to Jews. She hoped her dyed blonde hair beneath her low-brimmed hat didn't draw any attention to herself as she strolled as casually as possible across the gardens.

But one person recognised her, knew her, and began following her; at first without a plan – yet with a low-burning, simmering resentment. She had heard that Vera was in England. She was mortified when she had seen her with Daniel at the student protest. Look how *she* had suffered, following him to Spain! Look how they had fought side by side! Had none of that meant anything? Did he think she had suffered and nearly died in Spain for the *Cause?* Hadn't he always shown her the greatest respect, affection, and admiration – didn't that all add up to *love?* No. It didn't. Admiration wasn't love.

Once she understood that, she also understood that it was Vera who stood between her and Daniel. In the place of hope grew hatred.

Unaware of being watched, Vera sat on a nearby bench in sight of the tree, waiting, hoping; remembering times when war hadn't yet come, when there had still been a chance that it wouldn't come. Remembering her school days in England, and her friendships with Gwen, Noor – and Dodo, whose sacrifice at Dunkirk had become a shining example to them all.

Suddenly, the grief and fears for her loved ones rose to the surface. She had learned a profound affection for her uncle – and even for her aunt, who had treated her so coldly. Her poor aunt, put in a concentration camp.

And above all, Louis, whom she loved as a brother. How could she bear it if she lost him as she had lost Ethan, and her mother and father? She sat rigidly, staring ahead like a statue; but a statue which wept.

It was past 3 p.m. Jeanne hadn't come. Vera felt an irresistible compulsion to see her home in the Rue d'Assas. She walked across the gardens and over the road, and paused at the big door. It was ajar, giving her sight of the courtyard within. Madame Boucher was in her window, bent over her knitting. Many a concierge had turned informer, and Vera feared her. She stared up at the windows of their apartment realising, with deep foreboding, that the shutters were closed.

A resident emerged – a youngish, confident looking woman, very fashionably dressed. She crossed the courtyard, her elegant high heels clicking incongruously across the cobbles. Vera didn't know her; good – it gave her the courage to stop her politely and ask: "Excuse me? I'm looking for the Blumstein family."

"The Blumsteins?" She spat out the name as though it contaminated her mouth. "Good heavens! Those Jews! They've gone long ago. And the Moskowskis too. The place has been cleansed. We live here now."

Her uncle had gone too? And Louis? The voice, the accent, went through her like a knife. The woman was German.

Vera replied automatically, "I see! Very well. Thank you," and walked away. She had a terrible impulse fling herself upon this enemy; this monster daring to call herself a human being. But almost as quickly it had overwhelmed her, the hatred sucked itself out, leaving her ashen-faced, and despairing.

She turned back like a ghost. She belonged nowhere. There was no place on this earth she could ever feel safe, ever call home. She saw no future. On and on she wandered, hardly caring where she was going, until she found herself at the banks of the Seine. She leaned over the bridge, stared longingly at the swirling waters, feeling herself irresistibly drawn into the dark depths.

Further down across the road, a figure silently urged her. *"Go on! Do it. Jump. What's there to live for?"*

But there was Louis to live for; Daniel to live for; maybe even Ethan. With a deep sigh, Vera stepped back, and walked away.

The figure continued to watch, then followed her to Marianne's.

CHAPTER 52

The Vél d'Hiv Roundup

JULY 1942

I t is blisteringly hot.

Wearing a sleeveless blouse and loose skirt, Vera cycles to an address in the 19th arrondissement, with all the documents required for the escape of the Goldberg family. They are a large family group: mother, father, three children and one set of grandparents. They greet her with joy and trepidation, clustering round the dining table as she lays out the documents for their escape from France and listening to Vera's instructions. They are to travel in separate groups to three different pick-up points; they are to dress inconspicuously, wear the yellow star, and especially not to go where Jews are not allowed. Each is only to take a small bag; the sort of cotton bag which would look as though they were on a day out. Once they make their rendezvous, they will receive further instructions.

She listens patiently to their qualms: what to do if anything goes wrong? She feels their fear. But what more can she do, except hope that the adults will be calm, and careful, and follow the plan? She reassures them that if anything does go wrong, help will come.

Her job done, she gets up to go – although she can almost feel their hands clutching her, trying to hold on to her, as if she were their life belt. She hugs and kisses them all, and wishes them luck. "God will be good to you," she murmurs.

She is descending the stairwell from their fourth-floor apartment when, with a shock, she hears the rumpus of police cars, and *gendarmes*, and brutal voices shouting, "Get out of our way! Return to your apartments!"

The boots of French police storm the building; orders are yelled. "Open up! Police!" Doors are thumped as if they would break them down.

Vera dashes back upstairs to the Goldbergs, who have already been drawn to their small balcony. Down below are two, three – four buses.

"Get out, get out!" Vera cries. "Take the children. Run. Go by the fire escape. Take your documents." She thrusts them into Mr Goldberg's hands. "Leave everything else. Go, go!"

The oldest girl of about fourteen takes command. "I'll take the little ones to the scrubland nearby. We have hiding places there. We'll wait for you."

"Good plan, Miriam," says Mr Goldberg. "Someone will come and find you – leave some marks to help us. Now go. *Vite, vite.*"

Vera herds the family to the back steps of the fire escape. The parents linger to help the old ones, but the old ones say, "Go! Look after the children. We'll follow." Vera has to practically push the parents down the steps. The grandparents make to follow, scooping up their faked identity cards.

Too late. Bang, bang, bang!

Vera snatches the remaining documents from the elder Goldbergs' hands. They exchange a mute moment of understanding before she pushes them between two books on the bookshelf. It is too late for them.

"*Ouvre la porte!*" Open up!

Vera motions to the Goldberg grandparents to stay calm.

Bang, bang, bang! "*Ouvre la porte immediatement!*"

Vera is thrust aside as the police barge in. Her breath freezes in her lungs. She knows the younger of the two policemen. He had been in her class at school before she had been sent away to England. He stares at her, then drops his eyes. When he looks up again, his gaze is stony and blank.

For a moment, all hope flees. This is it; her fate is sealed. Her dyed blonde hair has not fooled him. Vera's inner self seems to lift outside her body, and float above everyone. Everything ends here, she thinks. She hasn't even said goodbye to Daniel.

"Is your name Goldberg?" barks the policeman.

"It is," says the old man. "This is my wife."

"Where are the rest of you?"

"Away. Summer holidays."

"Papers please."

Monsieur Goldberg heaves himself from the chair and walks slowly to a desk, as if trying to put off the fate that awaits them. He hands his papers over. Vera's eyes catch sight of the edge of the brown envelope between the books where she has thrust the fake documents. The younger policeman follows her gaze then turns his icy attention back to her.

"Your name, *mademoiselle*?"

"Aimée Dubois," says Vera calmly, taking out her own identity card and travel documents.

"What are you doing here?"

"My friends live here. I promised to check on *monsieur et madame* while the family was away, to make sure they're all right." She speaks calmly and naturally.

The young policeman checks her photograph. Then he thrusts the documents back into her hand. "She's legit," he announces firmly.

"Very well. You may go," says the older policeman.

"I want to stay and cook a meal for my friends," says Vera. "That's why I came."

"Your friends are coming with us." The older officer turns to the Goldbergs. "Get up, *madame*, please. Come on, come on!"

"What rule have we broken?" asks old Monsieur Goldberg with courteous patience. He puts an arm round his wife. "We wear the yellow star when we go out. We obey all the rules. Are our papers not in order?"

"Your papers are in perfect order. They confirm you are Jews. That's enough. We're cleaning the Jews out of Paris. Get going."

Madame Goldberg gets to her feet. Her husband kisses her tenderly, in case it is their farewell. "Come Anna, darling. We'd better do as they say."

The old lady looks transparent with shock. She sways and he puts both arms round her. "Be brave," he whispers.

Vera asks, "What should they take with them? Toiletries? Food?"

"They won't need anything. Get on with it!"

The younger officer tries to take Madame Goldberg's arm to help her outside. She politely withdraws. "I can manage thank you."

Vera hugs the old couple in one embrace. "Dear ones! All this will be over one day. Don't lose hope."

Then they are gone, leaving Vera inside. No one closes the door.

She is cold and shaking, though outside, the temperature has risen even higher. A pitiless sun burns over the city. Every building, tree, and object casts a hard iron-like shadow, as if the whole of Paris has become encaged. Down below is the queue of buses; the pathetic families, shuffling, terrified, distraught, coaxing along their infants, and young children, and elderly relatives; all to be driven away. Echoes of their voices continue to hang in the stifling air. "Feed my dog, my cats; will someone look after my birds and my rabbits? Please . . . please . . ."

"Where are they taking them?" Vera heards someone ask.

"The Vél d'Hiv," comes the answer.

The Vélodrome d'Hiver – the once proudly built Olympic cycling track. During two blazing July days, the authorities round up thousands, and turn the glorious velodrome into a pitiless holding camp.

"And then where?" ask others.

The names are whispered with dread: Drancy, Auschwitz, Dachau, Belsen . . .

After waiting an hour, Vera extricates the forged documents from between the books, and leaves the apartment, gently shutting the door.

Sitting in the living room of Marianne's house that night, with all the windows open to get a through-draught from the oppressive heat, they wait. Daniel and Yves have gone to find the remainder of the Goldberg family hiding in the nearby scrubland. They will try and shuffle them along from safe house to safe house, until they are out of Paris. It will take weeks, but they will be passed along a chain heading south, where they can either hide out until the war is over, or get across the Pyrénées into Spain.

News is coming in about the latest roundups. No one has any illusions. Whether you are a factory worker, a bus driver, a tailor, a teacher, a banker, an art dealer, a philosopher – if you are the world's greatest scientist, or a chemist; a street busker, or the most a famous musician; you become as nothing when you enter the Vél d'Hiv. You are stripped of dignity and status. Old, young, a babe, a mother, a grandparent – these terms become defunct. You are nothing, nothing, nothing, and you deserve nothing; not food, not water, not medical help. Nothing.

And along with the theft of your identity, they steal away all hope.

I think of nothing. I do not see the streets and the people walking to and fro; I do not hear the birds singing in the trees, or the rushing brook. I tell myself, all this pain will pass, and soon I'll be myself again.

A CHILD IN AUSCHWITZ 1940

CHAPTER 53

Meeting Lily

LONDON 1944

I've taken to sleeping in the coal cellar. In fact, I've managed to make it quite homey. I've made up a camp bed with pillows, blankets and cushions, a couple of rugs, and even my camping paraffin stove and kettle. Sometimes, I feel like a mole; or like Thumbelina, trapped underground, wondering when I will next see a swallow.

I prefer being down in the coal cellar. It's safer and, anyway, there are too many memories in the flat. Dodo's room, untouched since her death, and Noor's veena still stands propped in the corner. I never hear from Noor or Vera, and have no idea if they are alive or dead. I am fatalistic and fear the worst. The news from France is awful.

Death is a constant presence. I try to make a friend of him. Sometimes, I feel as though he enters my cellar. Why *do* I say *he* or *him*? If mother is birth, do I assume father or male is Death? I hear the cellar door open; hear his footsteps coming down softly, confidently; like an intimate.

He peers around the corner; bends over my paralysed body. Death has no face. I am alive; I am dead. I sleep; I awake.

Even when bombs drop on nearby St James's, Piccadilly, on Holborn and Leicester Square, when everything shakes as if in an earthquake; when windows blow in; when roofs implode with incendiaries, exploding gas pipes, crackling electricity wires, and the cascading rush of burst water mains – our building stays standing. After the all-clear, when the sound of bombers gives way to the sirens of ambulances and fire engines, I hurry up to find our block has no worse damage than shattered window panes and choking dust.

I could almost lull myself into thinking that we have a magic ring of protection around us; that Death is my friend.

If I am out, I barely bother to take shelter when the sirens sound. I once rushed for the underground stations; but they were always so packed, and reeking with the stench of overcrowding, with people even sleeping between the rail tracks, so now I prefer to take my chances above ground.

Since the first long Blitz at the beginning of the war, the bombing has eased a bit in London, but other British cities, like Bristol, Hull, and Coventry are being reduced to rubble.

Somehow we all keep going. A year passes, then another and another. We suffer more from food shortages, housing shortages, destroyed hospitals and destroyed self-esteem.

Could it be that the fury of war is exhausting itself? Across Europe, cities and lives have been shattered to bits. We begin to think that perhaps they've done their worst. The machine of Government carries on – and there has even been a by-election.

In September of '44, everything changes again. If we thought the terror of the Blitz could never be repeated, another weapon is suddenly unleashed. Silent in flight, thunderous and devasting in its impact.

The military call them V-2s or flying bombs, because they are not dropped from aeroplanes, but are unmanned; rocket-propelled. We call them doodlebugs, or buzz bombs. Typical British humour, to give strangely friendly terms for the deadliest weapon ever known.

The Germans call them revenge bombers. It feels like that. They arrive with an intermittent buzzing sound, like a monstrous mosquito churning through the air. How sneaky; how deadly. But it isn't the buzz that scares people as their eyes scour the skies. It's trying to decide which way to run when the buzzing is followed by silence; the silence of that last breath before death. The calculation; how many seconds does it take for the bomb to fall? Then the explosion; the thunderous shock that kills babies in their prams without a mark on them.

Those of us who dare to go out are always staring up

into the sky, listening for the deadly pitch of the doodlebugs which bring terror from the west end to the east end, from the south in Croydon to the north in Finchley. The combined banshee howling of the air-raid sirens, and the thundering booms of the anti-aircraft guns, send everyone scuttling to the nearest shelter.

Day and night the rockets rain down. Down in my cellar I listen, feeling helplessly entombed. Yet still I go to work.

Returning late from the War Office one night, I heard the buzzing. The air-raid siren went off. I had just reached Leicester Square when there was one almighty roar and a vast explosion. Everything shook. People began to run – some towards the underground, others towards Trafalgar Square to shelter in the crypt of St Martin-in-the-Fields. I was near enough to make a dash for home, when I noticed a young Lyons Corner House nippy crouched under a tree in total terror, her hands over her head, screaming hysterically. I rushed over and pulled her to her feet.

"Come with me!" I yelled, and began to drag her towards Orange Street. She felt limp and floppy, and stumbled in the rubble. I heard another bomb whistling overhead the dreaded buzzing coming closer and closer. "For God's sake – *move!*"

The buzzing stopped. We heard the hit a street away. With debris and dust flying around us, I got the door to the flat open and shoved her inside.

I was now well organised down in the cellar. I switched on my torch and fumbled for my stack of matches and lit a storm lantern. Then I flopped down next to her in the swaying shadows.

"It's all right now," I said reassuringly. "Look – I can even make you a cup of tea." I had my Primus stove, a kettle of water and some milk. "Good old Larry makes it through, come hell or high water, to deliver our milk to any house still standing. He's a blooming angel of a milkman." I boiled the water and made a pot of tea, then poured it into two enamelled mugs.

The girl had now gained control of herself and sat up apologetically, rubbing her tear-stained cheeks with her apron, and pushing back her hair. Then she gave a pathetic wail. "My cap! I've lost my cap! I won't half catch it!" Beneath all the soot and plaster, I saw she was only a girl of about fourteen.

"Hey, hey! Hang on. You can't go out there," I cried, grabbing her arm as she struggled to her feet, ready to rush out again. "Of course you won't get into trouble. We'll look for it after the all-clear, and if you don't find your cap, I'll go back with you tomorrow and explain everything to your boss. Now drink this tea; it will calm you down."

Her name was Lily. Yes, she worked at the Lyons Corner House. Yes, they were always expected to turn up if they and the building was still in one piece. After the anxiety over her lost cap had receded, she was overwhelmed by another terror. "Oh lawks!" she groaned as she beat the dust from her uniform. "I've got to get home. The little ones will be worried sick."

"Little ones?"

"My brother and sister: Johnny and Violet. They'll be frantic. The neighbours are kind and keep an eye as I have to go to work, but they've got their own kiddies to see to. I hate leaving them. Every time I go, we never know if we'll see each other again." Lily began to cry again.

"If your neighbours are as kind as you say, they'll watch out for Johnny and Violet," I reassured her. "Where are your parents?"

"Me dad's in the navy, and me mum . . ." She swallowed hard, dabbing her eyes with her apron. "She's . . . she was killed in an air raid – you know – last year when she was at work at the tool factory down the docks. So, I have to work. See? War or no war, we still need money to pay the rent. They would take the little ones away from me if I didn't have a job. I'm all they've got till Dad gets back after the war." She headed determinedly for the cellar door.

"Wait, wait!" I cried. "Where do you live?"

"Vauxhall," she said. "Over the river."

"Finish your tea, and I'll go with you."

"Oh no miss! You don't need to do that," she protested.

I was sure I did. She was such a thin, scraggy little thing. I felt I had to see her home.

I managed to extend the tea-drinking tea and chatting until, at last, we heard the wailing of the all-clear.

"We'll take my bike. You don't look very heavy. You

can sit on the back, and we'll be at your place in no time," I said.

My bike was propped in the hall, as usual. I opened the front door and bounced it down the steps into the road. We stepped into a glistening night of burning cinders and stars. There was a strange peace, after all the bedlam. Only the air balloons drifted like ghosts against a rosy light, which was not the dawn, but the red of burning fires behind the Swan & Edgar department store.

Lily perched on the back of my bike, her arms clasped round my waist, and we wobbled off, my eyes straining into the darkness as I wove in and out of the rubble. I pedalled over Waterloo Bridge with the smell of parched ash drifting through the night air, clogging our nostrils. The vast dark river writhed beaneath us like a huge animal.

My instinct to take Lily home had been entirely right.

Even in the darkness, I could see her neighbourhood was a slum area of cramped little houses, glued together with cheap bricks and mortar, blackened by soot and grime. I switched on my torch; she took out her key and fumbled at the door. We stepped immediately into a living room – if you could call it a room. It was worse than my coal cellar, with a gut-wrenching smell of dank, mouldy walls and remnants of old cooking.

We heard a whimper. Huddled together on a sunken sofa, half covered with a pile of grubby blankets and still fully dressed, were a girl and a boy of between eight and five years old. They can't have been deeply asleep, for at the sound of our arrival into the room, their eyes flew open. With cries of joy and relief they flung themselves into Lily's arms.

"We heard the bombs and saw the fires. We thought they might have gotcha this time!" gasped the boy, hugging the breath out of her. He and his sister as thin as toothpicks, and as scraggy as their older sister.

"This is Johnny and Violet. Little blighters they are too," Lila said, covering them in kisses. "Kids, this is the kind lady who brought me home."

"Where do you go when there's an air raid?" I asked, looking round their unbearably poor home, with torn curtains and just black paper for the blackout.

"We grab the blankets and get under the table," said Johnny. "We don't have no shelters round here."

"Lily," I said. "You know where I live. Come and see me again, won't you? I know where you live and work, so I can find you too."

She nodded passionately. "Yes, miss."

Cycling back over Waterloo bridge, I paused to gaze down into the river. Moored ships and barges seemed to breathe uneasily, like sleeping dinosaurs. An idea formed in my head.

As soon as possible the next day, I managed to get a phone call through to Aunt Madge.

"Everything all right, dear?" she asked anxiously.

"Fine, Aunty," I reassured her. "But – you know you've got Land Girls working on the farm, and people in the village have taken in evacuees? Do you think you have room for another Land Girl and her little brother and sister?" I told her all about Lily, Johnny, and Violet.

Darling Aunt Madge – she knew I never asked for favours unless they were really necessary. "Of course, darling," she replied without question or hesitation. "Send them to me. I'll speak to our local organiser. As a matter of fact, a group of evacuees went back to London last week. They couldn't stand it in the country; too quiet, would you believe? They said they would rather put up with the bombs! In any case, they missed their mother too much. So we have room for the three of them, and more hands on the farm are always welcome."

"I love you, Aunt Madge."

When a couple of days later, I was able to put the idea to Lily, she was flabbergasted, reluctant, and fearful. She'd never left London in her life; had never even crossed the river until war broke out. It was only the war which had made her cross the Thames when she was forced to go looking for a job. And she'd never been on a train. To go to the country was like going to the moon.

"You'll all be together," I said, "and it's safer in the country. There are other children from London there, and my aunt and uncle are the kindest people in the world. They'll look after you. Please say you'll go. I'll come and visit at the first opportunity."

I went with her to the Lyons supervisor so she could hand in her notice. Lily couldn't stop saying thank you.

When we got to Paddington, the family was speechless with awe at the sight of the vast steam engine huffing and puffing, and the cathedral-like station with its vast glass roof and pillars and beams.

"Oh my Gawd," Lily kept exclaiming, as I settled them into a carriage with their bags.

"You'll be all right," I reassured them. "What an adventure! Think what stories you'll be able to tell your dad! I've told the guard to keep an eye on you. Say a big hello to my aunt and uncle. They're like my mother and father!"

The guard's whistle blew, and the train whistle shrieked its departure. It was raining as I stood watching them slowly pulling out of the station with grinding wheels, and three hands waving and waving out of the window, till they disappeared into a black cloud of smoke and steam.

CHAPTER 54

Betrayal

PARIS 1944

Betrayal was always the biggest fear. From where and by whom might it come? A friend, a colleague, a trusted member? A concierge, a neighbour, a shopkeeper, someone with a grudge? The mind of another is the greatest mystery; those inner thoughts, those tangled feelings lying dormant like seeds in the earth, waiting to be activated and spring into action for good or ill; for love or hate.

The one who had been so faithful, had fought so bravely and been wounded on the battle front – she who had never understood the cause, not like Daniel, who seemed to understand everything. This was Simone.

She had gone to Spain to be with him, Daniel: to fight by his side, die by his side; not for the cause, but for him. But this was Daniel, who had no doubts about anything. His view of the world was clear. Just as in Spain, he had no doubt why he was fighting the Nazis in France – no doubt which woman he loved. He had told Simone – gently, sweetly – how much he admired her. She was a heroine. But he had always loved Vera, and always would. He even kissed Simone; begged her to understand.

Was that the moment Simone became a traitor? Could gentle rejection from the man she loved override everything: her nationality, her love of country, her morality? Did real love turn so easily to hatred – and not just hatred, but a desire to avenge and destroy? Did she truly believe that if she destroyed Vera, Daniel would turn to her?

When she saw Vera leaning in despair on the bridge, she had hoped Vera might simply destroy herself. *Go on – jump – jump. Get out of my life. Give me Daniel*! But Vera hadn't jumped. After several minutes, she had lifted her head and strangely raised both hands to her heart and shouted words into the sky, then strode away.

Simone followed her to Rue Monceau. She had stood outside for a long time. She stood till it was nearly the hour of the curfew, but she saw no one else go in or out. But now that she knew where Vera lived, she felt she had regained some power.

Now she could destroy her with just one phone call.

CHAPTER 55

The Radio Game

Geneviève was on the run.

She was on a list as a British agent; they were out to find her. Although Avalon had reformed under the name of Pegasus, they too had been betrayed. First the Courvets; then the Lejeunes, Claude Janvier and Christine Martell. It was still not clear what had happened to Leo Masson. All over France, resistance fighters and known critics of the Occupation were being exposed, arrested, disappeared, or found dead.

The radio transmitters rattled along in full tilt, filling the airways from London to Berlin to Paris to Moscow, playing their radio games. Codes were broken; messages flew to and fro between the Allies, traitors and Germans, both sides intercepting them, sending false messages to confuse each other; both sides trying to second guess the truth.

For the moment, Geneviève was the only British radio operator still free in Paris. The only link between the various underground sabotage teams, and London; the only go-between taking instructions and passing on plans to blow up a railway track, a bridge, or a military convoy, or liaising with those drops of ammunition and supplies from London. The Germans were desperate to get their hands on her. An allied invasion was rumoured; she might know the truth.

Marianne's shed in the garden was a safe haven. Here she could be Noor again, and talk to her fairies.

To a casual eye it looked like a garden shed with tools and lawn mower, but tucked away into a false cupboard was a mattress, pillow, and blankets. She could get to it through a hidden back door in the wall that opened on to an alleyway. Marianne warned her not to come too often – but if she was ever desperate, it was there for her. "Don't tell me when you come and go. I don't want to know. It's safer that way. If you have a message, leave it in the false cubby hole: I'll check from time to time."

Sometimes, Noor would creep into the house in the middle of the night, desperate to make music. The sounds of her veena filtered through the walls and up the stairs. For Pascal, lying there so helplessly, it made the tears roll down his cheeks as he remembered deeply valued friendships. Fatal he knew, to recall the past. Nostalgia these days was useless; it led to regret, to despair, that things could ever be the same again. Happiness was a phantom – sometimes glimpsed, then lost in a mist; but sometimes recalled by a turn of the head, a smell of cooking, a child laughing, an accordionist busking in the street, or Noor plucking the strings of a veena in the middle of the night.

"When this war is over, we'll all meet again," Noor whispered to Vera, who crept down one night to sit near her friend, and listen. "Perhaps in England – you, me, and Gwen – we'll remember Dodo – and we'll remember our school days."

I believe and I trust. Belief and trust will make you stronger and will help you to let go of uneasiness of hopelessness. Trust follows from hope.

Another plane came in from England, for a drop in the woods near Jean Melot's farm house. Geneviève and the Maquis were to attend. The farmer had his horse and cart ready to hide the goods. But they were betrayed.

Up among the quiet leaves of an apple tree, Geneviève saw it all. As the Resistance fighters approached the cart with the parachutes, a burst of machine-gun fire came out of nowhere, mortally wounding them. Then the guns were turned on old Jean Melot. He fell by his horse. His daughter ran out screaming, followed by their old dog. Geneviève couldn't help yelling out, "No! Go back!" But they too went down in a blaze of gunfire.

Silence. Geneviève hugged the tree.

A man looking like a farm worker appeared from behind the barn with a rifle. He had heard her cry and was looking for her. If he came into the orchard, he would see her case beneath the tree. She knew no one from Pegasus would have stayed to help her. In the event of a botched assignment, the instruction was to get away; no heroics. But if the enemy found her code book in the case she had left at the foot of the apple tree . . .

Cursing herself for her carelessness, she pressed her cheek so hard into the bark. Blood sprang from the broken skin, but all she could feel was her gun. The gun she never wanted to have; the gun she swore she would never use. She remembered Jack Court's words: the only crime you could commit was to let down your colleagues. She reached for the weapon. As the man crept closer and closer, his rifle panning across the trees before him, she cocked her pistol. Braced herself against the trunk. *Go away! Don't make me do this. Oh Papa!*

The man stopped. He had seen her case. His eyes looked upwards into the branches; saw her pale face peering down among the moon-struck apples, like some fairy or angel. Almost unwillingly, he lifted his rifle.

Geneviève pulled the trigger. Bang. He fell face down.

An alarmed night jar flew on to the upper branch above her head, its churring pulsating like the blood in her ears. She would have stayed there forever, just listening to the night bird, ignoring the life she had just extinguished lying there in the grass beneath her; but she heard a voice; high, fragile, almost like one of her fairies. It forced her to move. Branch by branch, she felt her way down and, stepping round her victim, ran out of the orchard towards the farm house.

Old Jean Melot was sprawled face down in the yard, his blood mingling with the dust; she checked him, and then his daughter, and then the dog – but all were lifeless.

There was the sound again: a whimper. It came from inside. She stood in the threshold of the open door, staring into the darkness. She called softly "Hello?"

A tiny shape emerged from between the dresser and a cupboard; so slight, so ephemeral in the darkness.

"Hello!" whispered Geneviève. "*Qui est tu?*"

"Babette," came a child's whisper.

Geneviève knelt down and opened her arms. "*Viens*, Babette," she cried softly. "Come! *Je suis* Geneviève, I'm your friend."

The child moved forward in a dreamlike state and clasped her. "I want Mummy," she whispered.

As if in a dream, Geneviève lifts and carries her outside into the night. She sees a church spire outlined by the moon across the fields. She feels herself float across the dark fields, edging between the great soft bodies of gathering cows. She reaches the far side, and takes a path, barely visible, which leads to the church. A low light gleams from inside.

She opens the old wooden door; it creaks. The priest at the altar doesn't turn, but continues kneeling with his back to her, his head resting on his clasped hands as if awaiting his executioner.

"Mon Père!" Geneviève calls out in a low voice.

He turns slowly; an old man with a face that speaks of a lifetime's experience of births, deaths, marriages, ferocity, and compassion. Seeing a young woman carrying a child, it is as if he is seeing the Virgin Mary herself.

"Mon Père," says Geneviève. "They have killed Farmer Melot and his daughter; they have even killed the dog. I found his grandchild hiding in the house. I don't know where to take her. Can you help me?"

"Ah! It's little Babette," the priest sighs. Gently, he releases the child's arms from around Geneviève's neck. "I'll take her, and make sure that she goes to a place of safety."

As Babette is transferred to the old priest's arms, the child succumbs as if into her own mother's arms, and falls into a deep sleep.

"Mon Père!" Weeping and broken, Geneviève falls to her knees, with head bowed. "I have killed a man. All killing is wrong, and I have killed a human being. I have sinned greatly. What will become of my soul?"

The priest lays the sleeping child in one of the pews. He kneels down next to the despairing young woman. "My child, only God knows everything; only God can judge you; and we believe God is merciful and forgiving. May I give you absolution?"

"I am not a Christian," she replies. But still, kneeling before him, she lets him lay his hands on her head and murmur the words of absolution.

"God be with you."

Geneviève returns across the fields. She can see a black Citroën parked in front of the farmhouse. It is clear that the bodies of the farmer, his daughter, and their dog have been removed and the farmhouse searched. A man leans against the car and strikes a match to light a cigarette. In the brief second of flame, Geneviève knows she is doomed.

A puff of cigarette smoke rises into the air as Marc Nadeau turns and looks hard at the orchard.

She falls to the ground, burying herself in the long grass. The cows cluster round her, protectively, snorting puffs of steam through their moist nostrils, their great bodies exuding warmth and comfort. She curls up in a tight ball like an unborn child.

Papa?

It's when you think Hope has died, that Hope is reborn, dearest daughter.

Geneviève sleeps.

When she awoke, the June sun was up and warm. The black car had gone. She rose shakily to her feet and stumbled towards the orchard with only one thought: her radio.

The body of the man she had killed had gone. The transmitter case was still lying in the long grass at the base of the tree. They had missed it in the dark, and the aerial, hanging loosely from a branch among the leaves and apples. With numb fingers she tapped a coded message to London: *Mission failed.*

She received a brief acknowledgment; and a second message: *Allies to invade France through Calais. June landing. Be prepared.*

Had hope been born?

Hope for whom? Never had the secret services been busier: the traitors, the secret agents, the double agents, the double-dealers; the gangsters and wheeler dealers. Meanwhile, the radio game went on: the coded messages, the false messages, the red herrings, the deliberate misinformation. And, when it was necessary for the good of the country, the deliberate offering of a sacrificial lamb – or the sacrifice of a hare.

Geneviève climbed the apple tree to recover her aerial. She was halfway down again when the smell of a cigarette rose into her nostrils. She clung to a branch, nearly fainting with terror, blackness swimming into her eyes.

Marc Nadeau was lolling against the trunk of the tree. He stubbed out his cigarette and held out both arms. "Can I help you down, *mademoiselle?*"

CHAPTER 56

There Are No Flowers Here

The car entered central Paris. Geneviève was ordered out. She knew the address: the dreaded 84 Avenue Foch – Gestapo headquarters. She knew what to expect.

She was taken up to the fourth floor and ushered into an office.

At first sight, the room was as pleasant a room as any you could find. It was furnished, carpeted, pictures on the wall, a fire burning in the grate, a table with a comfy, cushioned chair. A vase of gleaming purple flowers stood on a table in the window. How beautiful. It was a room to relax you, make you feel welcomed; a reminder of luxury after all the grimness, the shortages of food and heating – except, of course, for those wise enough to cooperate and collaborate.

They were giving her a chance.

A man sat behind the polished desk. His reflection in the shiny surface was familiar to her, even before she looked up into his eyes: that surprisingly soft, almost baby-like face, with his pouty lips, and floppy brown hair parted down the middle. His slim languid body sprawled lazily in the chair. Her eyes fixed on his ear with the black mole. Oh yes, she knew him.

He smiled, and held out his hand to shake. "*Bonjour*. Or should I say, 'Good day'?"

She ignored his hand.

Brown eyes are rarely described as cold; but these eyes had none of the warmth of wood, or earth, or walnuts – just the blank lack of pity.

"*Kaffee, Fräulein?*"

She shook her head.

He pushed a bowl of sugared almonds in front of her. "Still warm from being roasted," he said enticingly.

She declined.

"You've been in Paris quite some time *Fräulein*, and have been rather troublesome, I hear," he said. "Many is the time we thought we'd have you shot, but it seemed wiser to leave you free for a bit, and learn more from your activities. But now, sadly, I have to inform you that we've had enough. I have sufficient evidence against you to have you executed. You killed one of my men."

His outrage seemed insincere. She stared at the floor.

"You are a British spy, are you not? Nothing can save you except – I like you. Marc likes you, too. Don't you Marc?"

She hadn't realised that Marc Nadeau had come silently into the room, and now stood behind her. He was holding her radio transmitter.

"Tch tch!" said Black Mole. "Further evidence – as if we needed any. Yours?"

Geneviève dropped her head and didn't answer.

"YOURS?" he bellowed, his body as liquid as a snake's, uncoiling and slithering across the desk.

Geneviève didn't answer. A blow across her head made her slump.

"Answer him, *mademoiselle*," advised Marc Nadeau.

Through surging pain, she kept her head bent and said nothing.

"Well, how about telling us your name?" asked Black Mole. "You're allowed to do that. My name is Gustave Kieser. Yours?"

"Geneviève Bisset."

"Your *real* name, *s'il te plaît*," he said sarcastically.

She didn't reply.

Another blow knocked her out of her chair to the floor.

"Take her up." Kieser tossed his head to indicate the fifth floor.

Marc Nadeau clicked his fingers at two uniformed soldiers. They lifted her – one under each arm. She spat at him as they dragged her past. "Traitor!"

This time, the room she was tossed into had none of the comfort of the office below. It was cold, hard, and bare: bare walls, bare floors, and a single wooden chair. It was grubby, with the smell of urine and carbolic. Brown stains splashed the walls. There were no flowers here.

As they flung her into the chair and bound her arms and legs, Noor called out, "Papa!"

She heard no inner voice of reply, but through her

bloodshot gaze, as the blows and kicks descended, she saw, in the far corner, a shimmering, silver creature, sitting as if in a pool of moonlight, with bejewelled eyes, and long ears like sheaves of corn; so gentle. A hare.

"I am a hare," she murmured.

"What was that?" demanded her interrogator. "Speak up."

She remained silent, and they struck her again. She slumped, unconscious.

She awoke, clothed in pain, into an impenetrably black, cold place of silence. How long she had lain on this hard, freezing floor, she had no idea. Time and darkness were all that existed. Time passed, because it had to, like a flowing river, on and on and on, coming from somewhere, going somewhere; looking for its ocean. She stretched herself out on the dark and gleaming back of the river of Time, trying to befriend the pain burning through her body.

She bumped gently to a stop on a reedy bank. Trickling water sounded like music; like her veena. In her darkness, a tall, gleaming man stood in his coat of gold.

Papa?

Close both eyes, and see with your third eye.

She did as she was told. A child glimmered there. Louis? Ethan? Babette? Or was it one of her fairy children – a beautiful rose, or a lily? For now she noticed there were banks of flowers: white, yellow, purple – all the summer flowers of the woods and fields and, sweetly emerging from everywhere, were her fairies.

Play, my daughter.

Noor, play! hummed the fairies.

Noor. Yes; that was her name. She would never more be Geneviève Bisset. She was Noor; a daughter, a sister, a friend. She was real; she was loved. Her body rocked with the rhythm of water lapping on the bank, as if she cradled herself in her mother's arms.

They broke my fingers. The river can play for you, she told them.

How sweet! Their breath trickled like streams through her hair, and soothed her brow and, in the light of the darkness, a million stars came out, and her father held her.

I am your companion.
We shall sail together,
You and I
On this ocean of dreams;
Far, far away
To a place of beauty
And tranquility.
Where suffering and pain do not exist,
Where we give praise
For our joy and happiness,
Where our Love intertwines
With Love for all things.

More time passed. The door rattled and was flung open. Rough hands grabbed her, and dragged her out, back up the steps, her feet banging painfully behind her. More corridors. Another door and she was back in the same comfortable room, and the same chair; the same torturer behind the desk. It helped her to focus on the black mole on his left ear. The fire burned in the grate, so warmly; only then did she realise how cold, cold, cold she had been; and that she smelled.

The questioning began again. Her name; her contacts; addresses of safe houses; her instructions. After each refusal to answer, she was struck.

Was it true that England was planning an invasion?

From which area would they leave? Where would they land? Calais?

They had broken into her radio. She sat, head bowed in dizzy silence.

"Well, no matter. We have time. You will speak. Everyone speaks in the end. We will soon penetrate all your codes and find the answers in your radio, *n'est-ce pas?*" Kieser nodded an instruction. "Show her!"

A barely suppressed groan of agony swept in, from a prisoner thrust into the room. He was hardly recognisable as a human being – so battered, bloody, and broken was he. But she knew him. Leo Masson. Bruised and blackened eyes lifted, and briefly met hers.

"*Vive la France!*" Noor cried out – hoping it would be heard all over France – but only a croak came from her dry throat.

Leo Masson nodded before his head dropped to his chest, and he was dragged out again.

"Pity we have to resort to such treatment," said Black Mole in disappointment. "All you have to do is cooperate, and save yourself all this pain."

Coffee and sweet, fresh-smelling croissants were brought in. The warm aromatic smells almost made her faint with longing. Kieser offered them to Marc Nadeau; Nadeau tantalisingly offered the plate to Noor. He was suddenly kind, tender even; as if he cared that she hadn't eaten for days, that she had a broken nose, and swollen eyes, that her teeth had been knocked out, and she had bald patches on her skull where they had pulled out clumps of her hair.

"Would you like to use the bathroom?" he asked. "Tidy up a bit? Have a wash?"

"Yes," she managed to say through bleeding lips.

He helped her to her feet gently, considerately, and led her just outside to another door. "I'll wait outside. When you're done, let's have a talk, you and me. I'm sure we can find a way to cooperate."

He suddenly drew her close and kissed her on the lips, just as he had done at Gare d'Austerlitz. With an overwhelming surge of fury she tried to bite through his lip – but she had no teeth.

She went inside, and shut the door. She would have locked it – but there was no lock or bolt. There was a small window above the lavatory. Could she escape? Overcoming the agony of broken fingers, she hauled herself up on to the lavatory bowl. From there she heaved herself up by her elbows on to the sill and pushed open the window. A blast of air struck her face. She stared down a sloping roof which plunged four floors to a cobbled yard below. There was no escape. If she jumped, she died; if she returned, she died. Better to die, trying to live?

Jump, Noor! Jump!

I won't.

She heard a far-off, low-pitched roar like an approaching tornado.

Alarmed voices rose from inside and out. Noor saw people coming to their windows and balconies; looking up at the skies. Between the chimney pots, she saw them: wave upon wave of aeroplanes. Not the insect whines of the German Stukas or Messerschmidts, nor the little British Moths, the Lysanders, or Spitfires, but the deep body-shuddering roar of British and American bombers: Typhoons, Boeings and Douglas Invaders, Avro Lancasters, Hurricanes, and de Havilands. Like a formation of half-human, half-bird *Walkyries*. Was Paris going to be bombed, just as London had been bombed? It was unthinkable.

All over the city, the sirens began screaming.

Painfully, Noor eased herself back and opened the door. Marc Nadeau had gone. Even the guards had gone. She was no longer the priority. What about Leo Masson? Could she find him? Forcing herself to put one painful foot in front of the other, she limped along the empty corridor and found the door with the stone steps leading down, down, down, to the underground cells.

There were so many doors; all locked. Groans came from some, but silence from others. "Is the Lion there?" she called through each door.

At last she heard a reply. *"C'est toi? My hare?"*

"C'est moi," she sobbed. "The door is locked. I can't free you. But something is happening. I've heard aeroplanes. The Allies are here. They're bombing Paris. The war might be ending at last, so don't lose heart, *mon ami!*"

Leo Masson was hoarsely singing the Marseillaise when she left him.

She found a side door out into the open; she paused a few seconds, amazed at the smell of fresh air. From the west of Paris came sounds of shuddering explosions. No one had believed anyone would bomb Paris; she had never believed it. But now she saw the smoke and flames bursting into the sky. She crept towards the gate. The guards' eyes were glued in consternation to the planes overhead.

She had reached the barrier when a hand took her arm, gentle but vice-like. A voice said regretfully, "Leaving us so soon? We still have questions."

Marc Nadeau led her back inside.

CHAPTER 57

Sacrifice

"Did she crack?" asked Pinstripe.

"No," answered Jack Court shortly, despairing and furious. "None of us bothered to understand her. We measure everything by physique; physical courage, passing tests; the old English public schools code of conduct – and do you know what? She passed all those tests when it came to it. We think the British are unique for their moral fibre and backbone; that others, not least brown or black people, have no stiff upper lip, no spine, no lasting power. But we never considered her inner courage; her conscience, her faith; we never evaluated her sense of sacrifice. I sometimes think we British are disgusting."

The grey-haired woman had the grace to lower her head.

Jack walked over to the window to hide the guilty tears which had welled up in his eyes. "I'm sorry to inform you, sir, that our agent, Noor Khan, refused to speak despite days of torture. They executed her this morning at dawn."

"Bad show." Pinstripe puffed on his pipe. "She didn't

give them that false information we planted, about an invasion beginning by sea with a Calais landing, instead of Normandy?" He tutted with disappointment. "Better let Winston know."

CHAPTER 58

The Tip Off

In the Rue Monceau, the Gestapo and police were responding to an anonymous tip off over a crackly telephone.

It was Pascal who heard the cars draw up; Pascal who, yelling to the others to get out, somehow stumbled from his bed and down to the front door to try and stall the police long enough for everyone to escape. But it was useless. They forced open the door and, within a few minutes were all rounded up – Pascal, Marianne, Léonie, Yves, Antoine – and bundled into a van.

Watching discreetly from a distance, the anonymous caller gave a sigh of satisfaction when she saw Vera shoved out through the door – until she saw Daniel, the last to leave, thrust violently down the steps to sprawl at the open rear door of the van. Vera reached out, and pulled him in.

Only as the van was driven away at speed was a despairing, high-pitched shriek to be heard, as of an animal caught in a trap.

CHAPTER 59

An Ancient and Tattered Airman

Everyone is going mad with revenge: finish the war, end the war; be victorious, be defeated – who will prevail? Each side brings in their best brains to devise the most murderous weapon.

Operation Overlord has begun. The Allies are landing on the Normandy beaches – not in Calais, as transmitted to Geneviève.

I'm back in Orange Street; a brief respite. It is midmorning; I've slept late, having got back from Glasgow where I had delivered another aircraft. There is a banging on the door. Clutching my dressing gown around me, I stagger up out of the cellar, and open the front door.

It's Uncle Harold.

I freeze. No hugs from me, no welcome; just shock, and the thought that only something serious could have brought him to London.

"Has something happened to Aunty Madge? Archie? Eric?" I exclaim, fearing the worst.

"You could say that, after a fashion," comes a beloved voice.

My brother Eric steps into the frame of the open doorway.

"Eric!" For the moment I am speechless with relief and joy; then aghast. He is alive, but he has been so terribly wounded: his face scarred, his hands burned, leaning on crutches with a leg missing. I fling my arms round him and burst into tears.

He laughs, holding me at arm's length. "Don't be upset! I'm now an illustrious member of the Ancient and Tattered Airmen! Aren't you going to ask us in?"

It is a painful ascent of the stairs to the flat – though Eric makes it look like bounding, with the help of his crutch, hopping up step by step. Uncle Harold follows, muttering, "What have we come to . . ."

"Oh Eric! I'm so sorry," I say. "You loved flying so much. Now I guess it's all over for you?"

"All over? Not a bit of it," he cries with glittering eyes. "They're so short of pilots that even if you are one-eyed, one-armed, or one-legged, anyone who can fly, will fly. They need us! And my God – do we need to be needed. You're flying now too. So, you know that. We can be scared for each other. I'm content with my lot and who I am. They tried to destroy me, but, here I am, alive, and I can still fly, Gwenny!"

Oh! I have slipped the surly bonds of Earth
And danced the skies on laughter-silvered wings;
Sunward I've climbed, and joined the tumbling mirth
Of sun-split clouds – and done a hundred things
You have not dreamed of – and wheeled and soared and swung
High in the sunlit silence. Hovering there,
I've chased the shouting wind along, and flung
My eager craft through footless halls of air....
Up, up the long, delirious burning blue
I've topped the wind-swept heights with easy grace
Where never lark, or ever eagle flew -
And, while with silent, lifting mind I've trod
The high untrespassed sanctity of space,
Put out my hand, and touched the face of God.

JOHN GILLESPIE MAGEE JNR

CHAPTER 60

World's End

It was a glittering June night; a good night for flying aeroplanes, with enough cloud to hide in, away from enemy eyes. I was on a mission to deliver a transport cargo plane over to France. While thousands of soldiers were landing on the beaches of Normandy, I was bringing a cargo of backup supplies to eastern France.

The last days of a war are the most dangerous days; when the enemy on all sides becomes ruthlessly vengeful. When he sacks, burns and pillages all in his wake; and humanity seems to be the last thing on earth anyone is fighting for. Now that the Allies had the upper hand, they were flying in great formations into enemy territory; those great bombers with enough tonnage of bombs to flatten cities and wipe out civilisation. Nothing was sacred: not cathedrals, churches, schools, hospitals; not ancient buildings left over from previous civilisations; no vestige of anything of human endeavour was spared – except by accident – the spire of Coventry cathedral, St Paul's in London, Notre-Dame, or the great mediaeval cathedral of Cologne; especially not humans.

The final defiant act of brutality of the Nazis was to find every last Jew and 'undesirable' they could, and send them to extermination; even as the Allies rolled across Europe.

Like Eric, I never know what mission I'll be sent on next. I do nothing but fly: aeroplanes for repair, aeroplanes for ambulance work; aeroplanes to replace those destroyed; aeroplanes for transport from factory to base, from aerodrome to aerodrome. We're working night and day with barely any sleep; victory or no victory – the losses continue to be terrible. I dare not think about it. I cram my heart and soul, and every bit of space in my head, with work – like now, as I head over to France.

I've delivered and landed heavy cargo planes before but always on home ground. The plane I've been asked to fly to France is an Avro York; probably the biggest plane I have yet flown into enemy territory. These were big planes, and this one was heavy, and loaded with supplies to be distributed all over the ex-occupied countries. I feel nervous and excited. Landing a full plane like this one is hazardous.

I never fail to get a thrill when I let down the undercarriage and feel that bouncing contact of the wheels with the ground. The lights on the runway are faint. I hope the war really is over. It hardly seems possible after all we've been through.

I go into reverse; the engines roar until we slow down, and eventually come to a standstill with the propellers whirring. It will be the same all over again tomorrow when I get back to Blighty. But that is the thrill of it.

Bobbing torches appear from the bushes, and guide me into a camouflaged hangar. I'm helped out of the cockpit, congratulated – presumably for being a woman and having succeeded in not crashing the plane. I am clapped on the back and led away to a jeep. We hurtle away through the night to a lonely inn, where I am to stay until the plane has disgorged its cargo, and is then put to the use of injured soldiers needing to get back to England. It might be a few days.

Next morning, when I go down to breakfast, enticed by the smell of coffee and freshly baked bread, a man in British army uniform strolls over to my table. He moves diffidently but with a purpose.

"Major John Battersby." He holds out a hand. "May I join you?"

He's tall and young, not much older than I am; but, like so many of us, too young for his position and status. That's what war does: advancing people before their time, and killing people before their time. He pulls out a chair and accommodates his long legs half under and half out of the table.

"I hear you brought in an Avro York last night."

I nod. "My body's all scrunched up by that rattling boneshaker."

He smiles sympathetically then launches straight in.

"My driver got blown up yesterday; one of those abandoned road mines."

I gasp with shock.

"I need a replacement, actually. As you can fly those lumbering giants, you can surely fly a Lysander. I need to get to Germany."

"Germany?" It confirms, if confirmation were needed, that the war really is as good as over.

"I thought perhaps you could fly me," says Major Battersby. "I have a Lysander standing by. Would you mind awfully? I need to get to Bergen, a small town in northern Germany. I've got all the coordinates. Not a bombing mission, thank the Lord, but a mercy mission – escorting the Red Cross and all that."

"I'd need permission, sir," I murmur.

"One phone call is all it will take," says the major.

Within two hours, we are at a small aerodrome, and I am in the cockpit of a Lysander.

I flew the Major over Germany. The destruction beneath us was like hell.

"Did we do that?" I asked, bewildered.

"'Fraid so, old bean," he replied grimly.

We touched down on a military airstrip near Bergen. The town was teeming with British and American soldiers with their trucks and jeeps and motorbikes – now fully in charge of this broken German town. Exhausted and frightened citizens peered out from behind shattered buildings. Ragged children played in the rubble, while head-scarved old ladies steadfastly trudged to the various charity centres providing food and water.

Major Battersby found the British commanding officer to tell him he was here to escort the Red Cross and a contingent of soldiers into the local displaced persons camp.

I had propped myself on the running board of a jeep when he returned.

"Any further requests?" I asked, jumping to attention. "Or shall I take the plane back to France?"

"You can see how busy everyone is," he said apologetically. "They can't spare me anyone. Would you be my driver?"

"I'll have to get permiss–" I began to say

"I've made the phone call already. Sorry to jump the gun. Do you mind?"

"Of course not. Where's the vehicle?"

"You've been sitting on it, actually."

Our convoy wound its way through the countryside. How pretty it looked with its hedgerows and trees, and perfectly furrowed ground; so neat and cared for with its little wooden farmhouses. The birdsong was so gentle, so sweet; for them the world hadn't changed. They still knew how to sing. I expected we would be collecting people displaced from the bombing.

As we drove along that gentle country road, a strange silence fell over the company. The loud voices which had been raised over the noise of vehicle engine stopped. No one spoke.

The charming domestic dwellings became low outlines of wooden huts, and the hedgerows turned into tall, impenetrable barbed wire fences. And what were those ragged bundles leaning against the wire, seemingly impervious to the barbs?

Major Battersby heard my gasp of horror.

"Sorry, old dear," he murmured. "They said it was a camp for displaced persons but – I had heard rumours. I didn't know what to expect, or how to warn you."

Even if I had heard the dread term 'concentration camp', he could never have warned me sufficiently. Neither of us was prepared, and nothing could have prepared us. Strange how no creature on earth hates human beings as much as humans hate themselves.

We entered the gates of hell, over which were the words BERGEN-BELSEN.

We abandoned the jeep. There was no clear way through the wasteland we saw before us. We stared with incomprehension: the squalor, the teetering piles of rubbish; and the stench, unlike anything I had ever smelled before.

The ground was a rubbish tip of scattered rags and bundles. Some of the rags were moving; scavenging animals? I wondered, till I saw a human hand, a foot, an upturned face. The rags were people: living people; yet hardly people at all, but starved skeletons, some on the verge of death, who crawled, or dragged their emaciated bodies along the ground. The stench was the smell of death, and the mounds of rubbish were pile upon pile of dead and living bodies.

Major Battersby had started off at a stride towards the Red Cross hut at the far end. Halfway there he faltered, lost; looking back at me as if for help. Tears streamed down his face. On all sides, British soldiers were leaping from their trucks. They too, for all the horrors of war they had seen, were bewildered and disbelieving. Gently, they began clearing a way through the bodies for the Red Cross vehicles.

Major Battersby regained his composure and continued towards a reception hut. Doctors, nurses, stretcher bearers, and volunteer soldiers, with medicines and food, and gentle hands, and compassionate faces, bent to tend these human remnants.

I found the will to follow the major, trying not to feel revulsion as claw-like hands stretched out to clasp my ankle, or grab my skirt. But then one hand in particular reached out and held my skirt, and wouldn't let go. I was forced to stop.

I looked down at a face that was barely recognisable as

a face: a skull, with bottomless dark eyes brimming up at me.

"Gwen . . ."

I looked and looked, and dropped to my knees, and looked again and again.

"I know you," I whispered, as I wound my arms round my friend: Vera. I held her gently, in case she should splinter into a hundred pieces.

CHAPTER 61
Never Forgotten

PARIS, 25 AUGUST 1944

We might have been invisible. No one took any notice of us, two young women walking, painfully slowly, away from the parades and celebrations of the Liberation of Paris, down the Boulevard Saint-Michel.

It was a dreamlike walk; a walk of fear, hope, anticipation, dread; and a walk of great exhaustion. Vera was still weak; she shouldn't have returned to Paris so soon. But nothing could persuade her to wait. She would have crawled on her knees if she had to. That Paris was liberated; that the war in Europe was all but over; that Vera herself was alive, had come out alive from the horrors of Belsen, meant almost nothing, till she knew what had become of Louis.

"Get me there, please, Gwen. Get me there." Her skeletal arms had clasped me like shackles when I had sat by her bed in the Red Cross hospital in Bergen.

I told her as gently as I could that we might not find

him. Louis could be dead; and if not dead, he could be anywhere in the utter chaos that was Europe.

"But our search must start in Paris," Vera had argued. "Jeanne may have saved him; someone may know. Please, Gwen. Take me back to Rue d'Assas."

Only if some brave person had hidden him was there a possibility that Louis was there. Many had hidden their Jewish neighbours; so I agreed to find a way as soon as possible to get her to Paris, and I would go with her.

That day – the day of Liberation – Paris went mad. Those with any strength in their bodies rushed out on to the streets as American troops and the armoured divisions of the Free French army came marching down the Champs-Élysées. The populace flocked around them, draped in red, white, and blue – those colours which for four years had been banned. Girls showered them with flowers and kisses; young men flung their arms round their liberators, shook their hands, patted them on their backs; while all around the crowds kept breaking out into the Marseillaise. It was joyful, passionate, bursting with relief. Others peered anxiously through the shutters of their apartments, some too ill, or too weak to join in; for many had been starving, forced to eat cats, and dogs, and leaves from the trees.

But there were those who were nervous too; those who had collaborated. They knew there would be a reckoning.

We reached the gates of the Jardin du Luxembourg, and made our way across the gardens, not pausing to admire the statues and flowers, the water fountains or lake. Like ghosts, we passed through the gates on the far side and on to the Rue d'Assas.

There it was: number 42. I had never visited Vera in Paris, though had written many letters to her – and it was strange to see the address become real.

Vera sank to the ground outside the large, wooden doors. "I can't, Gwen! What if . . .?"

I held her lovingly, and raised her to her feet. I put my arm round her waist and walked her gently into the courtyard. The concierge wasn't at her window. Perhaps she was too busy out on the balcony of her own apartment a further floor up, listening to the sounds of rejoicing, mixed with the splattering *pah pah pah* of gunshots as snipers from both sides tried to have the last say.

Slowly, slowly, we climbed the stone stairs and came to the apartment door which had once had the name 'Moskowski' by the bell.

Vera bent over the parched cheese plant that had never been moved or replaced in all the years she'd lived there. Yes, just as always, a key lay beneath the soil. She drew it out. With a deep breath, she inserted the key into the lock and turned it.

A slight click and the door opened.

I saw the apartment for the first time, and remembered Noor's description of how lavish it had been. What faced me was a hollowed out, empty, echoing, dusty, bleak corridor, with doors left open through which I saw more emptiness. Everything had been removed except, miraculously, the piano.

Vera went over to it, easing her painful body on to the piano stool. She began to play the French folk song we had learned once at school, and I found myself singing quietly along with it:

> *A la claire fontaine*
> *M'en allant promener*
> *J'ai trouvé l'eau si belle*
> *Que je m'y suis baigné*
> *Il y a longtemps que je t'aime*
> *Jamais je ne t'oublierai*
> *Il y a longtemps que je t'aime*
> *Jamais je ne t'oublierai*

On the repeat of "*Il y a longtemps que je t'aime*," another voice joined in: a shaky, young, treble voice: "*Jamais je ne t'oublierai.*"

I have loved you for a long time.

Never will I ever forget you.

Vera turned as if she had invoked a ghost. There in the doorway stood a boy; a tallish boy; a thin, white-faced boy whose pale skin hadn't been touched by the sun for months and months; a blinking, scraggy, unkempt boy, with hair falling round his shoulders.

"Veroshka?" His voice trembled.

Vera would have fallen, had I not clasped her round her shoulders. She slid to her knees as Louis rushed into her arms.

"Oh Louis!" she wept. "How you've grown."

For nearly a year he had been hiding in his very own special hiding place: the one no one had known of – not even Jeanne.

Where was Jeanne? Louis shook his head sadly. One day there had been a heavy knock on the door; not a neighbourly knock but a loud, insistent policeman's knock. Jeanne had said, "Quick! Hide, Louis!" He had rushed off and hidden. He heard voices shouting –

"We were told there were Jews here!"

"You are wrong," Jeanne had said calmly. "They have all gone."

But they still rampaged through the apartment, upturning any possible hiding place.

"I told you – they've all gone."

"And not you?" they challenged Jeanne. "Didn't you know it was forbidden for Aryans to be in a household of Jews?"

Louis had stayed hidden all night, expecting Jeanne to call out an all-clear, but it never came. When, finally, he emerged, she had gone. Since then, every morning, he had found a bowl of milk and bread on the kitchen window sill; sometimes an apple. Someone knew he was there, but didn't give him away.

"One night I stayed hiding in the kitchen to see who

brought me the food. Do you know who it was?" he exclaimed with wide eyes. "It was the German officer who had moved into the flat next door."

We were silent.

Then Vera asked, "Is he there still?"

"No – he's gone. They all left a few days ago. But he didn't forget me; he left me bread and apples and cheese – enough for a while. Enough maybe till Jeanne comes back. But Jeanne has never came back. I thought you too wouldn't come back," said Louis, clutching Vera's hand as though she might vanish into thin air. "I thought everyone had forgotten me."

"I told you," whispered Vera, holding him tightly. "Never would I ever forget you."

POSTSCRIPT

Marianne and Pascal were shot for espionage. Their children continue to live with their grandparents.

Noor was shot as a spy, and was posthumously decorated with the Croix de Guerre by France, and the George Cross by the British.

Charles was declared missing at Dunkirk, presumed dead.

Dodo died trying to save Charles and other servicemen at Dunkirk. She was awarded the George Cross. Her parents never returned to England.

Daniel was deported to a concentration camp in Germany, but escaped en route when his train was bombed. He fought with the Resistance till the end of the war. He and Vera married in Paris, and live on with Louis in the Rue d'Assas.

Neither Vera's baby brother, Ethan, nor her aunt and uncle, nor any other member of Vera's family, reappeared after the war.

Daniel's parents made it to safety first in Spain, then later in Israel.

Simone was a broken woman and never recovered from her treachery.

Jeanne was arrested by the Nazis and imprisoned. After the war, she was released by the Allies and returned to Rue d'Assas, where she was overjoyed to be reunited with Louis, Vera, and Daniel.

Raymonde Gilles disappeared into obscurity.

Georgie still serves in the Café Rigaud on the Boulevard Saint-Germain.

Eric survived the war, continuing to fly, albeit with terrible wounds. He went to live with his aunt and uncle in Wales.

Ralph returned from the war, and found Gwen waiting at Orange Street. They took the next possible passenger ship to India to marry in the presence of Gwen's parents.

NEVER SHALL WE EVER FORGET THEM.

EPILOGUE

Above the Himalayan peaks of the everlasting snows, an eagle soared high in the cloudless skies, wheeling and circling, scouring the land beneath for the unwary hare, a young deer, or a musk rat; watching the black bear lumber forth from his winter hibernation, or the stalking prowl of the snow leopard.

It was still very cold. From October to March snow had lain thick on the mountain slopes. It had buried the tracks through forests and canyons, isolating remote villages, shrines, and monasteries. It had blocked the trails and halted the laden mule and yak caravans which traded along the routes from China, Tibet and Bhutan into India.

But, at last, with temperatures rising day by day, melting snow was now pouring into gullies and mountains streams, and rushing down into the rivers; down, down, to the great Gangetic Plain, where it threaded out across the land, bringing sustenance and life to the parched fields of India.

Perhaps the eagle saw two tiny specks toiling their way

up the steep mountain paths. A little early for pilgrims; but on they plodded, higher and higher. Every now and then, when they met a farmer, or came to a village, they checked the way and asked if anyone knew of a certain name. Quicker than any telegraph system, word flew ahead of them, so that when they arrived at a farm or an inn to seek shelter for the night, the inhabitants already knew that that two *Ingrezi* – English – were coming: a man and a woman. They were looking for a Sufi hermit.

They trekked on for several days more, accepting the hospitality of villagers, or huddling into cowsheds to find warmth for the night with the animals. Now they were at such a height that the air became thin; they struggled for breath, and they could hardly place one foot in front of the other.

At last, they came to a village where a young boy came dancing down the track to greet them. Yes – word had already reached them. The boy asked a question, but because he spoke a language of the hills, they didn't understand him. Then the rest of the family clustered round, and when the boy asked his question again, the old grandfather translated into English.

"Are you looking for a man in a coat of gold?"

The English woman nodded.

"He has been here for four years, all alone; speaking to no one. We don't even know his name – but we call him the Man in the Coat of Gold. He lives in a cave." He gestured further up the mountain. "He won't speak to you,

you know. He never comes out. He's only alive because we leave food for him every day. It is our duty. We believe he is very holy, so we venerate him. In return, he sometimes scrawls a message or a prayer in the earth outside his cave for us to find – in our language, although he is not from here. Yesterday, he wrote: *In a world of darkness and hate, look for illumination and love.*"

"Can someone guide us to this cave?" asked the Englishman.

"The boy will take you," replied the old man.

"What is your name?" the English woman asked the boy.

"Lakshman. And what is your name?" he asked in careful English – the only phrase he knew.

"My name is Gwen, and this is Ralph."

They were surprised by how far they still had to climb. The sun was already past its zenith when they crossed a rocky river, leaping from stone to stone. The boy pointed to a cave on the other side, gouged into the side of a great cliff. "Man in Coat of Gold," he announced.

The two stood silently. Ralph took Gwen's hand. "Well, old girl! Are you ready for this?"

Lakshman stayed behind as they began their last climb. They followed the skinny little goat path that zigzagged up to the mouth of the cave. They hadn't quite reached it when suddenly a figure appeared in the entrance. He was dazzlingly gold in the sunlight, so at first, they could hardly see his face. But, as they drew nearer, Gwen knew this was the man they had come to find.

Noor's father. He was just as Gwen remembered him coming into their classroom all those years ago: tall, looming and gaunt, as if carved out of rock, wearing the same gold-threaded coat. And now he stood, like a statue of a god, surveying the two young English visitors. Gwen was about to call out to him and introduce themselves, but he spoke first.

"Noor has gone to Paradise."

His voice was deep, as if it came from the throat of the cave in which he stood.

Gwen nodded sorrowfully. "Yes."

"Yet she lives," he said.

They sat in silence for a while. He offered them two tin mugs of tea and some bread. They talked, crouched on their haunches, and Gwen told him everything she knew about his daughter, and how much everyone had loved her.

The sun was sliding down a fading blue sky, and the canyons were filling with a wild darkness. The air was chill now. Gwen shivered. A hare suddenly leaped down the mountain side; it stopped before them, transfixed and quivering, as the shadow of the eagle passed overhead.

"Noor always loved you, and longed only for what was right and just," said Gwen.

My daughter was a hare; her sacrifice defeated the power of evil.

The sun dropped lower. The hare sprang into the air and sped away.

It was time to go.

THE END

Others think they know me
But I am mine; what I am, I am.
A CHILD'S HOLOCAUST DIARY

NOOR INAYAT KHAN

NEVER FORGET YOU is a tribute to Noor Inayat Khan, the children's writer and British resistance agent in France during the Second World War. She was the first inspiration behind this book.

In 2005 I contributed a very short story about Noor, called *Princess Spy*, for an anthology of war stories for Michael Morpurgo. Her story still resonated in my mind. I thought at first I would write a novel about her, but felt the only way I could do it – and feel totally free to respond to the kind of person I felt she was – was to fictionalise her. Although all the qualities of the real Noor will be apparent to anyone who knows about her, I hope I have captured the essence of her in my fictionalised context. I should add that all other characters are entirely fiction, and will only, coincidentally, bear any resemblance to other real people.

ACKNOWLEDGEMENTS

I am profoundly grateful to Cally Poplak, a protégée editor of Miriam Hodgson, and now Executive Publisher of Farshore and HCCB. She took on this book when all seemed lost. She provided me with support, encouragement, and a wonderful team to see me through – especially Liz Bankes and Lucy Courtenay for their rigour and attention to detail, and Olivia Adams for her beautiful design. Thanks also to my agent, Veronique Baxter, for her endless patience throughout this endeavour.

I would like to thank Professor Gavin Schaffer, who cast his historian's eye over the book; and my sister, Romie Singh, who accompanied me to Paris, involving herself in the spirit of the research I was doing. I also thank many friends who read the drafts throughout long years – longer than the Second World War – and made valuable suggestions, especially Jane Serraillier, Elizabeth Lindsay, Elisabeth Chatelain, and friend and historian, Donald Sassoon. I must also add a thanks to my friend Joanna West who, while describing her life at RADA, gave me the inimitable line:

"It was mainly tights for movement, scripts for learning, and bone props between your teeth for diction."

Last but not least, I thank Beverley Naidoo, for being there at the end of a telephone to reassure, commiserate, and finally share my relief when the book was concluded. *Merci mille fois.*

JAMILA GAVIN

WINNER OF THE WHITBREAD CHILDREN'S BOOK AWARD

'A rich and almost gothic drama'
Philip Pullman,
Guardian

CORAM
BOY

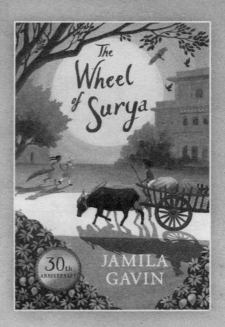

The
WHEEL
of Surya

30th ANNIVERSARY

JAMILA GAVIN

The
EYE of the
Horse

JAMILA
GAVIN

Winner of the Whitbread Children's Award

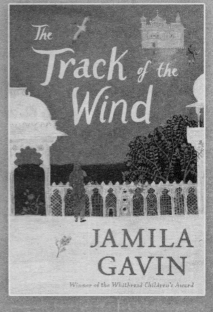

The
TRACK of the
Wind

JAMILA
GAVIN

Winner of the Whitbread Children's Award